CARSON'S TREE

By

Monica Ruthizer

LIBRARY OF CONGRESS
OCT 30 2002

© 2002 by Monica Ruthizer. All rights reserved.

No part of this book may be reproduced, stored in a
retrieval system, or transmitted by any means,
electronic, mechanical, photocopying, recording, or
otherwise, without written permission from the author.

ISBN: 1-4033-1150-1 (e-book)
ISBN: 1-4033-1151-X (Paperback)

Library of Congress Control Number: 2002103514

This book is printed on acid free paper.

Printed in the United States of America
Bloomington, IN

1stBooks - rev. 9/6/02

CHAPTER ONE

The skylight in the spacious studio threw natural light into every corner of the huge room, its strongest rays shining directly underneath the glass, onto the artist's easel. Constructed out of three attic rooms on the top floor of a London townhouse, it was a huge area, filled with canvasses, some complete, and others in various stages of work, shelves holding brushes, paints, palette knives, rags, a dozen palettes, and a bottle of turpentine. In one corner of the room rested a child's easel, complete with a collection of small brushes and jars of paints, as well as a camp bed and a toy box. In the opposite corner, a small refrigerator, stove and a few cabinets lent the only domestic touch to the entire room. On the wall directly opposite the easel was placed a couch, laughingly called an "old fashioned beast" by the artist, resplendent in faded burgundy velvet, edged with a tasseled silk border, and covered at the moment by an enormous fringed pink and peach flowered silk shawl, placed strategically to hide the bulging spring on the left hand side.

For the past month, the studio had been deserted, silent and waiting. The streaming sunshine played along the floor, without an audience to applaud its yellow and shiny beauty. On the easel sat the artist's latest work, the third in a series of color studies. "The Lilac Woman" was almost completed, ready to join the two companion pictures leaning against the wall, one a sea green and the other silvery blue.

*   *   *   *   *

Juliet Macallister put her key into the door of the Mayfair townhouse she shared with her husband, Donald, and their three children, a girl and a boy from his first marriage, and their son, Carson, her hand shaking as she turned the lock. Quietly, without any drama, she let herself into the small foyer and let the heavy door close behind her. The sound echoed through the empty house, as she half listened for the sound of her eight year old son running down the stairs to announce his news of the day. But today there would be no thudding of childish feet on the stairs, no arms around her neck, no kissing her hello, no breathless report on the latest goings on at school.

She took a deep, shaky breath and climbed the stairs to the parlor, usually her favorite room, decorated in shades of yellow, from pale lemon to deep mustard, with greens and pinks scattered as accents, the morning sun she loved giving it the appearance of an exotic jewel box. Stopping for a moment to look at herself in the mirror to the left of the parlor door, what should have been the familiarity of her reflection was not there. Rather, she saw her face, thin and pale, with huge blue shadows under her tawny eyes. Her long red hair hung lankly, with none of its usual glimmer and bounce, as if it too were exhausted and depressed. Sighing, she kicked off her shoes and sat down at the desk. The telephone, sitting silent at the right hand corner of the desk, refused to ring, and after a few minutes of staring into space, she picked up the receiver and dialed her husband's private line. He answered on the first ring.

"Juliet, darling, you're home?" His voice was gentle, calm, undemanding.   •

"Donald, it's so quiet here. I keep forgetting that he's gone to stay with your father."

2

"What did the doctor say?" A note of anxiety crept into his voice.

"I'm not a match." Her voice shook as she wiped away a tear as it rolled halfway down her cheek.

"Darling, we knew that this would happen at some point, that he would have to be told that I'm not his father, at least not his biological one."

"Not now, when he's sick and so young and vulnerable. I'll have to go to New York, to try and find Tony. Perhaps he or one of his family will be a match."

"Before you do that, we have to decide what to tell him, and when. Perhaps after you come back from New York, we can tell him together. I'd rather not do it now, in case things don't work out." Donald forced a confidence he did not feel.

"Can you make the arrangements, Concorde, tomorrow?" From one second to the next, she was suddenly so tired that even speaking simple words was a physical effort.

"Of course, darling. Right away. I'm leaving here in ten minutes. See you in an hour." Standing up, Donald Macallister wrote out the instructions for his secretary, airline flight, car service, hotels and wire transfer to his New York account, and collected his jacket, coat and briefcase.

"Sylvia, here are the plans for Juliet's flight tomorrow. Please have a messenger bring it all to the house when it's ready." Sylvia Barstow, his secretary of ten years, was forty five years old. In spite of her position as private secretary and assistant to the Chief Operating Officer of Macallister Industries, everything about her was quiet and subdued, from her brown hair always gathered into a neat bun, to her sensible clothing and shoes. She was referred to by Donald in hushed tones, out of her hearing, as his irreplaceable factotum.

"Of course, by five o'clock. Is everything all right, Lord Donald?" A look of uncertainty flashed across her brown eyes.

"No, Sylvia, as a matter of fact, everything could not be worse."

* * * * *

Her bags were packed and sitting by the door. As if by rote, she checked her documents for the third time, the marriage certificate and divorce decree from her marriage to Tony Graniston, Carson's birth certificate, with Tony's name on it, the form that terminated Tony's parental rights, and her passport and ticket, the two things that usually excited her imagination, the unknown vistas of a trip away from home.

"Try not to worry. I'll be there with him every day, and my father and your parents said they would be there as well." Donald looked up at her over his glasses, the morning paper on his lap.

"How can I not worry? He's our child, and he's going to die unless we can find a donor." She checked her watch again, it was only three minutes since she had checked it the last time.

"We may still have some time, not much, I'll grant you, but enough so that even if Tony won't cooperate, the international network might help. Now, try and have some fun while you're there. Why don't you call Paul and show him the photos of your new series." He put his arm around her shoulders and kissed her forehead.

"Life has to go on as normally as possible. Carson is not stupid, Juliet. He picks up on everything these days. If you miss a chance to sell your series, he'll know something is wrong." She nodded and turned to the door.

"The car is here. I have to go, or I'll miss my flight. Kiss Carson for me and tell him I'll be home soon." She reached up her hand and touched his face. Smiling, he bent down and brushed her lips with his. Turning around, she took one last look and closed the door behind her.

* * * * *

Juliet spent the three hour flight sketching out a new series of paintings, playing with a pastoral idea she had had while watching a huge oak tree outside of Carson's hospital room window. She had had months to stare at the tree, tall with a spread of large branches reaching skywards, its look different with each passing season. Now, in the middle of April, its branches would have tight buds, each one holding back the promise of the pale green early leaves that would appear at the end of the month. In spite of her fear for her son's life, her artistic instincts had taken over, and she had begun to see the tree in a different light. Smiling, she finished the sketches and wrote down the color chart at the bottom of the last page. Packing the pages away into her portfolio, she checked her watch. In twenty minutes the plane would land at Kennedy Airport, the limousine would pick her up and the long odyssey to save her son's life would begin.

* * * * *

As she walked by on her way to the study, Emily Graniston tweaked a large orchid in the flower arrangement on the round highly polished table in the center of the foyer. She had only to collect her briefcase before she left for her weekly staff meeting at the real estate agency she owned in downtown Greenwich. Halfway back to the door, the telephone began to ring. After the third ring, she walked back to the desk and picked it up, irritated that Maria, her live-in housekeeper for the past twenty years, had missed the call.

"Mother, how nice to hear that you answered for a change." Tony Graniston's voice teased gently over the line.

"Don't tease me, I'm not in the mood. How is Laurel, and how are the girls?"

Emily checked her watch and unconsciously began to tap her foot against the chair, a sure sign that she was both annoyed and impatient.

"Laurel is enormous, and assures me that this time it will be a boy. And my daughters are driving their preschool teachers to distraction. Other than that, Dad and I are on our way to a dinner meeting with our new clients, and he asked me to call you and tell you not to expect him before eleven."

"Thank you, I'll stop by and visit Laurel and the girls, and then bring them back here for dinner. Good luck to both of you, and now I really have to go, or I'll have to postpone my meeting again." Emily hung up and picked up her briefcase. She checked her watch and sighed. It was almost eleven o'clock, too late for her to be on time for her own meeting. She picked up her cellular telephone and punched in the number of her office as she walked towards the door.

"Janet, it's me. I'm late again. Is everyone there?"

"I'm glad you called, Emily. Amy and Michelle are still out on sales calls, and Michael had to go into Stamford to close on the McAllen house. They all extend their apologies and asked if we could meet tomorrow instead." Emily drummed her fingers against the wall.

"Not tomorrow. Tell them Thursday at ten, it's not an emergency. I'm taking the rest of the day off. Call me if you need me." Emily turned off the phone and walked towards the staircase. For an unknown reason, she stopped and looked around the downstairs of her brick house, enormous by anyone's standards, but her beloved home for thirty years, still as beautiful and pleasing as it had been the day she had moved in, pregnant with her first child, and her husband far away in Vietnam. The ceiling of the foyer soared to the second story, her grandmother's massive Waterford chandelier shedding soft, starry light over the entire staircase as well as the downstairs. The oak floor, recently stripped down to its original golden color, shone brightly, covered randomly with several antique oriental rugs, their original colors now faded to pastel blues, oranges and greens. But the centerpiece of the downstairs foyer and sitting room was her latest acquisition, a lyrical painting, a study of a park bench, all of its colors muted by the misty silver of an early spring rain. It had been delivered only yesterday, after a six month search of several art dealers, and acquired only after she had agreed to an exorbitant purchase price. All worth it, as she stood and watched as it shimmered, slowly taking command over everything in the room. As Emily smiled and turned to go up the staircase, the doorbell rang. Sighing, she turned as Maria walked through the foyer towards the door.

"Whoever it is, let them wait in the foyer until I know who it is. I'll be down presently." She reached the head of the staircase and turned into her bedroom.

*   *   *   *   *

Immigration, customs and retrieving her bag were all a blur. Juliet saw Edward Carstairs, the managing director of Macallister Industries' New York office, waiting for her in the room just outside customs. He handed her a large envelope with one hand, as he picked up her bag with the other.

"Your Grace, the detective Lord Donald hired left this report for you, and there is also a cellular phone, with battery and charger for you to use while you are here in New York. I took the liberty of confirming your reservation at the Park Lane, the company suite, and the car and driver will be available for you as long as needed." He smiled at her, secretly admiring the combination of her artistic clothing and her unusual beauty.

"Edward, it's wonderful to see someone smile. I haven't seen that for over a month, and it makes me feel wonderful."

"I think you need more smiles to help you through this. How is Carson?" He was suddenly all business again, serious, a small frown of concentration replacing his easy smile.

"I think the best way to put it is as well as can be expected for an eight year old at the end of his last remission. He needs a bone marrow transplant, and I'm not a match. My ex-husband might be, that's why I'm here." She stood at the curb outside the terminal, and adjusted her watch to New York time.

"How long has it been since you've seen him?" Edward Carstairs sighed. Normally a man whose life was entirely wrapped up in his position as head of Macallister Industries America, he was ill at ease and awkward when it came to making small talk.

"Almost nine years, since before the divorce." He raised an eyebrow, thinking carefully about whether to respond or keep silent.

"Does he know about Carson?" His head came up and nodded at the sight of the limousine.

"Yes, he knew that I was pregnant, but he terminated his parental rights before Carson was born." She smiled ruefully and put her hand onto the car door.

"The driver will take you to Greenwich. He has the address of Tony's parents. I imagine you can take it from there." Edward leaned into the window of the limousine.

"Thank you. Please, call Lord Donald at Dunodeen House and tell him I'll speak to him this afternoon. Thank you, Edward." The window rolled up slowly as the car pulled away from the curb. As the car edged out onto the highway, she opened the envelope and began to read the detective's report.

"Countess Juliet, the following is a record of the last nine years of Tony Graniston's private and professional life. After he returned from England in 1988, he entered Harvard Law School, graduating third in his class in 1991. He is now a partner at his father's law firm, Graniston, Blair and Mackinnon. In 1989, he married Laurel Davenport, a debutante and daughter of old family friends. They have twin daughters, aged four years, and are expecting their third child. Currently, they are living in a mansion in Greenwich, which Emily and Jordan Graniston, Tony's parents, gave them as a wedding present.

"Tony is not a faithful husband. To date, he has had numerous encounters and four serious affairs, all with very young and vulnerable women. He gambles, and is in debt up to his eyebrows. He also has a drinking problem, which he has succeeded in hiding for quite some time.

"Your husband asked me to find out about all of these things, thinking that perhaps you might need an extra something to persuade him to cooperate. My very best wishes for a successful conclusion, and if you need me, just press the star key and the number 12 on your new phone and I will be more than happy to help you."

Steven James, private investigator

Juliet closed the folder, sighed and looked out of the window. The car had just pulled onto the Hutchinson River Parkway.

"Your Grace, we're about forty minutes from Greenwich, give or take." The limousine driver had rolled down the glass window just enough to allow conversation with his passenger.

"Thank you for the warning. Just take me directly to the address you were given, and if you could wait, I would appreciate it."

"Of course, no problem."

Exactly forty minutes later, the car pulled into the driveway. As the driver opened the door for her, Juliet took several deep breaths. She clutched her calling card, one of the ones Carson had given her for her birthday last year, laughing as he had insisted that since she was now a famous painter, she should have business cards, just like Donald's. Swallowing the lump in her throat, she rang the doorbell.

The woman who answered it had a heavy accent. Juliet breathed a sigh of relief, she had received a coward's gift of a few more moments. Smiling, she handed over her card.

"Please ask Mrs. Graniston if she would be kind enough to see me. I don't have an appointment."

"Please come in, you can wait in the foyer. I will see if Mrs. Graniston is at home." The door swung wide and Juliet stepped inside, reminded for an instant of a story from her childhood, of a brave young princess entering the castle of the evil Queen. She stood quietly, near the door, appraising the room with an artist's eye. It was superbly decorated, with all the colors working off each other, but with nothing out of place, a museum instead of a house. She thought suddenly of her townhouse across the street from Hyde Park, with the baggage of a young boy appearing almost as if by magic, football boots in the kitchen, a rugby shirt in her bathroom, small reminders of the life of her child.

Emily Graniston smoothed the gray cashmere cardigan, tugging it into place and picked up the silver-backed hairbrush to tidy her hair. She had let it go to gray after her granddaughters had been born, laughing as she insisted that being a grandmother meant she didn't have to pretend to be thirty anymore. Turning her head as Maria knocked on the door, she rose and took the card. For a moment, she couldn't believe what she was seeing. Countess Juliet Macallister, the painter of her beloved new acquisition, was actually waiting downstairs, in her house.

"Of course I'll see her. Put her into the sitting room, and make some tea. The English all like tea, I believe." Smiling, she sprayed herself with Madame Rochas and looked in the mirror one last time. What a coup! Perhaps a dinner party for the family and a few friends to show off her new painting, and the artist. The thought made her shiver with delight. She turned out the light and hurried down the stairs.

11

*   *   *   *   *

"How do you do, Countess, I'm Emily Graniston." Juliet looked at the woman who was her son's other grandmother. She looked like a typical rich American, trying to be as English as possible. A small smile played around her lips as she extended her hand.

"Mrs. Graniston, please call me Juliet. The title is really only for very formal occasions, or at least that is what I keep telling my husband."

"I love your work and as a matter of fact, I just hung 'Silver Rain' last night. It's a bit unnerving, having you sitting here, directly across from your own painting." Emily couldn't remember the last time she had been so nervous.

"I noticed it when I sat down. I'm flattered that you like my work, but that isn't why I'm here. As a matter of fact, I've come because I have no other options and no where else to go." Emily raised an eyebrow.

"I've ordered some tea. Let's have a cup and you can tell me all about whatever it is that only I seem to be able to solve." Maria brought the tray and put it down on the table. Juliet watched as the tea was poured from an ornate silver pot into a delicate bone china cup. Emily made a fuss over lemon or milk, and then handed the cup to her guest.

"I don't really know where to begin. How much do you know about your son Tony's year in England?" The question sounded strange now that the moment had come. It had sounded perfectly normal when she had practiced it on the plane.

"Only that he did well at Oxford and that he enjoyed the year away from home. He never had much to say about what he did during that time. Why do you ask?"

"I don't understand it. He never said anything about what he did outside of university during that year?"

"No, nothing." Juliet felt a moment of panic as she saw the puzzled look on the other woman's face.

"I might as well start with this. Perhaps it will explain far better than I could." She took the marriage certificate out of her portfolio and handed it over. Emily read it, at least three times.

"I don't understand. It says here that you are Tony's wife. It can't be possible, he's married to someone else." Her eyes, stunned and shocked, stared at Juliet. Quietly, Juliet handed over the divorce decree as well.

"Why did you get a divorce?"

"When I met Tony, I was eighteen, a first year student at the Slade, and we fell madly in love. We ran off and got married, and managed to keep it a secret for about a month. My father was completely opposed to the marriage, I was too young, he was too irresponsible, all the things that in retrospect were absolutely correct, but of course, one never listens under those kinds of circumstances. Four months later, Tony had disappeared, gone back to America. My father was very kind, more than I deserved. He had the divorce pushed through, sent off Tony's copy of the papers, and he thought, that was that."

"Only it wasn't that, was it?" Emily looked down at her clenched fists, and slowly relaxed her fingers.

"No, it wasn't. A month after Tony returned the papers, I found out that I was pregnant. I wanted that baby more than anything. My father kept insisting that just because I wanted to be a painter, I didn't have to behave like one, but all I could think of was that baby growing inside me, an innocent, a person who never asked to be born, and who certainly shouldn't be

13

made to suffer because his father had run off to America."

"And the child?" Emily pinched the skin near her wrist, just to make sure she was awake.

"Carson, my son, or rather, Tony's and my son. The most marvelous thing that has ever happened to me. My inspiration, the food for my spirit, all the things that artists insist they have to have are wrapped up in that child. He looks just like Tony, down to the dimple on his chin." Juliet smiled the smile of all loving mothers.

"And your husband, does he love Carson?"

"He adores him. We met when I was in my seventh month, and married a week before Carson was born. When I went into labor, he was there, coaching me and holding my hand. He was the one who insisted that Tony's name should be on the birth certificate, not his. He said that one day, I might need to prove that Tony is Carson's biological father."

"You have no other children?"

"Two from Donald's first marriage. Miranda and Dylan adore Carson, and vice-versa."

"Tell me something, why have you come here now, all these years later? What do you want?" Emily couldn't help running down a list of possible reasons for the visit.

"Carson is sick, he has leukemia. He needs a bone marrow transplant. I'm not a match. Tony is my last hope. Without him, I'll lose my child." A hint of Juliet's desperation had come out at last. As she looked at Emily she wondered if, under the circumstances, the amount of desperation shown had been appropriate.

"I see. And Tony never got in touch with you, after the divorce?"

"Only once. When I wrote to his attorney to inform him that I was pregnant, Tony sent back a stinging letter and terminated his parental rights. He was convinced that somehow I had gotten pregnant by another man." Silently, Juliet held out the termination.

"I can't believe that Tony would do that. He wouldn't just walk away from his child." Still in shock, Emily's hand came up automatically to take it.

"He did, of his own free will. I didn't force him into it. I was prepared to share custody of Carson if Tony had wanted. There's one other thing. The adoption certificate. Donald adopted him when he was six months old." Juliet's hand stretched out with the last of the packet of papers. Emily lowered her head to look at the paper in her hand.

"I have a grandson. I can't wait to tell my husband."

"I would be grateful if I could tell him myself, and then talk to Tony. As well, there is a time factor. I have to be back in London by Friday. Tell me, what is Tony like these days?" Juliet sat back, cautious, but appearing relaxed.

Emily weighed the choice, and made a quick decision. Her visitor sat across from her, quiet and confident. It would serve no purpose to avoid the truth.

"I could lie to you and tell you that my son is a wonderful person, kind to everyone, a pillar of his community. But he isn't. He thinks he has his father and me fooled, but he hasn't. He drinks and gambles, not very successfully and he cheats on his wife." A light flush crept up Emily's neck.

"Tell me something, Emily, you're his mother. Do you think that he will agree to be tested?"

"For a price. Macallister Industries will be a tempting target. I guess that forewarned is forearmed." Emily's bitterness and disappointment bled through her self-control.

"Carson is Tony's child. Even he can't deny the resemblance." Suddenly, doubt settled in Juliet's mind. What if Tony refused to accept his son?

"You haven't seen him for nine years. A great many things have happened since then." Juliet chose to ignore any hidden traps and moved on.

"When will I be able to see your husband and Tony?" Emily sighed with relief. Emotions had been put aside in favor of the business at hand.

"Not until tomorrow. They're at an important meeting in Manhattan tonight, a new client. Where are you staying?"

"At the Park Lane. Why don't all of you come and have breakfast with me, tomorrow morning at about half past nine?"

"Fine. I'll arrange it." Emily walked across the room, then turned, almost as an afterthought.

"Tell me, do you have a picture of Carson?" Emily's hand shook as she took the picture and held it to the light.

"You're right. He looks just like Tony did at that age. Tell me about him."

"He's eight years old, and very smart. He has a tutor, when he's up to it, and when he gets well, he'll go away to boarding school. Later on, he'll go to Eton, that's where Donald went, and then, if he can make it, to Oxford or Cambridge. He's caring and sensitive, and very charming, like Tony. He paints together with me, at his own easel in my studio. I think, though, that he will have to stick to business rather than art. That's our private joke, that he really is Donald's son, in every way except the one that we need the most." Swallowing her tears, Juliet managed a small smile.

"Would you like something stronger than tea? I know I do." Emily's laugh sounded as hollow as she felt. "I never understood how men could toss back whiskey during a crisis. Now I think I could drink a whole bottle."

"I'm sorry, it must be a great deal to take in all at once. Perhaps I should go." She moved slightly, sitting on the edge of her chair.

"No, please, it's all been a shock, that's all." Emily held out one of the glasses.

"Really, I'm a bit tired, and I should go to the hotel and I have a few other things to do. I'll see you in the morning." Juliet kissed her on the cheek, and picked up her coat. Startled at the spontaneous display of affection, Emily put her arm around Juliet's shoulder.

"I'm happy that you like my work. I couldn't imagine 'Silver Rain' anywhere else." Juliet smiled and walked through the foyer, opened the door and closed it softly behind her. Inhaling deeply, she walked towards the waiting car, the first leg of her ordeal behind her.

CHAPTER TWO

"Countess, welcome back to the Park Lane. Is there anything that we can do for you?" The manager smiled warmly as he handed back Juliet's passport.

"Actually, Mr. Madison, there is one thing you can do for me. I'll be entertaining three guests for breakfast tomorrow morning, at nine thirty. I'd like it served in the suite."

"The usual breakfast that Lord Donald orders?."

"Yes, that would be fine. Just send a pot of coffee and some orange juice up at about seven, and that should be all." She held her hand out for the key to the suite.

"Here are your messages. Your husband and Mr. Carstairs. Can I reserve for you in the restaurant, or perhaps somewhere else?" The manager's hand rubbed themselves together.

"Tonight, I'm not sure about, but tomorrow night, see if you can get me into the Oak Room at the Plaza, for two, nine o'clock." She smiled inwardly at the sudden interest in the manager's eyes at the suggestion of two for dinner.

"Of course. Please let me know if you need anything, anything at all." He called after her as she left the reception desk and walked towards the elevators. The bellman followed her, carrying her suitcase and portfolio.

The suite was just as she had remembered it, from their last trip to New York. A year ago, Carson had joined them for a week, and she had seen New York through new eyes. She had made sketches, toying with the idea of exploring pen and ink for a series on New York skyscrapers. He had fallen in love with the bustle and diversity of the city, and had cried at the end of his holiday. Donald had consoled him, promising other trips for other holidays, telling Carson that he was now old enough to be a "delightful companion for his decrepit parents," bringing a gleam of humor to his eye, and a twitch to Juliet's mouth as she struggled not to laugh.

"Darling, how did it go?" Donald picked up the phone on the first ring.

"How did you know it was me?"

"Your father just called, and your mother is here, playing Snakes and Ladders with Carson."

"Anything new?"

"His red blood count is up a bit, Edgar is cautiously hopeful." The sardonic tone of his voice came across clearly. She could hear the phone being moved and then the sound of her son's voice.

"Mummy, how is New York? Have you seen Uncle Paul yet?"

"No, darling, I just got here. I'll see him tomorrow. How are you feeling?"

"Fine. I'm whipping Granny at Snakes and Ladders. She's doesn't like it. Are you bringing me a present?" He laughed.

"Greedy boy, of course I am, from FAO Schwartz. Anything I should look for?"

"Something to put together, staying in bed so much is boring. Bye, Mummy, I love you and kiss good night. Here's Daddy."

"Juliet, I'm leaving in a few minutes. I'll call you when I get home, about eleven my time. I have to go back to the office for a few hours."

"Fine. I'll wait for your call. I love you."

"As well, darling. Smile and swallow. Talk to you soon." He hung up gently, kissed his son good night, and put on his jacket and coat. His mother-in-law followed him to the door.

19

"Did she say anything at all?"

"No, Rose, she did not. Not a good sign at all, but I'm sure she'll tell me more when I call her later on." He patted her on the shoulder, and walked slowly down the driveway towards his car.

* * * * *

The bathtub filled with scented bubbles. Juliet took off her silk gown and stepped into the perfumed tub. She had braided and pinned up her hair, and she sighed with satisfaction as the water crept higher. Closing her eyes, she tried to remember what Tony had been like for the short time they had been married. The only things that sprang to mind were the small irritations that had eventually driven them apart. The cycle of quarreling, always begun by his unexplained absences, followed by the arguments about money, and his complaints about the lack of it, had ended one day about four months after the marriage. At the time, her father had rejoiced at Tony's departure, stating that a divorce under these circumstances, with no children and no real property was easy to come by, especially if one's first cousin sat on the civil bench in London. Once the divorce had become final, she had heard from Tony only once more, shortly after she had discovered that she was pregnant. His letter had been abusive and insulting, the termination of his parental rights an outright relief.

Afterwards, it had been as if he had dropped off the edge of the earth, living in a void, a spatial plane from which she was excluded. Seven months pregnant, she had met Donald, a shy twenty-eight year old, who had fallen in love with the artist and her paintings at the same time. They had both been suffering from the scars left by broken marriages, hers to Tony, and his to Delia, who had seen only the fortune he would inherit. Tired of waiting for his father to pass on the millions produced by Macallister Industries, she had vanished on a trip to the South of France, only to resurface six months later in a French divorce court. He had not contested her suit, but had retained custody of their two small children, Miranda, aged four, and Dylan, aged two. It cost him half a million pounds, a price which his father always insisted was a bargain.

She smiled as she remembered her first meeting with her father-in-law. His eyes had traveled downwards, from her red hair to her pregnancy and back to her face again. Donald had explained it all, insisting that he didn't care who had created the child, that he intended to be its father, and that he loved it almost as much as he loved its mother. She had caught her father-in-law's eye as it twinkled, and had then kissed him on the cheek. He had coughed and then told Donald it was high time that he had acquired the backbone to marry someone normal, even if she was an artist. His only request was that they name the child after him, Carson Macallister III, if it was a boy, or Fiona, after Donald's mother, if it was a girl.

Since Carson's illness, he had been a regular visitor at the townhouse on Great George Street. Each afternoon he would arrive promptly at three, staying an hour or two. During the frequent hospitalizations, he had shared visitations with Donald and Juliet, and her parents.

Reluctantly, Juliet climbed out of the tub, put on her gown and robe and went back into the bedroom. She looked out of the window, over the trees in Central Park, and thought about the meeting she would have with Tony. Whatever unpleasantness was bound to come up, she promised herself that she would stay focused on what was important, saving her son's life.

* * * * *

She picked up on the first ring.

"Juliet, shame on you. I had to hear from Donald that you are here in New York." Paul Townsend's voice came over the line, amused, but gently chiding.

"I'm so sorry, Paul, I was going to call you after I'd gotten myself settled. It's been a long day. How are you?"

"Very well. You are making me a rich man." He chuckled at his joke, and then turned very serious.

"Have you seen that scum Tony yet?"

"No, tomorrow morning. Don't tell me you know him?"

"Of him only. A nasty piece of work. You are well rid of him."

"You sound just like my father."

"I always said he was a wise man. To business. Donald tells me the new series is almost finished."

"It's wonderful. The best I've ever done. I'm thinking about keeping them for myself." She couldn't resist putting the teasing tone into her voice.

"Shame on you. I sold your silver bench for half a million dollars, to none other than Tony's mother."

"I know. I saw it this morning."

"You are a fast worker. How is my dear boy?" He listened more closely to her voice, searching for despair.

"Not well at all. I need to convince Tony to submit to a blood test, to see if he could be a donor for a bone marrow transplant. I'm not a match. If he comes up negative, we're back at the beginning again." She swallowed hard, forcing her tears down past her throat.

"Darling Juliet, I will be tested. Perhaps we will be lucky."

"Paul, thank you. Do, by all means, and we will hope for the best. Dinner is at nine tomorrow night, at your favorite place."

"Dear girl, the Oak Room. You spoil me."

"I love doing it. Good night, and dream of my women, they're wonderful." She laughed softly and hung up.

*　　*　　*　　*　　*

The ringing of the telephone interrupted her room service tea and cakes. Sighing, she swallowed and picked up the receiver.

"Juliet, are you well?"

"Mummy, I'm fine. And yes, I'm in the middle of eating."

"Darling, please. I feel so helpless, not being able to do anything for all of you, allow me the luxury of worrying just a bit. I wanted to let you know about Carson. He seems all right, a bit low on energy and appetite, but the doctor says he's holding his own. And your father wants to talk to you, so I'll sign off. See you in a few days." She could hear whispers as the phone changed hands.

"Daddy, stop worrying. Everything is going according to plan, so all I have to do is wait." She decided to avoid any arguments and spoke first.

"Juliet, tell me about this morning. Did you see Tony?"

"No, just his mother. I can't decide who was the more surprised, Emily at the discovery that her son had a wife and child she knew nothing about, or me at the fact that he never told them he was married."

"You aren't serious."

"Oh, yes, I am. Tony never told them that he was married, or that it ended in divorce. Once she was over the shock, she was very curious about Carson."

"Did she talk about Tony at all?"

"Oh, yes. I could see her wavering, but she did tell me the truth. Everything in the detective's report is confirmed. Quite scary, the near miss I had. Daddy, I want you to humor me and do me a huge favor. Go to the solicitor and drag out the file, and make sure that the divorce is completely legal and binding. I don't want any surprises." He could hear the anxiety in her voice coming through.

"I'm ahead of you. I'm seeing David Graham on my way home, and although he assures me that everything is in order, I want to see it for myself."

"Please, ring me here as soon as you've seen it. They will be here at half past nine tomorrow morning, for breakfast."

"Of course. Try to sleep, and don't worry too much. Whatever happens, we'll deal with it as it comes."

Thoughtfully, Juliet hung up the phone and sat down to wait for her husband to call. When the phone rang again, she picked it up, expecting to hear one voice, and getting another.

"Juliet, this is Jordan Graniston, Tony's father. I'm in the lobby, and I was wondering if I could impose on you for a few minutes?"

"Are you alone, Mr. Graniston?"

"Yes, I sent Tony ahead with our dinner companions. I made up an excuse. He doesn't know that you're here yet. I believe we have something to discuss."

"Why don't you go into the bar? I'll join you in ten minutes."

* * * * *

Juliet stopped at the desk and had her calls held before going into the bar. She had decided to wear her favorite black dress, short, snug and almost dangerous. As she had come down in the elevator, she caught a glimpse of herself in the mirror. Smiling, she blew herself a mental kiss for luck. Nothing wrong with letting the man know what his son had thrown away.

"Mr. Graniston, how do you do. I'm Countess Juliet Macallister." And the battle lines were drawn. She had thrown the gauntlet and it remained to be seen if he would pick it up.

"Please, call me Jordan, if I may call you Juliet."

"Of course. Shall we sit down?" Juliet led the way to Donald's favorite table, in the far left corner, the best to see and be seen. As they sat down, she looked at him more closely. He was an older version of Tony, seemingly more collected and in control. An amused smile played across her lips as she watched him counting her assets, from the neck down. It was not difficult to see from whom Tony had gotten his winning smile and incredible charm. It was all there, the cleft in the chin, the passionate mouth, with its even white teeth, the straight nose and the wide-set dark eyes. The only difference was the gray at the temples and the wrinkles around the eyes that she knew came from squinting into the sun without sunglasses, a habit of Tony's that had always annoyed her.

Jordan Graniston was stunned. He had barely recovered from the news that his son had been married to an English art student, that he had deserted her, she had gotten a divorce, and she had had a child, which Tony had rejected, all without him knowing. He had not believed his wife when she had told him that Juliet was beautiful, in an exotic sort of way, a famous painter and also married to an aristocrat. Prepared to deal with his worst fears, he was shocked to discover that his wife had understated the truth, at least about Juliet's physical beauty. Tall, slender, with shapely legs and ankles, with what he sensed were sensational breasts, and that amazing red hair, long, smooth and silky, cascading down her back. Paired with that short, tight and quite dangerous dress, it was a devastating combination. He cleared his throat, but Juliet spoke before he could open his mouth.

"Jordan, I'm sure that you have a great many questions to ask me. Before you begin, let me show you the same documents that I showed Emily this morning." She pushed the envelope across the table. As he picked it up, the waiter appeared and poured the champagne. As he slid out the four pieces of paper, he knew it was all there; the sordid history of his son's weak nature.

"Have either of you told Tony that I'm here?" Watching his face carefully, she sipped the champagne to be polite.

"No, I don't have a clue as to how to tell him that the part of his life that he chose to keep hidden has just come back to slap him in the face."

"Jordan, please understand. I'm not here to punish Tony. If Carson weren't in need of a bone marrow donor, none of this would be happening. Donald is Carson's father in every respect, except for this, and it is the only thing I want from Tony. A blood test to see if he would be a suitable donor."

"And suppose that he isn't?"

"There is an international donor network. If Tony is not a match, it is the last option we have. We thought about a transplant using his own marrow, but he is so young and it seems that the disease is too advanced for that."

"And if all that fails?"

"We take him home and watch him die. It's as simple and as terrible as that."

"I'll make sure that he gets the blood test, tomorrow if possible. We'll all take the test, just to be sure. Tony's sister, Jennifer, lives in Los Angeles. I'll call her and make sure she gets tested as well. I want my grandson to have every chance. He's my only one, so far, and I'd like to have him around for a while." She smiled at his predictability.

"Jordan, I understand that learning about Carson's existence presents all sorts of possibilities for you, but I must caution you that he already has two sets of grandparents who love him and care for him. It may be too much for him right now to be told the truth, that Donald isn't his biological father, and that he has another set of grandparents anxious to love and spoil him, although that part of it will delight him, I'm sure. It's Tony's involvement with him that concerns me. The day that he left he made it quite plain that he never wanted to see me again, or have anything to do with me as long as he lived. He took our last five hundred pounds, packed his bags and left for America. I haven't heard from him in nine years, although I understand that he has married again and has other children." Deliberately, she kept her face solemn, her voice low, without emotion.

"Juliet, I thought that I knew everything there was to know about my son, but all this has proved me dead wrong. I gather that my wife told you a little bit about what he is like now. She said you were not surprised to hear what she had to say." She looked at him steadily, and sipped her glass of champagne. He broke eye contact and looked down at the table.

"You must have known before you went to my house. Your detective did a good job. You must know about his affairs, as well. You don't have to raise an eyebrow, your husband is not the only one who can hire a detective." He registered the look of surprise on her face.

"It all fits the pattern. Thinking back on it, I believe that he must have had affairs while we were married. Unexplained absences, that sort of thing, always led to loud quarrels." Her voice trailed off as she looked around the room.

"Will you tell me about Carson? Emily said he looks just like Tony."

"He's a wonderful little boy, eight his last birthday. He's smart, athletic, a great football, or soccer, player, but not artistic in the least, just like Donald. Right now he's at home with his father, waiting for a miracle. We all are." She took the picture out of her purse.

Carson's smiling face brought a host of memories back, unbidden. Jordan remembered flashes, bits and pieces of his son's life, now framed by regret, of time not spent together, and lessons taught, but never learned.

"He's a handsome kid, if I may say so. I hope we'll meet, one day soon." Reluctantly, he handed the picture back.

"That depends on a great many things. What do you want to do about tomorrow morning?"

"We'll all be here at nine thirty, as you requested. I think it best if Tony is not told anything at all until he sees you."

"I see. Emily did say something about him demanding a sort of bribe, money to do the right thing. I understand he is in debt. If paying them off on a one time basis will get his attention and cooperation, I can have my solicitor draw up the papers as soon as he agrees to have the blood test." She twirled the stem of the champagne flute in her hands.

"A word of advice. Let him do the asking. He may be my son, but I am not going anywhere near this one. See what he wants first. Emily and I will be there to back you up."

"And what do you want out of all this, for your support and cooperation?"

"Spoken like a businessman's wife. We'd like to meet our grandson and get to know him, maybe have him come to visit, with you and your husband, of course. But first things first. Let's get him healthy and then we'll worry." He smiled at her over his champagne glass and drained it. Standing up, he shook hands with her and paid the bill. Walking quickly across the room, he headed across the lobby and disappeared through the front door.

*   *   *   *   *

Juliet finished her glass of champagne, thoughtfully tracing her finger through the puddle left by the dripping champagne bottle. Tony's father was complex, but too eager to please. A small shudder traveled down her spine as she put down her glass and gathered her purse and key. As an afterthought, she checked the envelope, and the four documents. All accounted for, as well as the picture of Carson. Checking her watch, she hurried out of the bar, anxious not to miss the call from her husband.

*   *   *   *   *

"Darling, where were you? This is the fourth time I tried to get through."

"In the bar with Tony's father. He came to check the merchandise."

"I see. A case of the like father like son, is it?"

"Rather close to that. Too nice by half, but I'm not sure if the father is as untrustworthy as the son. For that, we'll have to wait and see. They want to visit Carson, and have him come to stay in Greenwich."

"Do they really? I hope you squashed that idea firmly."

"As firmly as I could. I need their support to get Tony to cooperate. Giving them a little hope without a promise seemed to be the way to go. How is my darling, greedy boy?"

"Tired, and pale. Tomorrow, Dad is taking him on a picnic, out on the grounds. Do him a world of good."

"How is he taking all of this?"

"He hides his grief well. I'm afraid what will happen if it all goes badly." Donald rubbed his eyes, trying to will the tears away.

"I know. My parents are trying to cope, but I can hear the tears when I talk to them. It makes me wish we had other children besides the three that we do have. How are Miranda and Dylan?"

"Devastated that they aren't a match. Looking forward to the school holidays and planning to spend every moment with Carson. They send their love, and Dylan said to put the screws to Tony. Where on earth does he learn language like that?"

"Too many American movies, I suppose. I like the suggestion, but don't tell him that. I can't help thinking about the divorce. I had a feeling tonight, while I was in the bar with Tony's father, that something is very wrong. I never saw the papers that Tony sent back to David Graham's office. Suppose that there is something wrong with them." She willed her voice to stop shaking.

"I'm going there tonight with Bertram. If there is a problem, I'll call you first and then come to New York. But for now, let's not buy any trouble. Paul called here today. Are you having dinner with him tomorrow night?"

"Of course. He's positively drooling over my three women."

"I'm so proud of you, my darling, not patronizing, I know how you hate that, but just because I'm so glad that you and I and the children are a family."

"I miss you terribly, Donald, and Carson and Miranda and Dylan. Send them my kisses, and call me the moment you've seen the papers. Good night." She blew a kiss into the receiver and hung up.

She checked her watch. It was six thirty. She picked up the <u>New York Times</u> and checked the theater section, but nothing attracted her attention. Suddenly, she smiled and picked up the telephone.

"City Fashions, Ms. Sherman's line." The secretary's voice purred into the telephone.

"Hello, this is Countess Juliet Macallister. Is Vivian Sherman still in the office?"

"Just a moment, please. I'll see if she's still in her office." Jane Lassiter pushed the hold button and leapt across the room.

"Vivian, it's Juliet Macallister, the artist, on line one."

"Juliet, welcome to New York. How long has it been since I was in London staying with you and Donald?"

"Three months, and much too long since I've seen you. Are you free for dinner tonight? Le Cirque, and

31

I'm buying. I've got a table for eight o'clock. Come to the Park Lane now, and we'll have a drink first."

"See you in half an hour. Usual room?"

"Yes. See you then."

*　　*　　*　　*　　*

"Juliet, I know you haven't come to New York just to sell your paintings, although I'm sure that Paul is besides himself with joy that your new series is ready to go. He certainly made enough on the last one he sold for you." Vivian took a sip of her wine.

"Vivian, how do know all these things. Paul has always assured me that he is the very soul of discretion." Laughing, she lifted her head in the air, imitating her agent's frosty outrage.

"You've chosen the wrong profession. You should have been an actress." Vivian reached across the coffee table and helped herself to a handful of peanuts.

"But seriously, I know how sick Carson is, and what a wonderful mother you are, so why are you here, instead of being with your son?"

"I don't even know where to begin, but I'll make it short. Nine years ago I ran off and married an American student. I was eighteen, he was twenty-three. It was an unqualified disaster from start to finish. My father pushed through a quick divorce, and it wasn't until it was all over that I realized that I was pregnant. I was in total shock, especially since the fact that I had missed three times never hit the right button. All I could think about was that little baby, a total innocent, my child. It ran across my mind that he was also my former husband's child, but he was very cooperative, terminating all his rights, and, of course, insisting he could not possibly be Carson's biological father."

"How absolutely ghastly." Vivian crunched another peanut.

"Oh, yes, I agree. But now, Carson needs a bone marrow transplant and I'm hoping that his father will be a match. I'm not." Juliet twirled the glass of wine in her hands.

"Can't they use his marrow?" Vivian washed the peanuts down with a sip of white wine.

"No. The remission is fading too quickly, and once that happens, there aren't any more conventional treatments left." She looked away, blinking her eyes against the tears.

"I see. So you are here to get your former husband to give you his bone marrow."

"Something like that, but there are problems." The glass of wine was put on the table untouched.

"Such as?"

"Tony Graniston has become an even more complicated person than he was when I married him." She shivered and rubbed her arms.

"He's the one? Oh, Juliet, that man is a scoundrel and a scandal. Drink, women, gambling, drugs, you name it, he's done it. I'd be surprised if he had any marrow left to donate."

"I know all that. Donald hired a detective. I've already seen his parents, who are, how shall I say, overwhelmed with the knowledge that Tony was married, then not married, and a father, all in the same breath."

"What do you think of them?"

"Emily is interesting, steel under the cashmere, that type of American my mother always told me was the most dangerous. She wants to be English."

"And the father?"

"What is that saying I keep hearing from Americans, the apple doesn't fall far from the tree? He's very charming, just like Tony, ruthless, powerful. He's already told me that he wants Carson to come and visit."

"Isn't that nice!!! I gather he was overjoyed to hear that he has a grandson."

"Ecstatic is more like it. Apparently Tony has only been able to sire girls, twins, and there is one more on the way. I feel almost sorry for his wife. She is about to have her life turned upside down." She smiled ruefully and finally took a sip of the wine.

"I wouldn't worry about Laurel. She can take care of Laurel very well."

"Do you know her?" Vivian, I don't like that appraising look you have just now.

"For years. Juliet, I grew up in Greenwich. I know Tony's family, too. A word to the wise. They may have something up their collective sleeve, they usually do. I wouldn't be surprised if Tony didn't try to sue for parental rights." Right now, dear friend, you look like a fluffy little lamb tethered to a stake waiting for the lions to come calling.

"Could he, after deserting me and then terminating his rights?"

"Nowadays, a reformed father is just what the courts and the media love. You're fortunate, Carson is a British citizen. That means that the hearings on final custody will have to take place there. I can't see the courts there being too anxious to hand him over to Tony." Juliet walked across the living room and stood at the window. Suddenly, the bustle of Manhattan had lost its charms.

"I'd never thought of that. Do you mean that he can apply for visitation here and get it? After nine years, the courts can simply hand over my child to a total stranger and tell him to go and stay with Daddy? It's too awful to think about. And right now, that is the least of my worries. All I can think of is that every day, my child is slipping away, getting thinner and weaker. That's what counts. If I have to promise Tony that he can visit Carson, then I'll do it, anything, as long as I can save my child."

"Be careful, Juliet, you may get more than you bargained for. Be very sure that he is a match before you promise anything. Tony owes money to all the wrong people. Your husband is a billionaire, and it doesn't take a genius to made the same connection that Tony is going to make." Oh, little lamb, I can hear the lions coming through the grass.

"I will. Now, enough gloom and doom. We're all dressed up, so let's go out and stuff ourselves." Laughing, she turned out the lights and closed the door.

*   *   *   *   *

It was after eleven o'clock when Juliet put her key into the door. The evening had passed quickly. Vivian was an old friend, and she had the ability to put a light touch onto any serious occasion. It had been just what she had needed. She opened the door, switched on the light, and dropped her kingfisher blue and gold silk jacket on the chair. The matching slipper dress flowed and clung to her body, culminating in a straight skirt, slit up the back. As an afterthought, she had swept up her hair into a ponytail and had braided it around a gold ribbon. Vivian had insisted that it was a case of the crow and the peacock, dining on the same worm. She had worn black from head to toe, a perfect counterpoint to Juliet's bright colors.

She picked up the telephone on the first ring.

35

"Darling, we have a problem." Donald's voice sounded unsure, wavering.

"Where are you?" She could not help the panic from rising up.

"It's not Carson. He was sleeping peacefully when I left my father's house. Juliet, I want you to listen to what I am going to say without interrupting. Then we can talk about it. I'm on the jet, on the way to New York. David Graham called me just after we hung up. He had the same feelings of disquiet that you and I and your father were having, and he went back to the office and took out the file himself. He's in a state of shock at the moment. It seems that Tony never actually signed the divorce agreement. He merely returned it, and the secretary who put it away never thought to double check that it was all in order. I've been to look at it, and it looks like a copy, and not the original that David sent to him. He may have kept the original, signed it, and sent back the blank copy to try and extract something from your father. When he didn't hear back from us, he probably counted on something happening eventually that would leave matters in his favor. The fact that he has remarried could signal that the papers were signed originally. I'll be with you by nine, and we'll face Tony together." She could feel the blood rushing to her feet.

"Donald, this is terrible. Tony is just the type who would marry with or without a divorce. My God, if he hasn't signed it, we're both bigamists. We aren't married, you're not Carson's legal father, and it just goes on and on. The publicity, and your poor father. It is just unspeakable."

"Juliet, don't buy trouble before it comes to you. The man has a family, a wife and children. He has a profession in New York, and I can't imagine that his parents would take kindly to his being a bigamist."

36

"Donald, I don't think Tony cares what they think. Life has always been about what is good for Tony and that's where it ends. I want you to call Carstairs, now, tonight, and have him consult the best family lawyer that America has to offer, and find out what can happen. And ask David to do the same. I have a feeling that this is only the beginning of our problems with Tony and I want to be prepared."

"All right. I'll take a helicopter from Kennedy. And try not to worry, we'll make it all work out."

"I'll try. See you tomorrow."

"Good night, my darling, and try to sleep." He hung up the phone softly, and rubbed his eyes, wishing for the optimism he had tried to pass on to his wife to come back and sit on his shoulder as well.

CHAPTER THREE

Donald's key turned in the lock half an hour before the deadline. He took a deep breath as he carried his bag and briefcase through the door. As he closed the door behind him, he saw his wife, her hair braided and wearing a severe black suit, standing at the window. He walked across the room and put his arms around her, holding her hands across her chest.

"I got here as soon as I could. I'm starving, I should have left more time." She leaned back against him and looked up into his face.

"No use. Carstairs and the divorce lawyer should be here momentarily. He wants us to be briefed before Tony gets here." She turned to face him and kissed him lightly on the lips.

"I'll take a rain check, tonight, no matter what, the world gets shoved out of the door."

"Something to look forward to. I need that." The doorbell rang and she crossed the room to open it.

"Lord Donald, Countess Juliet, I'd like you to meet Scott Barnes, a partner at Felder and Felder. I thought it best to retain the firm immediately. They are the best, and I wanted to avoid any conflict of interest. Why don't we all sit down, as there isn't much time before the Granistons arrive." Edward Carstairs found a chair and sat down.

"Lord Donald, let me begin by saying that my firm is honored that you have retained us, and we will do everything in our power to make sure that you and your wife retain custody of your son. In cases like this, even if the natural father files to reverse the termination, chances are that the most that he could get is supervised visitation. I know that is not what you want to hear, but we have to face up to all eventualities. The child's illness will be a factor. No American judge wants to appear unsympathetic to the mother of a dying child. And of course, the unfortunate reputation of the natural father will have a great deal to say for itself. But as far as the divorce goes, I urge you to try and settle out of court. The publicity surrounding a double bigamy case in which a celebrity is involved can be pretty horrible." Scott unscrewed the top of his fountain pen and sat with it poised over his legal pad.

"At this moment, I am not sure that bigamy is even an issue. Tony could have signed the agreement, and sent back a blank copy, just to be difficult." Donald tried to sound more confident than he felt.

"Tony Graniston has a reputation as an attorney who skates as close to the edge of the illegal as he can. Don't count on him having signed anything until you see it in front of your face."

"This is dreadful. Donald and I have no children of our own, only Carson, and two others from his first marriage. The only ones who can really be hurt will be Tony's family, and his parents." Juliet listened for a sound other than the scratching of pen on paper.

"Have either of you given any thought as to what you will offer Tony in return for his agreeing to be tested and subsequently, to be a donor, and of course, there is the matter of the divorce." The fountain pen raced across the page.

"My wife tells me that he owes a great deal of money to the wrong people." Donald could feel his stomach sinking lower and lower.

"That amount comes to almost half a million dollars. Considering the assets of Macallister Industries, it is a given that he will ask for a great deal more than what he owes. And the blood test itself is strictly voluntary. The word around the courthouse is that he has never done anything voluntary in his entire life, unless someone makes it worth his while." Scott checked his watch. "It's almost time. Would you like me to stay, or should I leave now and wait downstairs?"

"Why don't you and Edward go downstairs and wait? I want to let them make the first move. We'll call you as soon as we know anything." Donald opened the door, to find the room service waiter about to ring the bell. He checked his watch. It was nine fifteen. Just enough time to finalize his strategy.

At nine thirty exactly, the doorbell rang. Juliet nodded at her husband and as prearranged, he walked into the bedroom, leaving the door slightly ajar, saving the element of surprise for himself.

*   *   *   *   *

By nine o'clock, the Granistons had met in the lobby of the Park Lane. Tony and Laurel had complied with his father's unequivocal invitation, and now sat in the lobby, completely mystified.

"Tony, in thirty minutes, you and I are going to go upstairs to the Macallister Industries suite, and talk to Countess Juliet Macallister. When you get there, I'm sure that you will recognize her. You remember Juliet Sadler, don't you?" Tony's face blanched, his forehead showing beads of sweat, as he swallowed hard and looked at his father.

"Tony, I'm waiting for an answer."

Tony cleared his throat and opened his mouth, but nothing came out. He suddenly remembered sending back the divorce papers, or the copy he had made, unsigned, a malicious act, done in the hope of extracting a few extra thousand dollars from his former father-in-law. The original, unsigned and forgotten for nine years, remained in his safety deposit box, lying in wait for just such a moment.

"She was my wife, while I lived in England." He turned and saw his wife's face, the ugly red color traveling up from her neck and over her face.

"And?" His father sat across from him, cross-examining his witness.

"She divorced me, about five months after we were married."

"And why was that, son? Weren't you a good husband to her?"

"It was just a fling. I never intended to marry her. When Oxford ended, I just left. She's an artist. I figured it wouldn't matter to her." He shrugged his shoulders.

"Tony, you did sign the papers and finalize the divorce before you married Laurel, didn't you?" Tony looked away.

"I sent back the papers when I got them." Jordan felt the anger rising as he watched his son hedging his answers.

"Did you sign them?" Tony squirmed.

"Not exactly. I always figured her old man would cough up some more money to get me to sign them. He never even contacted me."

"So, let's review and get this straight. You are still married to Juliet, and she is married to her husband, and you are married to Laurel, but not exactly." Jordan Graniston fought for control. For the past seven years, ever since rumors of his son's behavior, both professionally and privately, had reached him, he had been in denial, unwilling to recognize the truth. In the past, he had counseled other men to muster the courage to cut their criminally inclined children out of their lives. He wondered, not without a sense of irony, who would now counsel him to do the same.

41

Sitting across from her husband, Emily Graniston felt sick, so nauseous in fact that with the slightest persuasion she would have vomited in the middle of the hotel lobby. She closed her eyes and breathed deeply, telling herself that soon it would be over, that she would wake up and discover that everything that had happened since yesterday had been a bad dream.

Jordan swallowed the bile that rose from his stomach. He checked his watch. It was twenty-five minutes past nine. It had taken that small amount of time for his life to be shattered. Any hope of salvaging the broken shards was, at best, fleeting. He looked across at Emily's face, and amended his thought. Her life, too, was in pieces. Neither of them would ever think about their son the same way again.

Emily turned to look at Laurel, eight months pregnant. The ugly angry red of her skin had faded to a pasty gray. Hastily, she got up and hurried her daughter-in-law into the ladies room.

*   *   *   *   *

"God! How am I going to fix this with Laurel? Not that it matters very much." Tony muttered under his breath.

"Son, It should come as no surprise to you that Laurel will handle this in the way that generations of wives with faithless husbands have. And don't think for a minute that she will ignore that part of your life that you thought you had hidden from all of us. Her lawyer will make sure you pay handsomely for all those good times." Jordan mopped his forehead with his handkerchief. He hadn't noticed how warm the lobby was until now.

"Tell me something, Tony, now that we're alone. What were you thinking when you took all her money and came home? Did it ever occur to you that one day somewhere, sometime, your past was going to come back to haunt you?" Jordan sighed. Tony was still looking away, anywhere except in his father's direction.

"For crying out loud, Dad, she was eighteen, and panting for it. Her father had money, a lot of it. He never gave us any of it while we were married. You can't blame me for wanting him to pay for her freedom." God, he's whining. Why didn't I ever notice this before, that awful whining.

About to answer his son, Jordan turned around and saw Emily beckoning to him. She was standing in front of the elevators, and as he joined her she whispered that she had put Laurel into a taxi and sent her home. Tony, following his father at a distance, was thinking about Juliet Sadler, or still Graniston, or Macallister, or whatever. He remembered her unusual beauty, that pale, creamy skin and tawny eyes and how he couldn't wait to make love to her every minute of the day that she was available. She had been such a willing partner, she was the best he had ever had, her passion for sex with him all too obvious. He had been a fool to run off and leave her. Now she must be twenty-seven, at the height of her beauty, and her body must be that of a woman. As he stood in the back of the elevator, he remembered how eager he had been to possess her, to own her forever, to make sure that no other man got near her body, except him. He closed his eyes and called back the memories of her hair, always smelling of lavender, long and silky, that amazing color of red. He had wrapped himself in its scented softness, teasing her and nicknaming her his very own Godiva. The soft jolt of the elevator

43

stopping on twelve brought him back to the moment. The thought of the particular advantages of still being married to her brought a smile to his face.

At the last note of the doorbell chime, Juliet took a deep breath, smoothed the sides of her hair and pulled down the jacket of her black suit. She reached out and turned the knob, swinging the door wide, and stepping back, afraid to look at her worst nightmare.

Tony had positioned himself in front of the door, so that he would be the first to enter. He said nothing, swaggering slightly as he walked into the room, his parents following at a distance. Looking straight ahead, he could see only the living room of the suite, decorated lavishly, in the soft pastels of most luxury hotel suites. Behind him, he heard the scrape of the bottom of the door on the carpet as it swung shut. His eye caught a brief movement, a glimpse of a tall woman dressed entirely in black, with a long red braid hanging down her back. A second later, she turned and they faced each other.

Tony was suddenly at a loss, his ability to speak or move temporarily stilled. She was so beautiful, more so than he had remembered, and for an instant, he could not remember one valid reason why he had left her nine years before.

Juliet was sure that everyone in the room could hear her heart leaping in her chest. His presence in the room had turned the clock back nine years, and again it was that last horrible day, when she had returned to their London apartment to find him with his bags packed, and a plane ticket in his hand. They had quarreled, and he had smacked her face so hard that she had had bruises around her mouth and nose for days afterwards. She could hear him laughing as he hit her, flaunting the money he had stolen, calling her an eighteen year old nobody, a worthless piece of shit.

And then he had assaulted her and told her she was nothing but a cheap whore who bored him, an ugly bitch he never wanted to see again. She had told her father, that day he had come with the doctor and the ambulance, to take her to the hospital. He had sworn never to tell another living soul, although he had insisted that his solicitor come to the emergency room to take both a full statement and photographs, in the event they were needed.

When she had fallen in love with Donald, she had told him everything, including showing him the file. He had cried and held her close and promised her that never again would she have to suffer that way, that he would love and cherish her and the child for the rest of his life. Now, looking at Tony, nine years and another lifetime later, he had become a stranger, part of a horror that could never be entirely forgotten.

"I think we should all get down to the business at hand. Tony, I'm sure you two remember each other. The first thing we should discuss is how we go about settling all of this like civilized people." Jordan settled back onto the couch, next to Emily, far away from his son.

"There's nothing to discuss. Juliet and I are still married, and I intend to keep it that way. Macallister isn't really her husband any more, but, if he wants to make it worth my while to sign the papers, then maybe we have something to talk about."

"I don't think that will work out quite that way, Tony. You have a wife and a family and somehow I don't think that your law practice will improve if your clients discover that you have committed bigamy." Juliet crossed over to the window and leaned against it.

"Compared to Macallister's money, my law practice isn't worth mentioning. I'll go for a lump sum

45

payment, let's say twenty million to start the negotiating." She took a deep breath, trying to ignore the smug look on his face.

"What makes you think that Donald would give you twenty cents, Tony? After all, we have no children of our own, and as you told me many times, artists are supposed to be unconventional. I doubt if anyone will even notice that we have been living together without being married. You, on the other hand, have a much larger problem. I understand that Americans are obsessed with, I believe it is called, family values. I wonder what all your friends in Greenwich and at your country club would say if they found out that you are a bigamist?" She clasped her arms tightly across her chest, using the pain as a distraction, willing the trembling to stop.

"Just a moment." Donald crossed the room, and put his arm around his wife.

"I'm sure you all know who I am. And since I am the one who will be signing the check, I would like to have something to say."

"Twenty million, and not a cent less."

"I think not. If you refuse to sign the divorce papers, and then try to use that to force me to pay you to sign them, that is blackmail, isn't it? As Juliet has told you, we don't care if someone points a finger at us. Actually, it would probably boost sales and improve the prices for her paintings." Donald allowed a ghost of a smile to cross his face. "I will happily pay off your gambling debts, and even round the figure off to give you a beginning of what you will need to hire your own lawyer to deal with your marital problems. But that is all, and if you push me any further with your ridiculous demands, you will get nothing." Juliet felt the slight pressure as Donald squeezed her shoulder.

"One million, my last offer." Tony licked his lips.

"With one other thing you must do. If you agree, you can have the check today." Donald whispered in Juliet's ear. Surprised, her eyes widened, but she nodded.

"What else do you want?"

"Tony, you do remember what happened that last day, before you deserted Juliet and ran off to America? Perhaps I should refresh your memory." Donald opened the desk drawer and took out the copies of the file that he had had made.

"There are enough here for everyone to have a copy. Shall I start with you, Jordan?" Donald walked around the room, handing copies of the file to the others in the room. Juliet looked out of the window, her back to the room, frozen with fear and shame, telling herself over and over again that she had to focus on the goal; she was fighting for Carson's life.

The suite was thickly carpeted, and despite its attractive appearance, had that hotel room feeling of still, dead air. There was no sound of a radio or television, or of polite conversation, only a deep and unfathomable silence, broken only by the rustling of paper. Jordan and Emily, overcome with shame and humiliation, looked down at their feet and said nothing. Tony merely glanced through the file and tossed it aside.

"Tony, something happened that day, something that turned out to be the most wonderful thing that has ever happened to Juliet and to me. When you raped your wife, you gave her a child and when you terminated your parental rights, you gave up all the experiences that I have had with him. That child is now eight years old, the most marvelous human being I have ever met. In every way, but one, he is my son. He calls me Daddy, and hugs and kisses me at night. I tell him stories and take him fishing and riding, and teach him to play tennis. All the things that you have missed." For a second, Donald allowed a smile of possession to cross his face.

"A son? I have a son? Why didn't you tell me?" Suddenly serious, Tony was finally paying attention.

"Would you have believed me if I had? If I recall the letter that accompanied your termination of your rights as a parent, you insisted that it was impossible that you could have fathered the child. In fact, you were very specific about the notion that in all likelihood I had, how did you put it, wound up in someone else's bed. There was one thing you forgot, Tony. I was in hospital for weeks after you left for America, and after that, let's just agree that I wasn't too keen on jumping into any man's bed." She held Donald's hand so tightly that he winced.

"He is not your son, Tony. You made that child by accident, the result of your act of violence against Juliet. You have no rights at all, except one."

"And what, pray tell, is that?" Tony walked across the room and sat down in an overstuffed chair.

"Carson has leukemia. The conventional treatments are no longer working and he needs a bone marrow transplant. Juliet is not a match. We need you to be tested, and if you are a match, you have the right to donate bone marrow to save his life."

"You're kidding me. Forget it, I'm not going to do it."

"So much for the sudden interest in your son, Tony. If you want the money we agree upon, and if you want the details of this file kept secret, you will have the blood test, and if you are a match, donate your marrow to save your son's life. There is no statute of limitations on rape in England. Do I make myself clear?" Donald's hands grasped the back of a chair as he leaned closer to Tony's face.

"No way, unless Juliet agrees to come back and be my wife. Just think, I have a son, and a beautiful, rich and talented wife. I'd be crazy to give that up." Donald backed away slightly from the menace in Tony's face.

"You already have. Jordan, I can see that your son is unwilling to be reasonable. My offer is off the table, and I will make sure that my London office delivers the original of this file to Scotland Yard." Donald turned away, as if disgusted with the entire process.

"Let's not be hasty. Tony, think this through carefully. You'll be out from under, a clean start, and you'll be able to do something to make up for what you did." Jordan found himself filled with self-loathing as he pleaded with his son.

"Donald, all this is pointless. I'm not waiting around listening to all of you bargain and argue while our son's life is slipping away. Tony, you disgust me as much as you did when I had to repeat what you said and what you did to my father's solicitor. Now you have a chance to do one decent thing in your entire miserable life, save a little boy whose misfortune seems to be that he is your biological child. Look at your parents, they are his grandparents, and they have never seen him, or held him or loved him. You owe them that, if nothing else." He began to clap, softly and slowly.

"Brilliant, Juliet, a worthy performance. Too bad this audience isn't buying. Start packing. We're going to London to be with our son. I want to get there as soon as possible." Juliet shuddered as she watched the superior smile creeping over his face.

"Over my dead body. You will never be allowed within one hundred yards of Carson. Tony, please, just have the blood test and let it go. Sign the divorce papers, and let all of us get our lives back." I will not cry, whatever I have to do, I will not cry.

"Why would I want to do that? There's nothing here for me. I hate my life, my wife is a pig, all my kids do is whine. I owe money to everyone I can think of, so as far as I can see, going to London will only improve my circumstances."

"Enough, all of you!" Emily had gotten off the couch and walked over to the window, to join Donald and Juliet. She was trembling with fury, not knowing what to do first. Jordan hesitated for only a moment.

"Juliet, I'm so sorry, about all of this. Tony, I want you to clean out your desk at the office, by close of business tomorrow. You're on your own, as of this moment. And, Donald, we'd both like to come to London to see Carson. If you need us, we'll be at home, packing." Jordan grasped Emily's elbow and guided her out of the suite.

"Wait a moment." Juliet slipped out of the door to catch Jordan and Emily.

"We haven't told Carson anything about all of this. Please, can you give us some time to tell him? I'm not trying to keep you away from him, it's just that all of this can be a shock for a healthy child, and he is so ill." After exchanging a glance with her husband, Emily patted Juliet's hand.

"Of course, however long it takes."

"Macallister's keeps a suite at Claridge's. I'll make the call, you can stay there. Be at the airport tomorrow at eight-thirty. Tell your driver to go the British Airways private hangar. We'll be flying on the Macallister jet." She kissed Emily on the cheek and went back into the room. Tony walked towards the window, obviously trying to choose his words carefully.

"Two million, and I'll have the test. And I want visitation rights with my son."

"Two and a half million and you never lay eyes on him. Take it or leave it." Donald crossed his arms across his chest.

"For God's sake! He's my son. I should be able to see him at least once."

"You gave up that right. The deal stands, as is." Juliet dug her fingers into her arms.

"Three million, I do it all. No questions asked."

"Done. My assistant is downstairs. I'll have him prepare the check and bring the papers for you to sign. You hand over the divorce papers, signed and notarized, and then we hand over the check." Donald could feel his body relaxing. It was over and he had won, at least for the foreseeable future.

"Just one thing, do you have a picture of him? Can I at least see that?" Juliet and Donald exchanged glances.

"No, that won't be possible. Now, I think you should go. You can wait downstairs until the papers and the check are ready."

*   *   *   *   *

"Jennifer, is that you?" Jordan wiped his nose with a handkerchief.

"Daddy, are you all right? You sound terrible." Her heart began to beat faster.

"I just wanted to tell you that your mother and I are going to London."

"London? I don't understand."

"Darling, listen to me. Do you remember when Tony went to Oxford nine years ago?"

"Yes, of course I do. I was in heaven with him gone. I finally got some peace and quiet. Why would you ask me that?"

"Did you know that he was married when he was in England?" Jordan's voice began to shake.

"Married? You're kidding me, right?" Is that all? Why am I not surprised that none of us ever knew.

"No, I'm not. He was married to Juliet Macallister, the painter, for five months, before she filed for divorce." He blew his nose again.

"Daddy, why don't you start at the beginning."

"She was an eighteen year old art student, and they ran off and got married. It lasted five months, and then your brother decided it was time to come home, without his wife, of course. God, Jenn, he raped her and beat her up and then left, with whatever money they had in the bank, and came home." Seemingly without control, he began to weep again.

"Daddy, try to calm down. What happened then?"

"Her father took her to the hospital, and kept pictures and a file of all the details of what happened. He arranged for the divorce, and sent your brother his copy of the papers, to be signed and sent back."

"Let me guess, he managed to avoid doing it, but everyone thought he did." The knowing tone of her voice was not lost on him.

"How did you know?"

"Daddy, what did you think happened all those years when I spent every waking moment I could away from the house? Remember you used to ask Mom if you really had a daughter, or was I a figment of your imagination?"

"Yes, I do."

"Daddy, I'm sure that I wasn't the only one he called a useless slut, it's just that neither of you believed me when I tried to tell you what was going on."

"I'm beginning to realize that I should have started listening a long time ago."

"It doesn't matter anymore. There's a healthy three thousand miles between the two of us. That's what's important, that he stay as far away from me as possible."

"There's more. There was a child afterwards, a boy, Carson. He's eight years old. I can't believe it, my grandson, your nephew."

"Are you sure?"

"Yes, he looks just like Tony did at that age. But there's a problem. He has leukemia, and needs a bone marrow transplant. Jenn, so far they haven't found a donor, and Tony may be the last chance the boy has. As a favor to me, would you and the kids get yourselves tested? Maybe one of you would be more reliable than Tony."

"And that's why you're going to London."

"Apparently, there's not much time left. If things don't work out, at least we'll have a chance to be with him for a little while." She could sniffling through the telephone.

"I'm so sorry, for both of you. No, that's not right. For all of us, I'm sorry for all of us. Where should I have the results of the blood tests faxed?"

"The Great Ormond Hospital for Children, to a Doctor Edgar Davis. Your doctor should be able to do it."

"Sure, no problem. Try to stay hopeful, Dad. Things have a way of working themselves out." Why do I sound more confident than I feel?

"Thanks. How are Marina and Lindsey?"

"Fine. They'll be thrilled that they have a new cousin. You know how they feel about Tony's kids, so he has to be an improvement. Look, if you need me, just call. We'll all pack up and come to London to be with you." Jennifer found herself staring at the school calendar.

53

"You'll like her, Jenn. She's a genuine, down to earth person."

"I'd like to meet her. I've seen pictures of her work. She's brilliant. How on earth did she marry Tony?"

"She was eighteen."

"That explains it. Look, I don't want to be rude, but I know you have things to do. Give my new nephew a huge kiss from his aunt Jennifer, and buy him a stuffed animal, Daddy, and tell him it's from all of us, that we're watching over him, you know what to do." Poor Daddy, how awful to finally have to confront the truth about your son.

"I've thrown him out of the firm. He's finished. He'll be calling you, probably when he's run through the money Juliet's husband paid him to be the donor for Carson."

"Don't worry, I can handle it. Now go, and keep in touch. I'll have the tests done today. Call me if any of us are a match. I love you, Daddy. Bye."

*   *   *   *   *

Once the door to the suite had closed for the last time, Juliet kicked off her black, high-heeled pumps, and flopped onto the bed. Donald sat on the other side of the bed and picked up the telephone.

"Hello, Father. How's my boy? Anything new?"

"Donald, he's fine, holding his own. I spoke to Edgar this morning, and he gave me a whole list of things to watch for. Did you get him to agree?"

"It cost us, but yes, he's agreed. He's such a swine that I almost hope that one of the other family members turns out to be the match. It would make things so much easier."

"How many others are there?"

"The parents, and a sister. The sister has two children. She might be a better match than Tony."

"And the divorce?"

"He'll sign and notarize it, or he won't get paid. I'm hoping that if I'm careful, not too much of his stink will wear off on to me."

"How is Juliet bearing up?"

"Like an Amazon, incredibly brave. She's here with me now, resting, and then we'll have dinner with her agent later tonight. Tomorrow, we'll pack up and take the jet back to London. Tony's parents, Jordan and Emily, are flying over with us as well. Can you make the arrangements, have a car pick them up and take them to Claridge's?"

"Of course. I'm glad you're staying the night. Juliet must be exhausted and you could both use an evening to yourselves. I'll come to pick all of you up at the airport. I'm sure Bertram and Rose can stay with Carson."

"We want to tell him first before he meets them. They can get themselves settled and tested while we're telling him."

"Right. See you tomorrow, and don't worry. Now, here's Carson with his list of goodies that he wants, and I'll say good night."

"Daddy, are you coming home tomorrow? Can you bring one of those hot dogs we had last year. I would love to have another one."

"Carson, how am I supposed to bring a grilled hot dog across the Atlantic?"

"You can do it, I know, you can do anything. With mustard and relish, please."

"Your wish is my command, oh noble one. Now here is your mother, and I'll say good night."

"Mummy, how are you? Have you sold the women yet?"

"No, darling, not yet. We're having dinner with Uncle Paul tonight and I'm sure he will love them as much as all of us do. How are you today?"

"The same, just a little tired. Grandpa rented 'Star Wars' for me to watch, and he got some popcorn, too. I have to go now, kisses to you and Daddy, and I'll see you tomorrow."

"Sweet dreams, my darling."

CHAPTER FOUR

Juliet got off the bed and walked over to the window. Through the door, she could hear her husband's voice coming from the living room. She checked her watch, it was only a little after ten and they had the entire morning to themselves before they had to meet with Tony to finalize the deal.

Standing in the doorway, she watched her husband as he continued to talk on the telephone. At an even 6 feet tall, he was as slim and handsome as he had been almost nine years ago, when they had met in the art classroom at the Slade. Even then he had worn the round horn-rimmed glasses that were so fashionable now. She remembered the first time she had looked into his face, with its even features, straight nose and well-defined mouth, but it was his eyes, large gray pools flecked with gold that had held her attention. All she had wanted to do was to run her hands through his dark hair and perhaps get him to make love to her. At that moment, she had blushed, as she had looked down at her pregnancy, two months from its end. He had noticed her blush, and had grinned, coloring slightly. She had caught him out, staring at her face, its clear ivory skin, small nose and passionate mouth, with those fawn colored eyes, and that incredible red hair, tumbling down over her bare shoulders. He had recovered and asked her to dinner, announcing to her professor that he would buy the entire goldfish series, and wanted to celebrate by dining with the artist.

They had eaten every lunch and dinner together over the next month, and fallen more deeply in love with each day. A month after they met, he proposed, and never hesitating, he had made love to her, helping to close the door on her disastrous first marriage. Two weeks later they found the time to get married, in between Lamaze classes and hunting for a place to live. They had been a truly happy and loving couple, raising three children, with everything to live for, until the day, shortly after Carson's sixth birthday, when he had complained of a sore throat. A trip to the doctor's office had developed into a long stay in the hospital, followed by the seesaws of brief remissions and painful rounds of chemotherapy. Carson had eked two years out of the treatments, but now his time was running out.

With a gentle smile tugging at her mouth, she turned and went back into the bedroom. There, after taking the coverlet off the bed, she undid the braid and brushed out her hair. She put her shoes back on, and checked herself in the mirror. At 5 feet nine inches, her legs were by far the longest limbs of her body. Under the black suit jacket, she had worn just a transparent bone silk shell. Added to the amazingly short suit skirt that barely covered her thighs, it was a potentially fatal combination. Locking and chaining the door to the suite, she turned to look at her husband. Still deep into his telephone call, he did not notice that she had drawn the sheers over the windows in both the living room and in the bedroom. Juliet returned and stood next to her husband. As he ended his call, she neatly unplugged the phone and tossed it onto the couch.

"You promised to shove the world out of the door." Laughing, she began to unbutton his shirt.

"That was for tonight, not now." Donald protested, but not convincingly.

"I just made it tonight, so, sorry, you're stuck. Say good-bye, for at least the next few hours, or until I get tired of you." She kissed him lightly beginning with his jawbone and traveling up across his face.

"Somehow, I don't think that will happen. I do have to call about the check in about two hours." His will to resist melting rapidly, he reached up and loosened his tie.

"Don't worry, we'll remember to do that. Now, aren't you supposed to be doing something?" She had undone the top button of his shirt and was taking off his tie.

"Yes, now come here and stand still." He held her head with his hand, feeling the softness of her hair between his fingers. Bringing her closer, he kissed her mouth, gently opening it with his tongue. His hand moved down and began to unbutton her suit jacket. As he pushed it off her shoulders, he looked down and laughed.

"Wicked woman, you knew I wouldn't be able to say no. Now you pay." The shell drifted down towards the floor as he unzipped her skirt. Her heart was pounding in her chest, so loudly she wondered if he could hear every beat. He swept her off her feet, and gently set her down on the bed.

Donald looked down at his wife, and he felt the same way he always did when he looked at her, so beautiful, with the steel of her resolve cloaked in the softness and vulnerability of her innocence. He loved her so much, and he always felt as if his love grew each and every time they were together. Quickly, his need for her overwhelming him, he began to make love to her. Juliet responded, feeling as if her body was melting, becoming one with his. Her lovemaking became more urgent as their passion dissolved together. Gasping for breath, she held him and kissed his neck, listening to the slowing of his heartbeat.

"Donald, I want to try again for another child. It's time, two years since the last one." He propped himself up on one elbow.

"Darling, remember what the doctor said after the last time, when I almost lost you, how fragile you were, and how dangerous it would be to try to have any more children." He stroked the hollow between her collarbones, finding it soft and irresistible.

"I promise I'll be good, and stay in bed if I have to, but please, I want to try again. I need to have another child. You don't understand, how wonderful it was to be pregnant with Carson. I wasn't sick a day, and all I could think about was that darling little baby that I would love for the rest of its life. Sometimes, my body feels as if it is actually hungry, starving for the feeling of carrying a child inside me, our child, someone to love Carson as a big brother. I'm only 27 years old, too young to have to give up on having children. I should have already had two more. Please, don't take this away from me."

"Juliet, I know I'm being entirely selfish, but I can't bear the thought of losing you. Last time, when you almost bled to death, I swore that no matter what, I was not going to put your life in danger again." He brushed away a strand of her hair.

"And you won't lose me. The minute I find out I'm pregnant, I'll go to one of those high risk doctors, and I promise to do whatever he tells me to, faithfully, and I won't cheat. Donald, please." He could feel her hand gently stroking his chest.

"All right. But I'll be the worst watchdog you've ever seen, believe me. If anything happens to you, I won't be able to go on without you. Just remember that."

"The only thing that will happen is that in nine months time, we'll be doing late night feeds again."

Her laughter began at her eyes, and ended up in a throaty giggle.

"You devilish woman. You planned this all along." He laughed, in spite of himself.

"Don't complain that I never consult you. Besides, when Carson was born, you did promise me a little girl, with hair as red as mine. I'm holding you to it."

"And you expect this to go just like that?"

"If we hit it right, or didn't you pay attention at Eton when they tried to explain all this to you?"

"Careful, or you'll pay."

"Please, right now, I'll pay as often as you like."

*　　*　　*　　*　　*

Tony Graniston sat in the bar at the Park Lane Hotel, sipping his third vodka martini. He had gulped down the first two to steady his nerves, and give him courage. God, he had ruined his life through his own stupidity. He must have been insane to abuse Juliet and then desert her. It was obvious, even to someone as egocentric as Tony that she genuinely loved Donald Macallister, sadly enough, the very same way she had once loved him.

He felt in his pocket for the divorce papers. He was fortunate, the bank, the safety deposit box and the notary public were around the corner from the hotel. It had taken less than twenty minutes to retrieve the papers and have them notarized, as they should have been eight years ago. His spirits rose as he thought of the three million dollar check he would be receiving in exchange for those papers. At least, if he couldn't have Juliet, the money would give him a fresh start.

Settling back in his chair, he began to think about his marriage to Laurel. The second time, he had chosen a more conventional path for his marriage.

Now, five years later, he had secretly grown to hate everything about her.

When he had met her again, the summer before his third year in law school, it felt comfortable and familiar, dating a girl from his own background that he had known for years. That summer he escorted her to all the right parties, and all the events at the country club, feeling that, at last, his life was going to be the way he wanted.

Their wedding had been lavish, the party continuing through the honeymoon and for quite a few weeks afterwards. By the time he had sobered up, a month before he was to begin working at his father's law firm, he knew he had made a second terrible mistake. For all of her pedigree, and healthy good looks, Laurel was conventional, so much so that he began to wonder what he had seen in her in the first place. This time, however, there would be no plane to take him three thousand miles away where no one would know what had happened. He would have to make the best of it.

By the end of the first year, he had lapsed back into the habits he had developed during his first marriage. Sullen and rebellious at losing his freedom again, this time to a woman not nearly as beautiful, fascinating and rich as his first wife, he began a heedless downward spiral of drinking, gambling and risky behavior with any woman who would sleep with him. On some occasions, he would pay for sexual favors, finding it intensely exciting.

Watching her husband slipping further and further away from her over the first two years of her marriage, Laurel tried to solve the problem in the same way that many of her conventional ancestors had done. She allowed herself to get pregnant. When she joyously announced the news over breakfast one day, about three years after their wedding, Tony could hear the metaphorical clang of the jailhouse door. Fatherhood was the last thing on his mind, but he forced himself to look and sound as if he was overjoyed. All he could think of was that he was trapped, more tightly, and more permanently than he had ever been with Juliet.

That evening, in between feeling very sorry for himself, and downing four glasses of vodka, he found himself becoming more and more depressed at the thought of what his life would become. A house full of children that he didn't really want, and probably would never really love, growing older and more bored and more trapped as he and Laurel raised their children, then finally, becoming so old that he would no longer be able to enjoy the kind of lifestyle he had always wanted.

But today, he had been given another chance. Once the shock of his former wife's appearance had worn off, and he had suddenly realized that he was free, the shackles of his unhappy marriage had fallen away. He picked up his fourth martini and drained the glass.

*   *   *   *   *

Edward Carstairs sat in the bar, directly across from Tony Graniston, nursing his mineral water. He looked at his watch, and shuddered. It was barely eleven, and Tony had already consumed four martinis. If that check did not come soon, he would be too drunk to sign the papers, or even understand what he was signing. Hesitating, he tried to decide whether or not to call upstairs and have Donald come down, just to keep an eye on things, when Lawrence Ames, Macallister Industries' American banker, arrived in the bar. Edward lifted his hand slightly, giving the signal to join him and sit down, while at the same time placing a call to the suite upstairs.

"Lord Donald, everyone is here, in the bar. Shall we all come upstairs?"

"I can come down, if you like."

"No, I think at this point that it would be good to get out of the bar for a bit."

"Carstairs, how much has he had to drink?"

"Four martinis and counting. We should do this quickly, or else we'll have to wait until he sobers up."

"Right. Give me ten minutes. I want to get Juliet out of here while all this is going on. She doesn't have to sign anything, does she?"

"No. Her set is already signed. All that remains is for Graniston to sign the papers I drew up, hand over the divorce papers, signed and notarized, and then Lawrence will hand over the check."

"Is there a custody provision in the papers?"

"Yes, there is. He agrees, when he accepts the check, never to attempt to contact or visit Carson, or to try to reverse the termination of rights."

"Will it stick?"

"I wish that I could tell you it would. But Scott emphasized that there is really no guarantee that an American court wouldn't reverse it if he makes his case convincing enough. We'll just have to hope that everything he said about the boy was just to get more money out of you."

"See you in ten minutes, and Carstairs, thank you for all you accomplished today."

"Think nothing of it, Lord Donald, just doing my job."

Juliet sat at the vanity and put on fresh make-up. She had dressed again, this time in jeans, a white shirt, and a navy blazer. Her husband walked by, and stopped to breathe in her scent. Lavender had always been her favorite, and even though she had a dozen or more bottles of perfume on her vanity at home, she still preferred its simplicity to any other. She had left her hair down, hanging freshly washed and smooth, to the center of her back, wearing only a navy blue headband to keep it back. As he stopped to bury his face in its scented silkiness, it enveloped him, bringing back the memory of their lovemaking, and he felt a great reluctance at making her go out, when what he really wanted to do was to take off her clothes and make love to her again.

"Donald, if you're not careful, you'll lead me astray, and then what would Carstairs and Tony say?"

"They would be completely and totally envious of me, as well they should be. And it's unfair of you to accuse me of leading you astray, when you are driving me crazy."

"That is what any wife is supposed to do to her husband. I'm ready, I have the list and I won't be back until I have bought everything on it, and more."

"How long will that take?"

"About two hours. Will you wait to have lunch until I get back?"

"I'm starving already. Go now, and we'll have a wonderful meal when you get back." He kissed her on the mouth, softly at first, and then harder. Reluctantly, she tore herself away.

"Wicked man! See you in two hours." Laughing, she walked down the corridor. Leaning back against the wall of the elevator, she wondered if she could be pregnant. Wistfully, she allowed herself to dream that this time, she would not lose the baby in the third month, as she had the last two times. The doorman caught her eye, and hailed a taxi, watching as it sped away.

*   *   *   *   *

Donald had just put on his tie and jacket when the doorbell rang. In front of the door, Tony swayed unsteadily on his feet, suddenly feeling the effects of four quick martinis on an empty stomach, part of which had spilled down the front of his blue shirt. His face was shiny with sweat, glistening in the light, as on either side of him, Edward Carstairs and Lawrence Ames each held an arm, supporting and holding him up.

As the door opened, he felt disappointed to see that only Donald was waiting inside the doorway. Throwing off the support of the other two men, he made the effort to walk across the room unaided, and wound up in the first available chair, more by luck than by design. Stretching out his legs, he crossed them at the ankle, folded his hands across his damp shirt, and waited for one of the others to make the first move.

"Carstairs, is he as drunk as I think he is?"

"No, but very close. Why don't we start before he passes out?" He took his briefcase and placed it on the table at the far side of the living room. Motioning to Lawrence Ames to sit down, he found a chair and made himself comfortable.

"Tony, we want to get started now. We all have other appointments, and I for one would like to get this over with." Donald stood in front of him, his hands in his pockets. His fists were clenched, and for an instant, inadvisable as it might be, he couldn't help imagining how satisfying it would be to land one good punch.

"Sure, I have all day now. Nothing else to do, but collect three million dollars." His speech was slurred as he made a vain attempt to get out of the chair.

Donald grabbed him under the shoulder and heaved him to his feet.

"Now, sit down over here, and try to concentrate." Donald dropped him into a chair, and then sat at the head of the table.

"Tony, this agreement touches on three major points: first, you agree to have the blood test within 24 hours; second, that if you are a match, that you come to London and donate your bone marrow, and third, that you promise faithfully not to try and visit or see Carson, and that you promise not to try to reverse the termination agreement." He pushed the documents and a pen towards Tony.

"Carstairs, please make sure he signs or initials every spot properly. Then, when he's done, and he hands over the divorce papers, check them over carefully. If they have been signed and notarized, give him the check and get him out of here."

The whole process took an hour, with Tony struggling to concentrate on his signature, and the others growing increasingly disgusted and impatient. At last, it was over, Tony had his check, and was taken down to the lobby. Edward Carstairs made sure that he was put into a taxi and taken anywhere as long as it was far away from the Park Lane.

*   *   *   *   *

Juliet shifted the shopping bags around so that each arm could carry an equal weight. Once she had finished buying the video games and other toys for Carson, she had stopped in at Saks. Heading for the boy's department, she bought jeans, shirts and a pair of cowboy boots for her son. As she tried to decide whether or not to buy a leather bomber jacket, she recalled how fussy he was about his clothes and how he followed fashion trends closely. Decisively, she tossed the jacket on the pile at the register, hoping that they would give him an incentive when it came time for the bone marrow transplant. Her next stop was the lingerie department. Her mouth twitched as she picked out several items, a black, lacy teddy, a pale peach gown and robe, and another gown, exquisite in its transparency. Once they had found their way into a shopping bag, she wandered through the dress department. Unable to resist, she bought a black dress she knew that Donald would describe as dangerously non-existent. It had no back, a plunging neckline, and its hem just covered the top of her thighs. As she matched it with a pair of three inch high-heeled black sandals, and hose with seams, she could not help but wonder what the reaction at the Oak Room might be if she arrived there wearing the dress.

After another quick stop to buy two suits, it was time to return to the Park Lane. Sighing with satisfaction, she leaned back in the taxi. Shopping was the one activity that she loved almost as much as painting. It wasn't that she was needlessly extravagant, but she loved beautiful clothes and accessories, and somehow always managed to wear and enjoy everything she purchased. The best part of it all was that she was now a wealthy woman in her own right. Her pictures had always sold well, and the current demand for them was at an all time high. It gave her immense satisfaction to be able to shop for whatever she wanted, and be able to pay for it out of her own money. Donald understood her need for financial independence, even while he would periodically indulge himself with giving her an extravagant gift, a luxury that she loved, but would never buy for herself. The memory of the sable coat he had given her for Christmas, the one to wear over the ruby necklace and black silk gown she had found in the beautifully wrapped boxes with her name on them, made her feel incredibly extravagant.

The taxi driver honked his horn in the mid-afternoon traffic. Looking out of the window, she saw that they were still ten blocks away from the hotel. Juliet leaned her head back on the seat, thinking about her husband. They would have to get married again, but this time at least they could do it ahead of the baby doctor. Maybe a romantic private ceremony, with their three children, and their parents present, in the South of France, or on top of the Eiffel Tower. She giggled and stretched out her arms. They had better hurry up. If she was pregnant, at least she should be able to wear normal clothes at her wedding.

At last, she was able to unload herself and all of her packages at the hotel. Keeping the bag with the lingerie, she left the rest to be delivered. As she opened the door to the suite, she could hear Donald on the telephone. She walked by and blew him a kiss as she headed into the bathroom. Turning on the tub, she added lavender bath salts and began to undress. Her back was to the door, and she didn't bother looking in the mirror. If she had, she would have seen her husband leaning against the door, watching her. Now, as he watched her take off her blouse and brassiere, he had to tamp down his desire, wanting to wait and watch as she gradually took off everything she had on before she reached into the Saks bag and took out the transparent negligee. She held it up to the light and giggled as she draped it on the hook near the tub. Dropping her panties on the floor, she picked up her hairbrush and began to brush her hair, slowly, luxuriously, tilting her head back, feeling its weight and its silky sweep against her back. Quickly putting it into a braid, and fastening it onto the top of her head, Juliet stepped into the tub. Sighing with pleasure and closing her eyes, she sank into the lavender scented bubbles and leaned her head against the back of the tub.

Donald had watched with a smile on his face. Her ritual of brushing her hair, letting it sweep down her back, the scent of warm lavender wafting towards him, never failed to excite him. In the days just after Carson was born, all three of their children had lived at home. When they had all been tucked in their beds, she would sit at her dressing table and brush her hair, long, sensual strokes that never failed to get his attention. His earliest fear, that the ten year difference in their ages would eventually create problems, had been put to rest on the very first of their "intimate evenings," nights filled with passion and lovemaking. Any worries he had had about satisfying a nineteen year old girl vanished during that first encounter, when they had made love unencumbered by her pregnancy. A memory flashed across his mind, the first time he had held her body after Carson's birth. Long and slender, her breasts incredibly warm, their lavender scent rising to his head, he had made love to her for the entire night, or at least until Carson's wails had had to be answered. Now, eight years later, he was well into his thirties, still as enthralled and bewitched by her sensuality as he had been the first time he had seen her.

He looked over at his wife. She had not moved since she had closed her eyes, and he quietly dropped his bathrobe and climbed into the bathtub with her. Juliet sat up and splashed water towards him.

"Not fair. Now you've seen my surprise!" She laughed as she pushed water over at him.

"Stop, the room is getting a bit damp. And I haven't seen that marvelous thing on you yet, so only half not fair. Besides, you shouldn't have brushed your hair like that, you know the effect it has on me."

"Poor man, always at my mercy." She leaned over and kissed him, her tongue caressing his mouth and her hand against his cheek.

"Juliet, don't do that. I'm likely to move suddenly and invade your half of this unbelievably small bathtub, the bathroom will flood and the hotel management will invite us to find somewhere else to stay. I have a brilliant idea. I'm going to get out of here, so you can dry off and put on your surprise. When you are finished, come into the bedroom, and bring your hair brush. This time, I think that I want to brush your hair for you. I haven't done it for far too long."

He stood up and was gone. Deciding to take her time, she dried off slowly, picked up her new bottle of lavender scent and sprayed herself, beginning with the top of her head and ending with her ankles. As a final act, she slipped the new negligee over her head. Her watch, laying on the sink, had silently ticked off the minutes since Donald had gone back to the bedroom. Fifteen of them had gone by, enough to draw out the tension. Impatience rising, she opened the door and stood in the doorway of the bedroom.

Donald had been busy while she had been taking her time. The bottle of Cristalle sat in the silver ice bucket, and soft music played in the background. He, however, was nowhere to be seen. Crossing the room and seeing that the telephone was lit up, she walked into the living room.

"Thank you, I'm so glad that you called to let me know. I'll be in touch with you in the morning."

"Donald, who was that?"

"Carstairs. He checked Tony into the Plaza so that he could sleep off his drunk and he's hired a detective to watch him. I need to know everything he does, at least until the results of the blood test come back."

"You're wonderful, do you know that?"

"Yes, but I love it when you remind me that I am. Looking at you in that gown, I would say that you are just as wonderful." He laughed and picked up the bottle of champagne. Expertly removing the cork, he poured two flutes and handed her one.

"To Carson, long life, and that daughter you keep promising me." Juliet took a swallow of champagne, and walked over to stand in front of her husband.

"To you, and to five daughters, if you can manage them." He looked down, into her eyes. Their color always reminded him of cats, feline beings who arched their backs and purred when their fur was stroked. His hand trembled as he picked up the hairbrush and began to brush her hair. The scent of lavender floated up and with each stroke, his control slipped a bit. He struggled and finally gave up, tossing the hairbrush on the floor. He loved her so much, he didn't think that he would ever be able to show the real depth of his feelings. Pushing his fears to the back of his mind, he began to make slow love to her, determined to give her the child she so desperately wanted.

CHAPTER FIVE

Gently, the tune of the little alarm clock that Donald took everywhere with him drew him up from a sound sleep. It was 5 P. M., time to get up. He swore under his breath as he got out of bed and put on his bathrobe. Turning around, he looked at his sleeping wife, her hair spread all over the bed and the pillow. Her arm, on the outside of the blanket, was completely relaxed. All the tension that she had carried for the past two years, since Carson had gone to the hospital for the first time, was gone, held at bay, if only for the moment. He hated to wake her up, but it was inevitable, that such a perfect sleep would have to be interrupted.

"Juliet, darling, it's time to get dressed to meet Paul. It's after five, and I know you want to take your time." He kissed her cheek and whispered softly into her ear. When she did not stir, he became more insistent, kissing her again, and gently stroking her neck.

"Insatiable beast! I heard you the first time." She opened one tawny eye and smiled.

"Shall I order something up from downstairs?"

"Yes, tea and sandwiches. I'm starving and we won't get any food for a long time. And don't look at me like that, it's dangerous." Laughing, she sat up in bed and tried to get the tangles out of her hair.

"How long was I asleep?"

"Since about three. We both slept, soundly, and satisfied."

Juliet lay back in bed, pulling the covers up to her chin. She couldn't remember the last time that they had had so much time for each other. Promising herself that once Carson was well, life would get back

73

to the way it had been before, she headed into the bathroom. Glancing at herself in the mirror, before turning on the tub and loading the water up again with lavender bath crystals, she smiled, pleased at how rested and satisfied she looked. While the tub.was filling up, she went to the closet and took out her new dress. As she held it up, she tried to decide if she was really in the mood to be that wicked. With a giggle, Juliet carried the dress and all of its accessories into the bathroom, and shut the door.

An hour and a half later, she emerged, almost dressed, wearing her robe over the hose, and the lace teddy. She had heard the doorbell, and the murmur of voices as Donald had settled with the room service waiter. He had already showered and dressed for the evening, for once grateful for the second bathroom in the suite.

"Lazy girl that you are, I've already made you a plate." Donald filled her cup with tea and placed it on the table next to her chair.

"Thanks. Did your father call?" She picked up the cup and took a sip.

"Yes, while you were bathing. Everything's fine, and no change in the red cell count. Dad took him out for a spin in that little red convertible of his, stuffing him full of ice creams, I imagine." He watched her nibble a tea sandwich.

"Delicious! Cucumber was always my favorite, so cool and green. My mother always insisted it was a perfect antidote to red hair and tantrums." She teased him over the edge of her sandwich.

"Your mother was a saint to put up with you, I don't know how I manage." He laughed as he crossed the room and sat down on the sofa.

"Are you going like that?"

"Not likely. What time is it?"

"Half past six. Why don't you hurry up, and we'll go down and have a drink in the bar, fortify ourselves for a long, gossipy evening with Paul."

"I thought I'd wear my new dress, give Paul something to talk about. Be right out." Five minutes later, she walked back into the living room, her legs seeming to stretch away endlessly beneath the skirt of the dress. The top, cut in a V, just skirted the edge of the lace teddy, and the curve of her breasts. The back swooped down, with just a hint of lace at the top. She had braided her hair, and twined it into a knot at the base of her neck.

"Well?" She pirouetted slowly, showing the dress off to its best advantage.

"I'm speechless. Do we need a bodyguard?" He couldn't take his eyes off her. Donald had always thought of his wife as an irresistible combination of brilliant artist and beautiful woman. From the second he had laid eyes on her, her magnetism had drawn and held his attention. In the earlier years of their marriage, he had been amused at the frequency with which he would have daydreams about her, even erotic fantasies. He had always thought that such things were meant for frustrated adolescent boys, not grown men approaching thirty, with three children and a business to run. There had been times, when Carson had been a toddler, and Juliet had been at home during the day, when he had given in to his daydreams, left the office in the middle of the day, and gone home to fulfill his fantasies. Not once had she said no, but had merely blown him a kiss, handed Carson over to the nanny, and reached for her bottle of lavender scent.

Their bedroom suite was on the second floor of the house, away from the living quarters, but within earshot of the nursery. The Regency furniture and the bedding and curtains in white satin and lace, and accents of rose and green, were all brought together with an antique Persian carpet, in beautiful tones of faded rose and green. During those afternoons, he had felt as if he could never have enough of Juliet, that there was an elusive element that he could not possess, that if he could only try harder she would be totally his.

One afternoon, three years after their marriage, he had received a telephone call in the middle of the afternoon. To the astonishment of his colleagues, and the knowing amusement of his father, he had simply left his business meeting, and gone home, this time to fulfill Juliet's fantasy. She was the one who came to him, softly, with incredible tenderness, and at that moment, that one illusory part of her being became his.

"No, I don't think so. Just think, darling, everyone will think I'm your mistress, and be totally envious of you, especially around bedtime."

"Juliet, you are a dangerous woman. Get your things and let's go, before I decide to show you how enticing that dress really is."

*   *   *   *   *

It was only one in the afternoon. Jordan Graniston turned the black Mercedes into the driveway, stopped at the head of the circle and turned off the ignition. In a figurative sense, he had begun a very long journey, starting at a place of profound disillusionment and pain. At the moment, he was stranded somewhere in the middle, any conclusion still hidden at some point far away from where reality lay. The underpinnings of his world had been rocked, assaulted by truths long denied, a reckoning long delayed. He was so tired it felt as if he had been awake for days.

Emily Graniston sat in the passenger seat, unable to make the effort to get out of the car. She looked at the outside of her house, warm rosy brick, with white framed windows and shutters. Where yesterday the pride of ownership had been so pleasing and gratifying, in its place today, there was nothing. When she had left the house earlier in the day, her mind had been preoccupied with her firm's three real estate closings that were taking place later in the day, and the details of the law firm's cocktail party, an annual event scheduled to take place in four weeks time. Sitting shocked and silent, as she had for the entire trip back from Manhattan, Emily could not fathom why they had been considered worthy of her attention.

"Em, let's get out and go inside. We have a lot to do before we leave tomorrow. We have to be at Kennedy by 8:30." Still gripping the steering wheel, he stared through the windshield, seeing nothing. Separated from the things that at any other moment would have grounded him in reality, he found himself in an alternate universe, in a place where nothing made any sense at all.

"Jordan, are we awake, or is this a nightmare? Will I be able to close my eyes for a few minutes, and then wake up to find that everything is the way it was yesterday, before she showed up on our doorstep?" She turned to look at her husband, but unseeing, he continued to stare straight ahead.

"It's a nightmare. I think that we've been living in it for years, but we were too blind to see it. Kids from this neighborhood, where they have everything and anything money can buy, aren't supposed to grow up and become criminals. They aren't supposed to rape their wives, desert them, and then commit bigamy, all because of a few thousand dollars that weren't paid. They aren't supposed to drink and gamble and sleep around on their wives, and do God only knows what else." As his stomach heaved, he felt nauseous and leaned his head on the steering wheel. Emily reached out and touched his shoulder.

"Darling, you have always been the one who told me that there comes a time when parents have to let go. We brought two children into the world and taught them what we thought were the important lessons, how honesty and hard work will pay off in the end, that respect and truthfulness can lead to happiness. And when children grow up and go out into the world, the best any parent can hope for is that they were listening. Jennifer was, and Tony wasn't. We have to accept that, and be grateful that we know it all now. There can't be any more surprises." Emily opened the door and got out. She leaned into the car, her hand on the door, ready to shut it.

"Come in the house. We'll have some tea, and then start packing. Maybe I'll cook tonight, I haven't done that in a long time." He nodded, and she shut the door.

Unlocking the front door, she disappeared inside. Jordan waited a moment, and then got out of the driver's seat. Pausing, he looked around at the house and grounds, focusing on them, wondering what it was that he should be seeing. Turning on his heel, he opened the front door, stepped inside and closed it gently, but firmly, against the outside world.

*   *   *   *   *

In his room at the Plaza, Tony lay on the bed, supposedly sleeping off his four martinis. When Edward Carstairs had checked him into the room, he had also taken him upstairs and dumped him onto the bed. In seconds, he seemed to be asleep, snoring and oblivious. Creeping out of the room, Carstairs went downstairs to telephone the private detective he had hired. Tony listened for the sound of the door closing before he reached for the telephone. Twenty minutes later, a young woman presented herself at the door of his room.

"You certainly took long enough." Tony began to kiss the girl while trying to take off her clothes.

"You're not my only client. I'd decided to take the day off and stay in bed. Once in a while I'm entitled to sleep alone. Tony, stop. You stink of booze. Why don't you take off those clothes and take a shower?"

"I had four martinis. That's why I smell, and yes, I'll take off my clothes, but no, I won't take a shower. I have other things in mind." His hands fumbled with the buttons on her blouse. Frustrated, he ripped them open and pulled her blouse off.

"Tony, just wait. I'll take off my clothes, and then yours. Just don't rip anything else." Cherry had learned from long experience that this was a client who did not take kindly to being criticized when he was drunk. Quickly, she stripped down to her panties, and then pushed him onto the bed. As she removed his clothes, he fumbled with her breasts. They were large, just the way he liked them. As he tried to kiss them, he remembered Juliet and how incredibly beautiful her body had been. She swam up out of his past, and he saw her as she had been when they were first married, and had spent every spare minute in bed. Juliet, even the name brought back the memory of her soft skin, scented with lavender, how she had loved it when he had kissed her breasts, and between her legs, how she had wept and begged him to make love to her, and how she in turn had made love to him, the silky sweep of her hair, with its flowery scent, lying across his chest.

The sound of Cherry's voice brought him back to the present. For a moment, he didn't know where he was, until he heard her calling his name. Sighing with pleasure, he lay back on the bed and let her do her job. After all, that was what he was paying her for. Closing his eyes, he fantasized that it was Juliet making love to him, shouting her name just as he passed out.

*   *   *   *   *

The dress was a sensation, especially on the woman who wore it. When Donald and Juliet presented themselves at the Oak Room, he could feel the heat of those who stared, openly and some quite longingly at her as she walked slowly through the restaurant. Fixing his gaze on the gentle sway of her body, and the way the dress clung and moved with every step, he struggled against the cool smile of possession that he longed to show to the world. Slightly ahead of him, she had stopped, and was kissing Paul on the cheek, as he stood alongside her and waited to shake Paul's hand.

"Juliet, darling, you look positively scrumptious in that dress. Donald, you're a brave man to let her go anywhere in.." Paul's voice trailed off as he met Donald's eye and grinned.

"We had a bet, Paul, and she won. Tell me, how many of the men here do you think are wondering, right at the moment, if she is my mistress, or not?"

"Donald, every man here, except me, and of course, Tony. He's draped across the bar in there, downing martinis as if they were plain water." Juliet could hear the disapproval in his voice.

"Just as long as he's sober enough tomorrow to take the blood test, and stays alive long enough to donate his marrow, I don't care about anything else." Juliet shivered as she pulled her wrap over her shoulders and moved closer to her husband.

"I gather he was well paid to do this, so he'll stay alive, at least until the check clears. I won't bore you with all the sordid little tales I've heard about him, too horrible and depressing. And tonight I'm in the mood to be excited, especially about your new paintings." Paul sipped his martini, as daintily as a well-groomed cat laps a saucer of milk. Slightly shorter than Donald, with regular features, brown hair and eyes, Paul Townsend had one distinguishing characteristic; he wore his brown hair plastered down onto his head, with a large swirl in the front. To complete his image, he always wore suits cut in a 1930's style, remarking to anyone who would listen that he was merely ahead of his time, and that every fifteen years or so, everyone else caught up. Juliet laughed and handed him the pictures.

"'The Lilac Woman' isn't quite finished yet. I had to stop work a month ago when Carson's remission began to fade. But, when he's better, I'll buckle down and finish it. You can spread the word that they will be for sale by Christmas, and this time I want them sold as a unit. Don't split them up like you did last time. I know that you make more money selling them separately, but this time I would appreciate it if you would sell them together."

"I'll try, but asking over a million dollars for the three paintings is going to make them very hard to sell. Individually, I can get half a million easily. It's the million dollar figure that is a barrier, not selling them as a series." Paul raised his hand slightly to signal the waiter to bring the menus.

"Think about it, Paul, otherwise I may not sell them at all. I can just as easily hang them in the townhouse, or in the country, and not miss the money." A small smile curled up the edges of her mouth.

"But my darling girl, I would miss the money. Let's order dinner, I'm starving, and I'm sure you two have other plans for tonight." His eyes twinkling, Paul studied the menu, ignoring the faint blush that stained Juliet's cheeks. The corners of Donald's mouth twitched as he struggled against a knowing smile.

*   *   *   *   *

Carson Macallister sat in the chair in his grandson's room and watched him sleep. He sighed, feeling all of his sixty-two years, as he looked at the little boy as he slept, clutching his teddy bear and dreaming a small boy's dreams of glory. That afternoon, as a reward for finishing both breakfast and lunch, he had taken the child for a ride in his red Maserati. The weather had been warm and sunny, and they had sneaked away for a spin and then had downed double scooped chocolate ice cream cones. The child had giggled and laughed, just as most children his age would, but it had given his grandfather a moment of incredible sadness, that this might be one of the last moments of joy he and the boy would share. He had two other grandchildren, those from his son's first marriage, but he had never liked their mother, and somehow that antipathy had been transferred to them. It made no sense that he should love Carson, who was not really his grandchild more than the two who were. But there was an appealing element of Carson's personality that could not be denied, a loving nature, and the ability to give a seemingly inexhaustible supply of that love to anyone with whom he came in contact.

He had bonded with his grandson from the moment he had held him, just two days after he was born. From that day until this, he had an established schedule; three times a week, when he was in London, he would go to his son's house and have dinner with Carson. As the boy grew older, these visits had expanded to trips to the zoo, to Hyde Park, and out to restaurants and movies. Now, he could not remember any of the details of these trips, only the memory of Carson's laughter, his ready smile and the huge hugs he would give his grandfather at the end of these expeditions.

Bertram Sadler, accompanied by his wife, Rose, knocked softly on the door frame, keeping to the schedule created to insure that someone familiar and loved was always in the room. The three shook hands, the daily report was passed on, and Carson Macallister departed. Although he was committed to staying at home twenty-four hours a day during Juliet and Donald's trip to New York, he had fallen into the routine of letting Juliet's parents stay overnight so that he could see to the demands of the business he shared with his son. In a few hours, they would all eat dinner together before retiring for the night.

The Sadlers stood next to Carson's bed and watched him sleep. They were struck, as they were every evening, at how small and frail he had become. He had always been a sturdy and athletic child, but tonight, his thinness and the bruise colored shadows under his eyes brought home the precariousness of his condition.

"Let's go to the door, so we can talk. We can still watch from there." Rose kissed Carson's cheek and walked across the room.

"I wonder how long it will take for the tests to come back." Bertram fidgeted as he stood in the doorway.

"A few days, I imagine. What will happen if Tony isn't a match?"

"I imagine they will try all the members of his family. If they aren't a match, then we'll have to try elsewhere, but I think that he will be. Carson looks just like him, so the DNA should match."

"Poor Juliet, having to see him again after what he did. I wonder how she is handling all of this."

"Very well, like she always does. Rose, she will be fine. Carson will be fine, and with any luck, Tony will drop dead right after he donates the bone marrow." He took out a large cigar and held it firmly between his teeth on one end. He had already had his ration of the two cigars per day that his doctor had mandated. No one, however, had forbidden a cigar that was held and not smoked.

"Bertram, behave. The most important thing is that he has agreed to be a donor. Everything else will have to take care of itself." She stroked the sleeve of his jacket.

"You're right, as usual. I'll go down and have them lay tea on a tray for us. Why don't you sit with Carson? The new book you got him is in my briefcase, in case he wakes up."

*　*　*　*　*

Tony Graniston sat at the bar in the Plaza Hotel, his second martini cradled in his hand, and a neighbor and commuting partner, Bob Davidson, seated next to him.

"It's the most fantastic story I ever heard, Tony. Does Laurel know yet?" Bob took a sip of his white

84

wine, and checked his watch. He had promised his wife, Mary, that he would be home before midnight.

"News like this seems to travel faster than the speed of light, Bob. By lunchtime, she was already on the phone. She's hired a lawyer, and I understand that I have been evicted from my own house. All my things are sitting on the front porch, so I guess I'll have to go out to Greenwich tomorrow and pick them up."

"Where will you live?"

"With three million dollars, I imagine that I can afford to rent a small apartment for the time being. After that, it depends. The money has to last me, at least until I get another job." He signaled the bartender for a refill.

"You're really going through with this, the transplant and everything."

"I have to, otherwise they'll take the money back. I would also like to see my son, although his mother seems to feel that I am the monster from hell, and therefore not fit to be with him." Tony took a large swallow of his third martini.

"I still have a hard time believing that you were married to Juliet Macallister. Did you love her?" Tony shook his head.

"Marrying her, it was all a big mistake."

"Why did you leave her? It doesn't make sense. She's so beautiful, and if you ask me, she must be unbelievable in bed." Bob could feel beads of sweat forming on his face.

"That last day, I was so sick of being married to her, I felt like a fish with a hook through its gills. I hated her for making me love her, and making me want her all the time, so I just let her have it. When it was over, I just left. I didn't see her again until this morning." Tony looked satisfied, like a cat that had just eaten a much desired bird. He didn't notice Bob staring at him, his horror mounting.

"Tony, I'm starving. Let's grab some dinner." Bob shuddered as he changed the subject.

"Good idea. I haven't eaten since this morning."

The two men walked slowly through the Oak Room, as the maitre d' showed them to their table. Bob wasn't really paying any attention to the other diners, but Tony was, noticing Donald and another man at a table set for three. As he and Bob found their table and sat down, Juliet was nowhere to be seen.

Paul picked up his brandy glass and looked around the restaurant. Sucking in his breath, he kicked Donald under the table, and when he caught his eye, raised his eyebrows and nodded in Tony's direction.

"Donald, I told you he was in the bar. Before you put him up here, you should have considered that you were bound to run into him tonight."

"Paul, it's all over. The divorce papers are signed, and all he has to do now is have the blood test tomorrow, and if he's a match, come to London to donate his bone marrow. He can't hurt her ever again."

"Won't he want to see Carson?" *You poor man, you don't have a clue as to what you are up against.*

"That will never happen. I'm going to have round the clock security outside his room when Carson has the transplant. No one gets in or out without my permission." Donald drained his brandy glass.

"Donald, how are you going to tell him about Tony?"

"Very gently, I imagine. If it weren't for his parents and sister, I wouldn't tell him at all." He played with his coffee spoon, dragging it across the tablecloth.

"I know that you want to spare him any pain, but he has to know sometime. He's a sensitive and intelligent child, he'll get over it." Paul's brown eyes were sympathetic. Not for the first time, Donald couldn't help comparing them to those of a cocker spaniel.

"I'm more worried about Juliet. This has all been exhausting for her, and if he starts making demands on her, to see Carson, just one time, to be able to call or write to him, a few times a year, she may fold entirely. For almost two years, now, she's been running on nervous energy." Automatically, Donald raised his coffee cup to his lips. Disappointed that it was empty, he put it back on the saucer.

"She looks radiant to me, almost as if... She's not pregnant, is she?"

"We're trying again. She wants, no, I think needs another baby more than anything, except Carson getting well."

"Best thing for her. Having a child changes the focus, makes one very strong and protective. Congratulations, in advance. You should take your gorgeous wife back to the Park Lane, rip off that dress and do what you have been thinking about all evening." Paul laughed as he finished his coffee.

"Is it that obvious? The woman is driving me mad with that dress."

"Telepathy. You're no different than any other man in here, including Tony. Now, here she comes, so I will say good night. Juliet, I'll talk to you soon. Kiss that wonderful boy for me." Paul stood up and walked out of the restaurant.

"Don't turn around, darling. Tony is sitting at a table behind us, about twenty feet away. He came in while you were in the cloakroom." Donald put her wrap around her shoulders, and kissed the nape of her neck.

"Do I have to talk to him?" He caught the note of fear in her voice, and squeezed her shoulder.

"Not if you don't want to. We can leave now, we're finished anyway." His hands stayed on her shoulders.

"You must think I'm a scared little mouse." She trembled, unable to control her emotions.

"Never. I keep thinking that if someone had done to me what he did to you, I would have killed him. Now, darling, I don't know about you, but I want to go back to the hotel. We have to pack up, and there is still the matter of your insistence on wearing that incredible dress." Distracted, she smiled and nodded as they turned to leave.

Looking up from behind the menu, Tony watched her. Her head was tilted back and turned to the side, and he stared at the perfection and symmetry of her features, the small, perfect nose, the full mouth and the classical chin, all set off by the weight of the hair at the nape of her neck. He felt a combination of anger and a strange sadness; she was the symbol of how he had ruined his life. Watching her leave, he was relieved. At least he didn't have to look at her and be reminded of what he had done to himself.

*   *   *   *   *

Juliet stood on the corner of Fifth Avenue and 60th Street and marveled at the never-ending ability of New York to attract, beguile and fascinate her. Sighing contentedly, she leaned her head on Donald's shoulder, as he put his arm around her and drew her closer.

"I just remembered something. I promised Carson a grilled hot dog. When we get back to the hotel, I'll call Carstairs, and have him deliver a dozen to the plane. That way we can hope that at least one will arrive in an edible condition."

"Have him separate the buns from the meat and mustard. That way, nothing will get soggy." Her eyes danced as she leaned into him, delicately sending a message whose meaning was all too clear. Their eyes met, and he could not help thinking that if he were not standing on a street corner in the middle of New York City, he would have made love to her right where they were.

"Tell me, oh mistress mine, shall I be the envy of all tonight?" Laughing, they crossed the street and walked up towards the hotel.

"Tell me, am I going to wear this dress again?"

"Absolutely not. Too risky."

"Good. Saves time taking it off. Here's the hotel. Let's hurry." She giggled as they slipped through the front door into the lobby, and headed for the elevator. Donald shoved the card into the lock, while loosening his tie and unbuttoning his shirt.

"Donald…" Juliet slipped by him, leaving her shoes on the floor. She faced him, her tawny eyes turned almost to black. Gasping, he grabbed the front of the dress, and ripped it downward. It fell away, leaving only the transparent teddy and the long, black hose. Lifting her up against him, he whispered in her ear. Wrapping her legs around his waist, he leaned her against the wall as she slowly removed first his tie and then his shirt. Taking her time, the exquisite slowness of her actions only increased his desire.

"Put me down, please." As he lowered her to the floor, she raised her arms to let down her hair. Mesmerized, he watched as she pulled out the pins. The heavy braid fell down past the middle of her back. She shook her head, and the braid became undone, the strands of her hair hanging down her back and over her shoulders. He buried his face in her hair, breathing in its familiar scent. Close to the edge, he began to remove the rest of his clothes, watching her as she removed the teddy, drawing it out, as she took off first one strap and then the other. His hand shaking, he stretched it out to help her, as the teddy fell away towards the floor. As if they were part of a separate being, his hands lifted her hair and then draped it across her breasts. Like skeins of silk, it lay across her shoulders, shimmering in the light. Her breath was sweet and warm against his ear.

"Darling, please, I can't wait any longer. Please, now, I need you." She pressed herself against him, as if by that action she could melt and become one with him. His breathing grew ragged as he lifted her up so that she could wrap her legs around him. All control disappeared as he could think only of possessing her, being part of her, creating himself within her, over and over. It seemed as if his desire was frozen in time, as if he had to repeat the act of love again and again, each time more passionately than the last. He sobbed as he held her, the warmth of her skin and the scent of lavender on his every breath.

CHAPTER SIX

Jordan and Emily Graniston sat at the kitchen table, dinner finished, the dirty plates sitting in front of them, just staring into space. Neither one made a move to clean up the table, or go upstairs and attempt to pack for their morning flight.

"We should go and pack. I booked the car service for 6 in the morning." Jordan held his chin on his hand and looked over at his wife. They had been married for over thirty years, and while he would never have described their relationship as anything other than a couple who had learned to live with each other with love and affection, tonight he would have added admiration to that description. He was awed by his wife's behavior. Not once had she lost her temper, but had accepted what was in fact reality, and gone on. Emily looked at him across the table, and was about to answer him when the doorbell rang. Jordan, needing to move around, got up and went to answer it.

"Daddy, we decided to come and go to London with you. It didn't seem fair to make you and Mom go through this alone." Jennifer, her husband, Herb Markham, and his two granddaughters stood on the doorstep.

"Aren't you going to invite us inside?" Jennifer laughed as she kissed her father on the cheek.

"Yes, of course. I'm just surprised to see you, that's all. You didn't have to disrupt your lives for this." He stepped aside as the others carried their bags and filed into the foyer.

"Daddy, we had to come. He's our nephew, and Marina's and Lindsey's cousin. I hope it's all right with you and Mom." Jennifer's linked her arm through his.

"Yes, of course."

"Herb came home from the office, and after I told him about Carson, he didn't say a word, he just picked up the phone. You've never seen four people throw clothes into suitcases as quickly as we did."

"Jenn? Whatever are all of you doing here?" Emily came out of the kitchen and embraced her daughter.

"We're going to London with you and Daddy, Mom. You shouldn't be alone, and if one of us is a match, then we can donate marrow right there, no delays."

"Well, then, Marina and Lindsey, how about a hug for us?" The two girls hugged their grandparents, leaning their heads against them.

"I'll get Maria to make up the rooms. There's dessert and coffee in the kitchen, and some dinner, if you're hungry." She put her arms around her granddaughters and moved off towards the kitchen.

*   *   *   *   *

Donald Macallister supervised as the bellman loaded the suitcases onto a luggage cart. Trying hard to concentrate on the task at hand, he felt dazed, incredibly satisfied and relaxed. After nine years of marriage, he had thought that he had known everything that there was to know about his wife. Last night had reminded him again never to underestimate her ability to surprise him. Regretfully, he closed the door to the suite and followed the bellman down the hall to the elevator. Juliet was downstairs, having breakfast and a last visit with Vivian.

"Juliet, do not allow Tony to get around you. Knowing what I do about him, he's going to try to see Carson, and I can feel it, he'll try and find a way to get custody. If you and Donald can manage it, get married again right away, and do it quickly."

"Vivian, he signed an agreement not to sue for custody." Juliet finished her herbal tea and leaned back in her chair.

"You haven't the foggiest idea how sleazy he is. Not the type of man you want within ten feet of Carson. I'm not trying to scare you, but Tony will stop at nothing, and I mean nothing to get what he wants." Vivian leaned forward in her chair, and rapped the table for emphasis.

"Vivian, darling, you're scaring me. Donald has insisted on having guards posted outside Carson's room, round the clock, to keep Tony out. You make it sound as if we will have to do this for a long time to come." Be careful, Juliet, the lion is getting closer to that fluffy little lamb.

"Exactly. Never take Tony at his word, or take it for granted that he will do the right thing. He doesn't know the meaning of the words." Vivian, you're scaring me with that determined look of yours.

"God, what am I going to do? Last night, he showed up at the Oak Room. I couldn't even bear to look at him and this was in a public place. Donald was amazing, strong and protective, but I was ashamed, so cowardly not even to turn around."

"Juliet, you're not a coward. You've stared the beast in the face and lived to tell the tale. Just be very careful." She reached her hand across the table, and patted Juliet's long, slender fingers.

"Here comes Donald. Time to go, I guess. Have a good flight, and call to let me know what's happening." Vivian got up, kissed Donald on the cheek and waved goodbye as she walked out of the restaurant.

"Ready, darling? The limo is packed, and we really must go now." She nodded, and grabbed her leather jacket. As she walked out of the restaurant, he followed her, resisting the urge to grin, as he watched

93

her body, clad in skin tight jeans, move through the lobby, and into the limousine.

*   *   *   *   *

The check-in had been completed, and Donald and Juliet sat in the lounge reserved for private jet passengers. All the bags had been loaded onto the plane, with the exception of Juliet's portfolio, and a shopping bag containing twelve freshly grilled Nathan's hot dogs, with buns, mustard and relish. He sat reading the Wall Street Journal, while she talked on the phone.

"Daddy, I can't thank you enough for moving in with Carson while we were gone. It meant a lot to both of us that all three of you were there with him while we were in New York. How did he sleep last night?" Bertram could hear the happiness in her voice. His heart was heavy, that it would not last.

"Soundly. Juliet, I'm afraid. What will we do if we don't get a transplant in time?"

"Daddy, we're doing our best. Hopefully, Tony or one of the others will be a match. If not, the international registry is hard at work as well. Other than that, there is nothing that we can do. I've never felt so helpless and neither has Donald."

"I know, darling, it's just that your mother and I feel so frustrated. It used to be that when you skinned your knee, or didn't feel well, that Mummy's kisses and Daddy's hugs were enough to make you feel better. With this, I've never felt so powerless." She could hear the catch of a sob in his voice.

"As soon as we land, we'll come straight home. Try to hang on until then."

"We will. Carson will be back here in an hour. He went to the office see to a few things."

"I love you, Daddy, and remember, our boy loves you with all his heart."

"I do. Give my best to Donald."

Juliet clicked off the cellular phone, and sighed, looking around the lounge. Jordan and Emily had not yet arrived, and without an overt reason, she checked her watch. A sudden worry crossed her mind, that they might not show up after all, that their cooperation might have been a sham, a bargaining chip to get Donald to hand over three million dollars. Shaking her head, she sternly told herself that she was becoming as paranoid as Vivian, and that in a minute they would walk through the door, and her fears would become meaningless. Turning her gaze towards the door of the lounge, she was surprised to see not only Tony's parents, but another family as well, entering the lounge. She watched for a few minutes while they all found seats and places for their carry-on baggage, before she walked across the room.

"Jordan, Emily, I'm so glad you're here."

"Juliet, I'm sorry, we cut it very close, but with all of these people, I had a tough time getting everyone out of the house. Let me introduce you to Tony's sister, Jennifer, her husband, Herb Markham, and their daughters Marina and Lindsey. They decided to come to London, in case one of the girls, or Jennifer is a match. It may speed things up a bit." He put his arm around his daughter, hugging her close.

Swinging her head to one side, Juliet looked at the woman who had grown up with Tony. Jennifer was a bit shorter than she was and strongly resembled her mother, with sandy brown hair and dark eyes. Despite being the mother of an eleven and a nine year old, she was as slender as her daughters.

"I'm Tony's sister, although that is something I don't admit to these days." Jennifer stuck out her

95

hand, smiling at Juliet. God, she's beautiful, she thought. My brother's an even bigger idiot than I thought. How any man could bear to let her go is beyond me. "I'm sorry, I was staring. Please forgive me."

"It's the hair. I'm used to it."

"I've seen your work in magazines. I couldn't believe it when my mother called me and told me she had managed to buy one of your paintings, and then the next day Daddy called to tell me about Carson. I'm so sorry for what you are going through. I can't imagine having to watch my child…" Her voice trailed off, not wanting to offend the other woman.

"Die. You can say it. Right now, it's a distinct possibility if we can't find a donor soon."

"We all ran out and had the tests yesterday before we got on the plane for New York. They told us that we would know by today, latest tomorrow." Jennifer put her arms around her daughters. "They can't wait to meet him. Frankly, Tony's children are horrible, spoiled little brats, and not much fun to be with. They're hoping he's different."

"He is, very different. Loving, charming, intelligent, funny, loves Star Wars and hot dogs. As a matter of fact, that bag over there has a dozen in it. Carson fell in love with them when we were in New York last year, during his second remission."

"My father told me a little bit about what Tony did to you. I'm surprised that you want to have anything to do with us as a family after what happened. I hope that you can look at us and think about us as something other than Tony's relatives." Jennifer smiled tentatively, taking her cue from Juliet.

"It never occurred to me to do otherwise, but you must understand, that I don't want to talk about your brother, ever. If I never have to see him again, it won't be long enough." She shivered, and rubbed her arms with her hands.

Jennifer nodded. There must be a lot more to the story than her father had told her. Poor woman, to have to live with those memories. Feeling a chill run down her spine, she remembered the stories she had heard about other girls her brother had dated. The conversation faded as the attendant signaled that the jet was ready. They gathered their belongings and filed slowly onto the plane.

*   *   *   *   *

The Mercedes limousines were waiting at the curb, as the passengers exited he terminal. Jordan, Emily, and Jennifer's family were ushered into one, and driven away to their hotel.

"Damn, the mobile is ringing. Hang on a minute and let me answer it. If I don't, they'll just keep trying. Hello, oh, it's you, Edgar. Edgar, you sound terrible, is anything wrong? Oh, my God. Yes, yes, of course, we're on our way. Thank you for calling us right away." Ashen faced, Donald disconnected the call.

"Donald, tell me. Please, just let him still be alive." The tears ran down her face as she clutched at her husband's arm.

"That was Edgar. The remission is over. They had to rush him to the hospital, an uncontrolled nosebleed. They're keeping him there, everyone is with him." His voice cracking, Donald turned away.

"Daddy was right. He told me this morning that he was afraid that the end was coming too fast." Crying harder, she shook her head. They held hands as the car sped on its way to the hospital.

"Pray, Donald, that one of them is a match. If not, I think our baby is doomed."

"Don't give up yet. I, for one, think that we are going to get lucky." Suddenly feeling a cold breeze cross over his arms, he put his arm around her and drew her close, drawing strength from the warmth of her body. Leaning her head against his shoulder, he stroked her hair, feeling the reality of its silky weight as it lay across his chest.

*   *   *   *   *

Donald and Juliet stood silently by their son's bedside. Carson was sleeping, an IV line already attached to his arm. He seemed smaller, thinner and more frail than when they had left.

"Donald," Edgar Davis stood at the door."Please come into my office when you're finished here." They exchanged glances, and nodded. Each one kissed Carson on the cheek before they went down the hall and sat down in the doctor's office.

"Tell me, Edgar, how long?" Donald's jaw worked, its muscles rippling under the skin.

"It depends how hard he wants to fight. I have the results of the blood tests. Good news, if it's not too late. Tony is a match, as well as the sister, Jennifer. If you want to rate them, Tony is a perfect match, or at least as perfect as these things get. The sister is not nearly as good. But, there is a problem."

"What problem?" Juliet leaned forward in her chair.

"The doctor who took Tony's blood this morning sent me a fax, telling me that he felt that Tony is in a high risk category."

"What does that mean?"

"Apparently, he was hung over when he showed up this morning, with your man Carstairs and a detective accompanying him. Donald, you know that nowadays, there are all sorts of other tests that we have to run on blood samples, to make sure that the donor is healthy, and doesn't have any nasty diseases that could come back to haunt the recipient." His hands moved across the desk, finding a pencil to ease their restlessness.

"What are you trying to say, Edgar?"

"That the doctor discovered a higher than normal level of white blood cells in Tony's blood. That could mean anything from starting a cold or flu to having been exposed to hepatitis or HIV. He feels that Tony has some unhealthy lifestyle habits, and recommends against using him as a donor." Every time I have to do this, I know why they used to shoot the messenger who brought the bad news.

"Oh, God! And what about the sister's blood?" Donald held his wife's hand tightly.

"She is only a fifty percent match. In his weak state, Carson could reject the transplant."

"And if we decide to chance it and go with Tony, when could we do it?" Juliet began to squeeze her husband's hand.

"As soon as you can get him over here. There isn't much time. If the disease progresses too much further, your son will be beyond help. If you can get Tony here say by tomorrow night or the day after, we can start preparing Carson for the transplant today."

"Does it hurt?" A single tear hovered on her eyelash, and then fell onto her cheek.

"Yes, from what others have told me, it hurts terribly. I'll make sure he's sedated so that he won't feel it so badly."

"And if we don't do it?" Donald felt if he didn't know the whole truth, he would go crazy.

"He'll die, for certain, probably within the next month. I'm so sorry, Juliet, he was doing so well." He lowered his eyes, unable to look at her directly.

"What would you do, Edgar?" Donald walked over to the window.

"I'd do it. Whatever Tony has, it can be treated. It will give Carson a chance. At the very least, we owe him that."

"And you're sure that he would reject the sister's marrow?"

"No, but I'm not willing to risk it. If he does, there may not be another chance."

"Donald, we have to do it, and just hope that all Tony has is a cold. Whatever happens in the future, we'll deal with it. Please." The tears flowed heavily now, unchecked, soaking the collar of her white shirt.

"All right. I'll call Carstairs. He'll put Tony on the next Concorde."

"Tell him not to let him drink any alcohol, or use any drugs. It could weaken the marrow."

"Yes, of course. When will you begin?"

"Tonight, right away. When we leave this office, I'll have the nurses take him to isolation. You'll have to make your good-byes now."

"He's asleep, he won't even know what's happening to him." Her voice quavered, as her husband put his arms around her.

"Juliet, it's better this way. He knows all the nurses, and when he wakes up, we'll call you. Look, I had wanted to try and not be too specific with you, but the cancer is moving very fast, and if he isn't in terrible pain now, he very soon will be, and, well, if there were no transplant, chances are that he wouldn't be awake very much until the end, anyway."

"But he was doing so well, just yesterday."

"That depends on what you call well, Juliet. Two weeks ago I would have said well, but since then he has barely been holding his own. That is the nature of this cancer. It breaks out, just when you think you have kept it away for a little while. Now, go and say good-bye to him. Make sure that Tony comes here straight from the airport. I have to run more tests before I can do the procedure."

* * * * *

Juliet lay on the bed, exhausted and drained. Donald was on the telephone, trying to reassure his father with a confidence he did not feel.

"We haven't a choice. If we don't go with Tony, Carson will die. If we do, he may die. We have to give him this chance."

"Have you spoken to Juliet's parents?"

"She called them earlier."

"How is she?"

"Devastated, but coping. We both are.

"Have you told him about Tony?"

"We couldn't. He was sleeping, and once the killing of the marrow begins, he'll be heavily sedated."

"It started this morning. He was fine at lunch, but about three I heard screaming coming from his room. He was covered in blood and it was just pumping right out of his nose. The ambulance came right away, and Edgar thought it best to put him to sleep until things calmed down. And now, of course, there are all the feelings to deal with. The what ifs and if onlys. Don't let Juliet succumb to that. It won't help."

"I understand. We'll see you in the morning. Tony should be in London by then."

"Donald, will she be able to stand it if he dies?"

"She doesn't have a choice, she'll have to."

* * * * *

Wearing an attitude of bravado mixed with fear, Tony Graniston sat on the Concorde, flanked by two private detectives. The call from London had come only two hours before, he was a match, and would he come immediately, there was very little time left. Leaning back, he closed his eyes. For the three hour flight, there wasn't much else to do but think.

In spite of the three million dollars he had received for agreeing to provide bone marrow to his son, he had great misgivings about the promise not to sue for visitation or custody. The reality that he had terminated all his rights to his son before he was even born did not concern him. The fact that his former wife was determined to hold him to it did. How was he to have known that the child was his, and a son. Not for an instant did he consider that what he had done could have created a child. After nine years, he still justified his behavior the same way-she made me love her and I hated her for tying me down. How could it be possible that she was pregnant, I don't understand it. Somehow he would have to find a way to break the agreement. He was not about to save his son's life, and then never be able to have any personal contact with him. It just wasn't fair.

*   *   *   *   *

The waiting room at the Great Ormond Hospital for Children was filled. An entire corner was occupied by Carson Macallister's relatives. He had been in isolation for almost two days, sedated to ease his pain, his diseased bone marrow killed while he waited for the transplant. Jordan and Emily Graniston kept vigil together with their daughter, Jennifer, her family, all the Macallisters, and Juliet's parents. In an operating room two floors below, Tony Graniston lay, heavily sedated, a machine drawing out the bone marrow to be used in the transplant. Once the process was completed, Carson would be taken into a different isolation room, and the bone marrow would be dripped into his body and hopefully, save his life.

Standing at the window of the isolation unit, Donald and Juliet watched their son as he slept, bruised and battered, under a blanket of pain killers. All pretense had vanished once the marrow had been killed. The short periods of wakefulness had been spent crying and screaming for his mother, who had been put into a special suit and allowed inside to comfort her child. After the second time, her husband had ordered that his son not be allowed to feel any more pain, that forcing him to wake up was little more than torture, for him and for his parents.

"Donald, it's time. We have the marrow, and we'll take him now. I only hope it isn't too late." They nodded, too numb and devastated to protest. Edgar Davis disappeared into the isolation unit. Juliet and Donald watched him from behind the glass, as the nurses closed the curtains.

"Darling, let's go and have a cup of tea. You haven't eaten anything since lunch." He held her in his arms, letting her bury her face in his chest.

"I can't help thinking how while we were together, having fun, he was beginning to die and I wasn't here." She cried, soaking the front of his shirt.

"Don't do this to yourself. Carson will need you to be strong for him during the recovery. Besides, just in case, you have to eat. Someone else shouldn't go hungry." She pulled away, head down and nodded. As they began to walk away, she looked at him and smiled.

"I hope it's true. I'd love to be able to tell him when he's better."

"That's more like the Juliet I know. No more tears, otherwise you'll have the entire visitor's room in floods. How about I order in tea and sandwiches and all sorts of goodies. We can all do with a diversion, at least for a while." His thumb stroked her cheek, soft and still damp from her tears.

"Donald, that sounds wonderful. Just the distraction I need. Please, just make sure that Tony can't get out of bed and start looking for me or for Carson. I just couldn't deal with him right now." Her head was bowed against his chest.

"He's in another part of the hospital, and as soon as he is back on his feet, he'll be discharged and put on the next plane to New York. Until then, I have guards posted inside and outside his room. Why don't you go and talk to your parents, and to Tony's family, reassure them that things are going as well as can be expected, and I'll go and order the food." She nodded and put her hand up to his cheek. He held it there and kissed her wrist, before turning and taking the elevator downstairs. Taking a deep breath, she went into the visitor's room, smiling, armed with her husband's love, to comfort the others who were waiting for good news.

*   *   *   *   *

Two hours later, an exhausted Edgar Davis opened the door of the visitor's lounge, and signaled Donald and Juliet to come outside.

"It's over, and he's back in his isolation room. He's being medicated with pain killers and anti-rejection drugs, at least for the time being. When he's able, we'll stop the pain medication, and then we wait until the marrow takes hold and begins to work on its own."

"And all the cancer is gone?"

"Yes, all gone. He's lucky, I think that we were just in time. All of his organs were still functioning, but a close call."

"Thank you a thousand times for what you have done for him. Can we see him now?" Wiping her eyes, Juliet smiled through her tears.

"Through the glass, yes. He will sleep, probably until tomorrow morning. Maybe then you can climb into that suit and go inside. My prescription for both of you is to go home and get some sleep. You've earned it."

"Edgar, what are his chances now?"

"Only time will tell, Donald. He's had the closest possible match to his own, and now the rest is up to him."

"Thank you, Edgar, for everything. Darling, let's go and then tell everyone the good news." After shaking hands, Donald put his arm around Juliet's shoulder, as they walked towards the isolation unit.

*　　*　　*　　*　　*

Relaxed, and free from pain, Carson Macallister slept, and smiled as he dreamed a young boy's dreams. The private duty nurse sat at his bedside, monitoring his vital signs, pulse, heartbeat, respiration, and the drip on the IV in his arm. The pump delivering oxygen whooshed and hissed, a comforting sound of normalcy, as the child breathed deeply, and slept.

On the other side of the hospital, Tony Graniston was waking up from the anesthetic administered during the procedure. He felt nauseous and he could feel the areas where the needle had penetrated his bones.

When he opened his eyes, he could see that it was dark outside, and that someone was sitting in the corner of the room.

"What time is it?"

"Eleven thirty."

"Is it over? Did they do the transplant yet?"

"Yes, they did."

"Did it work?"

"It's too soon to tell."

"Who are you?"

Someone leaned over and turned on the light. Saying nothing, he merely sat in the chair, waiting for Tony to make the first move.

"How kind of you to be here to bring me news of my son." The sarcasm dripped as Tony struggled to sit up in bed.

"I wouldn't do that, if I were you. You're going to hurt for a few days. Sitting up will be difficult." Donald continued to sit quietly in the chair.

"I want to see my son."

"I'm sorry, but that will not be possible. You signed an agreement promising not to try to see or contact him. I never expected you to keep your word, that seems to be something you don't understand, so I have taken some precautions. And when you are able to travel, you will be taken to the airport and put on the first plane to New York."

"You can't do that. I have rights, even if you and that bitch say that I don't."

"Tony, listen to me and listen very carefully. You have no rights, you never wanted any, and if you fail to abide by the terms of the agreement, I will hand over that file to Scotland Yard, and I will make sure that you are apprehended, tried and convicted for what you did to my wife. And just in case you are thinking about trying to escape, there will be guards posted inside and outside your room, in front of the door to Carson's room, as well as in the visitor's lounge. Let's be adult about this. We made a deal, a straightforward business arrangement: you donated bone marrow and signed the divorce papers, and promised not to see Carson. For those things I paid you three million dollars. I don't need to thank you for that, the money should be enough."

"You're a heartless bastard, you know that, Macallister."

Donald walked to the door. He stood and turned halfway through it. "Why, Tony, how kind of you to notice. I've been taking lessons from the best. You're an even bigger bastard than I am." As he left the room, the guard stepped inside and locked the door behind him.

CHAPTER SEVEN

Two weeks after the transplant, Carson began to rally. By the end of the third week after the procedure, he had demanded and received one of the hot dogs he had asked for, complete with the mustard and relish. Although he could only eat a few small bites, it was the first milestone on the long road to recovery. Ten days after that he was back in his room, and with their worries eased, Juliet and Donald had gone home and slept for twelve hours. Even then, the sounds of their other two children brought them back to reality.

"Mummy, when can we go and see Carson? You promised." At fourteen, Miranda was tall and slender, with Delia's blond hair and blue gray eyes. Her brother, Dylan, twelve years old, resembled his father almost exactly, with his dark hair, and gray eyes.

"Miranda, darling, what time is it?" Juliet mumbled sleepily, as she brushed her hair away from her face.

"It's going on noon. You've slept the day away." Miranda giggled as her father tossed a magazine at her to shoo her away.

"Wretched child! Give us an hour, and then we'll make up a picnic basket and you can go and visit your brother, after I talk to him privately, and maybe tomorrow, you and Dylan can spend the day." Donald propped himself on his elbow, and smiled at his daughter.

"You haven't told him yet, about Tony, have you? Really, Daddy, it's too much."

"Well, little mother, we couldn't do it before, because he was too sick. Today is the first day that he's well enough."

"Dad, are Tony's parents still sitting there waiting?" Dylan leaned against the door, trying to appear casual and nonchalant.

"Yes, Dylan, they are and very patiently at that. And they will continue to do so, unless you two go away and let us get dressed. Why don't you go and tell Marjorie to pack up a hamper with a picnic lunch."

"Mummy, aren't you going to be there?"

"No, I have an appointment. Now, please, disappear so that we can get dressed." Her last words were punctuated with the thump and clatter of two children running down the stairs. Faintly, through the door, they could hear Dylan bellowing for Marjorie, their long suffering cook of nine years.

"Are we safe?" He nuzzled her neck.

"Stop, you know I'm ticklish there. And remember how dangerous it is to tickle me. We haven't time today." Suppressing a smile, she sternly wagged a finger at her husband, as she walked to the bathroom. He could hear the sound of the shower running, and then the hum of the hair dryer.

"What are you going to do with your precious afternoon off?" Turning over on his back, he watched as his wife slipped out of her robe and began to dress. For some reason, her body looked different. Her skin had a peach colored glow, and her natural slenderness had begun to fill out.

"Doctor's appointment. I missed this month." She turned around and smiled, her entire face lighting up.

"I thought so. You look luscious, just like you did when I met you, like a ripe peach, ready to be licked all over." Laughing, he kissed her lips and disappeared to shower and dress.

Juliet sat at her dressing table and looked at herself in the mirror. She did look radiant, and she had noticed other signs while she was in the shower. Well aware that a third miscarriage would be her last attempt, she crossed her fingers, and prayed that this time, she would be able to keep her baby.

*　*　*　*　*

Lawrence Tinsdale sat at his desk and stared at his patient. He sighed, took off his glasses and rubbed his eyes.

"Juliet, you are five weeks pregnant. Let me congratulate you, and say that I admire your courage, and your persistence. I have made an appointment for you with a high risk obstetrical doctor, for tomorrow morning. For now, I want you to give up jogging and any other exercise, until after the third month. Then you may walk, without running, and I want you to eat, proper meals, not just nibbles like you skinny girls love to munch. Here are the prescriptions for your vitamins and iron pills. And please, I know how sick your son has been, but you must rest, and get plenty of sleep."

"I have been very tired the past week, and not just from worrying about Carson. I wasn't sick a day with him, but today I felt really ill when I woke up, not like the last two times, when I didn't feel pregnant at all."

"That's to be expected. Come back in a month, and we'll take a look at you."

*　*　*　*　*

"Carson, are you awake?" Donald put the picnic basket down on the floor and pulled the chair up to the bed.

"Daddy, have you come to spend the afternoon?" Carson smiled sleepily at his father.

"No, just half an hour or so. I need to tell you something, and I also need you to be quiet and pay attention to what I am saying. Can you do that?" The boy nodded as Donald sat down on the edge of the bed, and held his son's hand.

"Carson, you trust me, don't you? You know that I would never do anything to hurt you, and that Mummy wouldn't either?"

"Of course."

"Good. Now I want you to listen carefully. Do you remember back a month ago, when you were so sick and Mummy went to New York?"

"Yes, she went to visit Uncle Paul and sell the ladies."

"That's right. But she went for a second reason, a much more important one. She went to try and find a bone marrow donor for you."

"She did find one, didn't she?"

"Yes, she did. The marrow came from the man who made you, your natural father."

"What does that mean?"

"Exactly what I said. He and Mummy were married, and they made you."

"If he made me, then does that mean you aren't my Daddy any more?"

"No, of course not. Carson, when I met Mummy, you were already made, living in her tummy, almost ready to come out and be my wonderful boy. Your natural father was someone who was mean and did terrible things to her. And then he ran away and left her. Grandpa Bertram fixed it so that Mummy wasn't married any more, but then she found out that you were coming, and she wanted you more than anything in the world. So, when we met, she was carrying you, and she was so beautiful, I loved her instantly. All I ever wanted was to love her and love you and take care of both of you. So, I'm your Daddy in every way, except that one. My marrow was not a match. That is why Mummy had to go to America to ask the man who made you to give you his marrow."

"And did she?"

"Yes, she did. But..." Donald gulped. He hadn't imagined that this would be so hard.

"But what, Daddy?"

"He wasn't very nice to Mummy, and I had to pay him a lot of money before he would give you the marrow."

"But didn't he know that he was the one who made me?"

"Yes, he did. But he wanted to take you away from Mummy and from me, and I couldn't let that happen. That's why I paid him the money."

"He sounds like a bad man."

"Carson, sometimes grownups do things that don't make sense. Tony has done some bad things, but I'm sure if we tried hard we could find some nice things as well. But there is good news, too. You have another set of grandparents, and an auntie and uncle, and two beautiful cousins. They have been here, waiting to see you, since before you got the transplant. Would you like to see them?"

Carson grinned. His eyes lit up, and Donald began to laugh.

"Greedy boy! Three sets of grandparents! You will be the most loved and spoiled boy in all of England."

"You won't let anyone take me away, will you, Daddy?" Carson sat up and crawled on to Donald's lap. "I don't want to leave you and Mummy, and Grandpa Carson and Grandpa Bertram, and Grandma Rose and Miranda and Dylan."

He held his son tightly, rocking him slightly, more as a comfort to himself than to the child. Too soon for him to start gaining weight again, his little body was so light and frail. "Never. You will always be our son, our very special son. We will always be here to love you and protect you, until you are old enough to do it for yourself."

"I don't have to see him, the daddy who made me, do I?"

"Not if you don't want to. I fixed it so that he cannot come and bother us and try to take you away."

"Daddy, do I look like him?" Donald took a deep breath to keep his voice from shaking. His throat felt tight and sore, as if a lump had become stuck halfway down.

"Yes, son, you do, about as much as you look like me."

"I thought I always looked just like you, except I don't have gray eyes. Daddy, do you look like him?"

"Not a chance. I'm more handsome, and you will be, as well. At least that is what Mummy tells me."

"Where is she? I thought she was coming today." Carson leaned against his father's chest and sighed with contentment. His world, which had teetered off it's normal path, had been righted again. He had his father's love, and his other daddy slipped into the back of his mind, unwanted and irrelevant.

"She had to go somewhere. After all, my boy, Mummy has to have a chance to have a little time to herself. She'll be here later on. But, Miranda and Dylan are waiting outside. That basket is full of all the goodies you love so much, and you have my permission to stuff yourself with them."

"Thanks, Daddy. Can my other grandparents come in later and see me? When you're here again?" A small hesitation of fear had crept into his voice. Donald tightened his grip.

"If that is what you want, Carson. And if you don't want to see them, it's all right as well."

"I'm a bit scared of them. I don't know them, and their son is my other daddy. They won't take me away, will they?"

"No, they will not. All they want to do is love you, and try to be good grandpas and grandmas. Any other questions?"

"When can I go home?"

"When Dr. Davis says so. You're not out of the woods yet." Carson giggled.

"Yes, I am. There's only one tree here, my tree, right outside this room. You know, the one Mummy watches all the time."

"On that note, I am going to get your brother and sister. They will entertain you until Mummy gets here, and I, believe it or not, have to go to the office. I'll see you tonight."

"Daddy, can you bring me a Tandoori for dinner?"

"Of course, Tandoori for fifteen, that should feed all of us very well. Shall I tell everyone that we'll all have dinner together?" Carson snuggled deeper into his father's chest.   •

"All right." Donald breathed a sigh of relief, it was over, and Tony was behind them.

"Jordan, can I have a word?" Donald stood at the door of the visitor's lounge.

"Yes, of course. Anything wrong?"

"No, nothing. As a matter of fact, Carson would like us all to have dinner together in his room tonight. Tandoori, his favorite. He's ready to meet all of you, but he's a bit scared, as well. Accepting the fact that Tony ran off and left his mother while she was pregnant with him is a bit much for him to understand. More than anything, he wants to be reassured that no one is going to take him away from us, so for the time being, I think that any talk about visits to America should be put on hold."

"Of course. Don't worry, we'll keep it light, until he's really ready to accept us."

"Thank you. My other two children are with him now. Perhaps Marina and Lindsey would like to go down and knock on the door by themselves. They are about the same age as Dylan, Carson's older brother. They might help to smooth the way. And I am sure that they will enjoy all of the goodies that were brought along for the picnic."

"That's very kind. I'll speak to Jennifer. Thank you again for letting us be a part of his life. You could have said no, and we would have understood."

"I know, but I think that Carson would have been the loser. The reality is that he is Tony's son, and he will have to get used to the idea, sooner or later."

"Tell me, if he hadn't needed the transplant, would you have told him?"

"I would have had to, eventually. Tony's name is on the birth certificate. I hate to be rude, but I have to go over to my office for a few hours. I'll be back by half past four, and then we can go in and say hello, and have an early dinner." Donald shook Jordan's hand, turned and was gone.

* * * * *

Marina and Lindsey Markham held hands as they walked down the corridor towards their cousin's room. They were obviously sisters, sharing not only the same chestnut color of hair inherited from their father, but the eyes and facial features of their mother, and grandmother. As they stopped in front the door, they hesitated, listening to the sounds of laughter on the other side.

"Maybe we should go back and wait until later." Lindsey began to lose her nerve and pulled away from her sister.

"Don't be silly, Lin. They're our cousins now, and I'll bet that they're as nervous about us as we are about them." Marina tightened her grip.

"Do you really think so?"

"Let's knock and find out." Marina lifted her hand and knocked twice. Her hand drifted down to her side as the two girls waited for the door to open.

On the other side, Dylan Macallister got off the floor and rolling his eyes at his uncooperative sister, went to answer the door.

"Hello, who are you?"

"Dylan, don't be rude. They haven't even opened their mouths yet." Miranda walked to the door and took a very close look. Smiling, she put out her hand.

"I'm Marina Markham and this is my sister Lindsey. We're Carson's cousins." Marina smiled back and shook Miranda's hand.

"I'm Miranda Macallister, Carson's sister and that dolt over there is our brother, Dylan. Why don't you come in and say hello? Maybe you can help us eat some of this food." She stepped back from the door and then closed it behind the two girls.

Carson sat on his bed, watching his cousins very carefully. They didn't look dangerous, but it was too soon to tell. His conversation with his father had scared him more than he would admit to anyone. Terrified that his other daddy would come and steal him away, he decided to be friendly, but adopt a wait and see attitude.

"I'm Marina, and this is Lindsey. We're your cousins, and we wanted to say hello, and that we're glad you're feeling better." Carson nodded and sat back on the bed. Miranda made the first move.

"My Dad says you live in Los Angeles. Do you see any movie stars?" Marina laughed.

"Sometimes. We live in the Valley, that's east of Los Angeles. Once in a while, when we go to L.A. with my parents, we'll see someone, but not very often. You probably meet more celebrities than we do, with your mother being a famous artist."

Lindsey looked around the room, and made eye contact with Dylan. He grinned and pushed the picnic basket towards her.

"Go ahead, there's some great stuff in there. We brought it from home, full of all sorts of goodies."

"Thank you." She peeped over the edge of the basket and spied an apple tart. Reaching out, she picked it up and took a bite. Sighing with pleasure, she brushed the crumbs from her chin.

"Is that good?" Carson was amazed. This girl ate an apple tart the same way that he did, down to the way she brushed away the crumbs. It must be true, they were related.

"Yes, it's wonderful, my favorite. My Mom loves them, too. She says everyone in the family does." Smiling with satisfaction, she ate the last bite, and grinned at her sister. Marina rolled her eyes.

"You'll have to excuse her, she's only nine. No class whatsoever." Dylan's mouth twitched.

"No matter, she'll grow out of it."

The two girls spent another hour getting acquainted with their new relatives. Miranda and Dylan liked the girls very much, Carson less. His fears made him separate himself, leaving space and distance between them.

*   *   *   *   *

Juliet put her shopping bags into the back seat of her Jaguar, slipped into the front seat and turned on the engine. Looking in the rearview mirror as she maneuvered out of the parking space, she smiled softly as she caught a glimpse of the bags sitting on the seat. Unable to control herself, she had bought some new clothes and a few maternity outfits. Beaming, she patted her stomach, undoing the button on her skirt, and sucking in a deep breath. It felt wonderful, not being squeezed in. Carson seemed to be getting better, she was pregnant and all was right with the world.

* * * * *

The picnic basket was almost empty. The five children had methodically munched their way through everything except a few sandwiches. Even Carson, who had not been able to eat for a long time, had stuffed himself. He sat back on the bed, listening to the giggles and chatter of the others. Although he had tried to put his conversation with his father into perspective, in his eight year old mind, Tony had taken the form of a monster, someone who didn't really care about him, but who wanted to steal him away from the parents who loved him. Suddenly, his stomach began to churn, and he felt nauseous. The combination of too much food coupled with his emotional distress became too much for him.

"Miranda, I feel sick." Carson began to perspire. He did not want to be sick in front of everyone, but he was losing control.

"Oh, God! Carson, do you have to chuck?" Ever practical, Miranda grabbed the wastebasket from the bathroom. "I told you not to stuff so much into yourself."

"I want Mummy, Miranda. I feel sick." He began to see spots as he struggled with his nausea.

"She's not here yet. Carson, don't be a dope. Chuck if you have to, we've all done the piglet routine." She shoved the basket under his nose. Suddenly, he began to heave uncontrollably. Crying, and gasping, he brought up all the food, but could not stop vomiting, the violence of his upheaval causing his nose to bleed.

"Lin, go get Mom and hurry!" Marina moved to Carson's side and stroked his arm. Her sister ran out of the room, screaming for her mother.

"It's all right. Try to calm down, and stop throwing up. Take a deep breath and try to stop." Carson could not stop, beginning to panic and scream as he felt the blood trickling out of his nose. Miranda and Dylan stood on the other side of the bed, trying to calm down their brother.

"Mom, please come! Carson's throwing up and he can't stop." Jennifer was out of her seat like a shot. Running down the hall, she began to shout for the nurses or a doctor. She flew into the room, and saw the three children all trying to comfort a screaming and hysterical Carson.

"Darling, I'm your aunt Jennifer, and I'm going to try and help you. First, let's get rid of the nasty can, so you don't have to see it. Marina, go and ask someone in the lounge to call his parents."

Carson looked at his new aunt and gave in to his terror. She was here, and she was going to steal him away from his Mummy and Daddy.

"No, no, leave me alone. I won't go with you, I don't want my other Daddy, I want Mummy. Miranda, send her away. She wants to steal me from Mummy and Daddy." He screamed and screamed, his terror all too obvious. No one, not even his beloved grandparents could comfort him as he screamed for his parents. At last, a nurse came and shooed everyone out of the room. She gave him a sedative, and had just sat down to hold him, when Juliet arrived.

"What's happened? I could hear you screaming downstairs." She waved the nurse out of the room, sat down on the bed and took him on her lap.

"Mummy, where were you? I was so frightened, that she was going to steal me and give me to my other Daddy. I don't want to see him, I don't want to be with him." Soothing him, she rocked him and stroked his back as the sedative began to relax him.

"Carson, tell me, darling, what frightened you so badly?"

"My cousins, they were so much like me, and then I ate too much, and I started thinking about my other Daddy, and I was so scared. I threw up and I couldn't stop, and then my nose started bleeding. Then she came in and I was sure she was going to steal me away from you and Daddy." Sobbing, he hid his face in her chest, his tears and the blood from his nose soaking the front of her shirt.

"Carson, I want you to listen to me. No one is ever going to steal you away from Daddy and me. We won't let them. Daddy has a policeman right outside the door to make sure that no one gets in here who shouldn't. Especially Tony. He's gone back to New York, and you don't ever have to see him."

"Never?"

"Not unless you want to."

"I'm sleepy. Stay with me until Daddy comes." Carson yawned and closed his eyes. Slowly, his body began to go limp, and his head sagged against her chest. Gently, she put him to bed and covered him up. With great care, she climbed onto the bed and held him as he slept.

*   *   *   *   *

Her composure shattered, Jennifer Markham sat in the waiting room, her husband's arms around her. She leaned her head on his shoulder, devastated by the scene she had just witnessed. Tony must have done something so unspeakable, so inhuman, so terrifying that her nephew could not bear the sight of her. Tears seeping out under her lashes, she dabbed at her eyes, and blew her nose.

"I was afraid of this." Bertram Sadler shook his head, picked up his wife's hand and held it tightly.

"I don't understand any of this." Jordan Graniston was completely bewildered.

"What is not to understand. Donald had to tell him that he is not his natural father. Children don't understand the fine distinctions that adults make to each other. To him, Tony is a real threat, someone he doesn't know, and on top of it, someone who did terrible things to the one person he adores the most, his mother. His greatest terror now is that Tony will come and take him away, and he will never see his parents again." Carson Macallister tamped down his fury. Donald should never have permitted these people to come to London.

"Jordan, let's go to the hotel. I think that now we should not be here when Donald gets here. He's going to have his hands full." Devastated, Emily began to gather her purse and book.

"No, Emily. Let's wait. We should talk to both of them first. Perhaps it might be better if we go back to New York, and try again when he's stronger." Jordan held his wife's hand.

"Daddy's right, Mom. I think that we should wait and discuss this with Donald and Juliet. He's been sedated, so he'll sleep for a couple of hours. By that time, he may feel differently, so let's not jump the gun just yet." Jennifer took a ragged breath and stood up. Whatever her brother had done to his first wife, she was now in a position to take away some of the hurt he had visited on her, and by proxy, their child. She was suddenly possessed by a determination to stay in London for a long time, if necessary, to prove to her nephew, and to herself, that she was nothing like her brother.

*   *   *   *   *

Tony Graniston sat in the waiting room of the lawyer's office. He had been calling lawyers for two days, looking for someone who was familiar with family law in both England and the United States. The previous twenty attorneys he had spoken with had all told him he hadn't a prayer to get custody or visitation rights, but if he wanted to meet with them, he could pay their regular hourly rate. The twenty-first, John Trent, had reluctantly allowed himself to be persuaded to accept a flat fee of five hundred dollars for a single meeting.

"Mr. Trent will see you now." The secretary, busy typing a brief, looked up for a second as she waved her hand towards the office door.

"Mr. Graniston, please sit down. Before I get started, I need to know if you are aware of the extreme difficulties this case represents. It won't be easy and I need to know how serious you are about filing for custody of your son." John Trent sat behind his desk and studied the man across the desk.

"Serious enough." Tony sat back in the chair, hoping that he gave the impression of wealth and power.

"I looked over the termination and the agreement that you faxed over. They both appear to be ironclad, and, short of a miracle, impossible to break. There isn't much I can promise or give you, other than some advice."

"Which is?" Don't tell me I'm going to be disappointed again.

"Before you can sue for visitation, and then custody, you first have to try and reverse the termination of rights. If you consider its meaning, termination means exactly that, a total and complete end to custodial responsibility and to any parental relationship with the child. And even if you can manage to overturn it, anything other than supervised visitation would be highly unlikely." John drank deeply from a glass of water his secretary had placed on his desk.

"What do you mean, supervised visitation?" John could see that Tony was struggling to control his anger.

"That means that you can only visit him if a child welfare professional is in the room. That person is usually the caseworker assigned to the case. He or she will investigate your home life and make a report on that, and on the nature of the visits that take place." His sense of caution thoroughly aroused by Tony's demeanor, John looked away, avoiding any kind of eye contact.

"How long will I have to put up with that?"

"For as long as child welfare thinks it's necessary. Mr. Graniston, tell yourself that you have to start from the beginning, as if your son were a newborn baby. Don't look like that, any social worker would tell you the same thing. You can't just walk into an eight year old's life without a period of adjustment. And in a case like this, there is no way that child welfare will allow anything else. Going a step further and suing for permanent custody is something else again, and you will have to face a trial in England. Your former wife will have all the advantages there, beginning with the fact that the British give custody to the mother in all cases, except if she is unfit. From what I have found out, she is far from that. And if she hasn't already done so, you must accept the certainty that your former wife will have you investigated thoroughly." John could feel perspiration trickling down his back.

"What else would I have to do?" Tony made a concerted effort to keep his temper in check.

"Well, you'll have to, how should I put it, undergo a radical change in your lifestyle. The kind of stories I've been hearing won't go over well in a courtroom. In addition, I would advise you to remarry your wife as quickly as possible. Judges like to see a loving and stable home life when they decide a case like this."

"Can I use the bigamy against her?"

"That would be very foolish. Both of you married others under questionable circumstances. If, as I was given to understand, you never signed the first set of divorce papers, then it would make you look worse, much worse."

"Can I win?" Tony's desperation seeped through his control.

"There are no guarantees about anything in a custody case. You were made aware of the pregnancy, yet you chose to terminate all your rights to the child, without even waiting for him to be born. That will work in her favor, that she informed you that you were going to be a father. You did give him your bone marrow, but the rumor on the street is that you were very well paid for it. The Macallisters are extremely wealthy and powerful. They have a fleet of lawyers here in the U.S., and I would be very surprised if they weren't already preparing for you to try and break the agreement you signed. They can tie up this case for years, and while it may bankrupt you, the money it will costs them will be what I like to call spare change. Right now, you have no job, and from what I understand no family life either." He gave a quick, surreptitious glance at his watch. Time to wind things up and make sure this one never comes back.

"What are you trying to tell me, John?" He could hear the menace in the voice clearly.

"I'm just being more polite than the other twenty lawyers you called before me. Your chances of winning this case are slim to none. There's always a chance that you will get a judge who takes a liking to you, but don't count on it. If you wait ten years, he will be eighteen, and legally, the issue becomes moot. If you want to go and visit him, you can, provided he wants to see you."

"John, he's my son. He should be Tony Graniston, Jr., and it just isn't fair that I can't even see him." John gritted his teeth, as he listened to Tony whining.

"Mr. Graniston, you're an adult, and I'm sure that on any number of occasions, someone in your life told you that not only is life unfair, but that fairness has very little to do with it. It is the considered opinion of some, including the twenty other lawyers you tried to hire, that you are getting exactly what you deserve. You signed the termination order nine years ago, and probably never gave it another thought. I would even venture a guess that you were incredibly relieved not to be involved with your former wife and your child. Now, you find out that child is yours, and a boy, so all of a sudden you're interested. For whatever reason, you made the deal with Macallister. He paid you for your services, and as far as he's concerned, that ends the relationship. If you wanted visitation, the time to fight for it was when they were desperate to find a donor for the child, and for you to refuse to be paid for the donation. That looks very bad, even to me. No judge wants to hear that a parent refused to help his child unless he got paid for it."

"So, there is really nothing I can do, is there?" Tony stood up to go.

"To be completely honest, not much. The best course of action for you is to wait for the child to become an adult. Go home, Mr. Graniston, and spend the next ten years doing good deeds and showing your son that you are not his worst nightmare. You can stop at my secretary's desk to arrange for payment." John stood up and shook Tony's hand. As soon as Tony had gone, he ran to the men's room and washed his hands thoroughly, shuddering as he did it. Ten minutes later, his hands raw and almost bleeding from being scrubbed over and over, he asked his secretary to put him through to Donald Macallister, at Macallister Industries, in London.

CHAPTER EIGHT

"Yes, I understand. And I'll make sure that everything here is covered as well. Thank you, John, for calling. If there is anything here that we can do for you in return, please let us know."

"Thank you, and if you ever need my help with anything here in New York, just call me. That's return enough. My best to your wife and son. And Donald, never ever forget what you are dealing with."

Donald Macallister leaned back in his chair and put his feet on the cherry wood desk, a position from which he did his best thinking. Smiling, he remembered his mother, Fiona's, tart comments about his breeding and background every time he had done it in her presence. He glanced across the highly polished surface of his desk at one of the silver picture frames. She was laughing, standing on the front steps of their ski lodge in Zermatt, wearing a red jacket and holding a pair of skis. Fifteen years ago, his parents had gone on a short skiing holiday to Switzerland. His father had taken that picture just before his mother had gone to the slopes alone. That day there had been an avalanche, unexpected and ferocious. Five people had been lost, one of them Fiona Macallister.

He had just married Delia Lawrence, and they were still on their wedding trip when the call had come. Delia never forgave him for choosing to go home to comfort his father and attend his mother's funeral, rather than finishing their honeymoon as planned. Donald had been in his last year at Oxford when they had met and he had fallen in love with her cool, blond beauty. At the age of twenty-two, his desire for her was so great that, against all advice to the contrary, he had proposed marriage after two months. The thought of being able to make love to her whenever he wanted was more than enough to push aside any misgivings he might have had. The cold disappointment that went with the discovery of her true feelings gave way to joy when he discovered, about a month after their return to London, that he was going to be a father. Miranda had entranced him, and after Delia had refused to care for the baby, he had been more than willing to be the parent responsible for raising her. Looking into her eyes never failed to remind him of how much he loved her.

By the time Miranda was two years old, he had already decided to file for divorce. Delia, sensing that he was drifting away, had staged a seduction of her susceptible husband. Donald, having remained faithful since Miranda's birth, was in no position to resist. Two months later, Delia triumphantly announced that she was pregnant again. Once again, Donald was present at the birth of Dylan, the deceit practiced on him by Delia forgotten once he had held his son.

The end came two years later. Delia simply disappeared, leaving her children behind. Six months later, she surfaced in a French court and filed for divorce. She was only too happy to take the payment promised her in the prenuptial agreement Carson and Fiona had insisted upon before the wedding could go forward. To both Donald and Carson, half a million pounds was a pittance, considering that he had rid himself of her and retained custody of his children.

Two years later, lonely, and longing for a meaningful relationship with a woman, he had gone to the Slade to look at a series of paintings done by a young artist who had already made a considerable reputation for herself. Juliet Sadler, seven months pregnant, and incredibly beautiful, had taken his heart in the very first instant he had seen her. He had pursued her, gently and cautiously, afraid of overwhelming the obviously fragile young artist. She, on the other hand, had been as wary as a frightened deer, reserved and deliberately off-putting. It wasn't until he had proposed, and she had told him the truth about Tony Graniston that everything had begun to make sense. The first time that he had made love to her, she had begged him not to hurt her, and had flinched as he had touched and kissed her. At the end, he had wept as he kissed her stomach and sworn that he would love and protect her child as his own. They were married five weeks later.

Now, the happiness that had been won through years of hard work was being threatened by Tony's reappearance, and there was not much he could do until Tony made the first move, other than keep his family as safe as possible. He smiled contentedly as he crossed his hands behind his head. Soon, Carson would be released from the hospital. Summer was coming, and they would be going down to the family's country home in Surrey until September. What better place to hold a wedding-this time with all the trimmings, although, as he grinned at the thought, he had better hurry up. Juliet's pregnancy was about to burst forth, and he had no wish to subject her to another wedding one step ahead of the baby doctor. Crossing his arms across his chest, he drowsed in the warm quiet of his office, dreaming of the warmth of his family. He felt so utterly at peace with life that it seemed as if nothing else could go wrong.

Waking with a start, Donald picked up his private line on the first ring, listened briefly and raced out of his office, calling to his secretary to have his calls forwarded as he was out of the glass doors and in the elevator.

* * * * *

Carson opened his eyes. He had slept for two hours after the nurse had given him a small dose of Valium. Relaxed and calm, he smiled and stretched. Tentatively, he lifted his hand up and stroked his scalp. He could feel the stubble of his hair growing back and he smiled again.

"Feeling better, darling?" Juliet had spent most of the time he had been sleeping sitting in the chair under the window, anxiously watching her son.

Looking down, he mumbled. As she urged him to speak up, he got out of bed and sat on her lap, hiding his head against her chest.

"I'm embarrassed, Mummy. I acted like a big baby in front of my cousins, and Miranda and Dylan. I was so scared when Auntie Jennifer came in and tried to help me. All I could think was that she was going to steal me and give me to my other Daddy."

"Carson, it's all right. We all know how frightened you were, and how hard it is to understand all the things that Daddy told you." She stroked his cheek with her hand.

"I'd like to apologize to them, if that's all right. Can I put on my new clothes, and then they can see me, not like a sick person, but as a real boy."

"A wonderful idea. How's your tummy? Daddy called from the car, and I told him to go ahead and get the Tandoori for tonight."

"Better. Next time, I won't eat everything I see all at once. Mummy, they'll still like me, won't they, even though I acted like a baby?"

"Of course they will. They understand that you've been sick, and it will take a while for you to get back to normal. Now, let's take a shower and find your new clothes. Daddy should be here any minute." She stood up, placing him firmly on the floor, before going into the bathroom and turning on the shower. Fifteen minutes later, he was dressed, looking remarkably like any other eight year old, in jeans, tee shirt and baseball cap.

"Mummy, can you ask Auntie Jennifer to come in and talk to me? Alone?"

"If you think that you're ready to behave properly, yes, I can do that." He nodded and sat on the edge of the bed.

Juliet walked down the hall to the visitor's lounge. Now it would begin, and whatever relationship her son wanted with his other family, she would have to accept, no matter what her own feelings were.

"Jennifer, he's awake, and would very much like if you could go in and talk with him." She stood at the door, looking at her former sister-in-law. Jennifer blew her nose and nodded at Juliet.

"Is he feeling better?"

"Yes, I think it was a case of too much too soon. Too much food and too much family. I think we're over the worst, and he's quite ashamed of the way he behaved. I know that he wants to apologize to you and to Marina and Lindsey."

"He doesn't have to apologize. He was obviously terrified of me and what I might do to him. Juliet, what did Tony do to you that makes you so afraid even to say his name?" Heading in the direction of Carson's room, the two women walked slowly while they were talking.

"If I tell you this, you have to swear that you will never tell anyone outside the family. That last day, before he left to go back to America, he was still at home when I came back from the Slade. His bags were packed, and he announced that he was going back to America, taking all the money we had in the

131

checking account, and just leaving. I was stunned. I remember asking him when I should join him, and he started laughing. Then he hit me in the face with his fist, more than once, and knocked me down, telling me that as far as he was concerned, I was a useless piece of shit, just a convenience. After I started to cry, he hit me a few more times, then ripped off all my clothes, and raped me, over and over. I could feel blood everywhere, from my nose and from where he had abused me. When he was done, I was so relieved, I thought it was over. I was wrong, it was just beginning. He turned me over and after he kicked me a few times, he.." The tears streamed down her face.

"What did he do, Juliet? Please, I have to know." Jennifer put her arm around her. Taking a deep breath, her voice shook as she managed to get it out.

"He sodomized me. Then he wiped himself off and raped me again. The whole time he was telling me what an ugly bitch I was, and how useless I was and how he would make sure that no man would ever want me again." Juliet hid her face in her hands. Jennifer pulled them away.

"You have nothing to be ashamed of. You did nothing wrong. That part of your life is over and done with. No matter what, we will try our best not to let Tony ever hurt you again.

"I must have fainted, and when I woke up, he was gone. I crawled to the telephone and called my parents. My father came with an ambulance and a doctor. I was in the hospital for four weeks, and after that I went back to the Slade and tried to rebuild at least the creative part of my life. My father pushed through a quick divorce, and when Tony sent the papers back, we thought it was over. A month after he sent the papers back, I discovered that I was pregnant with Carson. I wanted him so badly, something clean and pure, someone to love and who would love me back. I needed a baby desperately, to reassure myself that I was still a functioning woman, that what Tony had said wasn't true." Juliet wiped her eyes and blew her nose.

"When did you meet Donald?"

"I was seven months pregnant, and he came to the Slade to look at my first series of paintings, the goldfish. He was so shy and sweet, I remembered thinking how handsome he was and how much I would love to run my hands through his hair. He was staring at my hair, like every other man, and I could tell that he was dying to touch it. After a bit of stammering, he asked me out to dinner. We fell in love and he married me a week before I had the baby. After Carson was born, when he held him in his arms and wept with joy, I knew I'd done the right thing. I felt normal and whole again."

"God, what an awful story! Why didn't you call the police and have him arrested?"

"I was unconscious and my father tells me, delirious for a day or so afterwards. When I came around, he told me that he couldn't bear the thought of the publicity and the trial, that he was afraid for my sanity. His solicitor took a statement and all the evidence and compiled a dossier, to be used if necessary, in case Tony came back."

"I gather that was what was shown to my parents."

"Most of it. I made Donald take out the really awful pictures, and parts of the report. I couldn't bear it for them to know every intimate detail, too shameful and shocking."

"I see. No wonder you're terrified of him, and Carson is terrified of me."

"He isn't, not now. He's ashamed of the way he behaved. It's a great deal to expect, for an eight year old who's been so ill, to be told the things Donald had to tell him, and then not to carry on a bit afterwards. But I think everything will work out now, you'll see. You can go in, he's waiting, and I think he'll want to talk to your daughters, and your parents, when Donald gets here."

"Thank you, for smoothing things over. We don't deserve any of this, Tony made sure of that."

"You're Carson's family. No matter what Tony did to me, I can't see any good coming out of keeping all of you out of his life."

*   *   *   *   *

Carson could see the door being opened. Taking a deep breath, he waited for his aunt to come into the room. There was a moment of awkward silence, as he hung his head, ashamed of his outburst.

"Carson, maybe we should say hello properly this time. I'm your aunt Jennifer."

"How do you do? I'm sorry for the way I acted, in front of you and everyone else. I was just so..."

"It's all right, or as we say in Los Angeles, AOK. I understand how scared you were and probably still are. I hope that one day we can learn to trust each other, and love each other, too." She smiled warmly as he grinned.

"Thank you, for being so understanding. Dylan says I was acting like a lunatic, a really barmy one. I promise, that won't happen again."

"I think I'll leave you now. Your brother and sister are outside and I know that they want to talk to you. I'll see you at dinner."

"Can you tell Marina and Lindsey that I'll talk to them later?"

"Of course, I'd be happy to." The door opened and she was gone.

"Monster, are you all right?" Miranda and Dylan stood in the doorway.

"Sorry, I was really pitiful. Shouldn't have stuffed myself that way." Carson hung his head, embarrassed by his behavior, in front of his adored older siblings.

"I told you, silly, we've all done the piglet thing, all those goodies and not being able to eat them for so long, and then, chuck time, or as Marina put it, hurling. How is your nose?"

"Fine, no more blood. I got Mummy fair full of it, right down her shirt." He rolled his eyes as his brother laughed.

"That's the last thing you should worry about. Big thing is getting out of here, going down to Surrey for the summer, and growing back your hair. Make you feel a lot better. Then maybe in the fall term, you can come up to Templeton with me."

"I can't wait." Carson sighed with happiness. His life would be the way he wanted, as long as he didn't have to worry about Tony.

*   *   *   *   *

Donald parked his dark blue Bentley in the visitor's lot and ran into the front entrance of the hospital. He should never have gone to the office after having told Carson the truth about Tony. Cowardly and shameful were what he accused himself of as he took the stairs two at a time. Worse, he had left Juliet with the burden of cleaning up his mess. While she rarely objected to handling these kinds of situations, this was one which he had hoped to handle all on his own. The floor was quiet as he walked down the hall to Carson's room.

"You asleep?" He poked his head around the door.

"No, Daddy. I'm awake." Carson sat on the bed, hanging his head. "They called you, didn't they?"

"By they, you mean your grandparents?"

"Which ones?"

"All three sets, actually. They were quite upset by what went on in this room."

Carson looked up at his father.

"I'm so ashamed. I acted like a baby, when what I really wanted to do was to get to know my cousins and the others."

Donald sat in the chair and pulled Carson on to his lap. The child leaned against his father's chest and sighed.

"You're not mad at me, are you, Daddy?"

"No, of course not. Just a bit surprised, that's all. I thought we understood each other, or I wouldn't have gone to the office. I'm sorry I wasn't here when you needed me."

"Mummy came just when I was really upset."

"Carson, tell me what started it all."

"First of all, I ate too much. Marjorie put all of this wonderful food in that basket, and I got greedy. Then Marina and Lindsey came in and Lindsey started to eat an apple tart, just like I do, even doing the thing with the crumbs on her chin, and I started remembering the things you had told me, and how I didn't want to go and live with my other Daddy. My tummy got all funny, and then I started being sick. Miranda gave me a garbage can, and I kept being sick. Then my nose started bleeding and I started screaming. Auntie Jennifer came and tried to help, but I just screamed and screamed. Then the nurse gave me a shot and Mummy came and I went to sleep."

"Are you feeling better now?"

"Yes, but I was just so frightened, thinking about having to go and live with my other Daddy."

136

"Carson, that will never happen. Try to put it into a real picture. Mummy and I really love you, and we won't let anything happen to you. Keep telling yourself that, and everything will work itself out." The boy's arms wrapped themselves around Donald's neck.

"I'll try. Thanks, Daddy."

*　　*　　*　　*　　*

Tandoori for fifteen, or more accurately for fourteen hungry souls, broke the ice and made everyone feel more at ease. As Miranda remarked, it was difficult to behave badly towards anyone when your face was full of yoghurt and spices.

Jordan took his plate and sat in a chair against the wall of the hospital room, where he could have an unobstructed view of his grandson. It was amazing, that this child, conceived in a moment of unspeakable brutality, should be such a loving person. On the surface, he resembled the child that Tony had been, but there the similarity ended. He could see what a wonderful job Juliet and Donald had done raising him and by what was obvious to anyone, loving and adoring him. As he took the last swallow of dinner, stood up and threw the paper plate away, he heard a voice behind him.

"Grandpa, can I sit on your lap and talk to you?" Jordan turned around to find Carson standing there, his eyes pleading for understanding.

"It would be my pleasure. It's been ages since a boy has asked to sit on my lap."

"Grandpa, I'm sorry, about the way I behaved this afternoon. I'm not scared of you, it's only that..."

"I understand, Carson, how afraid you are. I'm your grandfather, and that means that we are supposed to have a special relationship, and part of that means that I'm supposed to try and keep you from being hurt, as much as I can. That includes trying to protect you from what makes you afraid."

"You'd choose me over my other Daddy?"

"Yes, I would. You see, Carson, in spite of what I tried to teach him, he's not as nice a person as you are. He's done some bad things in his life. Choosing you will help me make it up to your mother, and to you, for what he has done." Hesitating for an instant, Jordan then reached out and held the boy close to his chest.

"Grandpa, that makes me feel safe. Will you do that for me whenever I feel scared of my other Daddy?" Carson reached up and put his arms around Jordan's neck.

Blinking back the tears, the older man held the boy tightly, whispering his promises into his ear. Emily and Jennifer had watched the first steps taken by boy and grandfather, and had hugged each other. They would be accepted, not immediately, but eventually, and they would all be a family. All that remained was to make sure that Tony could not interfere.

*　*　*　*　*

."What a day! Tomorrow can't come soon enough." Donald kicked off his shoes and dove onto the bed. The brass headboard shrieked as it was bumped into the wall, and the screws that held it together scraped against the brass footings.

"Donald, stop. You'll collapse the bed, and then you'll have to sleep on the floor." Juliet turned around in the little chair that matched her vanity table, decorated with pale rose silk.

"Where will you sleep?"

"In the nanny's bed, of course. I'm too delicate right now to sleep on the floor."

He stood up and came up behind her. Picking up her hairbrush, he began to brush her hair in long, loving strokes. Juliet stretched back her head, allowing the feel of the gentle strokes to radiate from the top of her head.

"That feels wonderful. Reminds me of being almost back to normal, like it was before Carson got sick." Placing the brush back on the vanity, he picked up the bottle of lavender scent, and gently lifting up the mane of her hair, sprayed it, slowly and thoroughly. She sighed with pleasure, as he worked his way around to the front of her body. Lifting the edges of her peach silk robe, he sprayed her breasts and neck first, and then worked his way down, all the way to her ankles.

"You're a lucky woman, that I can afford to buy you a truckload of scent, if I have to." Donald knelt down and buried his face in her breasts.

"Rather forward, aren't you? I don't recall inviting you to..." Catching her breath in mid-word as his hands pushed aside the robe, and began to explore underneath her silk teddy, she ran her hands through his hair. Whispering softly, she reached up and began to take off the teddy.

He slapped her hands away, while at the same time, removing first one strap and then the other. As he pulled her to her feet, the teddy slipped, like a sigh, to the floor.

Teasing her, he gently caressed first her back and then her stomach. His tongue circled her lips, at first gently, until they swelled under his touch. Breathing hard, his control began to slip. Inhaling the lavender fragrance with each breath, he was becoming increasingly distracted. She began to move away, closer to the bed. He followed, mesmerized by her scent and the sweep of her hair.

Juliet stretched out her hand, lightly stroking the side of his face. To him, it felt like scented silk being drawn across his face. For a moment he looked up, and into her eyes, huge and black, with a rim of the tawny gold that he loved. Caught off balance, she took advantage and pushed him back, onto the bed. Stretching out his arms, he pulled her down towards him.

"You are so beautiful, I can't stand it."

"You'll have to, at least for now. I feel this overwhelming need to make love to you, and to make you my prisoner, at least for tonight." Her throaty laugh echoed in his mind as he lay back, drunk on the smell of lavender, his senses floating as she drew him closer. Feeling completely helpless as she kept on, relentlessly loving him and whispering as she did, he could not fight his need any longer. He was powerless, unable to move. Closing his eyes, he gave way to each sensation as he floated, his passion increasing with each soft word and touch.

"Please, make love to me." He didn't realize the words were his, until he felt her body on top of his. Slowly, she moved, urging him on, with soft whispers and softer touch. The end surprised him, filling his consciousness with regret that it was over, and a moment of uneasiness, that he had imagined the moments of incredible sweetness, that it was all a dream from which he would wake up, cold and alone. Sleepily, his eyes opened, the pupils still enlarged, black against the gray of the iris. Focusing, he saw her face, and felt her body as she lay, half on top of him. Lazily, she reached out her hand and traced the shape of his mouth with her finger.

"Wicked girl! Taking advantage of an old man!" Laughter bubbled up out of her, as she giggled.

"Never let it be said that I don't know how to take advantage of your weak nature, just like I expect you to do to me." Bending over, she brushed his lips with her tongue, gently caressing, searching for a reaction.

Dazed by her lovemaking, and now overpowered again by the softness of her skin, he stretched out his hand, and began to caress her back. She preened like a cat, almost purring, as his hand moved slowly across her body.

"You can tell me what the doctor said, if you like." A smile tugged at the edges of Donald's mouth, as he continued to stroke her back.

"He said that we can expect another little baby in eight months. I have to go and see a high risk obstetrical doctor tomorrow morning. He said the usual, no jogging, running types of activity, lots of rest, plenty of real food, all that nonsense, and he gave me the usual prescriptions, all that boring stuff."

"Did he say how incredibly chesty you've gotten?" Donald nuzzled her neck as she giggled.

"Yes, we did talk about the fact that my clothes are feeling a bit snug around the waistline. He told me to wear loose clothing between now and the time I have to wear maternity clothes. I had to drive to the hospital with my skirt unbuttoned, it was so tight. So, tomorrow, I start wearing some of the new stuff I bought this afternoon."

"Ah, late night feeds and nappies, I can hardly wait. Come here woman, so I can enjoy all the benefits of a new baby."

*   *   *   *   *

Donald stirred and turned over, reaching his arm out to touch his wife. Her side of the bed was empty, and as he came fully awake, he could hear the sounds of her morning sickness through the bathroom door. Struggling into his robe, he knocked on the door.

"Are you all right?"

"Just a minute." The door opened, as Juliet emerged, pale and exhausted.

"This is terrible, and it's just beginning. I was never sick a day with Carson, or even the two others."

"How long did the doctor say this would go on?"

"About two months."

"Can I have Marjorie make you something? I'm sorry, but I have a meeting at 9:30, and I can't miss it."

"I'm fine, feel better already. He told me that it would probably be like this, once in the morning, and maybe some nausea later on. Imagine, he told me that some women throw up for the entire nine months." She shuddered as he smiled.

"Go back to bed, at least until I finish getting ready. I'll tell Marjorie to fix your tisane and some toast." He kissed her quickly before disappearing down the stairs. Ten minutes later, he returned, carrying her breakfast tray. Balancing it across her knees, he sat down on the edge of the bed.

"Feel up to talking?" She nodded as she nibbled on a slice of toast.

"I've been giving our wedding some thought. Would you like to get married down in the country, or at somewhere elegant here in London, like Claridge's or the Dorchester?"

"I can't get my last conversation with Vivian out of my mind. She told me to get married again as quickly as possible. She was quite adamant, seemed to feel that Tony would stop at nothing to try and get custody." She sipped the tea slowly.

"She's right, at least about Tony. I had a call from a lawyer in New York yesterday, shortly before I came back to the hospital. It seems that Tony has been calling lawyers, trying to find a way to break both the termination and our financial agreement. This man was the twenty-first one."

"You can't be serious."

"I am. He advised Tony to go home and wait for Carson to turn eighteen. Then and only if he wants to see Tony, will a meeting ever come to pass."

"Donald, he can't do that, can he?" Panic edged into her voice.

"Once Carson reaches his eighteenth birthday, there is nothing we can do to keep Tony away. My hope is that ten years from now he'll either be dead or have forgotten about Carson altogether."

"Fat chance of that happening. I think we should take Vivian's advice. How about a quiet wedding, just our families, and then a breakfast at the Dorchester?"

"Sounds wonderful. I'll book a private room, champagne and the works for all of us, ginger ale for you." Smothering a laugh, he sat back and looked at her.

"You're a dangerous woman, Juliet. If I'm not careful, my business will go to rack and ruin." He heard the thud of a throw pillow hitting the bathroom door, just as it swung closed.

CHAPTER NINE

Jordan Graniston sat at his antique Regency desk, his chin propped on his right hand, staring at the picture sitting at the right hand corner of the polished mahogany surface. Nestled in an Art Deco silver frame was the picture that had been taken of himself and Carson, the day after his grandson's release from the hospital. He smiled as he thought of the boy, how wonderful it had been to have him sitting on his lap, laughing at a harmless joke, while Juliet had snapped the picture. The knock on the door interrupted him, and he reluctantly looked up to see who it was.

"Tony's here. He wants to see you." Sheila Linden had come to work for Jordan Graniston twenty years earlier, arriving two weeks after her boss. They had quickly grown comfortable with each other, almost as if they had been married, the law firm in joke that never failed to amuse her. Looking at her over the top of his reading glasses, Jordan noticed her look of frank disapproval.

"Tell him I'm not here." He felt the sour taste in his mouth, the one that now appeared every time he had to see or talk to his son.

"I tried that. He's very insistent. He'll just sit here until you give in. It's better to get it over with." He saw that her face had changed, her expression now one of sympathetic pity.

"If I must. Time me for a minute, then manufacture a meeting across town so that I can leave three minutes after that." He avoided her eyes, feeling guilty.

"Jordan, he's drunk, or fairly close to it."

"Where did I go wrong, Sheila? I keep asking myself that." He sighed and rubbed his forehead.

144

"You didn't. Sometimes kids are just born bad." She patted him on the shoulder. In twenty years, she hadn't changed much, still slim and blonde, but with a few more wrinkles around her hazel eyes.

"When I leave for the meeting, call security and have them help you get him out of here." Reaching across the desk, he grabbed the picture and put it in his desk drawer. Using a small key from his key chain, he locked it, and nodded to her to show his son into the office.

"Tony, take a chair." Jordan stood up and walked around the desk.

"Have fun in London, Dad, you and Mom and Jennifer?" Tony flopped into a chair in front of the desk. His appearance had not improved in the six weeks since he had donated his bone marrow. Considering it pointless to dress for a job he no longer had, he was wearing wrinkled slacks and a filthy blue oxford shirt, with the sleeves rolled up.

"I'd hardly call what we went through fun." Jordan pushed his chair away, back towards the wall. The odor of stale alcohol emanating from the other side of the desk was overpowering.

"I want to come back to work, Dad. I need the money." Tony tried to focus his eyes on a central point in the room.

"That's not possible, and you know it. Donald gave you three million dollars ten weeks ago. How much of it is left?"

"I've had expenses."

"You mean gambling and women, don't you?" Jordan could barely swallow his distaste.

"I need to have a job if I'm going to sue for custody. Judges like to see a father with a job." Tony pronounced each syllable carefully, convinced that his condition would not be noticed.

145

"You are aware that the agreement you signed can't be broken. I've read it over several times. It's ironclad, I couldn't have done a better job myself." Jordan's face was expressionless.

"You're a lawyer, Dad. You should know better than anyone that there is no such thing as ironclad. There's always a way to break it, or get around it. All I have to do is be patient." Tony couldn't control the smug look on his face.

"There's the little matter of that dossier, Tony. If you try to go for custody, Donald will hand it all over to the police. You know as well as the next lawyer that there is no statute of limitations on rape over in England."

"I didn't do anything so terrible to her, I didn't give her anything that she hadn't asked for."

"Tony, when are you going to get it through your thick skull that after what you did to her, Juliet will never allow you within a hundred yards of her son."

"Everyone seems to ignore the fact that he's my son, too." Jordan checked his watch.

"That is a matter of biology, Tony, not parenting. I doubt that any court will decide that there is anything other than that to your relationship with Carson. I have a meeting to go to, and it's across town, so if you'll excuse me. One last word of advice. You will never win a case against her. You signed away your rights and insisted that you couldn't possibly be the father. And, in case you might forget, you wouldn't donate the bone marrow to save your son's life unless you got paid. From where I'm standing, neither will count well in your favor." He moved across the room, grabbed his briefcase and opened the door.

"Do me a favor, Tony. Don't come back here again, unless you're sober." The door closed quietly behind him.

Tony sat in his chair and looked around the room. As a child, he had loved spending a holiday or Saturday with his father. Jordan had let him sit at his desk, and pretend to be a lawyer at the firm. At the back of his mind during college and law school had always been the thought that one day, when his father retired, he would inherit the firm, the senior partnership and the office that went with it, down to the antique desk and exquisite Renoir paintings on the wall. But that was a dream, and it was dead, all because of his former wife and her new husband. He was content, as always, to blame everyone except himself for his misfortunes.

Checking his watch, he got up to leave. If he hurried, he could shower and change clothes and catch a train to Greenwich. Reconciling himself with his wife was an important part of his new strategy. A stable home life, even if it wasn't particularly happy or loving was another piece of the puzzle he needed for his plan to win custody of his son.

*　　*　　*　　*　　*

"I now pronounce you man and wife, for the second time." A ripple of laughter could be heard at the back of the chapel. Reverend Everett Armstrong, the same cleric who had performed Juliet and Donald's marriage the first time, allowed himself the ghost of a smile and winked at Donald.

"You may now kiss the bride." Juliet looked at her husband sideways, from behind the brim of her cream colored straw picture hat. She had trimmed it with lilac streamers, to match the cream and lilac tea gown she had bought for the occasion. Her mother had found it in an out of the way boutique during what Juliet later called her wedding gown odyssey. At the end of five hours of looking, trying on and rejecting everything, she and Rose had gone for lunch at a favorite restaurant. Once the meal was over, they had stood on the sidewalk trying to decide where to look next, when her mother had looked across the street and had seen the dress in the window of a tiny antique clothing store.

"Darling, look, it's even a size larger than you normally wear. It should fit perfectly." Rose enthused as she held it against Juliet's complexion. "It's divine, shows off your hair and eyes. And afterwards, you can have it taken in." Exhausted, Juliet reluctantly consented to try it on, secretly wanting only her bed and a long nap. Looking at herself in the mirror, she had been transformed, as if the dress had been waiting for her to come and find it. A vision of herself, in a picture hat, her hair braided into a bun at the nape of her neck, with white afternoon length gloves, strapped pumps and a lace trimmed shawl floated in front of her eyes.

Now, she stood in the chapel, dressed exactly as she had imagined. Carrying one glove, she looked down at her left hand. Her new wedding ring, thick strands of gold entwined with diamonds and emeralds, winked up at her. In spite of her protests, Donald had insisted on completely new rings, and had taken away the first set.

"It's a superstition. I can't marry you for the second time, using the ring from the first. So, start our new marriage with a new engagement ring as well." And he had placed a delicate ring, of three round diamonds entwined with gold, on her finger. Donald turned her head with his hand and kissed her gently. Laughing, he then pulled her close and kissed her properly, knocking off the hat in the process.

"Well, Your Grace, are we happily wedded?"

"Yes, milord, we most certainly are." Turning to smile at her three children, sitting in the first row, applauding their parents, she took her husband's arm and sedately walked up the aisle. There were no newspaper photographers present, at the bride's request. It had been an easy solution to the problem of shielding her children from anyone who might comment about their mother's need to marry a second time. Her father, armed with his favorite camera, had set up his tripod in front of the church. Smiling happily, the bride and groom posed for family pictures, with and without their children, until, sated with self-absorption, the groom announced that he was starving and was leaving.

The quiet party planned by Donald and Rose went off without a hitch. A piano, placed in the corner of the private dining room, played soft romantic music, while the guests celebrated what to them was a very special occasion. By two o'clock, everyone had made their farewells, and the exhausted bride, rebellious at last, was insisting on some time alone with her husband.

"Daddy, all the things for the children are in the back of Donald's car. You can take the Bentley and leave it in our garage, can't you? And, kids, remember, do not let Carson overdo or overstuff. Now kisses, and then leave us alone. Grandpa will bring you back next Sunday afternoon." Juliet and Donald hugged each of their children, and then waved as the car pulled away.

"Please, can we go up to the room now. I'm so tired I can hardly stand up." Juliet put her arm around her husband's waist.

"Yes, of course. Our flight to Nice doesn't leave for another four hours, so that should leave plenty of time."

"For what, Mr. Macallister?" Her eyes sparkled as they walked through the lobby of the Dorchester.

"A nap and then a bit of packing, I imagine. I'm a patient man, Juliet, other things can wait until later." He nuzzled the nape of her neck.

"What shall we pack? I didn't bring anything for France with me." While she struggled to control her laughter, her eyes were all innocence.

"Don't tease me. I know you saw all the goodies that I bought. They're in the closet in the suite upstairs, and those carriers are full of all sorts of dangerous things."

"Caught again. Darling, those little filmy teddies, and the gowns, I'm only relieved that I can still fit into them. In another month, I'll be fat and wearing huge clothes."

"Well, then let's enjoy them." Donald put the key into the lock of the bridal suite, turned and picked up his wife. With great care, he carried her over the threshold and set her down inside the room.

"What a romantic you are." Juliet giggled as she took off her gloves, and bent down to undo her shoes.

"Well, I couldn't do it the first time around. Admit it, you were a bit large then." Smothering a laugh, he held her close, his arms wrapped around her waist.

"Mm. Now who's being dangerous?" Leaning back against him, she raised her arm and held the back of his head.

"Too tempting by far. I'm going to bed for a bit. Can you undo the back of the dress for me?" Smiling, she waited until he had unbuttoned almost all of the buttons before she raised her arms and pulled the pins out of the bun sitting on her neck. Her hair cascaded down her back, its spicy scent, warmed by the heat of her body, rising and moving with each toss of her head.

"Unfair, and you wanting to sleep. I protest." Donald buried his face in her hair.

"Who said anything about sleep? And why do you still have all your clothes on? I thought this was part of our honeymoon." She turned to face him, dressed in nothing more than a skimpy camisole and pants. Hypnotized, he reached out his hand and touched her hair. Impatiently, she began to unbutton his shirt. Quickly, she pushed down his suspenders, and unbuttoned his trousers. Before he knew it, she had removed all of his clothes, and was standing in front of him, smiling, beckoning him to do the same for her. He felt the same way he always did when she made love to him, thick, powerless, drugged by her presence. No matter how many times he tried, he could not lift his hand to push down the strap of the camisole.

"Donald." She whispered in his ear, taking his hand and leading him to the bed. Obediently, he followed, sleepwalking through the scent of her body. As if from far away, he could feel desire pumping through his body, but he had become incapable of independent movement. Dazed, he watched her undress, and then spray herself and the bed with a spicy perfume.

"I should be making love to you, not the other way around." He sighed as she caressed him, her hair spread out on his chest. All too soon it was over, he felt even before it had really begun. As his breathing slowed, he reached out and pulled his wife close to him. Juliet smiled with contentment as she laid her head on his shoulder, closed her eyes and fell asleep.

*   *   *   *   *

"Juliet, lazy girl, wake up. It's ten o'clock, the sun is shining, and the pool, which you insisted I had to put

151

in, is waiting." Carefully, he put the breakfast tray down on the bed.

"I heard you the first time. Sorry I slept so late. Babies make you tired, even before you have them." She smiled and stretched, lying back against the lacy white pillows, and leaning over on one elbow, she poured out one cup of coffee, and one cup of herbal tea.

"How do you feel this morning?" Reaching for the raspberry jam, he spread some on a slice of toast.

"Starving, tummy quiet. Maybe the awful part is over." Juliet leaned back on the pillows, her hair pushed back from her face, and sipped her tea. "What shall we do today, after we swim?"

"Clive and Lydia are here, quite by chance. I thought that we could have dinner with them, if that's all right." He licked the raspberry jam off his fingers.

"Darling, he's your school chum, and I enjoy his company. I keep asking myself how he wound up with her. Men are really thick sometimes."

"I know, she is can be rather dim, but they seem to be happy with each other, so who are we to wonder? Now, up and let's put on our suits and use that incredibly expensive pool." Laughing, he tossed her bathing suit onto the bed.

"I haven't noticed you refusing to swim in it, and we did agree, or rather you gave in to Miranda's pleadings, that it would be a wonderful way to entertain the children, and keep them at home for a while longer." Pouting over the twitch of a smile, she put aside her tea and headed for the bathroom.

"Make sure there's an umbrella up, will you? I have to stay out of the direct sun, or I'll get brown spots." The door to the bathroom closed firmly.

"This is marvelous, I have to admit." Donald stretched and looked out over the hills. In spite of the teasing he did over the subject of the pool, it was the one spot on the entire property that never failed to give him enjoyment and a tremendous sense of peace and contentment. Turning his head, he looked over at his wife. Sitting under a large hat, she had placed herself under the umbrella. The new bathing suit he had bought her fit perfectly, in fact too perfectly.

"You shouldn't do that, it really isn't fair." Her teasing voice floated across the chairs.

"What was I doing that I shouldn't?"

"Staring."

"That's my privilege, as your husband and as an expectant father. I was just thinking how incredibly beautiful you are, just sitting there, and how I can see your body changing, almost before my eyes."

"Don't remind me. I can't imagine being that fat again, ever."

"You will. Darling, I'm starving. It's after one. Do you want to eat here, or in the house?"

"What's for lunch?"

"Lobster salad, bread and cheese."

"Indoors, very indoors. There's something overpowering about feeding lobster to each other. Give me half an hour so I can bathe and change." With a wave of her hand she was gone, through the glass doors, across the living room and into the bedroom wing. He could hear the telephone ringing through the open window, and sighing, he got up and went inside to answer it.

"Hallo, Donald? Clive here."

"Clive, Juliet and I were just talking about you. We're on for dinner tonight, aren't we?"

"Yes, we are, but that's not why I rang you. I couldn't really talk properly when you called. Someone was here two days ago, asking a lot of questions about you and Juliet, when you use the house, how

153

long you stay here, do your children come here as well. He came to our house after there was no one at home at your place. Very intrusive fellow, not at all trustworthy." He listened closely for any reaction.

"You didn't talk to him, did you?" Donald could feel his heart traveling down towards his feet.

"No, I didn't. He wouldn't identify himself, or explain what he was doing here or why he was so interested in you and your family. Lydia had just rung up the gendarmes when he ran off, and I never saw him again." It must be serious, Donald never sounds this strung up.

"I see." Donald's voice tightened with each word.

"Is there anything you want to tell me? Donald, you can trust me, we've been friends for years." The wounded tone in Clive's voice came through the receiver.

"I know that. Look, Clive, this is a very serious matter, and not one I want to discuss over the phone. Why don't we talk tonight, over dinner?"

"Is everything all right over there? I don't like the way this sounds."

"As far as I know, everything is in order. We'll talk later." Donald hung up and sat down in his favorite chair to think. His eyes swept the room, decorated in the vibrant colors so reminiscent of the south of France. Deep blues, reds, yellows and greens played as accents to the white couches and chairs. The tiled floor of deep blue stone, always cool to the touch, gave a strange, but artistic touch to the room. On the wall behind him hung one of the first paintings Juliet had done after their first marriage. Against a background of the hills of Nice, she had painted his portrait. Under protest, he had posed in casual clothing, white slacks and a pale blue linen shirt, sandals on his feet during their summer holiday, three months after Carson was born. She had captured him in a moment of total relaxation, his skin tanned by the sun, his hair tousled, his smile engaging and open. Whenever she looked at the portrait, she laughed, teasing him that he should always be painted or photographed after three hours of lovemaking. Always, he responded by throwing a pillow across the room, aiming it so that it would land, as if by chance, in her lap.

The way in which they teased each other hid no undercurrents. If other couples used teasing as a way to settle their differences, Donald and Juliet teased each other for no other reason than they were totally at ease with one another. It was their private language, creating laughter and memories, and on more than one occasion, fueling their desire for each other. Their ability to communicate with each other on various levels had existed almost from the beginning, from the moment when he had seen her in a classroom at the Slade. He had stood in the doorway, hidden for a moment, watching as she appraised her work, marveling at the loving way in which she stroked the canvasses, and finally, falling in love with her face, her hair, her essential being. In turn, she had watched him as he admired her work, as he soaked up the colors of the paintings, and had fallen in love with his manner, his glasses and the way he fingered his spectacles while he was talking. Juliet had thought that she was going mad, finding a total stranger, and the buyer of her paintings at that, physically attractive. It had only been seven months since Tony had disappeared, back to his life in America, and she was carrying his child. Not, she was convinced, much of a recommendation to someone like Donald Lord Macallister. The first dinner had proven her wrong.

155

Donald, battered by his marriage and divorce, was completely vulnerable, even desperate in his loneliness. Caring for two young children was fulfilling without question, but they hardly filled the void in his emotional life. Her gentleness and innocent humor filled his soul with wonder, and his dreams with love, and, gradually, his quiet and caring pursuit won her over. Struggling against her fears, her new feelings began to overwhelm her terror of any man, and her shame at loving one man and carrying the child of another.

The beginning of their life together, the one experience that defined their relationship, came during their first physical encounter. Never for an instant, in all the years they had been together, had Juliet forgotten the sensitivity shown by her husband. She had not been able to control the shudders of revulsion as he began to make love to her. Weeping, she had begged him to stop, feeling that she would never get over the trauma of the abuse. Thankfully, he had ignored her, and let passion take over and sweep aside her fears.

It had taken three years after the marriage before she had finally let go of the last of her fear. That day, for the first time since they had met, she had made love to him, an incredible gift that he had never forgotten. The almost unbearable sweetness of the experience, the unbelievable feelings of drifting between passion and reality on a cloud of her scent, closed the gap between them.

Now, he could feel the threat that lay behind the stranger's questions. Instinctively, he knew beyond all doubt, in spite of every precaution he had taken, that Tony was preparing to challenge the agreement he had signed, and sue for custody of Carson. Donald didn't know how he planned to do it, or how long he had before he would have to fight for his family, but he shuddered at the thought of what was to come, and worse, how he was going to tell his wife that their nightmare was just beginning. His solicitor had given him his opinion the day before the wedding, urging him to tell his wife as quickly as possible.

"Lord Donald, I must caution you that this is a most pressing situation. In spite of the termination of rights which he signed nine years ago, I must advise you that in my opinion, for whatever reason, the man is suffering a change of heart. And in spite of the fact that you adopted your son legally after your first marriage, the circumstances of the second ceremony could cast a shadow on your chances of fighting him off. I'll look into the law on this kind of thing. Discuss this with Countess Juliet, and then come and see me after your wedding trip."

Sighing, Donald got up and walked into the kitchen. The tray that Francoise, the housekeeper who had taken care of the family and the house for eight years, had prepared sat on the counter. Smiling, he noticed the small blue vase of wild flowers that sat in the far left corner of the tray. Each time that Francoise prepared a tray for Juliet, she placed flowers on it, dressing it up and making it an occasion. He opened the refrigerator and took out the salad, a bottle of white wine for himself, and mineral water for his wife. Carefully, so that nothing would spill, he placed everything on the white lace tray liner. The bread and cheese were on the counter, and he balanced them on top of the plates, already in the center of the tray. For a moment, he recalled their trip to the house after Juliet's last miscarriage.

Pale and weak, she had had to be carried into the bedroom when they arrived. For days, she had lain in bed, refusing to talk, or to eat, blaming herself for losing the child she so desperately wanted. Four or five times a day, the tray had arrived from the kitchen, adorned with flowers, and a small portion of a delicacy that Francoise had made especially to try to tempt Juliet to eat. Donald had stayed in the room with her, never leaving her side, possessed by a terrible fear that if he left her alone, she would try to kill herself. Drawn by a horrible fascination, he had stared at her arms, battered and bruised from a week of blood transfusions, fearful that in a moment of desperation, she would rip apart her veins and bleed to death.

For hours on end, he had held her, stroking her hair, talking to her, trying to keep her mind in the real world, even going so far as having a doctor come to the house to give her strong sedatives, so that she would sleep heavily, and he could sleep as well. No matter how strong the dose, she had not slept peacefully, but had shouted and wept, her dreams of blood and death playing out over and over again. Even their son had not been able to comfort his mother, and finally, Donald had sent for her parents, begging them to take the child back to England, so that he would not be traumatized by Juliet's breakdown.

His father-in-law had patted him on the shoulder and told him that it was Tony's fault, that after he had assaulted Juliet, she had lain in the hospital for four weeks, never speaking a word about the assault, never shedding a tear, and when she was released, she had gone back to the Slade, throwing herself into her work and refusing to even acknowledge what had happened to her. Numb, Donald had nodded, kissed Carson good-bye and returned to the bedroom.

A week later, she had begun to scream, pulling her hair and trying to scratch open her veins. Over and over, she had screamed Tony's name, that he was a curse, and that she would never be able to live like a normal woman. Terrified, he had sent again for the doctor, who had ordered intravenous sedatives to be given around the clock. He had also suggested that she be sent to a psychiatric hospital. Donald had refused, wanting to believe that eventually things would improve. A week later, praying that seven days of oblivion would have balanced things enough so that Juliet could begin to recover, he had ordered that the sedatives be stopped.

Emaciated and numbed, she had set out on the long road back to sanity. Initially, she had wept for hours, until there were no tears left to shed. Donald had fed her small portions of food, almost losing faith when for the first few times she had been unable swallow anything other than water. Gradually, she was able to eat and drink normally, although it took months before her appetite came back. Every two hours, the tray would arrive from the kitchen, always with the small blue pottery vase filled with flowers, brightly colored and arranged with an artist's touch.

Two weeks later, Donald had taken Juliet, still thin and pale, home to England. In spite of his father's attempts to keep things running smoothly, the business had suffered during his absence. Juliet, weak and listless, had taken to her bed, refusing to even go upstairs to look at the new studio Donald had ordered to be built in their absence. As soon as the front door closed, and she could hear the Bentley driving out of the garage into the street, she would begin to cry. With Carson and the nanny, Elizabeth Price, still living with her parents, only Marjorie Walters, the cook, and Caroline Evans, the housekeeper, were at home, and Juliet made sure that the door to her room was locked, with the radio turned on loudly, to muffle the sounds of her sobs. Alone and feeling completely abandoned, she cried for hours, often hysterically, rocking back and forth as if her grief would never heal. Each afternoon, after lunch, she would lock the door again, and take out the baby clothes she had bought. Lovingly, she would stroke them and then cry again, rocking back and forth, holding them against her chest.

The final crisis came the night she tried to cut off her hair and shave her head. Donald had bought her some new clothes, hoping that they would spark enough interest to get her out of bed. She had responded by insisting that she would not be bribed, and had taken a pair of scissors and tried to cut off her hair. Screaming that she wanted to be bald, that she did not deserve anything else, he had finally lost his temper. Grabbing the scissors, he had slapped her across the face, twice, as hard as he dared. Shocked, she had slapped him back. Breathing hard, he had kissed her, and then ripped off her nightgown, dropping it in shreds onto the floor.

Grimly, without saying a word, she had stood there, staring, wild-eyed for a moment, before she had begun to cry. Throwing her arms around him, she kissed him and removed his clothes, announcing that she was tired of self-pity and wanted to be normal again. Eagerly, he had made love to her, his pent-up desire pushing him to take her, almost brutally. She had responded, whispering how much she loved him, how she had longed for him to make love to her, and begging him to love her again and again.

The next morning, she was up at dawn. By ten o'clock, she had collected Carson and brought him home again, and during his nap, she was up in her new studio, planning her next series of paintings. Donald knew that the worst was over, when he found the shredded remains of the baby clothes in the wastebasket in their bedroom. Their loss was never mentioned again.

* * * * *

Wrapped in a robe after his own shower, Donald kicked the bedroom door open and carried the tray inside. He could hear Juliet singing as she lay in the bathtub. Putting the tray down on the bed, he opened a drawer in his desk and drew out a long, slim red box. Opening it, he admired the heavy gold necklace, with the four rectangles. Three were filled with the names of their children, spelled out in diamonds and sapphires. One remained blank, waiting for the birth of the baby. The matching earrings were gold squares, filled with diamond and sapphire chips. Softly, he closed the box and put it on the tray. Bad news would keep, at least for a few hours. For the moment, he was going to enjoy his honeymoon, feed his bride lobster salad and make long and passionate love to her for the entire afternoon, and if it wasn't enough, he would postpone their dinner plans for another night.

CHAPTER TEN

Juliet stood in front of the full-length mirror and preened, admiring herself, and her new necklace. Turning sideways, she pulled the cream silk shift tightly around her stomach. Detecting a slight bulge, she sighed with happiness and placed her hand over the small mound. Smiling, she gave her hair a final brush. In honor of her honeymoon, she had left it down, cascading to the center of her back. It was not without amusement that she checked her watch, wondering how quickly they would finish dinner and rush back to the villa.

"Plotting again?" Donald had been standing in the doorway, watching her in front of the mirror. Her small moments of vanity always reminded him of how complicated a person she really was. Most days, she wore no makeup or jewelry, dressed in blue jeans and her favorite paint stained shirts that at one time or another had been in his closet. Her hair was braided any old way, and she frequently met him at the end of the day with paint all over her face and arms. It was only on the occasions when they went out alone, as a couple, that she bothered to dress up and wear make-up. At those moments, she was breathtaking, so much so that on more than one evening, they hadn't even made the trip downstairs before he had canceled dinner and made love to his wife instead.

"If you're not careful, you won't get any dinner, and neither will someone else." He rested his chin on her shoulder, clasping his arms around her waist.

"I'm sure there's plenty in the kitchen that we can have for dinner, so don't tease me." She locked her hands over his.

"I'm not. There should be a rule, that you are not allowed to look so beautiful, and smell so good, right before I'm to take you out. Bad for my self-control." He smothered a laugh.

"Let's set a time then, to be back. How about nine thirty?"

"Not quite. Dinner isn't until eight. Too rude to Clive and Lydia."

"Darling, they know what we're like. We've canceled them at the last minute often enough." Her throaty laugh echoed in his ear.

"Not tonight. There' s something happening, and I have to discuss things with Clive." She wheeled around and looked at his face, not liking what she saw.

"I think you'd better tell me what's going on." He dropped his arms and turned away.

"I'd hoped to spare us what is coming, you in particular. Clive called today, while you were bathing. Someone has been here, probably a detective, asking questions about us, when we come here, how long we stay, do the children ever come with us. There's no need for secrecy any longer. I'm convinced that Tony is going to break the agreement. I don't know where or how it will begin, but if I were him, I would appear suddenly and try and see Carson." She sighed and turned away for a moment.

"I knew it was too easy. He's not the type to give up. Donald, we have to fight him every inch of the way. I can't bear the thought of him being in Carson's life."

"Darling, I know that. From now on, we'll have to be very cautious about everything. Perhaps we shouldn't come here with the children for a while, now that Tony knows where it is."

"What about Miranda and Dylan? They live for their holidays here."

"They'll understand. We'll take them to Florida instead. I'll have the house in Palm Beach opened up, and they can swim all they want there. We can use that until further notice." She walked across the room and put her arms around him.

"It's a nightmare, but we'll manage. I'll be fine, I promise."

The conversation at dinner was awkward. Clive and Lydia had sat in stunned silence while Donald had told them the story of Juliet and Tony. Lydia, shivering with horror at the end of the story, gulped her brandy, trying to stop the shaking.

"What a dreadful story! I had no idea. What can Clive and I do to help you?"

"Nothing, except to keep quiet, and to call the gendarmes immediately if someone else comes back asking questions about us." Juliet sipped her herbal tea and prayed for the evening to end. Gratefully, Clive stood up a few minutes later and announced their departure.

"I have a headache, and I'm sure that you're both exhausted. Donald, ring me tomorrow and we'll talk further." He pulled his wife out of her chair and left as gracefully as possible. Juliet finished her tea while Donald paid the check. Slowly, they walked out of the restaurant, and up the hill to their villa.

"I'm sorry, Tony seems to have ruined the evening." He put his arm around her shoulder.

"He can't ruin anything. I swore when I recovered two years ago that I would never let him control my life again, and I mean it." She had stopped, and turned to face him. "Darling, I want you to promise me something. I want to fix it so that he can never hurt me or Carson or you again. Knock him down, Donald, and make sure he can't get up."

"My idea entirely. Now enough of Tony and our other troubles. The night is young, and I'm in the mood for a swim." They began walking up the hill again.

"In the bare altogether? No one can see and Francoise is gone for the day." Her eyes sparkled.

"I have plans for us tonight, so be patient. Let's get home first."

*　　*　　*　　*　　*

Bertram Sadler closed the door of Carson's room quietly. He had already checked on Miranda and Dylan and all three of his grandchildren were fast asleep. When their daughter had married Donald Macallister, and taken on his two children, Miranda, six, and Dylan, four, Bertram and Rose had said very little. As almost an observer in the beginning, Bertram had been appalled at Delia's behavior, abandoning two young children and leaving them with their father. Donald had done an excellent job with them, but he was not a mother, and a woman's love was the one element that had been missing from Miranda and Dylan's lives. They, in turn, had embraced their new mother and never let go.

The first time that Miranda had climbed onto his lap, followed by Dylan, anxious that he should receive equal attention from their grandfather, Bertram had lost his heart to them completely. When he had held them close, hugging and kissing them, they had responded, calling him Grandpa. Eight years later, he had a hard time remembering what his life had been like before he had acquired three grandchildren. Smiling to himself as he went downstairs to the sitting room, he realized that it must have been meaningless.

Try as he might, he could not remember a thing about it as sharply as he could the last eight years.

The lamps in the sitting room were lit, and he could hear the chink of cup against saucer as he walked across the room. Rose put down her cup of tea and smiled up at him. She had always thought that the last look at one's grandchildren traditionally belonged to the grandmother. Her husband's insistence on having that privilege had touched her heart. He had never been overly demonstrative, preferring instead to be gruff in his public declarations of love, but she had never doubted his devotion to her and their daughter, not for an instant. The arrival of ready-made grandchildren had changed her perspective on his way of showing affection, to the point where he had grudgingly admitted that it was rather nice to be able to kiss his grandchildren in public.

"All snug in their beds?" She handed him a plate of cookies and put a cup of tea down on the table next to his chair. He looked as tall and slender as he always had, if even a bit younger than his fifty-two years. He had aged well, with only a few lines on his face, his aquiline nose as well shaped as it had been when he was a young man. The blue eyes whose twinkle had captured her heart were still as clear as ever. His only concession to age was a pair of half glasses that he used for reading, and his liking for the distinguished look his graying temples gave his dark hair.

"Yes, Carson was a bit restless, talking in his sleep. He's afraid of Tony, won't show it to anyone, but he's afraid." He nibbled at a cookie, brushing the crumbs away from his jacket.

"What will they do, if he challenges them for Carson?" He looked across at Rose, the love of his life. She was still so lovely, as beautiful as she had been at eighteen, tall, slender, with delicate Titan features, masses of auburn hair and those tawny colored eyes she had passed on to their daughter. It was hard to believe that they had been married almost thirty years.

"Fight to the last breath. If need be, take him and run." Startled at the way he had been gripping the cup, and grateful that it hadn't shattered, he put it gently on the saucer.

"That's rather grim, don't you think? Donald has a business, Juliet has her own career, they'd be throwing all that away." Rose distracted herself by pouring another cup of tea for both of them.

"Rose, that boy means more to them than any business or paintings. Juliet will never allow Tony to get his hands on her son, and take my word for it, if she has to run with him, she will." Restless, he got out of the chair and walked over to the window. Flicking the curtain aside, he looked down into the street. The street lamps were lit, and the street was deserted, except for a blue sedan that had been parked in front of the house across the street at odd times for the past two days. He could see the outline of two men just sitting in the car, one of them drinking from a paper cup.

"We're being watched, you know. That car across the street has been here for two days. I'm calling the police, have them shooed away, at least for tonight. Tomorrow, I want you to pack them up. We'll slip out and go away for two days." He walked across the room to the telephone table.

"You don't think that they work for Tony, do you?" Rose had begun to feel fear in the pit of her stomach, the same fear she had had when she had seen Juliet for the first time after the assault.

"I'm sure that they do. How about we take them down to Bath for the weekend? Today's Thursday, we'll have two more days there before we have to come back on Sunday. I'll call the Royal Crescent and book rooms for all of us, and we'll let Tony's men bore themselves to death." He picked up the phone and punched in the numbers to the police station. Five minutes later, a patrol car had arrived, and the blue sedan pulled away.

* * * * *

"Donald, how are you two enjoying yourself? Weather warm?"

"Bertram, we were just swimming and talking about you. Are the children behaving themselves?"

"Perfectly, as good grandchildren should. The reason I'm calling is to tell you that we are taking them away tomorrow, for a short vacation."

"Can you fax me all the particulars, right here to the house?"

"Yes, of course. How is Juliet?" He could hear her laughing and splashing in the background.

"Waiting for the other shoe to drop."

"I see. When you hear from me, fax me back. Have fun, and we'll see you on Sunday."

"Right." Donald hung up the phone, and sat back in the lounge chair. Distracted, he watched his wife climb out of the pool. Somehow, she had managed to lose her bathing suit in the pool, and her long red hair clung to the front of her body, as she rose out of the water and climbed the ladder.

"You look like Venus, rising out of the sea." He laughed and threw her a towel.

"I feel like it, too." Catching the towel, she began to rub her hair dry. "What did my father have to say?"

"Something's going on. He called to tell us that they are taking the children out of town for the weekend."

"Did he say where?"

"No, he didn't. He's faxing us with the details."

"Donald, I don't like this at all."

"Let's try not to panic. Your father will not let anything happen to them. I would venture a guess that someone is watching the house, and he simply wants to avoid giving them anything that Tony can use."

"Should we go home tomorrow?"

"No, I don't think so. This is our honeymoon, and I'm afraid that this may be the last moments of joy and peace we'll have for a very long time. So, wicked girl, stop trying to wrap that tiny towel around yourself, it won't work. Come here and I'll put your robe around you, and we'll go inside." Standing up, he held her robe so that she could get into it, his hand brushing against her breast as she turned around. A single tear rolled down her cheek. Without thinking, he bent down and kissed it away.

"It isn't fair. I wish that none of this had ever happened, that Tony would drop off the face of the earth."

"Juliet, no one has ever said that life is fair. Some of us are luckier than others, but that's fate, or destiny, or whatever you want to call it. And believe me, no one wants Tony to disappear more than I do."

"Can we go home tomorrow, please? Let's join my parents, wherever they are. I feel a tremendous need to hug my children." Trembling, she buried her face in his chest. "I'm so afraid, of Tony, of losing Carson to him, so stupid and childish."

"Nothing stupid and childish about it. You are more than entitled to be afraid."

"Donald, promise me something. After the baby comes, and if all goes well, promise me I can have more children."

"Yes, of course, as many as you can chase at one time. Darling, nothing is going to go wrong. Carson will not leave us, I promise."

"For now, I'll believe it, but even you can't see the future. I have the strangest feeling, I'm almost sorry I'm already pregnant, I feel as if making love tonight has magic in it, making a child, and all that." Using his right hand, he lifted her chin. Her face was wet with silent tears, her eyes washed clean of fear.

"Then let's not waste it. If we're going home in the morning, we have a lot to do before then."

*   *   *   *   *

Donald lay in bed, looking out of the window and watching the sun come up. When he and Juliet had redecorated the villa, about six months into their marriage, she had insisted on removing a wall. and replacing it with a soaring floor to ceiling window. The view from the window was spectacular, skipping across the pool, and to the hills beyond. In the days when Carson was a baby, and had to be nursed early in the morning, she had drawn the shades back and sat at the window, feeding the baby and watching the sun come up. Teasing, Donald had insisted that she was really a Viking savage, thrilling to the early hour and the beauty of the sun.

Today, however, their positions were reversed. He was sleepless, staring out at the first rays of the sun as they peeped across the hills, while she slept, smiling and happy, her arms around his chest. He absentmindedly stroked her hair and held her closer, before he gently removed her arms and got out of bed.

Struggling with temptation, he resisted the impulse to wake her up and make love to her once more before they had to leave for the airport. From now on, they would fly the Macallister private jet wherever they had to go. Just one more precaution, a sacrifice for her peace of mind. The telephone rang once, and he could hear the low whine of the fax machine. Walking into the study, he waited as his father-in-law's fax came across.

"Sleepy girl, wake up. We have to get ready to go."

"What time is it?"

"Almost seven. I've got your tea ready, and then we really have to go, if you want to get to Bath at a reasonable hour."

"Bath? Whatever will we do there?"

"Your father has taken everyone there for the weekend. Apparently Tony had someone watching the house. They all slipped away early this morning, while the police were still in front of the house, watching."

"Is this what we have to look forward to from now on?" She sat up in bed and pushed her hair out of her face.

"I expect so. It looks as if he is going to become quite a nuisance."

"He already has. Where are we staying in Bath?"

"The Royal Crescent. Hurry. I'm almost ready to go."

*   *   *   *   *

Tony Graniston closed the study door behind him and sat down at his desk. With a great deal of pleading and begging, he had achieved a reconciliation of sorts with his wife. They had decided to wait until after the baby was born to remarry quietly, and on the surface, life seemed to be close to normal again. He had stopped drinking as heavily as in the past, and stayed close to home, foregoing his usual evening occupations of gambling and patronizing prostitutes. Each morning when he looked in the mirror, he grudgingly had to admit to himself that healthier living had its benefits. His face had lost that white, puffy look he always had when he was hung over, and he had lost ten pounds.

Laurel was due to have her baby any day now, and Tony had, for the time being, given up on looking for another job. Instead, he spent his time planning his upcoming bid for custody of his son. Checking his watch, he picked up the telephone and placed a call to Chicago.

"Bill, it's Tony. How are things going?"

"It's still to early to have anything substantial to report. I told you from the beginning that as far as I can tell there is absolutely nothing you can use against your former wife. She is a devoted mother, and the child lives in a loving home. As the primary custodial parent, she is the one you will have to fight. Macallister is the child's legal father, and much as you might want to go after him, he's the wrong person."

"And you've been digging?"

"As deep as I dare right now. I don't want to get the husband's attention just yet. I've sent people out asking questions, and I have people watching them. That's the best I can recommend right now."

"Where are they now?"

"On their way back from a week-end in France. Rumor has it that they got married again, and took a few days vacation."

"Where is my son?" Bill gritted his teeth at the tone of his client's voice. If Tony Graniston weren't paying three times the rate card, he would have nothing to do with him.

"He was with his brother and sister, at her parents' house. I had a car outside watching, but they had to withdraw. Your former father-in-law is sharp. He spotted them and called the police. There was a squad car parked outside his house for the following day, so by the time we got back onto the street, all of them were gone."

"I'm worried. If she even suspects that I'm planning to sue for custody, all of Macallister's power will be used to fight me. How long will I have to wait?" Tony tried, without much success, to keep his voice calm and dispassionate.

"Don't keep asking me that, Tony. I don't know. In order to win custody, you will have to find something that will be so overwhelming that no judge will be able to deny your case. Right now, there isn't anything that I can find to use against her, and you have to accept that there is a very strong chance that you may never gain custody of your son. You could always wait until he turns eighteen."

"Ten years is too long."

"I can't help that. Just keep your nose clean, and pray that they don't have anything on you."

"And if they did?" Bill looked at the clock on his desk. Five more minutes, and he would cut Tony off.

"Then you haven't even got a prayer. Your ex-wife is a world class artist, and from what my people tell me, doesn't have an enemy in the world. Charming, gracious, beautiful and she dotes on her children. The only chink in the armor is Macallister's ex-wife."

"Can we use it?"

"No. She abandoned her children ten years ago, and filed for divorce. The kids haven't seen her since. Macallister paid her half a million pounds to give him sole custody, no visitation. She jumped at it. From what I've managed to dig up, she was never what you

173

would call an ideal mother. He was always the primary parent, from the beginning."

"Where is she now?"

"Married to a French industrialist. Mega millions, no kids. You won't get to first base with her, Tony. She's happy and satisfied with the way things are. Remember, she hasn't seen her children in ten years."

"Too bad. Keep me informed as to what happens."

Tony hung up and leaned back in the leather chair. The study had been furnished along the same lines as his father's office. From the exquisite Persian carpet on the floor, to the Art Deco desk and the Louis XV clock on the mantelpiece, it exuded power and position. In the first years of his marriage, he and Laurel had chosen the furnishings for the room, keeping in mind the day when he would inherit his father's place in the firm. That dream was dead now, but someday there would be another job, another partnership, another dream. As he sat in the chair, it seemed as if all of his troubles had begun when he had married Juliet Sadler. Now, beginning with the custody suit, it was his turn to settle the score.

* * * * *

The rented limousine glided into a parking spot across the street from the Royal Crescent. The driver, Val Lenox, one of Donald's team of private detectives, checked the street first before opening the rear door.

"Lord Donald, the street appears to be clear."

"Good. Val, we'll check in to the hotel. You know what to do next." Donald got out of the car, and, taking his wife's hand, walked into the Royal Crescent. Val remained behind, checking the street carefully as the bellman was unloading the luggage.

On the flight over from France, a plan had been worked out, designed to give Tony's detectives as much difficulty as possible. A great show had been made at the airport, with the Macallister car picking them up and taking them back to the townhouse. The small blue sedan had followed them, at a discreet distance. Once home, they had repacked their bags. April Connors, a female detective and Brian Saunders, Val's partner, drove the Bentley out of the garage. As it rounded the corner of the street, the blue sedan followed. Five minutes later, the taxi Donald had called picked them up and drove them to a Macallister construction site in Southwark. There, Val waited with a rented limousine. April and Brian had driven the Bentley back to the house. Once safe inside, she had called the police and registered a complaint against the driver of the small blue car.

"Mummy, you're back." A small blue-jeaned blur flung himself into his mother's arms. Carson hugged her fiercely, did the same for his father, and then bowed and pulled off his baseball cap.

"Look, it's growing back. Grandpa said that in a week or two, I'll just look as if I'd had an American haircut." He beamed with pleasure.

"That's the best news I've had today." Juliet stretched out her arm and stroked the fuzz on her son's head. He looked wonderful, happy and smiling, and looked as if he had gained a few pounds.

"Did you bring us presents?" He had his arms wrapped around Donald's legs.

"Greedy boy, will you never stop?"

"Sorry, Daddy, but I made a bet with Miranda. If you did, I get her dessert tonight. Otherwise, I have to give her mine." Carson grinned as he looked up at his father.

175

"Tell her to be sure to order something truly gooey and disgusting. Then you can eat every bite." Swallowing his laughter, Donald's eyes twinkled.

"I told her you would. She said you and Mummy would be too busy to buy things this time."

"Never that. Now let us get to our rooms and unpack, and we'll see you later. Where's Grandpa?"

"In your room, waiting for you. He said to go right along, it was important." He turned and disappeared around the corner of the hotel.

"What a difference. Darling, are you feeling all right?"

"Just for a second, I was feeling quite ill. I think I'll go to the room, and lie down for a while."

"Shall I call a doctor?" His skin grew paler.

"No, I just have to be sick again, that's all. So much for an early end to this. Then I need my rest for half an hour. I seem to be tired all the time right now."

"I'll have to tell our baby not to abuse its mother." Laughing, he kissed her cheek, breathing in the scent of lavender.

"Go and rest. I'll take your father to the garden and talk there."

"Just don't talk too long. It's still our honeymoon, at least until Sunday night." Laughing, she opened the door to the suite, kissed her father hello, and walked through to the bathroom.

"She all right?" Bertram closed the door to the room.

"She's tired, just worn out from the last two years, and now she has to worry about Tony." Donald sighed and rubbed his eyes.

"It's only beginning, you know that, Donald."

"Yes, I know. Now it's a waiting game, to see how long it takes for him to make a move."

"Damn him, trying to turn me into a prisoner in my own home. I could wring his neck, quite easily." Bertram bit down on his fourth cigar of the day.

"The blue car you chased off followed us home from the airport. The detectives gave them the slip. The police have been called again, and this time I've asked them to make sure they don't come back. Monday morning, first thing, I'll go down to Scotland Yard and file a complaint. That should keep them busy for a while."

"What do you think he's up to?"

"He wants custody of Carson. Plain and simple. Juliet's friend Vivian warned us that he would stop at nothing to get what he wants. It's ironic, him using the money I paid him to make Juliet's life miserable. Thank God I adopted Carson all those years ago. It will be extraordinarily difficult for him to gain full custody."

"What will you do when Carson turns eighteen?"

"Nothing. He will have reached his majority, at least in the United States, and Tony can visit him any time he wants."

"I'm convinced that he wants revenge, to get even with her for God knows what."

"She says the same thing. Tony can try whatever he likes, he will never take my son away." Donald poured two whiskeys from the tray he had ordered.

"Say, worst scenario, he wins shared custody. What will she do?"

"It won't happen. He'll rot in prison before that happens."

"And if he decides to just take Carson?"

"I'll hunt him down."

"I see. Donald, don't let this get out of control. Hit him and hit him so hard that he can't ever recover."

"That's what she said, to knock him down and make sure he can't ever get up again."

"A wise woman, my daughter."

"Agreed. And now, I'm going to the room to change, and spend some time with my bride, and we'll see all of you later."

"Of course. We're taking them on the tour of the baths, and then to the Pump Room for tea. If you like, join us. Otherwise, see you at dinner, say about eight?"

"Done." Donald stood up and walked across the garden. An image floated in front of his eyes, of his wife, holding out her arms, and suddenly the smell of lavender was overpowering, beckoning, wrapping itself around him. He lengthened his stride, walking faster towards his fantasy.

CHAPTER ELEVEN

Jordan hoisted his golf bag onto his shoulder, slammed the trunk of his car shut and walked towards the clubhouse. He had been a member of the Stanwich Club for almost thirty years, playing with the same three friends each weekend that he had been able for all of that time. Today he walked with new purpose. His son's wife had given birth to her baby, yet another girl. They had named her Emily. He was happy to have a new grandchild, in spite of knowing that he was being manipulated. He waved to his regular partners, standing a short distance away, ready and waiting. Walking rapidly, he had just moved his arm to drop his clubs into the back of the golf cart when he heard the chimes of his cellular telephone. Grumbling, he turned away to answer it..

"Jordan, Donald Macallister here. I hope I'm not interrupting anything important."

"No, just my golf game. It can wait. Nothing's wrong, is it?"

"Everything is fine. Carson is well, and overjoyed because his hair is growing back."

"You wouldn't have tracked me down here just to tell me that, Donald, so why don't you just tell me what is so important." Swallowing hard, he ignored the onset of the nausea that he now associated with any discussion of his son.

"It looks as if Tony is going to break the agreement. He's got people watching us, and someone was in Nice, asking questions about my family, and how often Juliet is there with Carson. My solicitor tells me that your son is probably getting ready to serve papers on her. I won't tolerate this, Jordan, and if he continues to push, I'll crush him."

"Let me ask around and see what I can come up with. Don't do anything until we speak again." Jordan could feel his heart beginning to thud rapidly.

"He's lucky, she's willing to ignore this, provided he gives up all ideas of suing for custody."

"Call me tomorrow, same time at the same number. I'll have some information for you then." Beads of sweat beginning to appear on his forehead, Jordan leaned against the wall of the clubhouse, closed his eyes and breathed deeply. When he had stopped trembling, he punched in Tony's number.

"Tony, I think we should have a talk. As soon as possible."

"I'm a little busy right now. How about sometime next week?"

"Make yourself free. I'll be there in twenty minutes. And make sure everyone else is out of the house."

"Sure, see you then." Tony replaced the receiver gently, wondering if by an outside chance, his father had found out about his decision to sue for custody of his son.

The ride from the Stanwich Club to Tony's house, on Lower Cross Road, seemed to take forever. Jordan found himself losing his focus as he became more and more upset. During a lengthy process of evaluation, every facet of their relationship had come under a microscope, even down to the law firm. He had long been aware of his son's hunger for his office and senior partnership. Recently, he had been asking himself a persistent question more often. Had his son merely tolerated his presence as a means to an end, the law firm, or was there really the possibility of a relationship that he might have missed? The Mercedes pulled into the driveway, and as he got out to ring the doorbell, he noticed that Laurel's minivan was gone. At least he could spare her one part of the ordeal.

"Dad, come on in. Laurel put out some lunch for us, if you're hungry." Tony held open the front door, his affability setting Jordan's teeth on edge.

"Let's go into your study. This won't take long, and I have a golf game in an hour." Grim-faced, he led the way, and motioned Tony to shut the door behind them.

"Where's Laurel?"

"She took the girls to the library. Emily is upstairs, asleep."

"Is there anything you want to tell me, Tony?" Jordan sat down in a chair, away from the desk, against the wall.

"No, I don't think so." Tony's facial expression was noncommittal and benign.

"I see. So you have nothing to say about the detectives you hired to follow Juliet and her family?" Jordan could feel his anger beginning to rise above his self-control.

"No, I don't." Tony sat down in the chair behind his desk, smiling and at ease.

"Tony, you are a damned liar." Jordan could feel himself losing control.

"No need to get so angry, Dad. After all, I have to do what's right for my son. I want full custody. She's had him for eight years. Now it's my turn. That boy is my son, much as she and Macallister might like to deny it."

"I see. And how do you plan to achieve this?"

"The normal way. Take her to court, and demand my rights."

"You'll have to give back the money. Once you break the agreement, Macallister will come after you. I'm warning you, don't ever underestimate him."

"He's got nothing to say, he isn't Carson's real father."

"On the contrary, he's the one who has been there for him and for his mother. When you first raped and abused your wife, then stole her money and came back here, he was there to pick up the pieces. Whatever happened afterwards, he was there, and you weren't. You weren't even interested in her, only in the money you could extort from her parents. You didn't even have enough respect for her to sign the divorce papers the first time around, and in case the fact may have slipped your mind, you signed termination papers before Carson was born. Macallister adopted him before he was a year old. You had your chance, Tony, and you threw it away. Now, all of a sudden, you find out that baby was a boy, and miraculously you become a concerned parent."

"That's absolutely right. All these years I thought that someone else had been in her bed, making love to her after I left, and she tried to palm her brat off on me. That's why I signed the termination. Now it's different. He's my son, and I intend to get full custody." Tony leaned against the desk, crossing his arms over his chest.

"Think about what you just said. I saw those pictures. Whatever gives you the idea that she would even be interested in another man? Or have you conveniently blocked out everything you did to her?" Jordan listened to the silence overwhelm him. All he could hear was the sound of his own breathing. "Tell me, what terrible thing did she do to you that made you hate her so much?"

"She made me love her. It got so bad that I couldn't breathe or think about anything anymore except her. It was like being possessed." In spite of himself, his voice became almost dreamy, as images of Juliet flashed across his memory.

"Son, no one makes you love them. You either do or you don't. And if you loved her that much, it doesn't surprise me that you aren't happy with Laurel. Feelings like that never die, no matter how hard you try to kill them. Juliet loved you, too, didn't she?"

"She was always saying she did. In the beginning, I was so proud that she loved me. When we went out somewhere, every man in the room would want her, but she was mine. That's why I married her, I couldn't stand the thought of another man touching her or making love to her. But after a while, I started to hate her. She had trapped me and I started to miss the life I had when I was single. When the year in London was over, I packed my bags and took the money out of the joint account. I was on my way out of the apartment, when she came back. I hadn't intended even saying good-bye and when she found out that I was leaving without her, and that it was over, she started crying.

"The next thing I knew, I was hitting her. It felt wonderful, feeling her face under my hands, like I was cutting away every connection to her. Something kept telling me I should stop, but I couldn't. Before I knew it, I had ripped her clothes off, and I was forcing her to make love to me. The whole experience felt like it was happening to someone else, not me. A Graniston doesn't rape and beat his wife, someone else does. It was like a bad dream, and someone else was doing awful things to someone I had sworn to love and cherish for the rest of my life. There was blood everywhere, and she was unconscious when I took my bags and left for the airport." Jordan could feel the burning of the acid in his throat.

"Your sister tells me you did something else to her." Tony hung his head and nodded.

183

"I thought that if I humiliated her, she would go away and leave me alone. I wanted to make her hate me for the rest of her life. It was so stupid. When I saw her again, I knew that I had made a terrible mistake, the worst one any man could make. I did a good job, Dad. She hates me so much she can't even stand to look at me."

"What were you thinking, then, to ask for money to save your son's life?"

"I wanted her to know that, even after what happened, there is still a connection."

"Is that why you want custody of Carson, so she will have to face you two or three times a year?"

"I want to spend time with the boy, get to know him. He's my only tie to her, the one thing that we have in common. I must have been insane to give up my rights to him."

"But you did. Juliet and Donald have made a life together, with Carson. There's no room for you anymore. Let it go, Tony. It won't end happily for any of us."

"How can I? He's my son. Every day that goes by he gets further and further away from me. If I don't start a relationship with him now, I never will."

"It's already too late. I'm sorry for you, Tony, but there is not now, nor will there ever be a relationship. You can't go on torturing yourself over a woman you threw away and a child you have lost through your own foolishness."

"All I can think about is having him living here as my son."

"Then you have a serious problem. Call off the detectives, or Donald will hand over the file on you to the police. I can't imagine that you would enjoy serving a life sentence in an English prison."

"How did you find out?"

"He called me at the club. Tony, he told me that if you don't call them off, he'll crush you, and that's an exact quote."

"I'll just have to take my chances. There's too much at stake for me to quit now. The custody suit is almost ready to go."

"You haven't listened to a single word I said, have you? Well, here's something else to think about. I won't back you on this." Jordan got out of the chair and walked to the door.

"It might interfere with your relationship with your grandson, right?" Jordan felt surprise, more than any other emotion. Not surprise that his son was back in character, but rather surprise that he had ever expected anything different.

"Yes, son, that is exactly right. You probably think I'm a selfish old man, but I wasn't the one who raped and abused my wife, and I didn't ask for three million dollars to save my son's life. Think about it, drop the detectives, and I'll beg her to let you visit the boy. That's the best I can do."

"Sorry, it's just not good enough. The answer is no." Jordan resisted the urge to slam the door on his way out.

*　　*　　*　　*　　*

The phone was answered on the first ring.

"Jordan, Donald Macallister."

"You're right on time, Donald."

"Do you have an answer for me?"

"He said he won't call them off. There's more. He's going to file for full custody, right here in Connecticut." There was a moment of silence, broken by Donald's sigh.

"I'd hoped to avoid him dragging Juliet through the mud. She's expecting another child, and she's fragile. I'll take it from here. Thank you for doing your best."

"I'm sorry I couldn't help you."

"I didn't expect that you could. Give my regards to Emily." The call was disconnected, the soft click on the other end telling Jordan that the call was over.

*   *   *   *   *

John Trent sighed as he swiveled his chair so that it faced the window. There was no sun, only a solid mass of gray clouds. The clouds reflected his sombre mood. He had no great desire either to take on Tony Graniston as a client, or to fight a case he had no hope of winning. His protestations that he was not an expert in such matters had failed to dissuade Tony, and he had finally gotten a reprieve by agreeing to consider the custody suit.

"Susan, put me through to Donald Macallister, at Macallister Industries. The number is in my private book."

"It will take a while, John, I'll buzz you when I have him on the line."

John crossed to the window, and looked out on lower Broadway. From his tenth floor office, he could see the traffic going by, and at this time, around the noon hour, he watched the lunchtime crowd going about their business. He felt overpowered by a desire to take a shower and change his clothes. Any contact with a user like Tony Graniston made him feel dirty and unclean. Turning as the buzzer went off, he shuddered momentarily.

"Lord Donald, this is John Trent calling, from New York."

"Yes, John, I remember you. How can I help you?"

"I just got off the phone with Mr. Graniston. He wants to hire me to file a custody suit, in Connecticut."

"Are you going to take the brief?"

"I don't want to take this case, not one bit. I just wanted to let you know that he is determined to pursue this."

"I never doubted it for a minute. Thank you for calling."

"Not at all. I'll keep in touch if I hear anything else." Squaring his shoulders, John walked out into the outer office.

"Susan, please, type the standard rejection letter to Tony Graniston, and send it to his home in Greenwich, and from now on I'm out when he calls. I never want to hear his voice again." The door to the inner office shut firmly behind him.

*   *   *   *   *

The table was decorated with flowers and balloons. Two plates had a gift box on them, going away gifts for Miranda and Dylan, who would be returning to boarding school the next morning. Juliet smiled as she put the finishing touches on the traditional last meal before the return to school. Six years before, when Miranda had gone away to school for the first time, she had started the tradition, trying to make the separation less painful than it could have been. Wistfully, she stopped at Carson's place. His plate was empty, but it would be so for the last time. In September, he would be leaving for school with Dylan, registered for the fall term. Touching her stomach, she was grateful for the new baby, a new beginning for herself and Donald. Tonight, she and Donald would tell the children that they would be having a new brother or sister in about seven months. She was in her sixth week, only six more until she was past the danger point. It was almost ridiculous, how careful about everything Donald was being, diet, exercise, enough rest during the day, enough sleep at night, and bringing her supper in bed if she showed the slightest fatigue during the day. He had closed her studio and forbidden her to paint until the doctor gave his permission for her to stand at her easel for more than ten minutes at a time.

There was very little she remembered about her last miscarriage. She had gone to bed early, and had slept as if she had been drugged. The next thing she knew, Donald was screaming and shaking her, and there was blood everywhere. She had opened her eyes for a second and then had fainted, not waking up until three days later, to find herself in a hospital room, hooked up to blood transfusions around the clock. For the next four days, she had gone in and out of wakefulness, too weak even to raise her hand. From far away, she had heard the doctor telling Donald that there must be no more children, that she could never have another child. Hot tears had begun to run down her face as she began to scream, over and over again, that she would never give up her child. With strength born of panic, she had ripped out the transfuser and tried to get out of bed. Too weak to run away, she had collapsed on the floor, hitting her head on the side of the bed. For another day, she lay unconscious, deeply sedated while the transfusions were finished.

The next six weeks were spent at the villa in Nice. To this day, she could only remember snatches, tearing her hair out, the doctor coming, Donald weeping and talking to her, and then coming home to London, and finally coming out of her depression, struggling on the long road back. Her father had said that she had had the breakdown she should have had after Tony had raped her, and let it go at that.

With a start, she heard the sound of running feet, as her children piled into the room, their voices ranging between laughter and sibling teasing.

"All of you, go and bathe and change. Daddy will be home in an hour, and we're going to sit down right away for supper."

"Mummy, do we have to back to school tomorrow? Can't we stay home longer?" Miranda put her arms around her mother, leaning her cheek against her shoulder.

Juliet laughed.

"No, you may not. Your A levels are approaching, and I'm sure you want that place at Oxford. And besides, the faster you go back to school, the faster the summer holidays will arrive."

"Are we going abroad somewhere?" Dylan looked over the table, his eyes lighting up at the sight of the small box on his plate.

"No, not this year. And don't pester me now, I can't discuss it. Daddy will be happy to answer all your questions. Now please, all of you, off and get ready, or Marjorie will have a few words to say about her overcooked food."

Carson stayed behind as the others climbed the stairs to their rooms. In the month since he had been released from the hospital, he had painfully, and with what his parents viewed as incredible slowness, begun to regain the ground he had lost. His hair was growing back, and he had put on some of the weight his illness had stripped away, but he still suffered from fear and insecurity, emotions that time alone could heal. When his brother and sister returned to school in the morning, he would also return to his studies. Over his loud protestations that his school friends would think that he was a sissy, Juliet had hired a private tutor to help him catch up on all the work he had missed.

"Mummy, please, can I go back to school tomorrow? I don't want to stay home with Mr. Jemson, please." Wheedling, he hugged her and looked up into her face.

"Carson, you have been in and out of school for over a year. You must do some serious work before you go back, or else you will have to repeat the year. I know how badly you want to see your friends, but if you have to repeat, they will be a form ahead of you. And I know how much you want to go to school with Dylan in the fall. If you don't measure up, they won't take you. And it's his last year before he sits for the exams for Eton. So, you decide, friends now, or school in the fall."

"Not fair. School in the fall. Promise me I can at least play football with them after school."

"Once in a while, yes, you can. Now, upstairs and bathe. I'm sure that Dylan is out of the bathroom by now."

"Probably not. He likes to stand in front of the mirror and put nasty goo on his hair, and then comb it in these awful hairstyles."

"Carson, he's almost thirteen. When you are that age, you will do the same thing. Now, off with you." She kissed the top of his head, and smiled as she watched him race up the stairs. There had been times in the past year, when the longing for some sign of normal health in her son had been overwhelming. Listening to the thumping of his feet on the stairs was reward enough for all the pain she had endured. Walking through the dining room, she turned into the hallway, and opened up the closet. Hidden in the back were the two gifts she had bought for Dylan and

Miranda. The attache case, with locking diary and new fountain pen inside was a perfect gift for Miranda, just the incentive she needed, and Dylan's biggest wish, a portable CD player, lay in its box on top of the case. Quietly, she closed the door and turned to go upstairs to change.

The two little boxes sat on the table all through dinner. Both children had learned that wheedling and begging for their presents got them nowhere, and so they were forced to wait all through dinner, allowing the anticipation to build. At last, dessert was put on the table, and Juliet served the apple pudding, what she would say, with a knowing smile, was the all-time favorite of all of her four children.

"Mummy, may we open our boxes now?" Dylan eyed the gift as it sat on the table in front of his plate.

"Yes, you may. In one minute. Daddy and I have something to tell all of you, and I think that the right time is now."

"Mummy and I are going to have another baby." Donald looked at the faces of his children as he made the announcement.

Carson and Dylan were overjoyed, but distress flickered across Miranda's face momentarily as she, too, expressed her joy. That brief second did not go unnoticed.

"Darling, so far everything is fine, and my two doctors tell me that it is very likely that I will have a healthy baby this time. I don't want any of you worrying about me, and just think, by Christmas, we'll have another wonderful baby to love." Juliet smiled and put her hand over that of her daughter. Miranda nodded, and kissed her on the cheek.

"In the hall closet are two boxes. The small one is for Dylan, and the big square one is for you. But first, open the small boxes."

Each child held up the contents, puzzled frowns on their faces. Miranda held up a small key, and Dylan a package of batteries.

"Now, go to the hall closet. Dylan's gift is the one on top, Miranda, so don't fight over the boxes." Juliet laughed as the two pushed back their chairs and elbowing each other, went to hunt for the boxes.

"You are too good to them, but they do appreciate and love you for it." Donald stood behind her chair and kissed her cheek. She put her hand over his and sighed. It was almost too perfect. Into this moment of perfect happiness, a dark cloud would surely come and spoil it all.

CHAPTER TWELVE

The bags had all been packed and stowed away in the back of the Bentley. The last hugs and kisses had been given, and Juliet and Carson stood on the steps, watching as the car disappeared around the corner.

"I can't wait until they come back. Mummy, it's only two months, right?"

"Right. And now, young man, you have to get ready for Mr. Jemson." Sighing, he made a face and nodded.

"I know, it's no use to argue about that. Are you painting today?"

"No, I won't be painting for a while. I think I'll just stay in the parlor and read a book. Later on, after lunch, if I feel up to it, we'll go to the park."

Mother and son turned away and walked up the steps to the front door. The detective hiding in the garden next door continued to snap pictures until the door closed behind them. Val Lenox, on his duty shift as bodyguard, watching from a window on the second floor, spoke briefly into a mobile telephone. Two seconds later, two men climbed over the wrought iron fence, collared the photographer and smashed the camera.

"Tell your employer, Mr. Graniston, that the Macallisters do not like being spied upon. The next time we catch you it won't be only the camera that gets smashed." Without so much as a backward glance, the man climbed the fence and ran down the street. The two men collected the remnants of the camera and the film and put them into a plastic bag. In an instant they had disappeared around the corner, leaving the street as empty as it had been only five minutes earlier.

*   *   *   *   *

Tony Graniston slammed down the telephone and pushed it across his desk, completely infuriated that no matter what he did, it never seemed to work out the way he had planned it. He leaned his chin on his hands, thinking about the irony of his situation. During the nine years since he had left England, he had never given a thought to the consequences of what he had done. Until the moment when he had seen her again, his memories of her had been banished, at least during the daylight hours. They were locked away, safely and securely, along with all the other things he did not wish to remember. But at night, if he was not watchful, the memory of what an incredible sexual partner she had been would surface, along with the relief that he no longer had to consciously deal with his obsession.

His relationship with her had begun with what could, in the best of circumstances, be described as selfish intentions. Beyond wanting to possess her body, and her fortune, he had not spent much time considering the realities of married life. He had known beforehand that her parents were wealthy, and that as their only daughter, she stood to inherit it all. It had been obvious that Rose and Bertram Sadler loved and adored their only child and would deny her nothing.

With gritted teeth and a wary, tentative handshake, Bertram had accepted his new son-in-law, setting down the rules of play that would govern their relationship during what was referred to as the trial period of the marriage. The first shock that Tony had received was that he and his wife would continue to live in her apartment on the upper floor of a brownstone owned by her parents. Gone were his fantasies of living in the style which he had taken for granted would be his. The second, and in the end, fatal shock was the allowance that Bertram announced that he would settle on the newlyweds. Seven hundred pounds a month would be put into their checking account, to cover all expenses, included the token rent that Juliet insisted on paying for their apartment. Tony had put on his blandest expression at the news, inwardly furious at being deprived of what he considered to be his entitlement. He had discovered Anabelle's and other exclusive after hours clubs in London and up to the time of his marriage had been able to enjoy them only on a very limited basis. His own parents kept him on a very strict allowance, one that did not leave much at the end of the month for recreational spending. Rapidly calculating that the excess of the two combined monthly checks could net him perhaps two evenings a month for gambling and drinking, he could barely hide his disappointment.

That moment had been the last genuinely happy one for Juliet. While she had been a glowing and happy bride, after the interview with her parents the tone of her life with Tony changed dramatically. He began to revert to the habits of his bachelor life, occasionally at the beginning, and then with increasing regularity. At first, he would be late for dinner once a week, charmingly insisting that he had been in the library studying. Proffering a bunch of flowers as an apology, he would then take his wife to bed and make passionate love to her, until her questions were forgotten. As time slipped by, he began to disappear one or two nights a week, sometimes not returning until after midnight. Initially, Juliet had waited up for him, frantic with worry. As the situation deteriorated at a faster pace, she was surprised to find that her worry had been replaced with dismay and fury. In spite of her best efforts to avoid thinking the worst, she smelled alcohol on his breath on more than one occasion and began to suspect that he was seeing other women.

As the end of his year in England approached, he gave up any pretense of trying to maintain a relationship with his wife. Juliet, bitter and disappointed, began to quarrel with him as soon as he came through the door. As he had never told her that he was leaving for the United States at the end of the academic term, Tony decided to teach his wife a lesson she would never forget. Ten days before his departure, Tony picked up his airline ticket and began to put his ideas into action. The next nine days were spent mending the damage that had been done over the previous months. He arrived home promptly at five every day, with flowers or candy, praised her cooking and made love to her every night. Juliet, at eighteen, still naive and innocent, did not ask any questions, but breathed a sigh of relief, believing that her marital problems were over.

Each morning at eight, Juliet would pick up her artist's case and leave the apartment to attend classes at the Slade. The morning of Tony's departure, trusting and unsuspecting, she had kissed him good-bye, reminding him that she would probably be home before three. He stood at the window, watching her cross the street. She turned around and waved as she quickened her step and disappeared around the corner. Feeling delighted with himself, he smiled as he took out his suitcases and began to pack. By ten o'clock, he had already been to the bank and cleaned out their checking account. An hour later, he had finished packing and was locking his suitcases. All that remained was to call for a taxi to take him to the airport, and as long as she stayed away until he was gone, his revenge would be complete. It was at that point that he heard her key in the lock. Any control that might have kept him from crossing over the line disappeared during the quarrel over his announcement that he was ending their marriage. Before he knew it, and could stop himself, he was gripped by an uncontrollable urge for power and violence. It wasn't until he had boarded the flight for New York that he was flooded by a momentary sense of shame, that he could have so horribly abused someone as innocent and beautiful as his wife. That brief feeling of remorse was the only moment in nine years he had thought of her with compassion.

The speed with which the divorce papers arrived surprised him, and after two weeks of waiting for a financial offer to be made for his signature, he had returned a copy of the papers, unsigned, counting on the vigilance of his father-in-law to offer a settlement to his advantage. When nothing was forthcoming, he shrugged his shoulders and soon forgot everything that had happened.

It was not without panic and shock that he received the letter from David Graham, Juliet's solicitor, forwarded by Oxford to his Harvard address. At first hoping that she had finally written to beg him to sign the papers, he was stunned at the news that she was pregnant. His mind flashed back to that terrible day, when he had raped her four or five times, but it stubbornly refused to acknowledge the not terribly remote possibility that he had created a child.

Convincing himself that the child could not possibly be his, he consulted one of his professors as to what to do. That worthy man, after listening to Tony's concoction of the story, urged him to file a termination of parental rights immediately. Smiling to himself at the thought that he had outsmarted his unfaithful wife, he filed it the next day. The existence of the child had never again crossed his mind again until the morning nine years later, when he had discovered that the child was indeed his, and a boy. From that moment on, he had been obsessed by a world of new possibilities. The fantasy of trips to the zoo, Saturday afternoon movies, football Sundays, all the things that he had dreamed of doing with a son for years, seemed now to be just within his reach.

From behind the locked door of the study, he could hear his twin daughters quarreling. Fighting over a beloved toy, their voices grew louder, their tone more threatening. Over their argument, he could hear his wife shouting, followed closely by the screams of the baby. Thirty seconds later, he heard two loud slaps, followed by noisy, desperate crying. He could hear Laurel screaming at them to shut up, followed again by two more slaps, and then suddenly, silence. Putting his head down on the desk, he tried to block out what had just taken place. Unbidden came the thought that had Juliet been the mother of his daughters, the fighting, screaming and the slaps would never have happened.

*   *   *   *   *

"Madame, your dinner and mine! Carson is dining with my father, and has been persuaded to go out for ice cream afterwards." With a flourish, Donald pushed the service cart across the room and maneuvered it next to the bed.

"Thank you. I'm so tired I can't keep my eyes open. Perhaps dinner will give me some energy." Juliet yawned and stretched, pushing her hair away from her face.

"Only five more weeks, and you won't feel so tired. Now eat up, and then we'll talk."

"What about?"

"Eat your dinner first." He lifted each tray carefully, placing hers across her legs, and his on the other side of the bed. She looked down at the meal, so carefully prepared by Marjorie, served on her favorite flowered china, complete with gleaming silver, lacy napkin, and a tiny vase filled with violets. She couldn't help thinking that the food looked so artistic, even if the smell made her feel ill.

"Juliet, are you feeling all right?"

"A bit nauseous all of a sudden. Could you take the food away for a while, until I feel like eating?"

"Now, look. Caroline tells me you haven't eaten all day, and she said she heard you being sick several times. You must eat something, or you'll get weak, and the baby will starve." He leaned over and stroked her hair.

"I feel sick every time I think of those men Tony hired to watch us. This morning, was too ridiculous. That man, hiding in Mrs. Nesbitt's garden, snapping photographs of Carson, your two men taking the camera away and destroying it, it's all too much for me. After that, I could barely make it to the bathroom, and that set the tone for the day. Every time I thought about eating, I had to be sick."

"Darling, you were the one who told me that Tony wasn't going to rule your life, ever again, I think were the words you used. Don't let him do this. He wants you to be upset, upset enough so that you will let him see Carson." He pushed the tray closer.

"I know. You don't have to remind me, but I feel so ill and useless. Guaranteed, if I get up now, I'll have to be sick again." She lay back against the pillows and closed her eyes.

"How about some crackers and sweet tea?" Smiling, Juliet opened one eye.

"No, thank you. I'll try and eat. Just talk to me, take my mind off being sick." Her hand stretched and slid the tray towards her.

"Did the high risk doctor, Charleton, tell you when you could travel a bit?" He swallowed the last bite of veal, and sipped his wine.

"Not until I give birth. He is worse than my mother. He said I can go down to the country in the summer, but trips abroad are forbidden. And, I fear, that he will make me stay in bed for the last two months."

"Did he say so?"

"Indirectly. He examined me at the last session, and frowned. Then he started to talk about getting more rest, staying off my feet as much as possible, no heavy lifting, and no stress."

"I see. At least it isn't forever, and there are compensations, staying in bed more often."

"Awful man! That is how I got this way in the first place." Putting the tray aside, she leaned over and kissed him lightly, her tongue tasting the wine on his breath.

"Mmm, good. Closest I'll get to wine until December." She giggled, and leaned back on the pillows.

"Juliet, I think that it's time for us to be practical. I think that we have to make some changes in our living arrangements until all this is over."

"Such as."

"We have a number of choices. We can move out and take an apartment, in an attended building. We can move in with my father, or your parents. Or…"

"Or, what?"

"My father thinks Carson should be smuggled out of London, to the place in Scotland. He can be tutored

200

there before he goes to Templeton in the fall, and no one will ever know where he is."

"That's a bit stiff. I can't leave London for the next seven months or so, and you have a business to run. Who will stay with him? He can't very well stay with your father's housekeeper."

"I was thinking perhaps of my cousin, Sophie."

"Absolutely not. She's a complete feather brain and besides, I don't want him to go so far away. Donald, if something goes wrong, and Tony finds him, he could take him, and I might never see him again."

"And if Tony wins custody, what then?" Donald put the trays back onto the service cart.

"Then you can take him and hide him away. I refuse to allow Tony to ruin Carson's life as well as mine." She crossed her arms over her chest, thrusting out her chin, full of determination. He began to laugh, as he always did when she looked that way. Stroking her hair with one hand, he kissed her gently. Sitting back down on her side of the bed, he gently picked up a section of her hair, and inhaled the scent of lavender, warm, embedded in the silky strands.

"You're leading me astray again. What shall I do?"

"What you've been thinking about for the past hour or so." She reached up and began to unbutton his shirt. Placing her hand on his chest, she could feel his heart beating, steady, reassuring.

"You're not going to be sick again, are you?"

"Only if you don't make love to me, for a few hours at least."

*   *   *   *   *

Donald looked across at the antique clock on his dresser. The hands read six o'clock, almost time to get up. Beside him, his wife slumbered peacefully, a gentle smile on her face. Carefully, he maneuvered so that he could hold her close, his security wrapped up in her presence. Gently, he whispered in her ear.

"What time is it?"

"A bit after six."

"Ungodly hour for a pregnant woman." She plumped up her pillow and tried to sleep.

"Juliet, I need to talk to you. We didn't finish last night, and I think the time has come for us to make some sort of decision." He propped his head up on one hand.

"Do you think that Tony is about to make a move?" Reluctantly, she opened her eyes.

"Yes, I do. Within six months, he will sue for visitation and custody, probably in the United States. Since you are Carson's mother, you will be the one most affected by all of this. You will have to testify and present your case. While we have excellent lawyers, there is no ironclad guarantee that he will not be awarded at least some kind of visitation. What you have to balance is the trauma of having to testify in public about what he did to you, the press all over you, the bigamy, which is sure to come out, and all of that may not prevent him from getting to see Carson in the end."

"Are you telling me that if he files, I should fold and let him have visiting privileges?" Sleep was now impossible. He had gotten her full attention.

"No, I'm not. What I'm trying to tell you is that trying to keep him away might not be worth it in the end, if you have to go through what I just told you."

"Darling, I understand all of that, and what's to prevent him trying the case in the press anyway. He could go public at any moment, just to embarrass me. And how do I know that he would be satisfied with simple visitation? We both know he wants full custody.

I'm afraid that if I give him an inch, he'll take the whole mile."

"I know, don't think I haven't thought about this. For the time being, I want us to move in with my father. Since Carson is being tutored, the problem of school is one we don't have to deal with right now. There will be plenty of help, and security there, and Tony's men won't be able to get near us. The way we live now, it's just too open and accessible. What happened this morning can't happen again if we move to his place."

"It's terrible, I feel as if we are being slowly squeezed into a corner. I don't want to give up my ability to choose. Have Carstairs contact that attorney he hired, and let's consult with him as to what to do next. And let's go and talk to someone at Scotland Yard, see what they can do to help us. We should know all the options before we decide what to do." She fluffed up her pillows and leaned against them.

"At least let's go to my father's on the week-ends. Carson can play outside without being worried that Tony is going to jump out from behind a bush."

"Or Mrs. Nesbitt's fence. Donald, all I could think of was how loud she would have screamed for the police if she had been at home. She would have come out in that coat she always wears when she brings out the trash, and she would have told them a thing or two. It made me laugh, even when I was being sick, to think of what would have happened if she hadn't been on her church trip to Brighton." A small smile crossed her lips.

"At least think about what will happen. It will get very ugly and unpleasant. I'm worried about you, what it could do to you right now."

"Let's not buy trouble. After all, nothing so terrible has happened yet, so maybe we still have a little time."

*   *   *   *   *

"Sheila, this is Tony. Is my father in the office today?"

"No, he isn't. I can relay a message when he calls in."

"Is he coming in tomorrow?"

"No, he isn't. He's on vacation." Her feelings of dislike rose to the surface, lending an edge to her voice that he could not miss.

"I see. Did he leave a forwarding number?"

"Yes, but it's only for emergencies, like the house burning down." A small smile crossed her face as she waited for his reaction.

"I want the number, Sheila. I'm his son."

"I'm very sorry, Tony, but I can't. I'll relay the message that you need to talk to him when he calls in. Thank you for calling." Gently, she replaced the receiver.

Thoughtfully, Tony hung up on his end, and sat back in his chair. His parents must be in England with Carson and Juliet, there was no other explanation. After a second's indecision, he picked up the telephone again and made a reservation on the morning flight to London. The arrangements completed, he picked up his detective's report, and read through the section on the house in Surrey, smiling at the thought of the reaction that his appearance would create.

*   *   *   *   *

204

The brightly painted red, blue and yellow wooden garden chairs had been placed in a circle, their colors set off by the intense green of the lawn. In the center sat a small round table, covered with a white tea cloth, with a stack of a dozen plates, with forks and spoons placed on the side. To the side of the table sat a small tea cart, with cups and saucers waiting for the tea to arrive, and glasses waiting as patiently for the lemonade. Childish laughter could be heard from the swimming pool, drowning out the shouts of the four players on the tennis court. Juliet, and her former sister-in-law, Jennifer reclined side by side, under a large beach umbrella.

"If heaven is like this, tell me I've died." Laughing, Jennifer swiveled in her seat, keeping a watchful eye on her two daughters, as they played in the pool with Carson and Dylan. Miranda had reluctantly agreed to partner her father in a doubles match with Jennifer's husband, Herb, and Jordan Graniston. Emily and Donald had volunteered for lifeguard duty, and sat at the pool with watchful eyes.

"It should be, but we won't find out, not for a long while. What a perfect day this has turned out to be. If you feel like a walk, we can go down and visit my roses."

"I didn't know you had roses this late in the summer. Ours never last until August. I'm lucky if they survive until the end of June." Jennifer turned her face to the sun and sighed with contentment.

"It's that dreadful English weather. It hardly ever gets this warm, so all the flowers last until September, at least." Juliet heaved herself out of the chair. Now at the end of the fourth month of her pregnancy, she had begun to show. Smiling, she stroked the shape of her child, cradling it for a moment through the fabric of her thin cotton dress. Her pregnancy had finally become almost as placid as her first, the only difference this time being that she had more doctors watching her progress. On her last visit, two weeks ago, she had had her first sonogram, and she and Donald had held hands as they watched their child move inside the womb. That night, he had presented her with a single large pearl, luminescent with its pinkish sheen.

"I'll give you one of these for each sonogram until the baby comes. Then I'll have them strung with a fabulous lock, and you can wear them to the christening."

"Darling, I have to have them every week from now on. That's eighteen of these. Really, you're too generous."

"They will look sensational around your throat, and I'm sure you'll be as beautiful as you were when Carson was christened." He had kissed her gently, and taken the pearl away for safekeeping.

"Juliet, hello, where are you?" Jennifer tugged at her dress.

"Oh, I'm sorry. I was just thinking about my first sonogram."

"Isn't it the most wonderful thing? I had one with Lindsey, and to watch them moving around, it's like magic."

"Better than that. I'm just so happy to be alive, and pregnant."

"You tried before, didn't you?" Jennifer followed her down the slight hill to the rose garden.

"Yes, twice. I lost them both. The second time I almost died. It happened in the middle of the night, and if Donald hadn't woken up early that day, I wouldn't be here now. I didn't wake up again until three days later."

"How horrible. This time must feel like vindication."

"Yes, it does. For the longest time, I felt that Tony had cursed me, that I would never be able to have another child after Carson. Now, how do you like my darlings? Over here in front of us are the Chinas, then the teas, and the Ena Harkness, and to the left are some American Beauties. In the corner are the peonies, and behind them are the miniatures I grow for the vases in the house. In the spring, we also have lilies of the valley and acres of violets. I bunch them with little lace doilies and put them everywhere, masses of them." Her eyes closed, Jennifer inhaled deeply.

"The smell of them all is wonderful, like being in a fantasy garden."

"All of them have a particular scent. Only the American Beauties don't, I keep them just for the color, such a wonderful counterpoint for the others." Picking up a basket and shears, Juliet began to clip yellow and peach roses, and white and pink peonies.

"Juliet, why does everyone call Carson, Car Three?"

"That's only when Donald's father is here. He is Carson the First, and since it skips a generation, Carson is the third in the line. We nicknamed him Car Three as a baby, and it stuck." Reaching across, Jennifer took the basket, now piled high with roses and peonies.

"This upcoming custody battle must be very hard on all of you. I'm sorry that my brother is such an idiot."

"I try not to think about it."

"I've tried talking to him, and so have Mom and Dad. He just seems to have a blind spot where you and Carson are concerned. I'm worried about him. It's not that I sympathize with him, but he seems to be so invested in this whole thing. He has this fantasy of the perfect father and son relationship. He told me about how much he is looking forward to football games, and Little League. It's creepy, the way he has it worked out, and the way he talks about it. It gives me the shivers." She shuddered for a second, cold even in the hot sun.

"Jennifer, your brother always wants to get his own way. And when he can't, it gets ugly. This time, there isn't going to be any giving way. You can tell him the next time you speak that I will do what I have to in order to protect my child."

"I understand." Juliet looked at her, and decided to change the subject.

"I don't know about you, but I'm starving and I'm sure the children have descended on all that lovely food. Let's go back and have some tea, and then we can decide what to do about dinner. We've eaten with them every night since you arrived, and I think that after a week of loud meals, we could all do with an evening out."

"That sounds terrific. What kind of restaurants are there near here?"

"None. I think that tonight, the children will be banished, and we'll have an adult dinner on the patio, with soft music, and dancing, slowly, of course. And we'll decorate, with flowers and trees in pots, lace tablecloths and candles."

"And floating bowls, with peonies in them, scattered around the table. The perfume will be just right."

"Exactly." Juliet turned and began to walk slowly up the hill. She sighed as she reached the top. Only two more weeks until the baby moved. She could hardly wait.

*   *   *   *   *

"Carrying our child suits you." Donald held her against him as she stood in front of the mirror.

"I'll bet you say that to all the girls." She slipped away and picked up her shawl. Raising her arms, she began to drape it over her shoulders.

"They're all very envious of you. Be careful, or I'll be led astray again, and you'll miss your own dinner."

"Much as I might like to, I can't. What would they say, if the host and hostess failed to appear?" Her mouth fought against curling up in a seductive smile.

"That they had the infinite good sense to go to bed early and stay there."

Her comeback was interrupted by the telephone. He answered, his voice and manner becoming tighter with every word.

"Yes, I see. Follow him from the airport and don't lose him, whatever happens. Report to me after he lands." Grim-faced, he hung up the receiver and turned to face Juliet.

"Tony just boarded a flight to London. I think he's on his way here. What would you like to do?"

"Give him a surprise. How long would it take all of us to pack and leave, go to an hotel?"

"A few hours at least. Where would you suggest?"

"Somewhere fairly inaccessible. Cornwall, or perhaps the Channel Islands?"

"Jersey is beautiful this time of year. I'd almost forgotten about the cottage, we haven't been there in so long. I'll phone and have it opened up, and order the plane for eight o'clock. Do you thing we can all be ready by then?"

"I don't see why not. Marjorie and Caroline will come along, so just tell everyone to throw things into the bags. We'll sort it all out when we get there. And ask Marjorie if she can make up two baskets. We'll eat on the plane." She turned around and faced him, a smile of satisfaction on her face.

"How long shall we stay, Donald?"

"I think three or four days. And then we should go home, and pack up the children to go back to school."

Donald watched her face as he spoke. There was a shadow that flitted across her eyes, just for a moment. Sighing, he reached out and held her close. He could feel her heart beating, quickly, like that of a frightened bird.

"I think the time has arrived for us to make a decision about our living arrangements once all three of them are away. That we move to a flat, or into my father's house until the baby comes. With Carson away at school, there will be no reason to endure Tony's detectives any longer."

"Your father's, then."

"Done. Why don't you tell the others while I make the calls to the hotel and the airport?" He waited until he heard the door close, and then counted to ten before he picked up the receiver. The first call was to the chief constable of the village, alerting him to the possibility of someone asking questions, and trying to gain entrance to the house. The call to the hotel took a bit longer. By the time the plane landed on the island, his private home on the grounds would be opened, aired and prepared, and detectives hired to watch the property around the clock.

CHAPTER THIRTEEN

Tony heaved his bag off the carousel, and lined up to go through passport control. Confident that the element of surprise was on his side, he waited patiently as the line inched forward. The immigration officer was polite, but thorough.

"The purpose of your visit, Mr. Graniston?"

"Vacation, with a little business mixed in."

"And your hotel while you're in London?"

"I'll be at Claridge's until tomorrow morning and after that I'll be traveling." He gave the inspector his most charming smile.

"Enjoy your stay, sir, and welcome to England." The officer watched as Tony walked quickly towards the exit. Nodding to his supervisor, he then continued with the next person in line. After a quick conference, the supervisor walked quickly to his office, locked the door, and picked up the telephone.

"Mr. Graham, this is Thomas Milton at Heathrow. Mr. Graniston has just passed through immigration. He'll be at Claridge's tonight, and plans to travel outside London in the morning. You're very welcome, and good luck."

*   *   *   *   *

Juliet had just zipped up the last of the suitcases when she heard the shrill of the telephone. Out of sight, she could hear Donald answer the phone, and also hear the changes in the tone of his voice. Through the open window, she could hear the crunch of gravel as the cars pulled up to the front door, ready to drive them to the airport. Walking over to the window, she looked down. Miranda and Dylan were already outside, along with Jordan and Emily, helping to load all the luggage into the cars. A soft knock at the door caught her attention, as Herb Markham stuck his head through the doorway.

"Jordan and I thought we'd take the bags now. Save a little time later on. Are they ready?"

"Yes, they're stacked at the end of the bed. Herb, I'm so sorry that we have to drag everyone away on such short notice, especially with only four days left to the holiday." Distractedly, she picked up her shawl and purse from the edge of the vanity table, and then dropped them again, this time on the side of the bed.

"Don't apologize. You and I have something in common, we both detest and fear Tony. Frankly, I like the idea of leaving now. When he gets here tomorrow, the only person to talk to will be the detective that Donald is leaving behind. Besides, I understand that Jersey is a beautiful island, and the kids will be able to enjoy the beach and the water." His smile was confident as he carried the bags out of the room.

"I'm afraid that this will only postpone the inevitable for a short while. My worst nightmare could come true, Tony could get custody of Carson." Her voice shook as she turned to face him.

"Then have him arrested, now, before he has a chance to file for custody. Let the police take over so that you can get on with your life." Herb leaned over to pick up the last bag.

"Ideally, that is what I should do, but I have three children, sensitive, vulnerable, wonderful children. The minute that I have him arrested, the whole horrible story will come out, and they will be the ones who will suffer. I'd like to protect them as long as possible." The sadness in her voice was unmistakable.

"Juliet, don't sell them short. Your kids are strong and smart, and they love you. If arresting Tony is what you have to do, they will go along with it. I'm sure that you and Donald can make some sort of arrangements with their schools to insure that no word of this reaches the other students."

"And the parents of the other students? I'm a famous person, Herb, and there are some people who like nothing better than to see someone like me brought low and humiliated. It gives them some sort of perverted satisfaction, and I can't bear the thought that even one parent of a classmate of my children should spread the horrible news that I was first raped and abused by my husband, and then committed bigamy because he refused to sign the divorce papers. It doesn't bear thinking about." Dejected, she sat down on the bed.

"Eventually, you will have to act, you know that. If you want my advice, which I'm sure you don't, do it now, while the children are young, and the social stigma that will go with the court case won't matter as much. In four years, Miranda will be eighteen, old enough to date, and go to college. If you wait too long, she could be devastated by the fallout." Herb sat down in a chair next to the bed.

"Don't think that I'm not haunted by that. She'll be presented at court as part of her debutante year. My father-in-law is an earl, he will insist on having his granddaughter receive her social due. Sometimes I wonder what will happen, if a presentable young man will even want to escort her to parties and balls. If I weren't pregnant, I wouldn't hesitate for a second. It isn't fair that I should have to choose."

"I agree, but in the end you may have to do just that. Jenn and I will stand by you all the way, whatever happens. The girls adore Carson, they can't get over how terrific he is, and they like your other children as well. You and Donald are part of our family now, and we Markhams always stick together." Herb smiled at her as he moved into the hallway.

Turning away from the door, she picked up her purse and shawl from the bed. Turning slowly, she mentally ran through her checklist to make sure that she had not forgotten an important item. As she stood in the middle of the room, eyes closed, and lips moving, Donald opened the door to the study, marveling, as he frequently did, at the difference between the two rooms. When he had bought the house shortly after his divorce from Delia, he had not bothered to decorate it before he married Juliet. She had laughed the first time she had seen the rooms, dark and dingy, with wallpaper dating from the 1920's.

She had been enormous, just a few weeks before Carson had been born, but with amazing energy had taken her sketch pad and drawn a plan for revitalizing their living space. Within a year of Carson's birth, the entire house had been redecorated and updated. The only thing she had insisted upon was that he not visit the house until it was finished. Under protest, he had agreed, secretly amused at his wife's jealous possession of her first decorating project. He had not been disappointed.

She had had the painters scrape all the paint off the walls, unmasking exquisite burled cypress paneling in the bedroom, and cherry paneling in the study. Working off the natural wood, she had recreated an old fashioned study in the room adjacent to the bedroom. Deep green velvet curtains worked off of an oriental carpet of green with a touch of red and white. In a junk shop in the Portobello road, she had unearthed a Victorian desk, and had paired it with a set of William Morris chairs, covered in deep green leather. Against the far wall, she had put a sofa, covered in an African fabric, its pattern repeating the colors of the rug and curtains. The only concessions to modern life that she had allowed were the computer and fax machine that seemed to follow her husband everywhere.

But it was in the bedroom that her artistic ability had taken flight. She had allowed the paneling to become the central focus of the room, choosing to stay with pure white accessories whenever possible. In the same shop where she had unearthed the desk, she had also found a set of bedroom pieces, a vanity, dresser and a gentleman's dresser, all of which she had stained a shade or two lighter than the paneling. The curtains, bedding, and other accessories had all been stark white, including a lacquered table which she placed under a window, and adorned with silver framed pictures of her beloved children. Scattered around the room were clusters of sterling silver objects, jewel cases and snuff boxes, things her mother and grandmother had collected over the last twenty years. She had also gutted the bathroom, replacing the fixtures with modern ones, and covering the walls with plain white paint over which she had sketched tiny flowers and plants.

Carson was seven months old when Juliet finally allowed her husband to see the rooms she had decorated. In addition to their rooms, she had also redone Miranda's and Dylan's and the three other bedrooms on the second floor, and had replaced the entire heating system as well. Smiling at her husband, she had begun the tour in the basement, gradually showing him the other rooms, and by the time they had reached their bedroom, she had lost all of her clothes, a piece in each room. Shyly, she stood in front of him, dressed only in a see through teddy, her hair tumbling about her shoulders, laughing at his amazement. Captivated, he had made love to her for hours, not even noticing the rooms he had really come to see, until well into the evening. Lit by the soft glow of the lamps in each room, he had marveled at their beauty, overwhelmed by the intricacy of her artistic vision.

"Be careful, you'll get dizzy and fall down and I'll have to catch you." Juliet heard his voice whispering in her ear.

"Be grateful I'm not as enormous as I was the day I saw this place for the first time." She leaned back, her head against his shoulder.

"Who was on the telephone?"

"David Graham. Tony has just passed through Immigration. He's in London tonight, supposedly, and will, in all likelihood, show up here tomorrow. Pity he won't get much of a welcome."

"I had a long talk with Herb. He thinks that I should have him arrested now, before the children get any older. He mentioned social traumas, all the things that give me bad dreams."

"It's up to you. You will be the one who will have to give evidence, and be cross-examined by his barrister. Most of the shame and fear will be yours, and much as I would love to be able to take it all away, I can't."

"I know. I'd like to wait until the baby comes, and then do it. By that time, it will be Christmas, and with any luck, nothing will happen until Easter term. With the three week break, things will die down a bit before they go back to school, and with any luck, they won't have to suffer much. Eventually, a new scandal will come along, and all this will become wrapping for tomorrow's fish."

"And if he decides to up the stakes? He could go to the scandal sheets any time he wants. And I don't think he cares much about any dirt that falls on him, only what falls on you."

"I know that, and I'm prepared. What I won't do is sacrifice my baby to all of this. We'll have to stall for as long as we can. It's only five more months, and then we're home free." She turned around and buried her face in his chest. He could feel the moisture from her tears seeping through his shirt onto his chest. Gently, he cupped her chin, and kissed the tears away, licking her skin dry, tasting the saltiness on his tongue.

"The others are waiting. If the children are ever to get to bed, we have to go." Nodding, she walked through the door and down the stairs. He turned out the lights and followed her out of the house.

*   *   *   *   *

After a few near misses, Tony adjusted to driving on the left side of the road and made good time as he drove to Surrey. Secure in his conviction that his arrival would be a complete surprise, he whistled to himself as he approached the exit. The English countryside was in all its glory, with green fields and magnificent flower gardens, heavy with the blooms of high summer. He noticed none of it, concentrating instead on his fantasies of the welcome he would get from his son. His daydreams had become so real that he could hear the excited calls of his son, and even feel his arms around his neck, and the kisses on his cheek.

Following the directions the detectives had given him, he arrived on the high street of the village at about two o'clock in the afternoon. The town seemed to be fast asleep, the shops deserted and no one on the street. He drove slowly down the street, looking from side to side, trying to absorb the environment in which his son spent his weekends and holidays.

From his office, the chief constable, Barney Grimes, watched the blue rental car drive slowly up the street. Earlier that morning, he had received a call from Val Lenox, giving him a description of the car that Tony had rented at Hertz's London office, and the number of the license plate. The car had arrived right on schedule, within ten minutes of the time he had been told to anticipate its arrival. Sighing deeply, he got out of his chair and straightened his uniform. He ran his fingers through his graying hair and looking in the mirror, positioned his hat to the regulation angle and walked out of his office onto the sidewalk. Tony, unsure of the way, spotted the policeman standing in front of his office. Relieved, he slowed down, and stopped, rolling down the window to ask for directions.

"Excuse me, I'm looking for The Groves, it's owned by the Macallisters?" He was at his most charming, sizing up and then dismissing the policeman as hopelessly stupid.

"Are they expecting you, sir?" Barney adopted his blandest expression, focusing his eyes on the steering wheel of the car.

"Yes, yes, of course they are. We're close friends." Tony lied, counting on what he perceived as Barney's hopeless stupidity.

"This is most peculiar. They've gone, sir. Closed up the house and left." Watching closely, Barney waited for a reaction.

"When did they leave?" Forcing himself not to react physically, Tony drummed his fingers on the steering wheel.

"Earlier in the week." A small bending of the truth, a lie matching a lie. Barney continued to keep his face without emotion, hiding his inward satisfaction.

"Do you know where they went?" The fingers moved faster and faster.

"No, I'm sorry, sir, they didn't give me their travel plans." Barney rocked back on his heels, never letting Tony out of his sight.

"I see. Do you know when they'll be back?" Tony adjusted his expression to an I don't understand what could have happened look.

"Hard to tell. Can't imagine why they left, knowing you were coming, sir. Not like them at all." Barney dismissed him, touching the brim of his hat. Tired of playing cat and mouse, Barney turned away and walked back to his office.

Tony watched him walk away, furious at once again having been outwitted by his ex-wife and her husband. Blinded by his fury, he made a decision. He would return home, and file for full custody. He would not tolerate any further denials of his rights. The next time he tried to see his son would be different. He would be armed with court papers that would have to be obeyed.

Out of the corner of his eye, Barney waited to see what Tony would do. He stood in front of his office, seemingly without a care in the world. From under the brim of his hat, his eyes narrowed as he watched the driver of the blue rental car. Tony, looking out of the rearview mirror, had no idea he was being watched so closely. He saw only the policeman, standing on the sidewalk, his face in shadow, hidden by the brim of his hat. To Tony's mind, he was an unbelievably dense individual who was probably sleeping standing up, his inattention hidden from anyone who cared to look. Wavering as to what to do next, he decided to follow a hunch. Picking up his mobile telephone, he placed a call to the local airport. Smiling with satisfaction at the answer, he made a careful U-turn and headed away from the high street, back towards the highway. Once out of town, he changed direction and headed for the airport. A flight to Jersey was leaving in an hour and a half, and he intended to be on it.

As he watched the blue car leave the village, all Barney's instincts were aroused. Leaving nothing to chance, he went back to his office and made a few telephone calls.

"Lord Donald, Barney Grimes. Yes, he was here. Wasn't too pleased to find all of you gone. The car sat here for about fifteen minutes after I gave him the news, and then he left the village, on the road to the highway. On a hunch, I called the airport. He was on the phone, inquiring about the Macallister jet, where it had gone, and when. I'm sorry, I tried to make it seem as if you left days ago, but he just didn't accept it. He's probably on his way to the island now, and it won't take long before he finds out where you are. It might be best to have it out with him now, Lord Donald. You have plenty of protection, and the island has so many hotels, it will be easy to hide your wife and son away for a short period of time. You're welcome, it was no trouble at all. My best to your family. Good-bye."

Barney replaced the receiver and sat back in his chair. The ingrained suspiciousness of the village policeman had been thoroughly awakened by Tony's appearance, and he only hoped that the Macallisters were prepared for what was headed in their direction.

*　　*　　*　　*　　*

Exercising extreme self-control, Donald hung up the telephone. As he always did when he was challenged by a problem, he took off his glasses and began to play with the frames. Staring into space as he worked the problem through, he was oblivious to everything around him.

The "cottage", as his wife was fond of teasing him, was in reality a stately country home acquired by Longueville Manor as part of a large parcel of land. The hotel itself had long been a favorite holiday spot while his mother had been alive, and when Dylan was born, Donald had approached the owners to negotiate the purchase of the slightly dilapidated manor. The renovation and expansion of the house had been halfway to completion when he had filed for divorce, and the half-completed house had stood empty until a year after his marriage to Juliet. Carson had just celebrated his first birthday when he had asked Juliet to undertake the completion of the cottage on the beach. When she had laughingly asked if she had to furnish a dozen bedrooms instantly, he had, in all seriousness, replied, "No, fourteen." She had then smiled mysteriously and asked for three months time and an army of twenty workmen to finish the task. In mock seriousness, he had given her until July, the month that they normally spent in Surrey, to finish the work.

On the first of July, insisting on leaving all three children in London, she had taken him to the island, and shown him the finished product. She had worked miracles, repairing what she saw as design flaws, opening up rooms and making the sea, only a short walk across the green stretch of lawn in the front of the house, a part of the living environment. Insisting on taking over the three bedrooms on the ground floor for herself and Donald, Juliet had knocked down walls, added floor to ceiling windows, combined two bathrooms into one, and turned the third into a small kitchen. Wooden floors had been ripped up, replaced with glistening sea green tiles. She had placed their bed so that they could look at the sea from any window, and had again relied upon pine furniture, stained a lighter shade of sea green, and white lace accessories. She had even had a small window installed, just above the bed, could be opened which automatically, to let in the smell and the sounds of the sea.

Upstairs, each of the remaining eleven bedrooms was decorated in different combinations of colors of the sea. Drawing on her love of tropical fish, she had made all the rooms a continuum, with all the colors drawn together in a feast for the eyes.

Donald had been speechless. Lost in the wonder of the colors and materials she had used in the house, he had stood in each room, more and more amazed with each one. She had led him gently through the living quarters and the kitchen, done in sky blue tiles, with terracotta accents, back to their bedroom. Silently pressing the switch for both the lights and the small window, the room had been plunged into darkness, the only light coming from the stars shining through the windows. The scent of the salt air and the sound of the crashing waves lay in the room as if they were afloat on the water.

Helpless, Donald had stood in the middle of the room, as Juliet gently unbuttoned his shirt, and began to seduce her husband. As she slowly removed her clothes, leaving only a wisp of transparent bodice, he heard a thundering in his ears. From that moment to this, he was never able to decide if what he heard was the waves crashing against the rocks, or his overwhelming desire for his wife pounding through his body. Before he knew what was happening, she was standing at the edge of the bed, mystical, beckoning, scented with violets and lilies of the valley. Surrounded by the pounding of the sea, and the headiness of her perfume, they made love for most of the night, only falling asleep as the rays of the sun had begun to streak the sky. Four weeks later, Juliet announced that she was pregnant, only to lose the child two months later. Unable to bear the house, he had had it closed and shuttered. Now, for the first time in six years, it was open and filled with the sea again.

"Daddy, please come and swim with us. Daddy, hello." Miranda stood in front of her father, watching him play with his glasses, his concentration on other things all too obvious. At last, impatient, she reached out and shook his shoulder.

"What is it?" Shaking himself, Donald looked up at her.

"Come and swim with us. Mummy shouldn't and Herb doesn't want to do it alone. Too many of us, he said."

"I have a few things I must do now, and then we'll swim. See if you can find Mummy and Jordan and tell them I need to talk to them."

"Tony's coming here, isn't he? I knew he would find us eventually. Daddy, why don't you have him arrested?" She tapped her foot impatiently. A smile of amusement at his daughter's resemblance to Juliet, he nodded.

"We will, eventually. That's why I have to talk to Mummy and Jordan. Now be a good girl and find them, and please, do not tell anyone what you know. The last thing I need now is for Carson to go into a panic."

"Right. I'll have Dylan take him fishing on the shore. Maybe they'll catch something completely disgusting, like the last time they put that slimy thing down my bathing suit."

"Very funny that was, I might add. A film star couldn't have screamed any better than you did. Be grateful that there are now two other younger women, your new cousins, who will most likely be the recipients of their generosity." Grinning, he got up and went back into the house. Miranda, after watching him disappear into the kitchen, turned and walked around to the side of the house, where Juliet, and the others sat on the stone patio, under beach umbrellas. Quietly, she whispered to her mother and Jordan, and as they got up, she turned and went in search of her brothers.

The house was dark and cool, filled with the salty breeze off the Channel. Juliet walked across the sky blue tiled floor towards the kitchen, where she could hear noises.

"Here we are, ready and waiting. Miranda said you absolutely had to see us and not a moment to lose." Her teasing tone and laughter vanished as Donald turned around and she looked into his face. Somber, almost depressed, his gray eyes looked back at her, their sparkle gone.

"The hound from hell has found us. He'll be here within the hour. Tell me now what you think I should do." Juliet felt her stomach hit the floor. Eyes wide, she stared at her husband, unable to take it all in.

"He called the airport and managed to get the flight plan. Admit it, once he calls around to all the hotels, he'll be here before you know it. You must tell me now what you want me to do." She could feel the room beginning to tilt to the right.

"I haven't a clue. All we can do is either have him arrested, or let him come here and deal with him then." Trembling, her voice shook. Try as she might, she could not manage to get over her memories or her fear.

"Donald, let me try to deal with him. After all, he's my son, my problem." Jordan sighed and rubbed his forehead.

"I may just take you up on that, Jordan. But first, I have to get Carson and Juliet to safety, before he gets here." He leaned across the wall, picked up the telephone and walked into the dining room. After a quick murmured conversation, and he returned to the kitchen.

"One of the company helicopters will be here in an hour or so and will fly the two of you to Guernsey for the rest of the day. Jordan and I will remain behind to deal with Tony." Donald ran his hand through his hair and looked at his wife. She had gone very pale, her skin tone almost greenish.

"Juliet, are you feeling all right? You look as if you have to be sick." His voice was very far away, as she swayed slightly and collapsed onto the kitchen floor.

"Damn. I knew this would happen." He knelt beside her, stroking her face, talking to her.

"Jennifer was a nurse before she got married. I'll go get her, and then go and find Carson." Jordan walked quickly across the kitchen, through the sliding glass door and disappeared around the side of the house.

A few minutes later, she opened her eyes, not realizing that she was still lying on the floor.

"What happened, you look as if you'd seen a ghost." His face, pale with fear, floated above her face.

"You fainted, dead away. Jennifer took a look at you and the baby, everything seems to be all right. If you can stand up, I'll put you to bed, and you will stay there until tomorrow." Gently, he knelt and helped her off the floor. When she was standing, he picked her up, as if she weighed nothing, and carried her into the bedroom. Quickly, he helped her put on a cotton shift, and tucked her into bed.

"I feel such a fool, fainting like that."

"Too much stress, not enough rest. As soon as Carson and the others are off at school, new rules. More bed rest, less worrying. Dr. Donald's orders." In spite of his terror, he managed a rueful smile as she put her hand up and stroked his cheek.

"Yes, sir. Anything you say. Now go away and let me sleep." She closed her eyes and slept, almost instantly. Holding her hand, he watched her sleep, a single tear finding its way onto his cheek.

CHAPTER FOURTEEN

Carson sat on the patio, his chair sandwiched between Donald and Jordan. The house was empty, except for the three seated together, and Jennifer, who had volunteered to keep an eye on Juliet.

"Daddy, Mummy will be well tomorrow, won't she?" The boy's voice shook slightly.

"Of course. She's just very tired and worn out. Having a baby is hard work, makes her very tired." Absently, Donald stroked his son's dark hair, so like his own.

"Carson, could you go and ask Marjorie to make some lemonade for us? I feel like some right now." Jordan smiled at his grandson, who got off his chair and ran into the house.

"Donald, Tony will be here soon. What do you want to do with Carson?" As Jordan leaned forward in his chair, Donald saw him as the image of the ever competent family solicitor.

"I'm still going back and forth over it. But more importantly, your son is determined to hound my wife for visitation until he kills her. I cannot allow this kind of stalking behavior to go on, Jordan. It has to stop, and it has to stop now."

"My advice is to send Emily to Guernsey with Carson until dinnertime. He'll love the helicopter ride, and she will take good care of him. Let Tony come here, and then we can deal with him without having to worry about him doing anything stupid." Jordan sighed and ran his hand through his hair.

"You don't think he'd try and take Carson, do you?"

"Donald, he's desperate, and quite capable of anything. How many people does the helicopter hold?"

"Eight or nine, I'm not sure."

"Why don't we send all the kids to Guernsey with Emily? Make it a dressed up outing, and let her give them dinner at a restaurant, go shopping for the afternoon."

A ghost of a smile crossed Donald's face.

"Brilliant. That way Carson won't feel that anything has gone wrong, Jennifer can stay here in case we need her and Herb can be our backup. I'll go and fetch them. Why don't you tell Emily to change clothes? The helicopter will be here soon." Turning around, he started. Carson had been standing at the screen door, listening to the entire conversation.

"Come here, Carson. Sit on my lap and we'll have a talk." Donald held out his arms to his son. Dragging his feet, the boy reluctantly climbed into his father's lap.

"I'm sorry, Daddy. I broke Mummy's rule, not ever to listen when I'm not supposed to." He hung his head, waiting for his father's answer.

"This time I think that it was all for the best, but don't do it as a habit. I don't like being spied on and neither does Mummy, and if someone did it to you, you wouldn't like it much either. How much did you hear?"

"Enough. My other Daddy is coming here, and you want me to run away in a helicopter to Guernsey. I don't think that I should. One day I'll have to see him, maybe it should be today."

"Carson, I don't look on this as exactly running away. In business, I would call it a strategic withdrawal. Sometimes it is better to postpone a meeting like this until people's feelings improve. This time, I do want you away from here when Tony arrives. He's not a reasonable man, and I don't want to take a chance of something bad happening." Donald's arms tightened around his son.

"All right. If you want me to, I'll go with all the others, and Grandma Emily. She's nice and I don't mind. Daddy, can I ask you a question."

"Of course. I'll give you an answer if I can."

"Why does he want to see me so badly? It doesn't make any sense, he asked for money to give me his marrow, but now he wants to be my Daddy. If he loved me, like a Daddy is supposed to, shouldn't he have given it to me for free?"

"He thinks that he has certain rights because he made you."

"Does he?"

"Carson, Tony was very mean to Mummy before you were born. At this moment, it looks as if he hasn't learned to behave much better. That's why I want to send you away for the day. Maybe sometime in the future, his attitude will get better, and you can meet him. Today is not the day."

"Do you think that if I told him myself, that I don't want to see him, and that I don't think that he loves me very much, he would listen?" Donald lifted Carson's chin and looked into his son's eyes.

"No, I don't think it would help. Tony is a man who doesn't listen very well."

"Are you afraid he might take me away?" Donald held his son tighter.

"That will never happen. Now, run along and change before the others come and want to get into the bathrooms."

"All right. Marjorie said that she's making iced tea instead of lemonade. Not enough lemons, she said. Before I get dressed, can we go and see Mummy, make sure she's not sick?"

"Right now. When I left her, she was sound asleep, so just tiptoe in and kiss her cheek. She needs her rest."

*   *   *   *   *

With a great deal of laughter and elbowing, the five children managed to climb on board the helicopter, followed by Emily. In only an hour, they had all managed to bathe and change, Emily and the girls into white dresses, and the boys into slacks and short sleeved shirts. The ungainly machine lifted itself off the ground, and in a minute had vanished from view.

On board, the six passengers spent the trip staring at the landscape passing by underneath and around the helicopter. Within half an hour, they were safely on the ground in St. Peter's Port, ready for an afternoon of shopping and general fun. Carson lagged behind, tugging at his sister's hand.

"Walk with me. I have to talk to you."

"What is it?" Miranda stopped and let the others go ahead.

"I'm worried about Tony coming, maybe we shouldn't have gone away."

"Don't worry about that. Jordan and Daddy are there, and Val and his men are on the grounds. Nothing will happen, especially now that you aren't there."

"What do you think? Should I have stayed there and met with Tony?"

"Absolutely not." She turned, bent down and kissed his cheek.

"Carson, we all love you a lot. No one will sit by and let Tony do anything to you, so stop worrying and enjoy yourself. Daddy gave me money to take everyone on a little shopping trip, so let's get started." The two children picked up the pace, and ran across the street to join the others.

*   *   *   *   *

Tony sat back in the taxi and looked out of the window, trying to control his mounting excitement. After only three calls, he had found what he was looking for. Twenty minutes after he had landed at the airport, the taxi pulled up to the front of the house. Under ordinary circumstances, Tony would have been impressed at the size and grandeur of his surroundings. But he was single minded and intent on his goal, of seeing and perhaps even leaving the island with his son. His only other emotion was a feeling of immense satisfaction at the surprise he was going to give his former wife.

Caroline Evans, well rehearsed by Jordan and Donald, opened the door, and without a word, stepped aside and let him enter. Stepping from the sunlight into the coolness of the living room, he was struck by what he could see as Juliet's artistic vision, the sky blue tile, the white sofas and chairs, all with sky blue and terra cotta throw pillows. A sound caught his attention, as Donald walked out of the kitchen and came towards him.

"I won't bother welcoming you to my home, because you aren't really an invited guest, just an intruder who can't take no for an answer." He took up a position behind the bar, just to the left of the kitchen.

"I want to see my son." Having dispensed with the formal niceties, Tony stood in the center of the room.

"He's not here. He's away from the island." Barely controlling his surging anger, Donald struggled not to raise his voice.

"I don't believe you." Tony listened carefully for any sound which would show him the way to his son.

"Tony, he's not here, but you're welcome to hunt for him all you want. It won't help you." Jordan leaned against the door leading to the master bedroom.

"Why does this not surprise me, Dad? It's too much to expect that you should be on my side." A small sneer spread across Tony's face.

"I made myself very clear the last time we spoke, Tony. My place now is with my grandson and his mother. It's the least I can do to make up for what you did."

"I have rights. We can do this like civilized people, or we can do it the hard way, in the courts. I don't care which way you want to do it, Macallister, but in the end, I will win." His chin thrust forward, Tony stood his ground.

"At the end of the day, Tony, you will not win. You have no rights, you signed them all away. I doubt that there is a judge anywhere who would award you so much as a supervised visit with Carson. I told you before, you had only one right left, to save his life. If I hadn't been forced to pay you to do it, we might not have been having this conversation, but that's irrelevant. My wife doesn't want to see you, or talk to you, and neither does my son." Donald's cool smile showed his confidence.

"Don't threaten me, Macallister. Do you actually think I'm scared that you will hand over that little file to the police? If you were serious about it you would have done it by now. So spare me the preaching, and produce my son. I'm not leaving until you do."

"I'm afraid that won't be possible. He isn't here, and I don't know when he will be back. Bullying me will get you exactly what you deserve, which is nothing. What I will give you, however, is a chance to leave my home voluntarily. If you refuse, the police will help you to do so."

"Call them, then, because I'm not leaving without seeing my son." Tony sat down on one of the white chairs, and crossed his arms over his chest.

"I have already called them. They should be arriving just about now." The front door had been left open, and the three men could hear the sound of tires crunching on the gravel. Thirty seconds later, a detective Inspector and several constables presented themselves at the front door.

"Lord Donald, I'm Detective Inspector Symonds. I understand you have an intruder on your property." The six foot four blond man shook hands with Donald, all the while taking in the position and build of the other two men in the room.

"That's right. He's on the white chair behind you. He's been stalking and harassing my wife and son for weeks now. We've tried to be civil about it, but he doesn't seem to be able to take no for an answer."

"Family problem, is it, sir?"

"Tony Graniston, her former husband, come back after nine years away. Very ugly story, if you ask me."

"Is it then? Well, I think that we'll just have to have a talk with this intruder of yours." The constables were scattered about the room, two standing in front of the chair, one at the front door and one near the door leading to the terrace, ready for any sort of confrontation. Tony, amazed at the conversation that had just taken place, was still sitting in the white chair. It was all about him, yet his presence in the room had been totally ignored.

"Sir, I'm going to have to ask you to come with us, down to the station house. I'd appreciate it if we could do this quietly, but if not, well, it's your choice." D.I. Symonds had on his most professional expression. For a split second, Tony sized up the situation. He was no longer in control, something potentially very dangerous. It would not look good to a judge if he was arrested at the home of his former wife and her husband.

"No need for that. I was just leaving. It's not over, Macallister, not by a long shot. Make sure that you tell Juliet to watch her back. Accidents can happen to anyone, even her." Tony got out of the chair and swaggered to the door.

"Excuse me, sir, but in this country we take threats of bodily harm very seriously. I'm afraid I will have to insist that you come down to the police station with us now, and then you can tell us all about the terrible things that the Countess Macallister has done to you, and then we'll come back here and listen to her side of the story." Tony began to squirm.

"I didn't mean what I said, I'm sorry if it came out the wrong way."

"Let him go. I'll deal with him in my own time. If you don't mind, Inspector, just take him to the airport and put him on the next plane for the mainland. My men will make sure he gets on a plane for America as soon as possible." Donald closed his hand around the glass of iced tea and drank from it, relaxed and confident.

"If you change your mind, Lord Donald, you know where to reach me." He shook hands with Donald, took Tony by the arm and ushered him out of the house. Within minutes, the cars had gone, and the house was quiet.

"Close call, Donald. You were too nice. It might have done him some good to spend a night in jail." Exhaling deeply, Jordan sat down on the sofa.

"And have the newspapers get hold of it tomorrow? Juliet wants to wait until December, after she has the baby. The schools will be on long holiday then, and the scandal may not land on the children quite as hard as it would at any other time. I'm going to check on her, and then, I think we're entitled to a real drink."

*   *   *   *   *

She was asleep, relaxed and smiling as she dreamed. He bent down and kissed her cheek, his heart pounding with fear. It was warm and soft, not cold as it had been the time she had almost died. He had just turned away when he heard her sigh and turn over. As he looked around, she opened her eyes and smiled.

"What time is it? I must have slept the afternoon away."

"Just on four o'clock. Would you like something to drink, or a snack before dinner?" He sat down on the edge of the bed.

"Herbal tea and some biscuits would be wonderful, but, first, stop looking so frightened. I fainted, that's all. No blood or anything else. Tony just got to me, his overwhelming arrogance at following us all over the place. I didn't eat much lunch, so it's partly my fault." She held his hand, stroking the palm.

"You terrified me completely. I saw all sorts of horrible things floating in front of me when you were lying on the floor. And Carson is fairly well scared as well."

"Poor darling! How about if I get up for dinner and he sees that I am walking around. That should make him feel better."

"Not necessary. Emily took the lot of them to Guernsey for the day, and out to dinner as well. The helicopter will bring them back about eight, and by that time, he can come in and say good night, and tomorrow will be another day. And I want you to stay in bed until tomorrow. No more funny business about not eating and not taking extra care of yourself. I'm going outside to have a drink with Jordan, while Marjorie makes a tray for you. We'll have dinner in here, and the others can eat in the dining room. If you like, we can spend the evening alone, just the two of us."

"Just the three of us!" She laughed as she shooed him out of the room. Sitting up, she ran her hands through her hair and then gave up. Too many snarls, and not enough energy to get up and find the hairbrush. Yawning, she lay back on the pillows and closed her eyes, falling back to sleep.

"She all right?" Jordan handed Donald a whiskey and soda, took his own and walked outside onto the patio.

"Yes, completely exhausted, but fine. It's been a hectic two weeks, not that we haven't loved having all of you for the holiday, but she insists on hiding how fatigued she is, and that makes for situations that could be dangerous."

"Like this morning."

"Exactly."

"I've been sitting here trying to compose an apology for the absolute arrogant stupidity of my son. One would think I would know my own child, but I'm beginning to discover that I don't know him at all. I never realized how important it was for him to have the validation of a son. He must have gotten it from me. I'm ashamed to admit that I feel something like that every time I look at Carson." He swirled the ice around the sides of the glass.

"I understand exactly how you feel. When I was born, my father was over the moon. I was healthy, but I was also a son, someone who could inherit the title and all the obligations that go with it."

"You never had any sisters or brothers?" Jordan sipped his drink slowly.

"I had an older sister. She was killed in a freak accident when she was a baby."

"How horrible for your parents. They must have rejoiced when you were born."

"Yes, they did. My mother in particular. She couldn't have any more children after me."

"And Miranda is named after your sister?"

"Yes, much to the dismay of my former wife, who wanted to name her Grace, after Princess Grace." Donald took a healthy sip of his whiskey.

"Miranda suits her better. And Dylan will inherit the title?"

"They will all have to deal with the title. Dylan will have to cope with the estate, and if he is so inclined, my business interests as well. All the others will be Lord or Countess, with an income to match."

"And Carson?"

"He will come into the business. He's second in line for the title, and one day will be known as Lord Carson."

"I'm glad you adopted him eight years ago. That way, if something should happen to Juliet, there will be no question about who retains custody. She should, however, make a will stating who will retain custody if something should happen to both of you before he reaches eighteen. If not, and you both die, Tony can legitimately claim custody by default."

"I'll discuss it with her when she's up to it. Here's the tray, and I'm going to bring it to her. Why don't you find Jennifer and Herb and have a swim or a round of golf, and I'll see you later." Donald picked up the tray, set daintily with a flowered teapot, cup and saucer, and a little brown vase filled with wildflowers. Marjorie had unearthed a small porcelain basket, which she had filled with Juliet's favorites, fairy cakes and chocolate biscuits.

* * * * *

"Sleepy head, wake up! Time to eat." He set the tray down, and sat on the bed. Smiling, he kissed her on the mouth, knowing full well that she had heard him the first time. Her throaty laugh bubbled up as he nuzzled her neck, traveling down her chest.

"Evil man! I'm supposed to be on my invalid's bed."

"Obviously, I was wrong about that. Now, sit up and have your tea. All your favorites today, and then I'll brush your hair for you, if you like."

"Wonderful. It's all snarled, and I was too tired to even get up and look for my hairbrush."

"Are you feeling better now?"

"Yes, restored to the picture of health. Now, if you're very good, and let me bathe after I eat, I'll let you brush my hair. Mmm, those long wonderful strokes." Her eyes danced as she looked up at him, all innocence with the crumbs from a chocolate biscuit around her mouth. His mouth twitched, as he struggled not to laugh. Gently, he reached out and wiped away the remains of the biscuit with his fingers, licking them afterwards to get rid of the mess.

"Delicious! How do you manage to get Marjorie to spoil you this way? I can't even get her to toast a muffin if you're not around to tell her to do it."

"It's all my evil plan, to get you to appreciate me, love me passionately, and be completely unable to live without me." Juliet leaned back against the pillows, satisfied and smiling.

"It's the last part I'm worried about. Seeing you lying on the floor in the kitchen was like living through my own personal nightmare. The thought of losing you, never being able to hear you laugh or tease me again, or watching you with the children, it was more than I could imagine. I don't think that I could survive without you." His head bowed, he stroked her hand, unable to look her squarely in the eye.

"You won't have to live without me, or even think about it, at least for now. I'm fine, and tomorrow it will be as if today never happened. I let myself get worn out with all the company, doing too much and not resting during the day. Tony took me by surprise, and I was overwhelmed. I promise that I will take more care of myself in the future." Reaching out her hand, she gently ran it through his hair.

"Now tell me about Tony's visit. I'm sure it was very pleasant and civilized, and I wish that I could say that I was sorry to have missed it, but it would be a terrible lie if I did." Settling back on the pillows, she waited for his reply.

"It was all rather like a Hollywood film, complete with the worst dialogue imaginable. He showed up, full of bluster and bravado, demanding to see Carson. I think his exact words were that he would wait all day until we produced his son. He refused to believe that Carson was not on the island, and even Jordan could not convince him that it was true."

"Poor man! How did he take the confrontation?"

"Badly. He's consumed with guilt over Tony's behavior, blames himself for the way he turned out."

"And then what?"

"The police came just at the right moment. I called them the second he arrived, figuring that however long it would take them to get here would be just enough time to allow Tony to cross the line."

"And did he?"

"You sound remarkably like my mother used to when questioning me about some offense I had

239

committed. He did, and in front of a Detective Inspector, no less. Threatened you, said you should watch your back, that accidents could happen, even to you. He backed down pretty quickly when it became clear that the police wanted to arrest him. It all ended with him apologizing for the threat, and then they escorted him to the airport and put him on a plane for London. My men there will make sure he gets right back onto a plane for New York."

"There's something else you haven't told me, isn't there?"

"Jordan seems to think that you should make a new will, laying out Carson's future in great detail. He reminded me that if something happens and we die before his eighteenth birthday, that Tony could, in the absence of your specific wishes, sue for and win custody." Her eyes narrowed as she listened to the end of the conversation.

"That will never happen. I'll take care of that as soon as all of them are off to school."

"Darling, I think that we should not delay moving in with my father as soon as everyone is at school. Aside from the care you will get until the baby arrives, he'll be terribly lonely when Carson goes off to school, missing his three evenings a week with him, and I think the company would be very good for him. And we'll be close to your parents, and your mother can come to visit every day if she wants."

"A wise choice. Our house and my parents' place are out of the question. I fear that very soon I will begin to have problems negotiating stairs, and even coping with ordinary day to day chores. I hadn't wanted to bother you, or scare you, but I haven't been feeling very well for the past few weeks, and the doctor has ordered that I do absolutely nothing after the children leave, and continue to do so until the baby arrives. I'm sorry, but that means months of rented video movies and trays in bed if I'm too tired to come to the dinner table."

"Juliet, I will buy out the video store and the book store, and order in any meal you want, and serve it to you on a tray, for years if I have to. But please, if you feel ill, you must tell me. I had a feeling that all of this company was too much for you right now, and while I understand that you want Carson to know his other family, there comes a point when you have to say no." He held her face between his hands, looking into her eyes to emphasize his thoughts.

"I promise to be good from now on. I want nothing more than to have a healthy baby, and even a few more after this one. It's just that every time I have to think about or talk about Tony, I feel sick and dizzy, and have to sit down. Today, I just couldn't control the dizziness any longer, and that's why I fainted."

"Right now, why don't you go and have your bath, and I'll see to dinner, and also keep our three guests company. The others will be back around eight, and I'm sure that the rest of the evening will be spent packing to leave tomorrow. Then if you're up to it, we'll go back to London the day after. And don't worry about packing them up, I've spoken to Caroline, and she'll have her cousin Mavis come up for a few days to help out." He kissed her on the forehead and then closed the door behind him.

CHAPTER FIFTEEN

The flight from London arrived at Kennedy Airport at two in the afternoon. Alerted by Tony's telephone call, Laurel was waiting on the other side of customs. Since the birth of her third daughter, she had made a tremendous effort to lose all the weight she had gained, both before and during her pregnancy. Her blond, blue-eyed prettiness had returned, and she looked almost the same as the day he had married her.

Tony, in turn, had become more attentive, in a removed sort of way, as if he were on automatic pilot, absent in mind, but present in body. His lovemaking was competent, intended to satisfy her, but he was careful never to drink before he made love to her. For some unknown reason, he remembered the night at the Plaza, when he had shouted Juliet's name during the encounter with Cherry. Whatever he thought of at the end of sex, he kept it to himself. As he had for all the years that he and Laurel had been lovers, he used the fantasies of a woman he had thrown away, but never ceased to want and desire to help him to gain sexual satisfaction. If either Tony or Laurel had sought self awareness and honesty, they would have seen that their daily lives together were founded on a steadfast refusal to acknowledge the truth. Their relationship as husband and wife, and as parents was based on a certain cynicism, he needing her to validate his quest for custody of his son, she whether unwilling or incapable, in spite of everything she knew that he had done, to go it alone.

Coming through the double doors, he saw her standing there, a tentative smile on her face. Frustrated and angry, he forced himself to put on a neutral expression, and kissed her lightly on the cheek.

"It didn't go well, did it?" She led the way through the terminal and out to the car.

"Is it that obvious?" He opened the trunk and heaved his bag inside.

"You might as well hold up a sign. What happened?"

"I got to the house in Surrey, but they had gone. I don't know how he does it, but Macallister knew I was coming. On a hunch, I went to the local airport, and managed to get the flight plan for his private jet. He flew everyone, my parents, Jennifer and her family and the boy over to Jersey, in the Channel Islands. By the time I got a flight, and found the house, he had gotten my son off the island. Even though I told him I would sit there all day if necessary to see my son, he called the police and had me put on a plane to London, and then one to New York. I feel as if I'm always one step behind him. At this rate, the boy will be eighteen before I get to see him."

Behind the steering wheel, she was silent, devoting her attention to the heavy traffic leaving the airport.

"Aren't you going to say anything? He's your stepson."

"There isn't anything I can say that hasn't been thought or said already. Maybe it's time to change your tactics."

"Why don't you mind your own business?"

"You don't have to get all huffy, Tony. All I meant was that you can catch more flies with honey than with vinegar, or didn't your grandmother tell you that on a regular basis?" Her eyes flicked over to look at him, and then went back to concentrate on driving.

"Obviously, you've been thinking about this while I was gone, and since we're in this car together, why don't you tell me and get it over with." Breathing deeply, he labored over maintaining his self-control.

"If you keep showing up and demanding to see the kid, they are going to do everything in their power to prevent it. A custody battle could take years, and even if you win in the end, more than likely it will have become a dead issue. He'll be almost an adult, and will probably want nothing to do with you. You just might have more luck being a nice guy, sending the kid presents, writing to him, letting him get to know you. Put yourself in his shoes, Tony. To him, you're an ogre, someone who is trying to take him away from his mother and the man he calls Daddy. And to add to that, when he was dying, you insisted on being paid to donate your bone marrow. Be honest, if you were Carson, wouldn't you wonder about someone who says he's your father, but refused to save your life unless he got paid?" Laurel changed lanes and made the turnoff for the bridge to the Bronx.

"I'm not even sure he knows about that." Avoiding her glance, he turned his head to look out of the passenger window.

"Tony, from what you've told me about Donald Macallister, he's made sure that Carson knows all about what you've done. He had to explain the existence of your parents and sister, so why on earth wouldn't he tell him about you? If the situation was reversed, you wouldn't be able to control yourself, giving the kid the good news about his new Daddy."

"I'm willing to try anything. Maybe then, I'll be able to show the court that I've been trying to be a good father, even though Juliet is doing everything she can to keep me away from my son. I think you have a very good idea, honey." He leaned across the gear shift and kissed her on the cheek.

The idea took hold. It was almost too good to be true, he couldn't possibly lose. Eventually Juliet would have to let him see the boy, especially if he kept the gifts that he would send at regular intervals. Turning his head, he looked at his wife. She was almost as pretty as she had been when they got married, now that she had lost all that weight. Things could be a lot worse.

*   *   *   *   *

"Jordan, Tony is on the telephone. He's asking to make an appointment to see you."

"I'll take it and talk to him now, Sheila. That's all I need, to have him coming here to argue about the boy, again." Grudgingly, he picked up the receiver, and forced himself to make a genuine effort to be cordial.

"Tony, it's good to hear your voice."

"Dad, your sincerity overwhelms me. You don't have to pretend that you're glad to hear from me, or that you want to see me. I just called to let you know, so that you can run and tell Juliet and her husband, that there won't be any more demands to see my son, at least not like the previous ones."

"I don't think I understand what you're getting at."

"I've decided to try being a nice guy for a change. The kid is scared to death of me, and it doesn't surprise me in the least. I should have tried harder to let him know how much I want to love him and how much I want to get to know him. Maybe that will open the door for me."

"What about the custody suit?"

"I don't want to lose out on a chance to try and get to know him, even if it's only through letters, and maybe a phone call, if he wants it. And by the time of the first hearing, he might actually like me." Tony's voice was a soft monotone, as if he were reading from cue cards.

"And what do you expect me to do about this?" Jordan clenched his teeth, reminding himself that he was talking to his own flesh and blood.

"Tell her I've turned over a new leaf, that I won't harass her any more, that all I want is a chance to be a father to my son."

"I see. I'll pass the message along. Is that all, Tony?"

"Good-bye, Dad. Give my best to Mom."

The connection was broken quietly, and Jordan sat at his desk and held his head in his hands. A feeling of deep unease sat at the back of his mind. It was impossible for him, knowing what his son was capable of, to believe that all Tony wanted was to be a nice guy.

*   *   *   *   *

"Mummy, why can't I take my old football boots to school with me?" Carson sat on the floor of his room, surrounded by all the items he was required to bring to boarding school.

"For two reasons, one, because they are almost worn out, and two, you've outgrown them. So you'll take new ones, and most likely by the time you come home for Christmas, you'll have outgrown them as well." Laughing, Juliet reached out her hand and stroked her son's hair. It had grown back as thick as it had been before his illness.

"Do I have to pack up all of this stuff myself?" Wheedling, he got up and sat on the edge of the chair and leaned his head on his mother's chest.

The door slammed shut downstairs, and both could hear the sound of someone running up the stairs.

"Yes, you have to pack it all up. This time, I can't bend over the trunk to help you, doctor's orders, and Mavis has her hands full with Miranda and Dylan. But, I believe help has arrived. Daddy's home, and will be more than happy to help you finish your packing."

"Did I hear my name being taken in vain?" Donald stood in the doorway, inwardly amused at the expression on his son's face.

"Can you help me finish my packing, please? Mummy can't bend over the trunk, and I'm stuck."

"Since you ask me so nicely, yes, I will help you. It shouldn't take too long, and Mummy can supervise. Carson, is this everything that has to go into the trunk?"

"Everything except the sweets that I have to hand over when I get there. That part doesn't make sense."

"Of course it does. Otherwise, you'd eat them all at once, have a terrific tummy ache, and there would be nothing to have as a treat for the entire term. A very satisfactory system, I might add." Suppressing a smile, Donald bent to the task at hand.

"Daddy, are you and Mummy going to miss me when I leave tomorrow?"

"Carson, of course we will miss you. We've had you at home for almost nine years now, and loved every minute of it. But now it's time for you to begin a new part of your life, learning to make your own decisions. It's a part of growing up, changing the importance that Mummy and I will have in your life. That doesn't mean that we don't love you as much as ever, or that we won't miss you." Carson hung his head, unsure of how to phrase the next question.

"What about the new baby? Will you love it more than you love me?" Juliet and Donald exchanged a look before she answered.

"Never. Carson, Daddy and I have three children, and we love all of you as much as ever. When you came along, I didn't stop loving Miranda and Dylan, and the same will hold true for the new baby. Darling, love grows all the time. It's something that has no limits at all, and so it never runs out, or fades away."

"Carson, you're not thinking that we're sending you away to school because of the baby, are you?" Donald sat on the floor and held his son close, his cheek resting on the top of his head. Carson shook his head, not very convincingly.

"Darling, when I have the baby, you'll be home for the term holiday, and you will be as big a part of its life as Miranda and Dylan were of yours when you were born. Just think, you'll be the only nine year old we know who can change a nappy."

"No, thank you. I think I'll leave that sort of stuff to Nanny. I'd rather play with it, anyway." The corners of Carson's mouth turned up in a smile.

The last of the items had been packed away, only the last few things left for the following morning. Juliet heaved herself out of the chair and went to check on the progress of her other two children. She was pleased to see that Mavis had packed up all of their things, and they had disappeared downstairs to wait for the rest of the family.

Dinner on the night before her children would return to boarding school was the same, except that this time all three of the children's plates had a small gift box on them. Marjorie had prepared all of their favorites, and as the children laughed and teased, both Juliet and Donald had bittersweet feelings. Tomorrow their little family would be divided, all of their children off to school, the only positive being that in a few months they would be beginning a whole new family. The lump in her throat grew larger as she looked at the three of them, Miranda and Dylan well on their way to university and Eton, Carson at the threshold of preparatory school, beginning on the same path.

"Can we open our boxes now?" Carson squirmed with excitement. He had waited so long to grow old enough to be part of the departure ritual. Opening his box would be the final step before tomorrow morning, when Donald would take him to school.

"Yes, you may. And then it's bedtime. We have to leave at six in order to have you there by the afternoon." Donald leaned back in his chair and smiled, remembering the night before he had been sent away to school for the first time. He had just celebrated his eighth birthday when his parents had packed him up and brought him to Templeton, the same school where he was sending his two sons. In his case, the night before had been like any other, and school had been an escape from what he knew was the unhappiness of his parents. It wasn't until he had turned ten that he had forced Mrs. Gregson, the housekeeper to tell him the truth. The horror of learning that his older sister had been killed in a tragic accident was compounded by the shocking realization that his parents had kept the knowledge to themselves, shutting him out of something that he should have known. His mother's behavior now made terrible sense, the strange silences, the unexplained bouts of crying, the almost suffocating protectiveness that he had lived with until he had gone away to school. The coldness of his parents' relationship had not escaped his notice either, and for years he had puzzled over the fact that neither of his parents seemed overly affectionate, towards him, or each other.

But at the same moment that Mrs. Gregson told him about his sister, he felt a terrible burden fall away. For years, he had blamed himself for the unhappiness of his parents, trying his best to be the perfect child, always to be well-behaved and obedient, never causing any problems. At the back of his mind had always hovered the fear that if he did anything wrong, he would lose his parents and his family would be shattered.

Donald felt a small shudder as he could not help but remember the emotional explosion at dinner the following night. In an unexplained instant of enormous courage, he had faced down his parents and demanded that they tell him about Miranda, and explain why he had never been told about his sister. The heavy silence that had followed his outburst had almost shattered his resolve. Looking around the table, he had, as if in a dream, seen more fresh tears rolling down his mother's face, and surprisingly, a path of tears on his father's face as well. His father's voice echoed down through the years of his memories. Stammering, he had tried to explain to his ten year old son what had happened to his family after the death of his sister.

"The worst thing that can happen to a parent is to lose a child, Donald, especially a loss that could have been avoided. A carriage left unattended, even for a second, can be a death trap. It felt as if my heart had died, that I could never love anyone again. When you were born, I was relieved. You were a son, someone who could inherit all I possess. I tried to feel love for you, just as I had felt for Miranda, but I couldn't." At that point, he had begun to cry, shaking his head, unable to go on. His mother, uncharacteristically, then spoke her mind.

"I was the one in charge of Nanny and the carriage. Nanny had gone to the kitchen to supervise Miranda's lunch, and I had gone into the house for just a moment to answer the telephone. When I came back, the carriage was on the grass below the terrace, lying on its side. I remember seeing the wheel spinning slowly, and I couldn't understand, because the brake had been put on. As soon as I reached the carriage, I knew there was no hope. After the police had finished their investigation, we discovered that the brake had failed, and that Miranda had hit a rock, smashing her skull. The surgeon told us that if she had landed on the grass, she would have lived. Your father and I were shattered, she was such a good baby, so smart and sweet. I couldn't forgive myself, and couldn't bring myself to ask your father to help me. When I found out I was pregnant again, I was consumed by fear, that for some other reason, I would lose my child. After you were born, I was afraid to hold you, get attached to you, to be a mother again. I'm so sorry for it all, we put a terrible burden onto you, making you feel responsible for keeping the family together. We've robbed you of so much, I hope that one day you can forgive us."

Donald had sat at his place, his head down, not daring to breathe, feeling his heart pounding loudly in his chest. Overwhelmed, he could not speak. The only sound he could hear was the scrape of a chair. In the next instant, his father had picked him up and had held him tightly, weeping. His mother had joined them, her hand stroking his face as she cried. For an instant, he had felt guilt, an intense, overwhelming guilt at having forced them to come to terms with the past, but it was swept away by the intense relief, the knowing and sharing of his parent's love.

After that terrible evening, life with his parents had felt like heaven. For the first time, he had felt loved and cherished, like a child instead of a little adult. Now, twenty-six years later, he rarely thought of that night, never realizing how it had shaped his emotional attitudes towards parenting and family life.

His thoughts were interrupted by Carson's squeals of delight, as he opened his gift. Juliet had managed, he had no idea how, to get him a rugby shirt, autographed by his favorite players, and for possibly the hundredth time, he dreaded having to bring his three children to school the following morning. He had been lulled by the joy of having one child at home while the older two were away. Tomorrow, the house would be completely silent, stripped of all childish presence, at least until December.

"Donald, do you want any pudding?" Juliet waved the dish under his nose. For years, the last night meal's dessert had been apple pudding, concocted out of cookies and applesauce.

"Daddy, you have to toast us with the pudding, you always do." Miranda smiled as she held up her spoon, loaded with dessert.

"To a successful term, and a quick return home to us." Donald swallowed the sticky treat.

"Bedtime, you lot. Up at five tomorrow morning, out by six." Juliet herded her children in the direction of their bedrooms. Stopping for only a moment to make sure that they were getting ready for bed, she moved on to her own room, willing herself to ignore her aching feet. She also changed into nightclothes, her cotton shift and robe, stopping for a moment to glance enviously at the sheer nightgown she had bought in New York. As an afterthought, she hung it in the back of her closet. No sense torturing herself with it until she could wear it again. Sitting down in front of her vanity table, she lifted her arms and began the nightly ritual of unbraiding and brushing her hair, and then rubbing the ends with silk. Smiling, as she rubbed her hair, she remembered watching her grandmother, Isabel Thornton, rubbing her hair the same way.

"Now, Juliet, my dear child, hair like ours is a responsibility. It isn't every day that someone is born with the color and texture that we have. It has to be protected, and loved, every single day. And one day, when you get married, your husband will fall in love with it, just like your grandfather Benjamin did." And her grandmother would laugh, and then tell her another story of how much fun she and her husband had had when they were young and newly married. Her mother had not approved of these stories, crossing her arms across her chest and tapping her foot on the floor to show her disapproval.

One night, unable to sleep, Juliet had crept upstairs and along the corridor towards her grandmother's bedroom. Hearing her mother and grandmother's voices, she had hidden in the shadows, afraid to announce her presence.

"Mother, really, you must not tell Juliet all those stories. She'll grow up thinking that her hair has magical properties. She's already so beautiful, it frightens me, and yesterday I had a visit from her teacher. Miss Butterfield thinks that she has artistic talent. She wants to put her in a competition for a special art school."

"Rose, I want you to listen to me, and please, do not interrupt. Try as you might, you will never be able to deny the magic that she possesses, from the tip of her head, all the way down to her toes. It isn't even her beauty, which will only grow as she does, or her artistic talent, which will also grow the same way, but her character, her innocence, her sweetness, it's a magnet that is surrounded by all those other things. Such things have to be nourished and protected, not stamped out or ridiculed. Juliet has a marvelous life ahead of her, I'm only sorry that I won't be around 'to see it. Just remember one thing, Rose. That child has no defense against evil, and never will. She is incapable of understanding that it exists in other people. To her, evil belongs in a story book, not in real life. That is what makes her so unique.

"One day, no matter how hard you and Bertram try to prevent it, she will be confronted by evil. She will be shattered by it, even devastated, but it will be her strength of character that will get her through it, along with love and support from the two of you. And Rose, when it's over, she will always be able to recognize it, to see it as clearly as she can see her own reflection in the mirror. That is a gift as unique as any God can give to a child."

At that point, the voices had fallen and she could not hear what was being said. A few minutes later, her mother had opened the door to her grandmother's room. As she had walked by, Juliet had squeezed herself against the wall of the landing, back into the shadows. Later, when she was certain that no one else would come, she crept back to her room, and covered herself completely with the sheet and blanket, creating a new universe for herself, in which she could think and digest everything that she had heard.

Until she met and married Tony, she never fully understood what her grandmother had meant. And even after he had abused and raped her, laughing as he had taken his suitcases and gone back to America, she had refused to admit that she had been touched by evil. Instead, she had sought a refuge, first in her work, spending long hours perfecting her first series of paintings, then in her pregnancy, relishing the growth of an innocent life within her, and finally in her marriage to Donald. From the first, she had sensed that he had loved her deeply and completely, but with the fear born of her experience with evil, she was reluctant to give that last ounce of trust, to commit herself without reservation. For three years, she questioned herself, constantly wondering if her feelings for Donald were really love or gratitude at being rescued by him at the last minute. He had responded by trying everything he knew to reach that last place in her soul, often coming home in the middle of the day to make love to her, drowning himself in her, but never being able to feel that everything about her had become part of him.

Juliet put down the hairbrush and picked up her bottle of lavender scent. Slowly, she raised her arm and began to spray herself with its heady, seductive aura. Smiling as she did so, she remembered the day when she had needed to express her love in her own way. She had telephoned the office, whispering words of love and pleading, bringing him home, as she knew they would. For the first time in their relationship, she had made love to him, surprising, and even shocking her husband with the deep sensual nature of the experience. At the moment of greatest pleasure, she finally understood the echo of her grandmother's words, that in her innocence and sweetness, she would ultimately find the truest meaning of love.

*   *   *   *   *

"Donald, wake up! I'm sorry, but it's five, time to get up!"

"Mm. Go away, I'm sleeping."

"If you get up now, there's still time for love, not too much, but enough." Her throaty laugh echoed in his ear as she stroked his hair.

"No, there isn't, never enough time at this ungodly hour." Yawning, he stretched and sighed.

"I've decided, I'm taking the rest of the week as a holiday. That way we can get ready to move by the weekend." Laughing, he buried his face in her hair.

"I'm ready for life to get a bit easier for a few months."

"I'll go and make sure that the children are up and almost ready. I'll shave and shower, and meet you downstairs in half an hour, so we can all have breakfast together." Kissing her lips lightly, he reached for his robe and belting it, opened the door to the bedroom and was gone.

Completely relaxed, she closed her eyes and dreamed for a moment, of holding her unborn child. Placing both of her hands across her abdomen, she could feel the butterfly movements of the child, reassuring her of its presence.

* * * * *

Tony paid for the toy, an enormous building set, took his receipt and walked out of FAO Schwartz without buying anything for his daughters. He got as far as the end of the block when he realized his mistake, and hurriedly returned to the store, choosing three moderately priced gifts.

Emotionally invested in a fantasy relationship with Carson, Tony went through the motions of family life as if he were sleepwalking. Automatically, he would drive the twins to preschool, come home and send out resumés, go out with Laurel and the baby until it was time to pick up the twins, come home, eat dinner, watch television, go to bed, dutifully make love to his wife, and finally fall asleep. In the months since he had moved back into the house, and decided to pursue some kind of relationship with his son, every day had passed this way, dreamlike with no hard edges. Periodically, he would allow himself to fantasize about being with his son, being able to do the kind of things that fathers and sons do together. These daydreams never included his wife, or his daughters, although on occasion he did allow himself to daydream about proving what a good father he was and receiving some kind of reaction from Juliet.

Now he waited anxiously to see if the gift would be accepted. After three weeks, when no word came that the package had been returned, he breathed a sigh of relief, and began to wait for a thank you note from Carson. Two weeks later, with no note forthcoming, he had called the store to ask if the package had, in fact, been delivered. It had not and coincidentally had arrived back at the warehouse the day before. Tony's initial feelings of anger and disappointment gave way to depression as he told the store to credit the full amount to his American Express Card.

CHAPTER SIXTEEN

Confined to bed, Juliet sighed and tried to fight off the crushing boredom that had become her constant companion. She had run out of useful projects, and even getting up for the limited amount of time allowed her each day exhausted her. In spite of Donald's efforts to keep her entertained and happy, she had reached the stage where even the prospect of the new baby, whose clothes she had lovingly stitched and decorated during her time in bed, did not cheer her up. To her embarrassment, she had even become weepy, bursting into tears for no reason, and then crying furiously when anyone would try to comfort her.

Even the specter of Tony had lost its edge, although she had had a few anxious moments when the package from FAO Schwartz had arrived. Luckily, her mother had been at the house fetching a few things when the delivery had been made, and she had refused it and sent it back to New York. Donald had reassured her that Mrs. Nesbitt, the next door neighbor, would take charge if anything else arrived, and she had promised to send whatever it was back where it came from. Inwardly, she prayed for the arrival of her baby immediately, or at least tomorrow. As she rang for the nurse to help her out of bed, she began to cry.

"Darling, what is the matter with you? I've never seen you like this, all weepy like a leaky faucet." Donald had answered the bell.

"I'm depressed, I'm sick of staying in bed and looking like a whale, and I haven't seen my feet for weeks. I'm so tired of being like this."

"You aren't the only one. I want my wife back, the old one, not the new one."

Stricken with guilt, she hung her head.

"I'm sorry to be such a bore. I'd like to be the old one, as soon as possible." Suddenly, she sucked in her breath as a flash of pain traveled up her back.

"It may come sooner than you think. It's time."

"Are you sure?"

"As sure of this as I'll ever be."

*   *   *   *   *

Holding his new daughter to his chest, Donald kissed the perfect hands and feet. Smiling with relief, Juliet stretched out her arms for her daughter, as promised with red hair.

"I wonder if she'll always be in a hurry." He sat on the edge of the bed, watching his daughter eat.

"If she's like I was as a small child, she will be. I'd like to call her Isabel, after my grandmother, and Fiona after your mother. I like the sound of it, Isabel Fiona Macallister, marvelous initials for her."

*   *   *   *   *

Isabel Macallister soon became the center of the household. After a short stay in the hospital, Juliet and Donald returned to their own home, with the baby taking up residence in the nursery, long vacated by her older brothers and sister.

So energized was Juliet, that she immediately began to think about planning for the Christmas holidays. Fully recovered, she felt reborn, finally free of whatever evil she had imagined had cursed her attempts to have a healthy child. Sitting at her desk, she compiled lists, each one longer than the one before it. In between, she found time to go to the studio and finally finish the last of her three paintings, the Lilac Lady. In two weeks, they would all be shipped to New York, where they would be delivered to the manager of a hedge fund.

Her greatest pleasure was to take her baby daughter up to her studio, and lie on the couch with her, feeding and holding her, for hours on end. She had unearthed the robe she had worn when Carson was a baby, an exact match for the shawl that lay across the couch. Donald had remarked, quite enviously, that she looked like a voluptuous model, lying in wait for a painter to come and commit her to canvas. She had merely smiled and turned to nurse Isabel again, beckoning her husband to join them on the couch.

*   *   *   *   *

"What shall we do for Christmas? Would you like to go somewhere warm, where the children can swim, and Isabel can sleep in the shade of a palm tree?" Donald lay on the bed, his head propped in his hand, as he gently stroked his daughter's cheek. Totally relaxed, he felt almost languid, caught in that gray area between alertness and almost sleep, feeling that the smallest push would send him to sleep for the night.

"I had started to plan the holidays here, but it suddenly occurred to me that the days after Christmas are many, and activities I can do with them very few. So, speak to me and suggest balmy skies, the sound of the surf, soft music and tropical smells."

"The house in Palm Beach is ready and waiting for us if we should decide to go there. Or, if you are feeling very adventurous, we can go to Barbados or to Hawaii."

"I think Palm Beach. It's only a six hour flight, and the weather has to be better than it is here." Juliet smothered a yawn, picked up her daughter and kissed her cheek. The baby slept on, completely satisfied and contented, not even noticing when the nanny took her and put her to bed.

"The day after Christmas, then? We'll do the usual here, with all the goodies I know you are planning, and then off to Florida. I'll book us into somewhere for a few days and we can take them to Disney World. I'll bet we'll all look wonderful in those mouse ears." He dodged the throw pillow as it bounced harmlessly off the bed.

"Don't do that, it's dangerous. I'm being patient, but six weeks is a long time to wait."

*   *   *   *   *

"Mummy, we're back!" Juliet could hear the thump of Carson's feet as he charged up the stairs, followed closely by Dylan and Miranda. At the top of the stairs, the three charged into her bedroom and flung themselves at her, hugging her and covering her with kisses.

"Can we see Isabel now? Mummy, we've been so patient, not nagging to be allowed to come home to see her. Please?" Miranda smiled as she put her head onto Juliet's shoulder.

"Go on, she's all dressed and awake and waiting to meet all of you. And remember, dinner is in half an hour, and you can discuss when Daddy is going to take you shopping. I hope all of you have your lists." Carson burst out laughing at his mother's effort to be stern. Laughing back, she hugged him and kissed the top of his head. He looked wonderful, the picture of health, rosy cheeked and at least half an inch taller.

The three children tiptoed into the nursery, holding their breath, waiting to see their sister for the first time. Leaning over the side of the crib, Dylan watched as the nanny lifted the baby up and held her, so that they could all have a good look at her.

"Look, she has red hair, just like Mummy's." Miranda stroked her sister's cheek softly. She bent down, kissed her and then stepped back. Her two brothers elbowed each other to get a closer look. Dylan kissed Isabel's cheek, while Carson kissed her hand and stroked her fingers.

"She's wonderful, isn't she. Just think, I won't be the only girl besides Mummy in the house anymore." Miranda sighed happily as she kissed the baby again and then chased her brothers out of the room.

"She needs to sleep, and I'm sure we'll see plenty of her while we're here, so let's go down and eat." Laughing and teasing, Isabel's older siblings headed down the stairs for dinner.

*   *   *   *   *

"Now, look, you lot, we have a lot of shopping to accomplish and only three days to do it, so let's try and get organized. Your mother has instructed me that since the christening will be held two days before you return to school, I'm to buy suits for you boys, and she will meet us for lunch so that she can buy Miranda something to wear as well." Donald wrapped his muffler around his neck.

Juliet stood at the foot of the stairs, checking shopping lists, and giving last minute instructions. "I'll meet you in front of Fortnum's at half-past eleven. That will get us in right away, and out to shop before the crowds arrive." The front door opened, and in a minute, they had all disappeared into an icy blast of cold.

*   *   *   *   *

Juliet sighed with happiness as she braided her hair, making sure that one of the gardenia blossoms from the indoor garden peeped out of the middle. Finished, she twirled in front of the mirror, her gray silk slipper dress hanging perfectly on her body. Aside from a larger chest, she didn't look as if she had had a baby only seven weeks ago. She added extra gardenia scent, then her necklace, the empty space filled in with Isabel's name, and her cranberry and gray silk shawl. Tonight was the first evening she and Donald would spend alone together since the baby's birth. Seven weeks old tomorrow, she was a sweet baby, filling out and becoming a bit chubby, and sleeping almost through the night. Her eyes were almost the same color as her father's, and her hair promised to be as red as that of her mother.

"Aren't you ready yet? If we don't leave now, we'll lose our reservations." Donald poked his head around the door, and caught his breath.

"Yes, I'm ready, just being vain. It feels wonderful to wear real clothes again, and to be able to see my feet."

"And beautiful you and your feet are." Laughing, he took her hand and led her out to the car.

"Are we dining alone?" Juliet stood outside the car and waited to get in.

"Of course we are. It's our first night together since Isabel, and I want it to be special."

"Then shut the car door, and take me back inside."

"You can't be serious, after you spent almost an hour and a half getting dressed."

"How long will it take you to reverse that process?" She slammed the door shut and stood on the pavement, her arms crossed, tapping her foot to signal her impatience. "Besides, I feel like pizza. We can order in, and have champagne with it. Donald, I'm feeling very dangerous right now, and you wouldn't want me to start undressing right here in the street, now would you?"

He walked around the car and stood in front of her, so close that they were almost touching. The heavy scent of gardenias seemed to wrap itself around him.

"I think all that I need is about five minutes, but only that long because I love that dress and don't want to rip it." Reaching out, he pulled her close and kissed her on the mouth, his passion all too obvious. With a life of their own, his hands moved to the straps of the dress, moving them down as he kissed her shoulders.

"Now who's being dangerous. I wouldn't do that right now if I were you, the children might be about watching." Her breath was warm and sweet against his ear, as he drew a ragged breath. Grabbing her hand, he led her back inside the house and into their suite, where he left instructions with the nanny and the housekeeper, and then locked the door. Turning around, he saw that Juliet was still in the same position he had left her when he had picked up the telephone. Transfixed, she was standing absolutely still, watching him. Slowly, he began to unbutton his shirt, and remove the rest of his clothes. As if her arms had become useless, she had dropped her shawl and purse on the floor. Still and silent, she watched him undress, her breathing rapid, her tawny eyes turning black with desire.

"Come here, darling. You still have all your clothes on." His ears registered that his voice shook, like a school boy at his first encounter. Desperate, he watched her glide across the room, the dress shimmering in the light. In spite of the fact that he knew every inch of her body so well, her mystery overwhelmed him, and he found himself wondering what she looked like under the dress.

"I love you so much, I can't live without you." His hands came up, and gently pulled the straps of her dress away from her shoulders. Bending his head, he kissed her on the mouth, so gently that she felt as if the softest of flowers had brushed her lips. Moving further down, he kissed her shoulders, his tongue tracing the shape of her collar bone. The straps of the dress fell to her elbows, allowing the dress to begin to fall down her body.

"Sure of yourself, aren't you?" He laughed as he ran his hand over her. She hadn't had a stitch on under the dress. Unable to wait another second, he reached up and undid the necklace. Tossing it onto the chair, he then undid the braid. As she shook her head to finish the job, he could feel the scent of the gardenias traveling across her chest towards him. Almost unnoticed, the single gardenia blossom floated down her chest towards the floor.

Donald was so intoxicated by the scent of gardenias, and by the attractions of her body that he didn't know what to do first. He felt like a boy, a nervous adolescent confronted with his first experience. He could sense her whispers in his ear, but couldn't understand a single word. All he could hear was what sounded like the crash and roar of the ocean, but it couldn't be that. The ocean was too far away to be heard like that. Maybe it was his blood pumping through his body. It was all her fault, that all he could hear was the pulse of his desire. He reached out for her. The last thing he remembered was her laugh and the smell of her hair, saturated with the essence of gardenias.

"Mmm. Definitely better than dining out." The last crunch of pizza disappeared as Donald washed it down with a swallow of champagne. Laughing, Juliet leaned over and kissed her husband, her hair falling all around him. The sound of the telephone, muffled by the pillow placed over it some time earlier, was insistent and unceasing. Sighing, Donald removed the pillow and picked up the receiver.

"Jordan, how nice to hear your voice. And Merry Christmas to you and Emily as well. How is she? Yes, we're all fine here, just enjoying some vacation time with the children and our new little girl, Isabel. Yes, as a matter of fact, she looks exactly like her mother." He couldn't help the wariness that crept into his voice.

"Donald, I hope that you don't mind that I called David Graham and asked him to tell me where you were. You know that I didn't call just for good wishes, although I'm always happy to speak to you and to Juliet. We're all in Miami, and, well, this isn't easy for me, but I think that you should let Tony see Carson, just this once. Now, please, hear me out. I have a very bad feeling about all of this, and I'm very worried that he might do something stupid, out of sheer desperation. If you let him see the boy, even if it's only for a few minutes, it will defuse the emotional issue. All of the gifts and letters he has sent to the boy were returned, unopened. He feels that he's out of options, and I'm afraid he'll do something drastic." Jordan's voice grew louder and more emotional with each sentence.

By this time, Donald was all attention. "What exactly do you mean by drastic? Should I be hiring extra security to guard my family?" Jordan's sigh came through the receiver.

"Maybe you should. Donald, he's been sitting in Greenwich for almost a year, waiting for an opportunity to right what he considers a grievous wrong. I agree with you that no wrong was done to him, and that he has no right to ask for anything, but I also know how unpredictable and even violent he can be if he doesn't get his own way."

"It's too late. Before we left England, I had my office forward the file to Scotland Yard. Even as we speak, I'm sure that they are petitioning to have him arrested and then extradited to England to stand trial. Jordan, I understand that this is very painful for you and the rest of your family, but you must understand that I don't trust Tony, and I don't want him anywhere near Juliet or Carson. That last time, when he followed us to Jersey, convinced me that he will never give up, and in spite of my trying not to, I keep worrying that he will try to take Carson away by force."

"Donald, I know you've done what you think is best, and I also want you to know that Emily and Jennifer and I don't hold any resentment against either of you. My son did a very bad thing, a criminal act against your wife, and like it or not, he has to pay for it. How long do you think it will be before they come for him?"

"I haven't any idea. I'd appreciate it if you kept silent about this. I know that's asking a great deal, Tony is your son and you love him, the same way I love Dylan and Carson, but we're not dealing with a petty criminal, but someone who could do a great deal of damage if he knew what was going to happen."

"Donald, that's a great deal to ask. It's not that I want to warn him so that he can disappear, but he will have to get his life in order and that takes time. I'll wait until after we're back in Greenwich to tell him. I can postpone it until then. And one more thing, the custody suit has been filed, but it's not on the calendar yet. I thought you'd like to know. We would have liked to have seen you, and Carson, we have all sorts of presents here, ready to be shipped to you, but I'll understand if you say no."

"I'm very sorry, but no it has to be. Wish everyone a happy holiday and New Year, and I'll make sure Carson calls you before he goes back to school. Good night, Jordan, and thank you for calling." Donald hung up the phone and lay back against the pillows, looking up at the ceiling.

"Bad news?"

"The worst possible. We're going to have to leave here, tomorrow most likely. That was Jordan. They're all in Miami, he called to beg me to let Tony see Carson. He's afraid that he may do something drastic. He even recommended that I hire extra security."

"Darling, we knew this would happen. Tony is a man who likes to get his own way. But I don't think we should run this time. Carson and I have had a number of talks together since he came home from school. He's accepted that Tony is his biological parent, and while he doesn't think it's the best thing that ever happened to him, he does understand that if he doesn't meet him at least once, Tony will continue to harass and annoy us for the next nine years. Perhaps you should have the call traced, and we can call Jordan back and arrange for a meeting, on our terms, with Val and the others scattered around so that Tony can't do anything drastic."

"You know he won't be satisfied with only a meeting. Next, he'll want an overnight visitation, and we might never see him again."

"Donald, David Graham and Scott have both told me that here in America, he will, in all likelihood, get some sort of visitation. Of course, the best thing that could happen is that Scotland Yard take him into custody as soon as possible, but that may not happen for some time. Until that happens, I'd prefer not to antagonize him any more than I have to, otherwise, he could steal him and we'd never see him again."

"So you want to let Carson meet Tony?"

"You know very well that is not what I want. Like it or not, this has to be partly Carson's decision, and if he's willing to take the chance, I think that we have to allow him to do it. I'm so proud of him. He's so brave and courageous, he puts me to shame."

"I'll call both David and Scott in the morning. David will be able to tell us how far along Scotland Yard is, Scott can advise us about our rights, and how long it will take until the custody hearing, and we can take it from there." He continued to stare at the ceiling.

"You're very upset about all of this, aren't you?" Juliet leaned over and rested her head on his chest.

"More than you'll ever know. I can sense that my relationship with Carson will never be the same again, once Tony is in the picture. It's inevitable, that with increased exposure, that they will establish some sort of rapport, one which won't include me." His voice shaking, Donald swallowed angrily.

"Darling, you are Carson's father, in every way but one. He even said that your feelings about all of this mean a great deal to him, that the last thing he wants is to hurt you in any way, and that if you don't want him to meet with Tony, he won't. He's only agreed to do it because he knows he will have to eventually anyway." Suddenly worried, she watched him wipe tears from his face.

"He means everything to me, Juliet. My relationship with him is so precious, it's different than the one I have with Dylan and Miranda. I adore them, and they feel very secure with that, but Carson is different. So special, so loving, and so much like me, it tears me apart to think that he isn't really my child."

"Donald, look at me and listen. Carson is your child, the child of your heart and your soul, and that is far more important than being the child of your body."

"Stop trying to make me feel better, it's not working. Right now, I'm sorry I ever put Tony's name on the birth certificate." He reached for a tissue and blew his nose.

"Likewise, but we have to deal with the reality of the here and now. Jordan and Emily won't let anything bad happen to him, and I don't think that Tony, in spite of his anger, would hurt the son he has longed for all these years. What he really wants is to have a son, even if the child happens to be mine, one he created in a moment of brutality. I think that he's so caught up in the fantasy of being a father to a boy that he isn't thinking rationally."

"Juliet, what would Tony do if the situation were reversed?"

"With him, no one can be sure of what he would do, but I think that he would try to avoid it for as long as possible, threaten everyone, fight it, but in the end, he would give in."

"It gives me great pain to know that in spite of all my power and all my wealth, I can't keep him away from Carson."

"I feel the same way. We'll just have to drag it out, stall for as long as we can. By then, perhaps he'll be in jail and all our worries will be for nothing."

Rolling over onto his side, Donald put his hand up to her face and stroked her cheek.

"That would be the most wonderful thing to happen out of this mess. No more talk about Tony for the time being. What would you like for dessert?"

"Nothing. The pizza was more than enough food for any normal person. Besides, I don't want to waste any time on food. Isabel will be calling for her last feed in a little while, and I would just like to spend that time with you, not thinking about Tony for a change." Smiling, she leaned over and turned out the light.

*   *   *   *   *

"Mummy, can I wear shorts today? My new red ones?" Carson sat next to his mother at the breakfast table, drawing out their time together to the last second.

"Yes, and a white polo shirt with it. Carson, I need to talk to you about what will happen later today. Daddy and I will take you into Fort Lauderdale, to a hotel near the ocean. Tony will be waiting there with his wife, Laurel, and Grandpa Jordan and Grandma Emily. When we sit down to have a meal together, you will sit between Jordan and Tony. For the two hours that we are there, you will be talking to Tony, and getting to know him, and Laurel. After the lunch, no matter what happens, you will be polite, shake Tony's hand, make your goodbyes properly, and we will leave."

"Nothing will happen, will it? Tony won't try and take me away, will he?" Carson fidgeted while he spoke.

"No, he won't. But just to make sure, we will have Val and the others stationed all over the hotel and the restaurant."

"I'm scared. I wish I didn't have to do this." Carson buried his head in Juliet's lap.

"Me, too. But you did suggest this, and so now it's better to do it with a smile. Now off with you, and tell Miranda if you see her that I need to talk to her."

Nodding, Carson got off his chair and walked through the kitchen and the living room towards the bedroom he shared with Dylan. She could hear him bellowing for his sister, and then being hushed by everyone as he passed the nursery.

"Mummy, is everything all right?" Miranda appeared silently and sat down in the same chair that Carson had occupied.

"Yes, of course. Darling, while Daddy and I are in Fort Lauderdale, I'd like you and Dylan to keep an eye on things for me, and play with Isabel when she wakes up. I left a bottle for her, and you can give it to her, if you like."

"Is Carson all right with what is happening? He seemed a bit shaky when I spoke to him."

"He's nervous, like all of us, but I'm sure that everything will work out. Tony is not going to mess up things for himself when he finally has what he wants. It's just a matter of getting through the lunch. Daddy and I don't want you or Dylan to worry. We'll be back before you know it, and tomorrow it's off to Disney World, so try to smile and not show it if you're worried."

Nodding, Miranda hugged Juliet fiercely, savoring the few seconds of contact. That had been her habit, since the day Juliet had come home with Donald, and had introduced herself, not as Mummy, but as Juliet. Miranda was then six years old, a grave and solemn child, very caring and watchful of her younger brother. Old enough to remember being abandoned by her mother, she had grown wary of any adult female who was not a nanny or a housekeeper. Sitting down in one of the straight backed chairs in the sitting room, Juliet had held out her arms, motioning to the child to climb into her lap. Donald had gently pushed her and whispered in her ear as she dragged her feet across the room.

Miranda had approached the chair, looking straight ahead, but seeing very little. She stopped in front of Juliet, and looked up into her face. Up close, she saw a young girl, with a very beautiful face. Juliet had smiled at her and had held out her arms again. Drawn closer by something she did not understand, Miranda climbed up into her lap, and allowed herself to be hugged, strongly and fiercely, the smell of lavender helping to engrave the moment in her memory forever. As her arms had found their way around Juliet's neck, she had felt a lump in her throat. Struck dumb for an instant, she had recovered, and still holding Juliet tightly, had whispered in her ear,"Are you going to stay here, with us and with Daddy?"

The single word, "Yes," had changed her life forever. In an instant, she had acquired a mother, a new set of grandparents, and a week later, a new baby brother. Surrounded by a woman's love and affection, Miranda lost her grave demeanor, and learned to laugh and to be a little girl. With the strength of Juliet's love at her back, she grew daring and even courageous, testing the limits of her self.

Now, at almost fifteen, she was lingering on the border between adolescence and young womanhood, that time when maturity happens almost overnight. As she sat back in her chair, Juliet looked at her daughter's face. When she had married Donald, Miranda had resembled her mother, with the same hair and eyes. Now, nine years later, her face had changed, taken on the form of what it would be when she reached adulthood. Her face had refined itself, honing out what had reminded her father and grandfather of that perpetually bored look that even photographs taken of Delia had captured, and bringing forth instead the intensely alive features of Fiona Macallister.

*   *   *   *   *

"How do I look?" Juliet turned around and looked at her husband. The blue blazer, white collared sport shirt, and pale blue slacks make him look younger, about the same age as when she had painted his portrait.

"Wonderful. Too good for Tony." Leaning forward, she brushed his lips, her lavender scent following her movements. Turning away, she twirled in front of the mirror one more time. The pale blue linen dress fit perfectly, and she had left her hair down, tucked behind her ears with a headband. She wore no jewelry, except her wedding rings, a square Cartier watch, and a simple gold bracelet, the first gift he had ever given her.

"You look beautiful, up to expectations." Donald stood behind her and wrapped his arms around her waist. "I wish that we didn't have to do this." He took a deep breath of her scent, almost as if seeking its protection.

"We have to, and anyway, once the custody hearing takes place we may not have much of a choice. Better to ease into it now." She leaned her head against his shoulder.

Sighing, he moved away and opened the door for her. Silently, she walked through and down the corridor, back straight, head held high, holding her breath against her fears.

CHAPTER SEVENTEEN

"Dad, we should go now. I want to get there first and scout out the territory." Tony, wearing a white golf shirt, gray slacks and black loafers, paced back and forth impatiently across the living room in his parents' hotel suite.

"Tony, what do you think is going to happen during this lunch?" Jordan took his wallet off the top of the dresser and put it in his pocket.

"You figure it out, Dad. Try using your imagination."

"Tony, if you're planning to do something such as taking the boy by force, if I were you I wouldn't even consider it. I can guarantee that Donald will have private detectives stationed around the hotel to insure nothing like that happens." Jordan pushed his feet into polished brown loafers, and checked himself in the mirror. Smiling, he noted that his gray hair made him look very much the grandfather, a reality that he enjoyed.

Tony reached into his pocket and took out the court papers he was planning to serve on his ex-wife. He had finally succeeded in getting a court date for the first week of January.

"What are those papers?" Jordan's heart sank into his shoes.

"What do you think they are? I can't afford to let her keep him any longer. The older he gets, the less chance I have to establish a relationship with him." Jordan gritted his teeth.

"You're whining, something I find revolting in a grown man. What kind of a relationship do you think you will have with him if you take him away from his mother and the man he looks on as his father? Do you actually imagine that he will suddenly realize that Macallister is not a good father, and decide that you are the absolutely ideal parent?"

"And, of course, you'd be the first to make sure of that, wouldn't you?"

"You should have told me about the hearing. I just finished telling them that it hadn't gotten on the calendar yet. I don't like to be made into a liar." Jordan had put his hands in his pockets, clenching his fists, searching for the control that was rapidly vanishing.

"Why would you think that would matter to me? You've spent the past nine months sucking up to my ex-wife and being with my son. After January 7th, everything is going to be on my side of this. Carson is going to be living with me and only me." From where he was standing, Jordan could see Tony's face reflected in the mirror. The combination of malevolence and triumph made the older man's stomach turn.

"Why don't you just talk to the boy and try to gain his trust? That's what you want, isn't it? That's a much easier way to accomplish what you want than going to court."

"Let me give you a piece of advice, Dad. Whatever I decide to do about my son is my business, and you'd be a lot better off if you'd remember that." Jordan's stomach felt the sinking feeling that always spelled trouble.

"Are you threatening me, Tony? Because if you are, be assured that you have chosen the wrong person to try to intimidate. Now, I'm going to fetch your mother and Laurel so that we can get going. My piece of advice to you is to calm down, and behave yourself today. Nothing will be accomplished if you lose your temper." Infuriated, Jordan turned on his heel and left the room.

Smiling to himself, Tony followed slowly, allowing his imagination to play out his favorite scenario. His son, on seeing him for the first time, would declare his love, and insist on going home to live with his Daddy. His mental pictures then switched to a Little League game, his son the star player. At that point, the images always faded, only to resurface as a sort of instant replay, a video tape on a loop, doomed to repeat the same images over and over. No matter how many times Tony indulged himself in this replay, he never tired of it, nor did he ever cease to imagine the moment when he would possess his son.

He had never understood the reality of fatherhood, the sacrifices, the need for unending patience and love, the deeper relationships that come between a man and his children. In his mind, his son was a prize, a trophy to be flaunted. Carson's humanity, in all of its dimensions, would remain forever foreign, unreachable and inexplicable to Tony, as foreign, unreachable and inexplicable as had been that of the boy's mother.

*   *   *   *   *

The restaurant at the Marriott had windows facing both the pool and the ocean. The Granistons were the first to arrive, and thinking that they had the choice of tables in the dining room, walked around trying to choose the best one. As the hostess approached, Tony turned to point out their choice. Apologetically, she showed them to the large round table strategically placed so that any activity taking place there could be seen from every part of the restaurant.

"Mr. Macallister telephoned yesterday, Mr. Graniston and specifically requested this table. And I'm very sorry, but all the other tables are already reserved, so I'm afraid that this is it." The unmistakable look of fury on Tony's face gave her a few anxious moments, as she pulled out Emily's chair and motioned to the busboy to fill the water glasses.

"I'll send your waiter over to take your drink orders in a minute. Enjoy your meal." Backing up, she walked away quickly, breathing a sigh of relief as she rounded the corner.

"Excuse me, I'm Donald Macallister, and we have a reservation for lunch." She turned and smiled, her welcoming gestures automatic. Grabbing the seven menus for the table, she walked towards the table.

"The other members of your party are already here, sir. I know it's probably none of my business, but one of them, the younger man, is in a very bad mood. In fact, I found him rather intimidating." She fingered the menus, her fingers making a slapping sound as the plastic folders fell against each other.

"It's all right. My wife and I are used to his behavior, and I will personally guarantee the furniture and the crockery." A small smile played around his mouth.

Juliet held Carson's hand, walking a step or two behind her husband. As they neared the table, she leaned over and spoke to him. Stroking his hair, she whispered a small joke, trying to break the tension that had been building since they had pulled away from the house.

"Now remember, be polite, no matter what. If Tony gets out of hand, we'll leave immediately. Now, go over and kiss your grandparents, and then introduce yourself to Tony. I'll be right here if you need me." Her hand lingered, holding his for a second longer, as if trying to pass her courage on to him. Raising his head, he looked into her eyes, peaceful tawny pools. He relaxed and let go of her hand. Speeding up, he passed Donald and waved, an impish grin on his face. As he approached the table, he slowed imperceptibly, taking in the four people at the table. His grandparents he knew and trusted. The other man, who looked a lot like him must be Tony, and the other woman, his stepmother, Laurel.

Jordan had not been watching the door, but had been deep in conversation with Emily and Laurel. Suddenly, he felt a tug on his sleeve, and as he looked down, Carson planted a kiss on his cheek.

"Grandpa Jordan, Merry Christmas! Grandma Emily, the same to you." Suddenly shy, he stepped within the circle of his grandfather's arm, and turned to face Tony.

"I'm Carson, how do you do?" Extending his hand, he waited for Tony to shake it. After half a minute, when there was no response, he let it fall to his side. Unsure of what to do next, he stood next to his grandfather, his hand creeping into Jordan's.

"You're supposed to call me Daddy, and kiss me." Ignoring the pain in his ankle from the well-placed kick administered by his wife, he stared at his son. The boy looked exactly as he had at that age, sturdy, dark haired, with an obviously happy nature and he could see traces of an impish sense of humor.

"Tony, you can hardly expect that kind of familiarity when Carson has never seen you before." Juliet's voice brought him back to reality.

"The boy doesn't have any manners, anyone can see that. I'm his father, whether any of you like it or not." Juliet could see the beads of sweat forming on his forehead.

"That is besides the point. You're a complete stranger as far as he's concerned, so I think that in this case, you're the one without the manners." Donald kept his temper on a tight rein. "I think that we should sit down and order some food. Carson, remember you're sitting between Jordan and Tony." As if this were something he did every day, Donald picked up a menu and pretended to study it, seeing nothing, every nerve ending jangling as he heard his son making conversation with his grandfather.

"Tell me, what did you get for Christmas?" Jordan's eyes twinkled as he teased his grandson.

"Besides a new baby sister? Two new cars for my train set, a couple of those kits to make aeroplanes, some Star Wars figures, some books, and a new suit for Isabel's christening. Oh, and a steamship ticket for Easter holidays, we're going on a Mediterranean cruise, all of us, even the baby. And some other things, a stocking full of candy and oranges, clothes, and a woodworking set from Miranda and Dylan."

"That's quite a haul. There's more stuff for you out in the car from your grandmother and myself. And I think that Tony and Laurel have a gift for you as well."

Carson chewed his lip and turned to talk to Tony. Unsure of the new set of rules, and not wanting to sit in silence, with Tony staring at him, he took a breath and began.

"Mummy told me that I have three sisters. How old are they?"

"The twins are four, and the baby is almost a year old. And they're your half-sisters, better than Miranda and Dylan, anyway, they aren't your brother and sister at all." Shocked at the venom of the answer, Carson shrank away, and looked pleadingly at his mother.

"Carson, if you have to go, now is the time to do it. I'll order you a hamburger and fried potatoes." Donald smiled at his son, his heart aching for his pain. Nodding, the boy got out of his chair and disappeared around the corner, followed discreetly by one of the detectives.

"Now look here, Tony. The boy is only nine years old, and this is all very painful for him. He's trying very hard to meet you half way, and you aren't making it any easier." Closing the menu, Donald sat back in his seat, calm, powerful, pretending he was negotiating a very difficult business deal.

"No, you look. That boy is my son, and I insist that he call me Daddy and show appropriate affection towards me. It all goes to how unfit your wife is as a mother, that she can't even get him to treat his father with respect." Tony's moment had arrived. He reached into his pocket and threw the court papers across the table.

"What are those?" Donald reached out and picked up the envelope.

"What do you think they are? On January 7th, everything is going to change. This time, Carson is going to be going home with me." Tony tossed back a second double vodka, the alcohol fueling the simmering rage from the previous four glasses he had consumed in the hotel room. The others sat in silence, stunned at the meeting's rapid degeneration.

Carson's soft step had not been noticed by anyone. He had been about to slide back into his seat when he had heard Tony's outburst. Inexperienced in the ways of hate or evil, he held his tongue and said nothing.

"Carson, darling, we're going now. Kiss Grandpa Jordan and Grandma Emily good-bye." Juliet got out of her seat and walked around the table. A few seconds later, flanked by five bodyguards, the Macallisters crossed the dining room and left the building.

*   *   *   *   *

"I'm so sorry that I have to interrupt your holidays, Scott. But it seems I don't have much of a choice." Donald took a swallow of tea while waiting for the other man to answer.

"Don't be ridiculous. This is the reason you are paying me that incredibly generous retainer. And we really don't have much time to waste. The seventh is only ten days away. When can you come back to New York to prepare for the hearing?" Scott unscrewed his fountain pen and pulled a pad towards him.

"We're planning on taking the children to Disney World for a few days before we go back. Isabel is being christened on the second."

"That gives me a little time to prepare the briefs I have to submit to the court. Let's see, Monday is the second, the day I go to Hartford to see the judge. Can you have Juliet in New York on the third? That will give us four days to prepare, although I don't think we'll need that much time. And Donald, you'll have to produce Carson at some point during the hearing. The judge will want to talk to him and don't worry, it's all pretty standard procedure."

"What about Miranda and Dylan? Do they need to be there?" Donald couldn't help the anxiety in his voice.

"How old are they?"

"Sixteen and thirteen."

"They should be there, not all the time, but certainly when I am examining your wife. It looks very good to a judge to see all the children sitting in the front row. When Tony crosses her, you can take them outside to wait."

"Isn't there anything you can do to stop this whole thing before it gets out of control?"

"I'm truly sorry, Donald. But even someone like Tony Graniston is entitled to his day in court. Despite the fact that he signed the termination of custody, the fact that he is Carson's biological father gives him a chance to try and reverse it. Put yourself in his place, if this were your child you would be moving heaven and earth to get a chance to be with him, I might add for all the right reasons."

"That doesn't exactly make me feel any better. The next major thing I want you to do is to start proceedings to recover the money. He broke the contract he signed, and now I want him to suffer the consequences."

"I was about to suggest that myself. I'll file the papers on Monday morning, before I go up to Hartford. That way we can bring that into the case if necessary. Try not to worry too much about the hearing. It doesn't help to build up the tension and stress beforehand. Neither of you have done anything wrong, and you should keep telling yourselves that."

"Thank you. We'll see you in New York on the third. We'll need another hotel this time. No use giving him any advantage. I'll call you and let you know." Donald heard the reply and then the click of the disconnect. He leaned back in his chair and closed his eyes. His mind moved past the hearing to the aftermath. If it went badly, he would have to be able to take Carson and hide him away immediately after the verdict, before anyone could move to take the child away.

"Father, nice to hear your voice. Look, I need you to come to New York after the New Year. Tony's gotten himself a custody hearing on the seventh and I want to prepare for every eventuality." He listened to the simple question.

"Prepare a list of countries where we don't have any interests. We'll talk again when you arrive. Have a good New Year. I will." Donald stared at the telephone. He still had to call Juliet's parents. Not a call he was looking forward to placing.

"Donald, shall I call Mummy and Daddy? Save you the pain?" She sat down in a chair next to his.

"Would you? I don't think I could face another call like the one I had with my father. He's terribly upset about all of this."

"I understand. My parents aren't going to be celebrating either. When do you want them in New York?" She reached across and picked up the telephone.

"The day after Isabel's christening. We can all fly together. Easier all around." He leaned back and closed his eyes, waiting for her to finish.

*　　*　　*　　*　　*

The ride back to Miami was silent, Jordan driving with Emily beside him. Neither one could bear to be the one to break the silence. Tony sat in the back with Laurel, who sat as far away from her husband as possible against the door on her side of the car. Any further, she thought, and I'll be on the outside looking in. Jordan swallowed another antacid, his third in less than half an hour. Sourly, he weighed the risk factor of escaping from all of this without an ulcer.

"If it were any more silent in here, I could be in the morgue." Tony belched and looked at his wife.

"What do want me to say? That I liked what you did in there, that I think you're a hero? Guess what, Tony. I didn't like what you did. It was sneaky and underhanded, and it certainly didn't win any prizes from your son. Can't you get it through your head? You won't get him to talk to you if you behave the way you did today. He may be only nine, but he's not stupid."

"Shut up, Laurel. This time I know what I'm doing, she won't be able to get out of this one by telling the judge what I did to her. This hearing is solely about parenting. Well, I'm a parent. I have a beautiful home, three children and a pretty wife. That makes me about even with Macallister, doesn't it?"

"Tony, you're drunker than I thought if you think that you can ever be on the same level as Donald Lord Macallister. He holds a title that is about three hundred years old. When his father dies, he will be an earl. Surprise, when your father passes on, you will still only be Tony Graniston. Sorry, Jordan, that didn't come out right."

"No, Laurel, you're absolutely right. When I die, Tony will get very little. He was supposed to get the law firm as his inheritance. As of now, he's no longer in line for that, so I guess you're right. He will still be the same wonderful person he is now." Ouch, that should hurt him more than it did me.

"There are other law firms, Dad, or hadn't you noticed, and when I'm ready, I'll get a job in one of them." So glad you think so, son. My congratulations in advance if you do. Jordan stared straight ahead, concentrating on the traffic.

*   *   *   *   *

"I christen thee Isabel Fiona Macallister, and command all evil spirits to depart forthwith." The ancient Scotch Presbyterian ritual was over. Smiling broadly, Donald retrieved his daughter from the arms of her godmother. Juliet, standing nearby, looked lovingly at her daughter. Unconsciously, she fingered the pearl necklace, made of the nineteen enormous pearls she had received as gifts during her pregnancy. They lay creamy against her neck, just above the line of her suit, black wool with a thin cream stripe. Always the watchful parent, she gazed over the crowd, picking out her other three children, assuring herself of their safety.

Donald, holding his daughter, stood next to his father, relaxing during a break from the House of Lords. Full of pride, he watched his grandchildren as they were put through their paces by the guests in the church.

"I never realized it before, but Miranda looks just like your mother. I always thought she looked like Delia, used to give me a turn every time I looked at her, but now it seems that she has matured, the right way I might add. Juliet looks radiant, actually exquisite would be a better word."

"Yes, she does look incredible, doesn't she? Now it's time to go to lunch, and that means everyone, especially Isabel. Can you take the others and Juliet's parents? We'll go alone so that she can feed the baby on the way."

Nodding, Carson walked over to the small cluster of children and adults and shepherded them all out of the door.

* * * * *

"Tony, this Bob Davis. Just wanted to let you know that your ex-wife and her family arrived in New York this afternoon. We haven't found the hotel where they are staying yet, but we will. Call me back if you have any questions." Tony listened to the beep ending the message, and then played it back three more times.

* * * * *

"Brilliant idea to let Vivian book the room on her credit card, darling. We just have to be careful not to run up any charges here that can be traced, and to take the underground when we go anywhere." Donald lay stretched out on the bed.

"The Waldorf Towers is lovely. I understand the President stays here when he is in town." Juliet dropped the information booklet back onto the glass coffee table.

"Why don't we have some tea and sandwiches? It's going to be a long time until dinner, and Scott is on his way over here."

"Good idea. The children must be starving. Shall we do the tourist thing tonight and go to Chinatown? One can hardly expect Tony's detective to follow us there." Juliet played with the baseball hat she had been using to hide her hair.

"Good idea. Why don't you call Vivian now and have her find a good place. She and Paul can meet us there."

"Donald, shame on you. Can you picture Paul in Chinatown? We'll all be in blue jeans, and he'll come in one of his tweed confections. I suppose Vivian might be able to force him into the present. I've never been able to do it." Laughing, she picked up the telephone and made two calls.

*   *   *   *   *

"Well, that does it. Juliet, you're ready for anything Tony can throw at you."

Scott Barnes leaned back against the sofa, his hands behind his head.

"I can't wait for tomorrow to be over." Juliet stood by the window, looking out onto Park Avenue.

"This could last for two or three days. Be prepared. Tony will try very hard to rake you over the coals and rattle you. Whatever he does, don't lose your temper, and try not to let it show if he gets to you." She flashed him a glance and turned back to the window. Donald looked at Scott and shrugged his shoulders. This would be the longest week of his life.

*   *   *   *   *

"Tony Graniston for the plaintiff, your Honor." Cold sober, but longing for a few shots of vodka, Tony looked every inch the lawyer in his black suit. On his side of the courtroom, Laurel sat alone, two seats away from Tony's only witness.

"Scott Barnes, Felder and Felder for the defendant, your Honor." The side of the courtroom behind the defense table was filled. The row at the very back of the defendant's side was filled with reporters, all of whom sat quietly, pads and pens at the ready,.

The Honorable Thomas Woolrich looked first at the plaintiff's side, and then at the defendant's, duly noting the emptiness of Tony's side of the room. Peering over his half glasses, he looked carefully at the defendant. Dressed quietly in a black suit with a white silk blouse, her hair in a bun, Juliet could almost have passed for a woman who was ordinary. Almost, but not quite. No matter what she does, she will always stand out in a crowd. The judge pondered for a moment what that must mean to her husband and children. And what that must have meant to her when she was married to Tony Graniston. Sighing, he rapped his gavel and cleared his throat.

"Are both of you ready to begin?" Both men leapt to their feet, assuring the judge that they were definitely ready to begin.

"Call Dr. Marvin Anderson." Tony's first witness, the quiet, unassuming man sitting in the same row as Laurel, came forward to take the stand.

"Dr. Anderson, please tell us about your professional qualifications." Tony hovered a bit too close to the witness box.

"I am a psychiatrist affiliated with the Yale University School of Medicine. I attended Harvard University and Yale Medical School. I am a member in good standing of the American Psychiatric Association and the American Medical Association. At present, I am a contributor to the American Journal of Psychiatry." The witness straightened his tie and moved his shoulders, waiting for the next question.

"Tell me, doctor, are you familiar with the case currently before the court?"

"Yes, the plaintiff consulted me several months ago."

"In reference to what, doctor?"

"What if any psychological damages could be present in a child brought up in a home without the biological father. There was also a discussion as to whether a woman who was, shall we say, not a full-time mother could do an adequate job raising a child."

"Objection. No basis in established fact, your Honor." Scott managed to sound as bored as possible, a direct contrast to how hard Tony was working to appear in control of his case.

"Sustained."

"I'll rephrase, your Honor. Doctor, did the plaintiff ever give you specific details as to why he was consulting you?"

"Yes, he did. Specifically, he wanted to know if his absence from the home for nine years would have any effect on his relationship with the boy. I had to answer yes, of course there was an effect. He was the missing person in the child's life."

"Objection. Sheer conjecture."

"Sustained. Wrap this up, counselor. You're starting to waste the court's time."

"Your Honor, this has a real basis in fact. The plaintiff did not know of the boy's existence for the first nine years of his life. We consider that a great detriment."

"So noted. Now get on with it. We don't have all day." God help me, he's whining and floundering. How do I always get stuck with the whiners?

"What specifically did you recommend to the plaintiff?"

"That he should do whatever he had to do to become a part of the child's life. If not, the child could suffer real harm at not having an emotional tie to the biological parent."

"Objection. No basis in fact presented." Scott stifled a yawn.

"Sustained. Tell me, Mr. Graniston, are you going to finish with the good doctor before the lunch break?" Donald looked at his watch. It was 9:45.

"No more questions. Your witness."

Scott walked slowly towards the witness box."Tell me, doctor, what is your affiliation with the Yale Medical School?"

"I lecture there on occasion."

"How many occasions might that be?"

"Twice."

"Twice. Doesn't that strike you as rather strange. You attended the medical school, shouldn't you be a big·part of things that go on there?"

290

"Objection."

"He opened the door, your Honor."

"Overruled."

"I was, for years. My practice demands all of my attention right now."

"I see. And what kind of practice do you have?

"I consult many parents like the plaintiff."

"In plain English, doctor, you try to help people get custody of their children. Is that correct?"

"Yes, in so many words."

"Do you ever treat the children involved?"

"Oh, no. I'm not a child psychologist."

"Please tell the court then how you are able to testify as to the effect on children if you do not treat them in your practice?"

"Objection. Badgering."

"Mr. Barnes, you've made your point. Move on." Tony sat down, a smug look on his face.

"How many cases a year do you testify in?"

"I don't know, maybe fifty."

"Isn't the total closer to a hundred and twenty?"

"Perhaps. What does that have to do with my testimony here today?"

"Good question. Is it not true that in the majority of the 120 cases you testified in late year, you testified for the plaintiff, and that most of the plaintiffs were fathers?"

"Yes, that's true."

"And is it also not true that were it not for your testimony, those cases would have been unsupportable in court?"

"I wouldn't know. I'm not a lawyer." Smiling at his own joke, Dr. Anderson sat back in his seat.

"Dr. Anderson, did the plaintiff discuss with you the fact that the child lives in a home with two parents?" Scott delivered the question almost as an afterthought.

"Objection."

"Don't even go there, Mr. Graniston. Overruled. You may continue, Mr. Barnes."

"Well, yes, he did mention it in passing."

"I see. Would it surprise you to know that Donald Macallister is a loving and involved parent, and is the legal father of the child?"

"No, it wouldn't. The plaintiff did discuss his former wife's husband."

"And what did he say?"

"That he was very worried that the boy was being influenced against him by his step-father. And that he was very anxious to repair whatever damage had been done."

"Just one last question, Dr. Anderson. Did you meet with the child before today's hearing?"

"No, I didn't feel it was necessary."

"No more questions."

"Call Tony Graniston to the stand. Your Honor, Laurel Graniston will read the prepared questions for the plaintiff." Laurel approached the witness box, carrying a thick, yellow pad. Juliet allowed herself a tentative smile. So far, things appeared to be going her way.

"Mr. Graniston, when did you learn of the existence of the minor child, Carson Macallister?"

"When my ex-wife, his mother, appeared at my parent's house in Greenwich, Connecticut to ask for help."

"And what kind of help did she ask for?"

"Her son was dying of leukemia and needed a bone marrow transplant. It was at that moment that she revealed that he was in fact my biological son, and that most likely, I would be a perfect donor match."

"And did you donate your marrow to your son?"

"Yes, I did." Scott smiled. Gotcha, you lying bastard.

"And after that, how many meetings, if any, were you allowed with your son?"

"Only one."

"And when was that?"

"Last week."

"And what happened during that meeting?"

"The boy refused to call me Daddy or show appropriate affection, or gratitude towards me for saving his life. After that, the Macallisters left the restaurant."

"Mr. Graniston, what plans have you made for including your son in your life?

"We, my wife and I, have fixed up a room at home for him. I bought him a baseball glove and a new bicycle, just a few things to make him feel at home. We're hoping to take a camping vacation out West this summer, just the three of us." Laurel bit her lip. That last sentence was not part of what they had rehearsed.

"How have your other children taken the news that they have an older brother?"

"The older girls, they're twins, are thrilled that they will have a big brother. The youngest is only a year old, but we're sure she'll grow to love Carson."

"How do you feel about the fact that your first wife kept his existence a secret?"

"That's why I filed the custody suit. I feel that I have a right to be a parent to Carson, just the same as she has."

"How did she react when you announced that you were filing for custody?"

"She and her husband were furious. They swore that I would never get my hands on their child."

"Objection. Hearsay." You absolute pig. I can't wait to rip you apart on the stand.

"Sustained."

"Nothing further, your Honor."

Thomas Woolrich smiled as he leaned over the bench. "Your witness, Mr. Barnes."

"Good morning, Mr. Graniston." Tony nodded, and gritted his teeth. Cross examination was always the worst part.

Scott drew blood the first time out. "Mr. Graniston, what were the terms of the agreement you signed when you promised to donate your bone marrow?"

"What agreement would that be?" Tony stalled for time.

"This agreement, Mr. Graniston. Defense exhibit 'A', your Honor." Scott handed one copy to Tony and one to the judge.

"Please read from pages one, three and four, the highlighted passages."

"The undersigned donor agrees to accept the sum of three million dollars in exchange for the following promises: he will not attempt to visit, telephone or write to Carson Macallister III, nor will he attempt to sue for custody. He will, at the given moment, and should he prove to be a matched donor, donate his bone marrow to above said child, Carson Macallister III. He will, with all possible speed, return the signed and notarized copy of the agreement finalizing his divorce from Juliet Sadler Graniston."

"And the next passage, on page three?"

"If he does break this agreement, he will have to repay Donald Macallister the sum of three million dollars plus any appreciated interest at the prime rate."

"And on page four, is that your signature, Mr. Graniston?" Scott stood next to the witness box, forceful, yet completely relaxed.

"Answer the question, Mr. Graniston. The clock is ticking."

"Yes, that's my signature. But I was drunk, I didn't know what I was signing."

"Really. Tell me, how long did it take you after Edward Carstairs, Lord Donald's President of American Operations, dropped you onto a bed at the Plaza Hotel, to have an amusement delivered to your room?" You stupid, arrogant bastard. I have you now.

"I don't know what you're talking about." Tony floundered.

"This entertainment, Mr. Graniston. Exhibit 'B', your Honor, a detective's report, and a photograph of the young lady who knocked on his door at 2:00 in the afternoon. Now, please answer the question."

"About twenty minutes. I wasn't ready to go to sleep yet."

"On four vodka martinis on an empty stomach? I congratulate you on your fortitude."

"Objection, your Honor. Argumentative."

"Sustained. Mr. Barnes, you know better."

"I apologize, your Honor. Now, Mr. Graniston, you testified that you only learned of your son's existence when your former wife appeared on your parents' doorstep. Is that correct?"

"Yes. That's right."

"Is it not true that nine years ago, you were made aware that your wife was expecting your child? Did you not receive a letter from David Graham, your former wife's attorney, telling you that she was pregnant?"

"Yes, I did."

"And is it not also true that you immediately consulted one of your law professors as to the best course of action to take?"

Tony began to sweat. "Yes, I did."

"And why did you do that? Wouldn't it have made more sense to acknowledge your child then? Perhaps Countess Macallister might even have been willing to share custody of the child."

"I felt it was impossible that the child could have been mine."

"Any why was that?"

"It seemed too convenient."

"I see. And what did you do next?"

"I filed a termination of parental rights."

"For the record, your Honor. A termination means exactly that, that there are no rights or responsibilities remaining for anyone who signs such a termination."

"Objection. Counsel is testifying."

"Don't try my patience any further, Mr. Graniston. Overruled. You may continue, Mr. Barnes."

"Now, Mr. Graniston, let us travel back to last summer, the week of July 20th. Where were you then?"

"I don't remember."

"Don't you? Defense three and four, your Honor. A copy of a passenger list of British Airways flight 201, and a copy of the defendant's immigration declaration for the date of July 20th."

"Now, let's do this again. Where were you the week of July 20th last year?"

"In London."

"Only in London?"

"Yes."

"How long did you stay in London?"

"I don't really remember."

"Please instruct the witness to answer the question, your Honor."

"How long did you stay in London, Mr. Graniston. And you will answer."

"A few days."

"Defense five and six, your Honor. Copies of the registry at Claridge's hotel, and the American Express charge for one night's stay."

"Did you change hotels in London, Mr. Graniston?"

"No."

"Well, then, did you sleep in Hyde Park? Where were you until you got back on the plane two days later?" Scott had raised his voice, just enough so that it thundered across the hushed courtroom.

"I was in Surrey and then on Jersey."

"And what were you doing there?"

"Trying to see my son. I wanted to get to know him, maybe even take him home with me." There was an outraged buzz from the defendant's side of the room.

"Did your former wife give you any indication that she would relinquish custody of the boy to you?"

"No. I never even saw the boy."

"And why was that, Mr. Graniston?"

"Macallister and my father had gotten him off the island."

"I see. And what reason did they give you when you arrived at the home of the Macallisters?"

"That I had no right to see the boy. That I had signed away the right to do that when I accepted the money. And it wasn't fair. All I wanted was to see my son and be a father to him."

"Objection, your Honor. Plaintiff is grandstanding."

"That's a new one, Mr. Barnes. I'll accept being irrelevant." Scott nodded and turned back to Tony.

"What happened when you arrived at Longueville Manor?"

"I told Macallister I wanted to see my son and that I wouldn't leave until I had."

"And what happened then?"

"He called the police and had me thrown out. They put me on a plane for London and New York."

"Is it not true that you threatened bodily harm to the defendant if you did not get to see your son? And is it not also true that DCI Symonds was prepared to arrest you for that?" Tony shook his head.

"Please instruct the witness to answer."

"Mr. Graniston, whatever the embarrassment, answer the question."

"Yes, I did. But I wasn't serious."

"Is that a fact?" Scott murmured as he turned towards the defense table.

"Objection."

"Mr. Barnes, no sniping in my courtroom. You're about to cross the line."

"I'm sorry, your Honor. Now, Mr. Graniston, let's talk about last June. Is it not true that you hired a Chicago detective agency to follow your former wife and your son? And is it not also true that these detectives attempted to gather information as to when she and the boy would be at their vacation home in France?"

"I didn't know what else to do. Every thing I did, they were one step ahead of me. I just wanted to see my son."

"Is it not true that in the back of your mind was the possibility that if you knew when they would be out of England that you could, how should I say, snatch your son away and bring him back to the U.S.? Is it not true that you knew that it would be next to impossible for your former wife to retrieve the boy once you had entered the United States with him?"

"That's a lie. I never thought about that."

"Come now, think again, Mr. Graniston. I can call witnesses who will testify that you did contemplate the possibility of simply taking your son."

"You mean my father? That's an unprejudiced witness."

"Objection. Plaintiff seeks to impugn credibility of a potential witness."

"Mr. Graniston, be very careful. What you did might just land you in my personal pokey on a contempt charge. I hope you have a toothbrush with you. Once more and you are my guest for the next seven days. Continue, Mr. Barnes."

"Nothing further. Thank you, your Honor. Defense is finished for now. We reserve the right to recall at a later time." Trembling and dying for a drink, Tony walked back to the plaintiff's table and sat down.

"Call your next witness, Mr. Graniston."

"Plaintiff rests, your Honor."

"Your Honor, move to dismiss."

"On what grounds?"

"Failure to provide proof of complaint."

"Denied. Step back and call your first witness."

* * * * *

"Darling, you were brilliant up there. So calm and composed I shouldn't wonder if the judge fell in love with you." Donald picked up his sandwich.

"I felt that way. I hope it will last this afternoon when Tony gets up there."

"He'll be very careful. He daren't go for you. It would only show what an absolute rat he is."

"Mummy, he's right. You were wonderful. I'm only sorry we can't stay with you this afternoon. I'd like to see Tony try anything." Dylan took a bite of his hamburger.

"Thank you for all your kind words. This afternoon I shall face the lion with only Vivian and Paul with me. All the others are instructed by our barrister to take the afternoon off. Grandpa has planned an activity for all of you, and we'll meet back at the courthouse at about three."

* * * * *

"We're back in session now, and, Countess, if you'll take the stand again, Mr. Graniston can begin his cross examination."

"Yes, of course. I'm ready." Juliet settled herself in the witness box, using the sides as a shield against any contact with Tony.

"Back when you were just plain Juliet, how old were you when you met your former husband?"

"Eighteen."

"And when you married, how old were you, and how old was he?"

"Eighteen, and he was twenty-three." This is ridiculous. He knows very well how old we were.

"And was the marriage a happy one?" Careful, this is a trick question.

"It was like most new marriages. There were a lot of adjustments to make."

"And what were those adjustments?"

"Objection. Leading the witness."

"Sustained."

"I'll rephrase. Did you love your husband while you were married?"

"Yes, I did. Very much. He was the most important thing in the world, at least in the beginning."

"And when did you fall out of love with him?"

"I never said I did. He began to stay out until all hours of the night, and several times he came home with alcohol on his breath and lipstick smeared all over his face. It made me very unhappy that try as I might, I couldn't seem to make him happy."

"And how long did the marriage last?"

"All told, about six months."

"What happened towards the end of the marriage?"

"It seemed as if the problems we had had were gone. He came home on time every night. We began to build a relationship, or so I was led to believe."

"Who filed for divorce, Countess?"

"I did. It was quite obvious that once my husband had gone back to America, that I would never see him again."

"And before that last day, did you and your husband have relations?"

"Yes, we did. Every night."

"Was the sex ever spontaneous?"

"By that, do you mean did we ever neglect to use birth control? No, we never did. I was afraid to get pregnant too soon. I wanted to be sure the marriage was on a sound footing before I had a child."

"When did you discover you were pregnant?"

"About three months after my husband left for America. We were divorced by then."

"Were you surprised at your pregnancy?"

"Extremely."

"How long did it take before you began to see other men after your husband left for the United States?"

"Objection."

"Sustained. Keep on track, Mr. Graniston."

"No other men, Countess? Think carefully before you answer. Is it not true that immediately on your husband's departure, you began an affair with another man?"

"No, it is not true."

"Objection, your Honor. This is ridiculous. Counsel is attempting to lose his own case. This line of questioning is totally besides the point."

"Sustained. This is the last time I will speak to you. Once more, Mr. Graniston and my bailiff is going to hand you a toothbrush and escort you downstairs for a cooling off period. Now stick to the point." God help me, I may not make it to the end of this hearing.

"Let me rephrase. Is there anything else you would like to tell the court now about your behavior after the divorce?" Tony's face, angry and full of hate, stayed about three inches away from Juliet's.

"When I discovered I was pregnant, my solicitor wrote to my former husband, informing him of the pregnancy."

"And what did he reply?"

"He filed to terminate his parental rights, and wrote a letter stating that the child could not possibly be his."

"And why would that be, Countess?"

"Objection. Relevance."

"No, I want to answer the question properly, please. I think we can clear up this problem quickly if I am allowed to answer." Scott smiled, his signal loud and clear.

"Good. Now tell the court about the affair that took place in the days after your husband left for the United States."

"There was no affair. I was in hospital in the critical care unit for two, no, three weeks after he left England. After that, I couldn't bear to look at another man until my husband, Donald, came to my studio at the Slade Art School." Tony was silent, suddenly aware of how he had put the noose around his neck.

"Mr. Graniston, aren't you going to ask her what happened?" Struck dumb, Tony could only shake his head. The judge sighed and turned towards the witness box.

"Well, then I'll ask her. How did you wind up in the hospital for a month, Countess?"

"My husband put me there. Before he left, he beat me savagely, and then raped and assaulted me. The whole time he was calling me a worthless piece of shit and telling me he was going to make me so ugly that no other man would want me."

"So when you discovered you were pregnant, it must have been very upsetting to you."

"Oh, no, far from it. I wanted that baby more than anything in the world, your Honor. He was the only clean thing to come out of the whole sordid nightmare. He's one of the most wonderful things that has ever happened to my husband and myself." The judge wheeled around and put his glasses back on.

"You can go and sit down now, Countess. Counsel in my chambers. Countess, you may join us if you wish. We'll have a short recess."

*   *   *   *   *

"Wow. Juliet, I can't believe how you testified up there, right in front of Tony." Vivian paced the hallway outside the courtroom.

"I was rather amazed myself. But the judge was very kind and sympathetic. It wasn't nearly as hard as I thought it would be." She looked at her watch. It was almost three o'clock. Behind her she heard determined footsteps.

"You were magnificent. The judge has just spent the last hour chewing Tony's arms, legs, whatever. He wants to see Carson in half an hour, and then he'll decide. He promised me a decision before five. I think we're home free."

"Does that mean Carson will never have to see Tony again?"

"I don't know. I think that supervised visitation, that is he will be able to see Carson as long as a social worker is in the room, will be all the judge will allow. What we have to watch is that this doesn't become a habit, with him running from judge to judge, until he gets a verdict that suits him."

*   *   *   *   *

"Carson, I'm going to leave you now. Just walk through that door and the judge will be waiting." Scott ruffled the boy's dark hair.

"Tony won't be in there, will he?"

"No, he's being kept away until the judge finishes talking to you." Carson nodded and pushed the door open.

"Come in, young man. Sit down right here next to my desk so that we can talk."

"How do you do, sir. My name is Carson Macallister III, but all my friends call me Car Three."

"How did you get that name?"

"My grandfather is Carson the first. It helps to know which one of us is in for it." Carson settled into the seat.

"I'm supposed to talk to you to find out what you want to do about your biological father. Do you know what that means?"

"Tony made me."

"That's right. Tell me, Carson, how do you feel about Tony?"

"He frightens me. I don't think he likes me very much. The only time I saw him he said mean things about Miranda and Dylan, and about my mother."

"I think I understand. You know why you're here, don't you?"

"Yes. You have to decide whether or not I have to go and live with Tony and Laurel."

"Do you think that if you tried once more to meet with him, that things might go better?"

"I don't know. What I do know is that I don't want to leave my mother and father and my brother and sisters. They're my only family." The judge sighed, and stood up behind his desk.

"You can leave now, if you like. If you go through the door behind my desk, a police officer will take you to your mother."

"Thank you. Please, don't send me to live with Tony. I couldn't bear it." The judge nodded as Carson left the room.

CHAPTER EIGHTEEN

"All rise. Court is back in session. I have reached a decision in the matter of Graniston v. Macallister. I am prepared, for the moment, to ignore the legal implications of the willful disregard for the true facts in this case exhibited by the plaintiff. I am not, however, that amenable in the matter of the minor child, Carson Macallister III. It is obvious from all the documentation I have received, that the boy is far better served to be left where he is. I direct that he is to be returned to his mother permanently. She is and will remain the primary custodial parent. As far as temporary visitation is concerned, I find that even the presence of a social worker would not create an atmosphere conducive to the proper conduct of the plaintiff. I will, however, leave it to the judgment and good sense of the child's mother to determine whether or not there is to be another meeting where the child's father can finally get it right. Court is adjourned."

*　　*　　*　　*　　*

"Champagne, Donald and lots of it. We all have a great deal to celebrate." Carson sat at the head of the long table.

"Father, for once I agree. I haven't felt this good since Juliet and I got married for the second time."

"Don't be too relaxed. They'll be on you for another one of those family get-togethers, I think that's what the Americans call it."

"An inescapable fact of life, I'm afraid. He may not have custody, but I imagine we'll have to suffer through at least one more meeting with him, so that if there is a next time we can tell the judge that we tried.

And of course, there is the suit to get the money back."

"If I were Jordan, I'd sit back and let him take the consequences of his foolishness. I wouldn't want anything to interfere with my ability to see Car III. I can't imagine what it must be like, being the parent of a monster like Tony. Now enough gloom, we have things to celebrate."

At the opposite end of the table, Bertram Sadler sat surrounded by his three grandchildren.

"Here's to a good term at school, and a wonderful Easter holiday." He lifted his glass to each one in turn.

*   *   *   *   *

"It's good to be home again. This place is looking better and better." Jordan dropped his bag by the front door.

"It's so quiet here, as still as if no one really lives here." Emily riffled through the pile of mail on the center table. She looked around, feeling dull and empty, as if everything inside had been sucked out by a huge emotional vacuum cleaner. For the first time, she acknowledged that the long journey she had begun only ten short months before had led to a place she had never considered. Until now, she had accepted everything that had been put in front of her, willing herself not to be judgmental, struggling to adopt a wait and see attitude. Now she had waited, and seen things she had never imagined would happen.

"Why don't I boil some water and you can make some of that tea Juliet gave us. Maybe that will make us feel better." Jordan felt as if he had aged ten years in two days. He had spent months being torn apart, first by loyalty to the son he didn't really know or like, and love for the grandson who had come to him like a gift from the Almighty. On the drive home, he had turned his mind back to the beginning of his journey, from the moment that Juliet had appeared on the doorstep, and followed it over time to the verdict in the courtroom. It only made him feel more tired.

"I'll take the bags upstairs. I'll be down in a few minutes, and then we'll have that tea." Emily nodded as she watched him climb the stairs, at once so familiar and strange at the same time. He crept up the stairs, rather than his usual quick pace. She turned away, unable to watch him suffer as he climbed, step by step.

*   *   *   *   *

"Well, I hope you're satisfied now." Laurel stood by the kitchen table, watching her husband make a sandwich.

"It's not over yet. I can still get my father to beg her to let me see him again, just one more time." He layered the ham and turkey in a three inch high mass, and put the sandwich on a plate. Swiftly cutting it in half, he grabbed the plate and a beer and sat down at the kitchen table.

"What makes you think he'll ever do anything like that for you again?"

"Because he's my father, and because he believes in love and trust and all that stuff. Right now, I have to keep my nose clean and play the sorrowful and hopeful father." She could hear the noisy slurps as he drank the beer directly from the can.

"All of this makes no sense. She doesn't want you, the boy doesn't want you. Why don't you just leave them and move on?"

"Because he's mine. I made him, and I'm entitled to have him. It's as simple as that." He wiped his mouth on a napkin and put his plate in the sink.

*   *   *   *   *

"Thank you for calling, Scott. Just keep me informed as to the court date. My best to your family as well." Donald hung up the phone and stretched his legs out so that his feet were propped on the desk. Closing his eyes, he listened to the silence, a silence that meant he had no more meetings for the day, a silence that meant he could leave for home at any time. He hadn't felt so relaxed and optimistic since the day Carson had left the hospital. Now at the end of what he privately called his "troubles" he had only to wait for the civil suit against Tony Graniston. All things being equal, he would be able to do what he had promised his wife he would accomplish. Knock Tony down so hard that he would never be able to get up again.

*   *   *   *   *

"I don't believe it. How could he do this? That money is mine. I earned every cent with every drop of my bone marrow." Tony held the notice informing him that he was being sued by Donald Macallister. It was just one more piece of lousy, rotten luck. He should have taken that money and disappeared, started a whole new life as a whole new person. Instead, he had stayed and whatever he had done had turned out to be a loser. Without hesitation, he did what he had done all his life when he was in trouble. He picked up the telephone and called his father.

"Dad, it's Tony. How are you? We haven't heard from you and Mom in a while."

"Since yesterday? So, tell me, what has gone wrong this time?"

"Since you ask, Macallister is suing me for the three million plus interest."

"Does it surprise you?"

"Are you eating something? I can hear crunching."

"Another antacid. I think I'm getting an ulcer. What is it that you expect me to do about this lawsuit?"

"Can't you talk to them, get him to drop it? What am I going to live on if I have to return the money?" Jordan clenched his teeth in an effort to control his temper.

"You should have thought of that before you sued for custody. You did promise certain things and you didn't keep your promise. Now you have to pay the piper."

"Please, Dad. Arrange a meeting so I can apologize and show them I'm not so terrible after all."

"Why I believe you is beyond me, but yes, I'll ask Juliet if she'll agree to see you."

"And the boy. So I can apologize to him, too."

"I'll ask. Don't expect miracles."

*　　*　　*　　*　　*

"Jordan, how nice to hear your voice. How are Emily and Jennifer?" Juliet cradled the phone against her ear while she mixed a silvery blue paint.

"They're very well, thank you. And all of you are keeping well? Marina and Lindsey wanted to be remembered to your three."

"How nice. Jordan, I'm sure that you didn't call just to inquire after the health of all the Macallisters, so what is it that I can help you with? I'm sorry if I seem a bit rude, but I'm mixing paints and working on a canvas."

"Tony called. They served him with Donald's lawsuit papers. He's rather upset about having to fight to keep the money. And before you say he should have known better, save your breath. I already said that and a lot more. He wants another meeting, he says to apologize for suing for custody, or whatever he thinks he can get away with. I told him I'd ask."

"I'm sorry for you. It must be so difficult to be the go-between. I'm not optimistic, but I'll talk to Donald. If not, we'll see all of you this summer for the usual visit, July in Surrey?" Dipping her finger into the paint, she held it up to the light to check the tint.

"We'll look forward to it. Let me know when you can. Thank you, Juliet."

* * * * *

"No, absolutely not. I will not put you or Carson through that again."

"Donald, please. What harm can he do now? We have the bodyguards and the power to crush him any time we please. I think that we can afford to help Jordan a bit and have another one of those lunches."

"All right, if you want to do this, we'll do it. Carson is ours forever. We can afford to be generous. Tell him we'll be in Florida for half-term."

* * * * *

"Why does this feel like instant replay?"

"Because it is. Three months ago, I stood here in the driveway insisting on pizza and champagne." She tapped her foot on the driveway and crossed her arms over her chest.

"At this rate, I don't think we'll ever see the inside of a Florida restaurant."

"Of course we will. Tomorrow for lunch with Jordan and company. Donald…" The warmth of her breath mingled with her perfume. "Donald, why are you keeping me waiting?"

"All the more to have fun, little Red Riding Hood."

*   *   *   *   *

The mid-winter Florida sun showed its usual warmth. Donald sat near the pool, watching Juliet and the children swimming laps. He sipped his iced tea and marveled at the almost instantaneous change of mood, from the depressing cold and rain of England to the sun and warmth of Florida.

"Aren't you coming in? We've only got a few days left. Bring Isabel in and we can give her a swimming lesson."

"I'm waiting for a call from Jordan. Afterwards, I'll join you, if you aren't too shriveled by then." He ducked to avoid a huge splash of water.

"We'll be waiting for you." Dylan laughed and dove underwater.

*   *   *   *   *

The doorman at the Fort Lauderdale Marriott opened the door of the Jaguar and gave Juliet his hand. She stood in the driveway and waited for her husband and son. In spite of the heat of the day, she shivered involuntarily.

"Cold? Here, I'll warm you up." Donald put his arm around her shoulder.

"No, not cold. Just a scary moment. It's the same hotel as last time. Let's hope the outcome will be different." There was no answer, just an embrace when he held her closer to his heart.

*   *   *   *   *

Jordan sat in an armchair in his Miami hotel room, watching his son pacing back and forth. Both men were dressed and ready, both were waiting for their wives. Automatically, Jordan hunted around in his pocket for the roll of antacids, and popped one into his mouth.

"You should lay off that stuff, Dad. It'll rot your stomach." Jordan watched him continue to pace, the second time around, same hotel, same situation, same problem. So much restless energy could mean only one thing. He wondered how many double vodkas Tony had consumed before he had come into the room.

"So tell me, what are you going to tell Juliet and Donald today?" As the last word left his mouth, the father could see the anger boiling over in the son.

"Whatever I have to so that I can keep the money he paid me."

"Sincerely, I hope."

"When have you known me not to grovel sincerely, Dad?" The tone of resentment in his voice grew louder.

"Just don't drink too much. For once, I would like all of us to eat the food we order when we go out for a meal with them."

"Sure, Dad, this time I promise it will be different."

*   *   *   *   *

"Grandpa Jordan, how are you?" Carson gave his grandfather a hug and a kiss, then turned to his

313

grandmother and gave her the same. He faced Tony, for once sitting quietly, with a smile on his face, and shook his outstretched hand.

"How are you, Carson? Enjoying your vacation?"

"Yes, thank you. I love the sun. England is very cold at this time of year." Tony could feel the boy's eyes, watching every move he made. He gulped the double vodka and raised his hand to order another one.

Their attempts at awkward conversation faded away as the food was served and the two families began to eat. Twenty minutes went by without a word, both Donald and Jordan watching Tony, now on his second beer. Carson was sitting between them, the same as the last time.

"I think you should begin saying whatever it is that you want to say to them. Lunch is almost over and you are going to lose your opportunity." Tony stared at his father through red-rimmed eyes as the older man whispered in his ear.

"Donald, I'd like to apologize for breaking the agreement. As it turned out, I could have saved myself the effort." Tony, you're drunk. Why does that not surprise me? And that isn't much of an apology, either.

"And Carson, I wish I had chosen to just get to know you instead of what happened."

"Tony, that was very pretty. I wish that I could believe you." Donald's eyes had turned cold.

"You don't really have a choice, do you Macallister? Just like I don't have a choice. I pay you the money you gave me, my family winds up in the street. I take you to court to get my son back, I lose again. He should have been sent to live with me. I made him, he's my son." Carson began to push his chair back slowly.

"Do you hear me? No matter what you do or say, he'll always be mine." Donald could feel the entire experience falling slowly to pieces. He was half out of his chair, ready to leave when Tony turned towards the boy.

"Carson, I am your father, and I insist that you call me Daddy." Tony, now so drunk that he no longer cared what he said or whom he offended, leaned towards the boy, his face filled with hate and anger.

Goaded by the look he saw on Tony's face, Carson had had enough. "You're not my Daddy. You never will be. The judge said so. A Daddy is supposed to love his child, and he isn't supposed to ask for money to save his child's life, either."

It happened almost before anyone had a chance to react. Tony's arm came up and flew through the air. The sound of the slap as it connected with the side of Carson's face reverberated in waves around the table. Tears welled up in the child's eyes as the pain traveled across his face.

"You little bastard. That's what you are, you know. I always knew you weren't really my child, that's why I never wanted anything to do with you. I don't care if she denies it in court a hundred times, your mother couldn't wait to get into another man's bed. I wonder which one of us was really your father." The last word out of Tony's mouth was enough for Donald. Heedless of the plates and glasses on the table, he leaped across it and threw himself on top of Tony, punching his face with every ounce of strength he possessed. In the distance, he could hear Carson screaming for his mother, and Juliet calling for the bodyguards.

"You son of a bitch. And here I thought that things were going so well. You wanted to apologize. That's right, say you're sorry, and then strike an innocent child. And don't go running to the judge to complain about this, because I have ten witnesses who will swear that you behaved like a drunken pig. I can't wait for the trial, so I can squeeze you for every single cent of that three million dollars." Out of breath, he continued hitting Tony until Val Lenox and the three other detectives pulled him away.

"Lord Donald, enough, he's drunk. Let's go, before the police arrive." Pulling on his arm, Val led him away from the table.

"Where are Juliet and Carson?" Donald paused to wrap his hand in a napkin.

"He was crying. Her Grace waited until I got there and then took him outside. She was trembling and shaking. Don't worry about anything here, we'll take care of it. Take your family home, and we will be outside on the property in about an hour and a half." Val hovered, as ever polite and attentive.

"Make sure that you and the guards cooperate fully with the police. Tell them that I will be more than happy to talk to them later today or tomorrow morning. Explain that I need some time to calm things down at home." His face grim, he turned and walked away towards the lobby.

As Donald had reached the front of the hotel, he found his wife and son, weeping and huddled together on a bench in a corner near the front door. Looking up at the sound of his shoes on the marble floor, Juliet had caught sight of his bandaged hand. Smiling weakly, she had tried to stand up, but Carson had wrapped himself around her, as a vine would wrap itself around a tree, and would not let go. Bending down, Donald gently pried him loose and carried him out to the car.

"Are you all right, Daddy? Tony didn't hurt you, did he?"

"No, son, I think that this time, I got a few good ones in."

"Did it feel good?"

"After listening to the hurtful things he said, and after he slapped you, each one felt wonderful, even if your mother may not approve. Carson, don't mention anything about how it felt to hit him in front of Mummy, please. She's very upset and I don't want to make it worse." Carson put his arms around his father.

"I love you, Daddy. Please, please don't ever make me do this again." Donald just held him close and kissed his cheek. When the car arrived, he opened the back door, and motioned Carson to climb in. That accomplished, he looked around at his wife. Her eyes were stricken, the same way that they had been the first time they had met. Gently, he put his hand under her chin and brought her head up.

"It's all over. I'm alive, and for once, Tony is the one who is the worse for wear. Please don't cry anymore. Darling, don't make me feel guilty for defending my son, it isn't fair." He used his good hand to retrieve his handkerchief and wiped her eyes gently.

"I'm not trying to do that, I'm so terrified that I can't help myself. I'm so proud of you, I'm ashamed to admit that when you were hitting him, I was hoping that you would do some serious damage." She smiled and looked into his eyes.

"And to think I told Carson not to ask me about how good it felt to hit him in front of you, bloodthirsty woman. Now, let's go back to Palm Beach. How about if we rent some videos for the children, order in spicy, fattening food and go to bed as soon as we decently can." Wincing, he took the keys from his pocket.

"Wicked, that's what you are, wicked. I think that before we go to bed, we should wait for the police to call. Whatever would they think if they found us in bed and not sleeping." Smiling a slow smile, she brushed his lips with hers, and got into the car.

"Sheer envy. That's what they would think."

"Donald, wait, please." Emily stood on the steps of the hotel.

"Emily, there is nothing left to say." Donald walked around the car and opened the driver's side door.

"You can't mean that. Jordan and I are attached to Carson, he's so proud of his grandson, please don't do this." Her eyes were pleading, more strongly than her words.

"Emily, at the risk of sounding slightly crazy, I just beat your drunken son senseless because he struck his son and then called him 'a little bastard.' Correct me if I'm wrong, but was I under the mistaken impression that this was supposed to be the time that Tony apologized for what he has done? It's obvious that he is not only a drunkard, but an abusive one at that. Tell Jordan I will speak to him in a few days when things have calmed down. Now, if you will excuse me, I have to get Juliet and Carson home. They've had quite enough for one day." Donald gunned the engine and shot out of the turnaround, leaving Emily on the front steps, weeping inconsolably.

*   *   *   *   *

Tony remained under the table, drunk and snoring, unaware of anything going on around him. Disgusted, Laurel had tried to kick him awake, and failing that, had announced that she would wait in the lobby. Ten minutes later, an unmarked police car and the ambulance arrived at the scene. Jordan stood to the side and watched the ambulance technicians treat Tony's face. Shocked and nauseated by everything that had happened, he popped another antacid and

318

listened with half an ear as his son cursed the paramedics as they tried to treat his facial cuts and bruises.

"Sir, your son will have to go to the hospital. He's still too drunk to cooperate with his treatment, and some of those cuts should be seen by a plastic surgeon. If it's all right with the police, we'll take him over to the emergency room at Northridge, and you can meet him there later." Turning, he helped his partner strap Tony onto a gurney, packed his bag, and after checking with the detective in charge, followed his partner and the gurney out to the truck.

"Mr. Graniston? I'm Detective Paul Morales, Fort Lauderdale Police Department. I was wondering if you could tell me what happened here today?" Looking at the older man, Paul couldn't help a feeling of pity.

"Of course, what would you like to know?" Jordan allowed the detective to initiate and carry the conversation along.

"For starters, how did your son get beaten up?"

"Believe it or not, detective, my son got exactly what was coming to him. I'm only sorry that I didn't think of it first." Raising an eyebrow, Paul waited for him to continue. He shifted position, leaning on his left leg for support. At six feet, two inches, he was every bit the policeman. Dressed in what his wife, Linda, loved to call his Mambo Kings outfit, red collared short sleeved shirt and dark blue jacket and jeans he looked anything but a highly decorated police officer.

Paul's change in position had not gone unnoticed. The right leg, damaged in a drug bust, had never healed properly, and standing grew painful if he did not move around. Referred to as a stubborn burro by his wife, Paul had refused to put in for disability, preferring to run two miles each day to build up his leg, and studiously ignoring the pain for the rest of the time.

"Can we sit down? It's been a long day, and we are all exhausted." Jordan found two chairs and sat in one of them. Paul sank down gratefully into the other and turned to face the other man.

"Tell me about the others who were here today." Paul took out his pad and flipped to an open page.

"There's my wife, Emily, and our son, Tony and his wife, Laurel. The others were Donald Lord Macallister, his wife, Countess Juliet, and their son, Carson."

"Sounds like a nice family outing. What happened?"

"Maybe I should begin at the beginning. Juliet Macallister is my son's former wife. Carson, the boy, is Tony's son. Let us say that the end of their marriage was not a happy one, and that none of us knew about the boy, or the marriage, for that matter, until ten months ago. She appeared on my doorstep one day, desperate to find a bone marrow donor for the boy. He had leukemia, final stages. Tony was a perfect match, but there were problems. The end result was that Macallister had to pay him three million dollars to donate his marrow. My son was overjoyed to discover that he had a son, filed for custody of the boy, and lost. He signed a contract promising not to sue for custody, and now Macallister is suing him to get the money back. Today Tony was supposed to apologize to Macallister and the boy."

"I see. So how did it all go wrong?"

"Detective, my son is an angry and frustrated person, has been all his life. He just couldn't handle losing the custody case. Coupled with the fact that he was dead drunk, it was a mix doomed to failure."

"What did the boy do?"

"Nothing, until the very end. He was very polite, a perfectly behaved child."

"What happened then?"

"Tony demanded that Carson kiss him and call him Daddy. I think that was the last straw. The boy stared him down."

"What did he say?"

"That Tony wasn't his father, and never would be. That a Daddy was supposed to love his child, not ask for money to save his life."

"What happened after that?"

"Tony slapped him across the face and called him a little bastard, said that he was sure that he wasn't the boy's father, that his mother had slept with other men. It was just horrible. After that, Macallister leapt across the table and pounded him until his bodyguards pulled him off. They're over there, at the corner table, waiting to talk to you."

"I see. Where is Macallister now?" Paul turned to a fresh page.

"Juliet and Carson were hysterical. He took them back to his house in Palm Beach, but he told the bodyguards and me that he would be at home waiting to talk to you whenever you wanted."

"You stated that your son was drunk, sir. How many drinks did he consume?"

"Here, two double vodkas on the rocks and two beers. Before here, I have no idea. You can ask his wife, she may know."

"Does your son get drunk often?"

"Not for the past ten months. Before that I believe he indulged on a regular basis."

"Every week, every day, how often?"

"Closer to every day, I believe."

"You don't like your son much, do you, sir?"

"No, detective, I do not. I'm stuck with him."

"I'll need to talk to your wife and daughter-in-law and I'll do it right away so that you can go over to Northridge." Paul maintained eye contact, his hands moving independently, closing his pad and putting the pen away.

"Thank you. I'll send them over to talk to you."

*   *   *   *   *

Tony lay on a gurney in the emergency room, waiting, it seemed to him endlessly, for a doctor.

"Nurse, am I going to have to stay here all night?" She turned as she hurried by.

"I'm sorry, sir, but we have a serious car accident ahead of you. As soon as a doctor is free, you're next." He shifted position, carefully avoiding any sudden movements. His head was throbbing, a sure sign of an approaching hangover, and he longed for a couple of shots of vodka.

"Mr. Graniston, I'm Dr. Cohen, and I'm going to look at your face."

"Took you long enough."

"Sorry, we don't run on a timer here. Serious cases come before everyone else. We had a car accident, three people were banged up pretty badly. Now, let's have a look." With an automatic gesture, the doctor pulled on a pair of surgical gloves.

"Well?"

"You have several wounds that need stitches, but it appears that there are several other things that need seeing to as well. Tell me, how long have you had this skin rash on your neck?" Before touching the skin, he turned his back on Tony and put on an extra pair of surgical gloves.

"A few months, it comes and goes. Why?" Tony winced as the gloved fingers poked and prodded.

"Could be a sign of something serious. Are you sexually active?" Now the fingers were probing his abdomen. Tony drew in a sharp breath as the gloves moved over his liver.

"I'm married." Tony gritted his teeth as the hands probed further down.

"That's not what I'm talking about." The fingers pulled delicately and then stopped, seeming to have found what they were looking for.

"Sure, what man wouldn't if given a chance." There was a sharp pain as the gloves dug and searched. Nausea danced across Tony's eyes.

"I see. I'm going to order some blood tests and get the plastic surgeon down here to look at your face. How long have you had the sores in your genital area?" Tony looked away.

"Not long, I think a day or two." The lie was written all over his face.

"Are you sure about that?" The fingers resumed their examination.

"Yes, I'm sure." Tony closed his eyes. His misery had become complete.

*　　*　　*　　*　　*

"Mrs. Graniston? I'm Dr. Cohen, your husband is under my care while he's in the emergency room."

"Is he all right? His face looked awful." Laurel looked up from her seat in the waiting room. For the moment, she was alone. She had sent Jordan and Emily to find the cafeteria, using the excuse of wanting a cup of coffee. Whatever the bad news was, she wanted to hear it alone.

"The plastic surgeon is working on him as we speak, but there are a few things I would like to discuss with you."

"Somehow, I don't like the sound of that."

"I'm sorry to have to give you bad news, but there isn't any way to avoid it. Your husband had some symptoms, and we ran a preliminary test. I'm afraid he has a venereal disease, syphilis, in fact." Laurel felt the room begin to shift.

"Excuse me, did you say syphilis?"

"Yes, unfortunately, I did. And I'm even more sorry to tell you that I have to test you as well, right now, to make sure that you don't have it. Do you have a skin rash, or any other unusual symptoms?"

"No, nothing."

"Any sores or other discomforts? And when was the last time you had intercourse?" Needing to keep his hands busy, he wrote on the chart in front of him.

"No, nothing like that. We made love a week ago, and we used a condom. I didn't want another child so soon after my third." Laurel felt a blush working its way up her neck, her discomfort at the questions passing across her face.

"Do you and your husband always use a condom with intercourse?" The blush grew deeper, along with Laurel's discomfiture.

"Yes, for years. Why do you ask?"

"It's a protection for a woman, if her partner has a sexually transmitted disease. It keeps the rate of infection down to almost nothing. Mrs. Graniston, I won't know anything, how far it's progressed, or what else is wrong with him until the rest of the blood work comes back. I'll put you in a room and send someone in to take a blood sample. It'll be a couple of hours before it comes back."

"You're sure, about the syphilis?"

"I'm sorry, but the test has no false positives, Mrs. Graniston. Unlike the people it screens, it doesn't know how to lie."

*   *   *   *   *

Laurel paced the length of the waiting room, up and down, and then across and back. Each time, she walked a perfect rectangle, always in the same direction. Her coffee sat on one of the little side tables, by now cold and curdled. Jordan and Emily sat in one of the corners, holding hands, shocked and silent.

"Why don't they come and tell us what's going on?" Hating herself for whining, Emily crossed and uncrossed her legs for what seemed like the fiftieth time.

"Because the tests haven't come back yet. I'm not in any hurry to hear the kind of news we're going to get." Jordan closed his eyes and leaned back in the molded plastic chair. He tried to think of something else, anything more pleasant than what he was about to hear.

"Mrs. Graniston?" Ben Cohen stood in the doorway, watching as both Emily and Laurel turned towards him.

"I have the tests back, on both you and your husband. Why don't we talk privately?" Paralyzed with fear, Laurel nodded and walked slowly across the room, her arms held stiffly at her sides, and her hands clenched into fists so hard that she could feel her nails biting into the flesh.

"First of all, you can exhale. Your test came back negative for syphilis."

"And Tony?" Her fear was gone now, replaced by bewilderment and anger.

"Positive. It's a pretty nasty strain that's working, and..."

"And what?" Her voice had sunk to a whisper.

"It's a peculiar kind of strain. We see it mostly in HIV patients."

"AIDS? Oh, God, not that. My daughters, what about my daughters?" He avoided looking directly into her face.

"We aren't absolutely sure yet. I ran a test, but it being Christmas week, everything is slow, so it won't be back until later tonight. How old are your children?"

"Five year old twins, and a ten month old."

"We'll have to take some blood from the baby, and from you, just to be sure."

"Does Tony know?"

"Not yet. He's sleeping off whatever it was that he drank today, but I'll talk to him when he wakes up." Laurel nodded and turned away.

*   *   *   *   *

"We're back, with ice cream and videos." Juliet walked through the living room towards the nursery. Checking that Isabel was still asleep, she walked out onto the patio, and leaned over the edge of the pool.

"You lot, we're back. Be careful you don't get all shriveled, like prunes."

Miranda surfaced first. Laughing, she swam across the pool and heaved herself over the side.

"That was quick. What happened, did Tony do one of his famous routines?"

"Worse than that. He slapped your brother and your father, how do you say it, knocked his lights out."

"Daddy punched Tony? How marvelous! I'm sorry I missed it. Did he do it properly?" Miranda's eyes danced.

"Oh, yes, that he did."

"What did Daddy do?" Dylan stood at the edge of the pool and reached for a towel.

326

"You won't believe it, Dylan. Tony slapped Carson, and Daddy punched his lights out." She didn't bother to hide the satisfaction in her voice.

"About time. He's too nice and patient. Glad he lost his temper for once."

"Complete sentences, darling, please. Your shorthanded speech is appalling. Did Isabel wake up?"Juliet handed Miranda a second towel.

"Yes, about an hour ago. I gave her a bottle, and burped her, too. Nanny was very proud of me. And, Dylan even changed her diaper. How do you like that?"

"Very much. Darlings, Carson's upset about Tony and being slapped. He snuffled all the way home, so I think he's in the mood for lots of sympathy. Try not to tease him too much for a few days. He's inside with Daddy, dishing up enormous loads of ice cream and toppings." Dylan grinned.

"Right. I promise to try not to throw him in the pool, and both of us will stay close to him for a while." He leaned over and kissed Juliet on the cheek. "Don't worry, Mummy. We adore him, and we won't let anything bad happen."

"Race you inside, I'm starving." Her towel wrapped around her waist, Miranda got a head start into the house.

CHAPTER NINETEEN

Juliet licked her fingers and washed down the stone crabs with a swallow of champagne.

"Much better than spicy, fattening food. I'd rather drown myself in ice cream, anyway." Looking across at her husband, she picked up his injured hand and kissed the palm.

"Ouch, don't touch, it's bruised. I hope it's not broken."

"It hasn't swelled or turned purple, so I think you're safe there. I'm just glad the skin wasn't broken."

"Why would you be worried about broken skin?"

"Because Tony's was all bloody, and one never knows what he's carrying around." She bit her lip and looked away.

"We'd have heard if there was a problem by now, wouldn't we?"

"Don't count on it. I think in this case the bad news may not travel as quickly as one thinks. Now, darling, eat up. I want my ice cream."

"You'll get fat. You won't like that." Ducking quickly, he watched the small lacy pillow sail over his head.

"Be careful. Remember how dangerous that is, and the police haven't been yet." Laughing, she leaned over and kissed him. Regretfully, he pulled away and looked at his watch, wishing that the police would get it over with, so that he could take his wife to bed.

"Donald, I'm going to have a bath. I'll have dessert later. Why don't you call the hotel and leave Jordan and Emily a message? I know you're angry, but, darling, none of this is really their fault. They were as shocked as the rest of us by Tony's behavior."

"All right, but don't take too long. Maybe we can still get to bed early."

*   *   *   *   *

The door to the cubicle in the emergency room at Northridge Hospital opened slowly. On the other side, Tony was now fully awake, with a pounding headache and longing for a drink. He watched the door open, waiting for a nurse to come in so that he could get an aspirin and something to drink before he went home.

"Mr. Graniston, I'm Detective Paul Morales, of the Fort Lauderdale Police Department, and I was wondering if you feel up to answering a few questions." Tony looked over and took in Paul's shirt and jacket, and closed his eyes.

"No, I don't mind. Have you arrested Macallister?"

"I haven't arrested anyone yet. The investigation of this incident is still ongoing. Why don't you tell me what happened in the restaurant?" Opening his pad, Paul stayed near the door, as far as he could get from the smell of stale alcohol.

"Today was supposed to be a visit with my son from a previous marriage. I didn't even know he existed until last year. My ex-wife came to New York to ask me to donate bone marrow to save his life."

"Did you?"

"Of course, what father wouldn't. We just had the first round of hearings. I'm suing for custody of the boy." Tony kept his eyes focused on the ceiling, not caring if his lies were believed or not.

"And the boy, how does he feel about all of this?" Paul's pen traveled across the page.

"He's badly behaved, a real little snot. He needs to show respect to his father. His mother doesn't discipline him enough."

"What led up to the beating?"

"The kid was fresh. I reminded him of the reality of his situation, he smart mouthed me back, and I smacked him a good one across the face. He had it coming. I made it clear that Macallister wasn't his real father, and I was, and then Macallister vaulted across the table and started pounding me." Paul snapped his pad shut and turned to leave.

"Mr. Graniston, I don't have any more questions right now, but you can give a true and accurate statement to a stenographer when you're feeling better. I'm sure that you will have it all straight in your mind by then." Before Tony had a chance to answer, the door had closed and the detective was gone. Now truly angry, he reached for the call button and pressed it.

"Mr. Graniston, how are you feeling?" Ben Cohen took out a pen and wrote on the chart, using the clipboard as a barrier between himself and Tony.

"Lousy. I have a headache and I need a drink, and not water."

"That won't be possible right now, but I can get you two Tylenol and a glass of water to wash them down. Mr. Graniston, I have a few things to discuss with you before we take you upstairs to a room."

"Upstairs, I'm not going upstairs. I'm getting dressed and leaving as soon as you're finished." Tony tried to swing his legs over the side of the gurney.

"I'm afraid not. That is one of the things that we have to discuss. First off, I ran some blood tests. You are suffering from a particularly nasty form of syphilis, and we want to treat you for a few days, and monitor how the antibiotics are working."

"Syphilis, that isn't possible."

"Oh, but it is. You have obviously engaged in risky sex, and you got caught. You do remember the answer you gave me outside, when I asked you if you engaged in extra-marital sex, and you answered, 'what man wouldn't?'"

"Does my wife know?"

"She had to be tested as well. Her test came back negative. But that's only the first part of the problem. Mr. Graniston, the type of syphilis that you have is normally found in patients who are either HIV positive, or who have full-blown AIDS. We ran an AIDS test, and found a very high level of antibodies that show that you are HIV positive." Tony began to laugh.

"That's rich, Dr. Cohen. For the past nine months, I have spent hours and a fortune trying to figure out how to get custody of my child. I don't have to any more. He's tied to me in a way that his mother will never be able to overcome."

"I don't understand."

"I gave the kid a bone marrow transplant ten months ago. Tell me, how long will it take before the kid is as sick as I am?" Ben Cohen swallowed his nausea at Tony's malicious amusement.

"That depends on when you were infected. I know that labs run very extensive tests before they allow a donation, so I would tend to say that even if you had been exposed before the transplant, it hadn't taken hold yet. If you like, I can arrange for the boy to be tested."

"By all means. His mother will be thrilled." The venom behind Tony's sneer could not be mistaken.

"I'll come by and see you in a few hours, after they hook you up to the antibiotics. And I'm afraid that alcohol is out of the question from now on, that is unless you want to ruin your liver completely." The door banged on his way out.

*   *   *   *   *

331

Donald sat in the living room, trying to concentrate on a book. In the other end of the house, he could hear his children laughing at one of the movies he had rented. From the nursery, he could hear Isabel cooing and getting ready for her next feeding. It was one of those times when his cup should have been running over with happiness, but instead an overpowering feeling of doom, a presentiment that something had gone terribly wrong, weighed him down. He got up to answer the telephone, grateful for the interruption.

"Mr. Macallister, my name is Dr. Benjamin Cohen, I'm treating Tony Graniston at Northridge Hospital. I was wondering if it would be possible for me to talk to you and your wife. It's a matter of some urgency."

"I really have no further interest in what happens to Mr. Graniston, Dr. Cohen. Please do not call here again."

"I don't think you understand my meaning. This is very serious, and yes, I believe that you do have an interest in this. Look, I live in Palm Beach, I'd be happy to come to your house on my way home and talk to you and your wife, say in an hour."

"Tell me, Dr. Cohen, have you made me an offer I can't refuse?" Ben laughed as he answered.

"Yes, I have, and please, call me Ben. I'll see you in an hour." Donald replaced the receiver thoughtfully, just as the doorbell rang.

"I'll get it, Daddy." Dylan came out of the kitchen, carrying a bowl of popcorn.

"No need. I have it. Go back to the movie, and please, keep Carson out of here for the next hour or so."

"Right. I'll say good night now, then. I'll make sure he goes straight to bed after the movie." Dylan hurried away, instinctively knowing that this was not the time to press his father.

"Yes, can I help you?" Donald looked out into the semi-darkness and saw a tall, slim, dark haired man dressed in clothes that he would have classified as attention getting.

"Donald Lord Macallister?" Paul consulted his pad to make sure he was addressing Donald correctly. "I'm Detective Paul Morales of the Fort Lauderdale Police Department. Can I come in?" Paul stood on the doorstep, assessing the man who stood facing him. Later that night, he would tell Linda that this lord was a serious hombre who dressed like a movie star from the 1930's.

"I've been expecting you. Please, come in, and you can drop the title, I only use it for formal occasions." Donald swung the door wide, smiling as the detective entered the house.

"My appearance here is obviously not a surprise." Paul smiled as he dug around for his pad and pen.

"No, my bodyguards told me that you were planning to come here. I've been waiting for you. Can I offer you something to drink? Soda, or tea?"

"Thank you, a soda would be very nice. And your wife, she's…?"

"Taking a bath. She's rather upset by all of this. Her history with her former husband is a very unhappy one. This meeting today began rather well, but it went downhill pretty quickly. Let's sit down while we talk." Donald had noticed Paul's pronounced limp.

"Tell me, how did you feel about your son's natural father being in the picture." Paul sighed inwardly as he sank into a chair.

"I wasn't overjoyed, but I was prepared to deal with the situation, provided Tony behaved himself. Today was a very bad day for that sort of thing." Donald moved around the bar, opening the refrigerator and pouring the soda.

"I understand that he slapped the boy for being fresh." He was determined, no matter how painful, to cover each and every item he had discussed with Jordan and Tony.

"According to my wife's former husband, I imagine. Detective, before that slap was administered, Tony said some terrible things to my son, and afterwards as well. He stood up to Tony, said he was not his father and never would be, that Daddy's were supposed to love their children, not ask for money to save their lives. Tony gave him a tremendous wallop after that, and then called him a bastard. He said some terrible things about my wife, as well. Being English, I took offense to that, and proceeded to give Tony a dose of his own medicine." Unconsciously, Donald tried to flex the bruised hand.

"Mr. Graniston did mention the transplant. He described his donation as routine, loving father to son." His pen poised above the paper, Paul wore his most neutral expression.

"He lied. I had to pay him three million dollars in order to get him to agree to it." Donald looked longingly at the bar, and the whiskey and soda set ups that were waiting.

"I see. Is there anything else you would like to tell me?"

"Just that when I paid him the money, he signed an agreement not to sue for custody. He broke that agreement, and lost at a hearing in January. Today was about apologizing and getting me to drop the lawsuit. I'm suing him to recover the money. And not because I need the money. Not at all. I want, no, that's not right, my wife and I want to make sure that he can't make a claim on her or our son ever again."

"That explains some of the anger. What about his relationship with your wife? Can you tell me anything about that?"

"Not without my wife's permission. She should be ready just about now." The bedroom door opened, and Juliet emerged, her hair still damp, wearing beige linen slacks and a matching shirt. Smiling, she came forward, her hand extended, a greeting on her lips.

Paul was speechless. He loved his wife and family, but he had never seen a woman as beautiful and innocent as Juliet Macallister. Everything about her radiated purity of heart and spirit, and in an instant, he understood every subtlety working in the case. At last, he forced himself back to duty, and rose, his hand extended, personal warmth covering his lapse.

"Mrs. Macallister, what can you tell me about your relationship with your former husband, namely what else did he have to agree to in order to get his three million dollars?" He had maneuvered himself so that he was sitting directly opposite Juliet and Donald.

"You've been working very hard, Detective Morales. Donald paid him the money for two reasons, one was to donate bone marrow to our son, and the other was to finally sign our divorce papers. He never signed the originals, and as both of us had subsequently remarried, we were bigamists. I didn't care, at that time Donald and I had no children of our own. Tony had twin girls, and another on the way. It must have been very traumatic for his wife. And since I know what your next question will be, he didn't sign the papers originally because he hoped to extort a few thousand pounds from my father. His plan didn't work because the secretary at the solicitor's office never looked closely enough to see that the papers hadn't been signed." Donald squeezed her shoulder as she put her hand up to cover his.

"Tell me about your marriage. What was it like?"

"Miserable. It lasted for five months. Our parting was, how shall I put it, less than cordial. I was assaulted, in the most revolting way imaginable, by my own husband, who then emptied our checking account and went home to America. Carson was conceived during that assault."

"And you kept the baby?"

"Of all the participants in this sordid episode, Detective, my child was an innocent. I've always believed that all life is innocent, and that evil is unspeakable. Even being brushed by it makes me feel ill, unclean." She shuddered as she shrank into the sofa.

Mesmerized by her voice, and her lavender scent, Paul found himself envying Donald Macallister. He wondered what it must be like, loving and being married to someone so innocent. Every day he dealt with evil in all its forms, and the consequences it created. Tonight was the first time in his life he had been confronted by the opposite. From a policeman's point of view, it was a miracle that complete innocence even existed.

"Mr. Macallister, we won't be pressing charges. No jury would convict a father who defended his child against a drunken bully, not in a million years. I'll save the taxpayers some money and close the case. I imagine you won't be pressing charges, either."

"No, we won't. We're going to enjoy the last few days of our holiday and then go back to England. By the end of the week, my hand will be healed, and this whole affair will pass into history, as well it should."

"Got a few bruises?" Paul prepared to wrap up the interview. He made a show of putting away his pen and pad.

"Badges of honor, my wife tells me." Donald grinned as he winked at his wife.

"Your son, how did he take all of this?" The pad was away, a sure sign that whatever was discussed was personal and off the record.

"As well as any nine year old would. The first meeting over Christmas was not a success. Tony served the papers for the custody hearing between the appetizer and the entree. But, he was willing to try this again. He's a brave little person, doing that, standing up to an adult like Tony." Paul rose and shook Donald's hand.

"I'll see myself out." He nodded to Juliet and headed for the door, swallowing the thousand things he wanted to say to her, crushing his need to touch everything about her.

"I think you've made yet another conquest. Poor Morales, he was as uncomfortable as a sixteen year old in your mother's front parlor." Nuzzling her neck, his hand slipped inside her shirt.

"He did seem a bit preoccupied. Anyway, he's a married man, I saw the wedding ring. Donald, in a moment I'm going to do something very disgraceful, and poor Isabel will go hungry."

"If I grumble at being tormented by my wife, you'll have to excuse me. I expect you to do just whatever it is you have in mind later, after Isabel is fed, and our Dr. Benjamin Cohen pays us a visit."

"Who is he?"

"Tony's doctor. He just made me an offer I couldn't refuse. He should be here any minute, wants to talk to us." A force of will brought him back to the serious business ahead of them.

"Donald, do you remember what Edgar Davis said just before the transplant, about Tony's lifestyle and how he wasn't really the right donor." His jaw dropped.

"What are you getting at? That Tony has some awful disease, which was passed on to Carson?" Mute, she nodded, her throat so tight she could not speak.

Shocked into silence, he got up and walked across the room, and poured himself a brandy. As if he had moved out of the realm of reality, he watched as his hands shook, so badly that the brandy spilled over onto the table and the tiled floor. Grasping the glass with both hands, he swallowed the contents in one gulp. The burning fire of the brandy brought tears to his eyes and slowly began to deaden the shock. Looking up, he saw her moving across the floor, answering the baby's call. Starting after her, he was interrupted by the sound of the doorbell.

"I'm Ben Cohen, sir. May I come in?" Ben stood on the doorstep, coolly assessing the man standing in the doorway. The eyes gave it all away, he thought, as he realized that someone, at least, had made the connection. Donald looked at the instrument of his doom, a sandy haired, brown eyed man, about five feet eleven, in his mid thirties, wearing a kind and sympathetic face, the kind that all doctors seemed to wear when they had bad news to impart.

"Call me Donald, and yes, of course, we've been expecting you. My wife is just feeding the baby. It won't take too long, so why don't we just sit down and wait for her?" As always, Donald played the kind and caring host. He put fresh glasses of soda on a tray and brought them into the living room.

"How old is the baby?" Ben picked up a glass of soda and watched the man sitting across from him.

"She's four months old tomorrow. Isabel is a remarkably good baby. Never cries when she shouldn't and loves to be held and talked to. Just like her brother, Carson. Must be my wife's genes."

Donald drained one of the glasses on the tray, feeling as if his thirst could never be quenched.

"Who does she look like, if you know that already?"

"Lucky girl, she looks like my wife. Same red hair, and features, but with my eyes." Donald smiled, the brandy taking the edge off his fear. Relaxing, he put the empty glass back on the tray, no longer needing something to hold.

"Do you have any children?" Ben smiled at the thought of his two sons, freshly bathed and waiting for him to read them a bedtime story. Not for them the horror that might be waiting for Carson.

"Yes, Deborah and I have two boys and she's expecting again in about four months. It's a girl, and that should be it. She laughs when she tells me that I'm lucky that she works at home, otherwise our children wouldn't have any parents."

"Mine is the same. What does your wife work at, when she isn't chasing children?"

"She's an infectious disease specialist. I work in emergency medicine and I'm a surgeon as well. The two seem to work well together. Deborah publishes an online newsletter for physicians, world-wide, and when she isn't pregnant, she manages three days a week in the research lab."

"Interesting. Juliet is a painter, has a studio on top of the house. When she's working, it's usually twelve hour days."

"She's that Juliet Macallister? I love her work, can't afford it, but I've seen some in galleries in New York, before the sale. Her talent is amazing, I've never seen total innocence on a canvas before."

"Tell me, Dr. Cohen, are you taking my name in vain?" Ben's head swiveled around as he followed the sound of her voice. His mental jaw dropped as he watched her walk across the room.

"No, of course not. I would never do that. Please, call me Ben."

"Ben, short for Benjamin I imagine." Juliet smiled and sat down next to her husband.

"Yes, it is. My mother insisted that all of the Cohen boys had to have Biblical names."

"And how many are there?"

"Six, five doctors and one heretic, a lawyer. Aaron, Benjamin, Joshua, Reuben, Jacob and Jeremiah. And also Sarah, Rebecca and Leah. My parents believe in large families."

"Nine children and all superbly educated as well?" He could see her sense of humor as it crossed her face.

"Yes, all at Harvard. The dean once told my father that all the tuition he had paid over the years was enough to put a down payment on a dormitory all his own."

"Are your sisters doctors as well?"

"No, Sarah is an anthropologist teaching at Stanford, Rebecca is a writer and Leah owns her own business, a brokerage firm in New York."

"Holidays must be wonderful, all those children and grandchildren. My four seem to be puny compared to that." Juliet had run out of idle conversation, and the silence dragged painfully.

"Well, now to the real reason I'm here. There's no sense beating around the proverbial bush. Mr. Graniston is a very sick man, and he has a disease that is very contagious. I understand he donated bone marrow to your son, Carson, last year."

"What exactly does Tony have?" Filled with fear, Juliet's voice came as a whisper.

"First of all, he has a severe form of syphilis, which in itself is not so bad, because there are drugs that can kill it. The bad part is that this version is usually found in patients who are HIV positive, or who have full-blown AIDS. The fast test we ran on him shows that he has antibodies present. We did the more thorough follow up test and it shows that he is indeed HIV positive." Ben forced himself not to look away.

"Our oncologist told us that the laboratory that conducted the genetic test told him that Tony was a high risk donor. Apparently he was drunk when he presented himself for the test, and they found a high white cell count. We had to go ahead with the transplant, our son was dying, and we were out of time. We've been hoping for months that nothing would go wrong." Her voice wavered as the unthinkable, no longer academic, took a permanent place in her universe.

"I wouldn't get yourselves worked up just yet. There is a chance that the infection was so new that there wasn't any in the marrow, but just to be safe, I want to run an AIDS test on your son." Grateful for something to do, Ben opened his medical bag and organized the instruments of Carson's doom.

"Will you draw the blood now?" Donald surprised himself, his voice was calm and steady.

"If that's agreeable. It's early, and I can go to the lab and have them do the tests tomorrow, first thing." Weeping silently, Juliet nodded, her head bowed.

The power of speech had abandoned her, leaving her in touch with her rawest emotions, but with no way of expressing them. She could almost feel her soul screaming, locked in a room without a key, running from the clutches of evil, never being able to actually escape.

"I'll get him." Running on automatic pilot, Donald got up and went to the other side of the house, calling for Carson.

"Juliet, what will you do now? Your former husband has some other side effects from years of heavy drinking, his liver is pretty well shot, and with his other problems, I don't give him too long before end stage liver disease sets in."

"I hope he burns in whatever hell is reserved for people like him. You don't understand someone like Tony. In this country, people don't believe in evil, only in insanity that can be cured with a little pill. Where I come from, evil is a presence in one's life, something that has to be dealt with. When I met Tony, I had never confronted evil before. He has given me so much pain and fear and horror, that if it weren't for Carson, I would have killed myself years ago.

"When I found out I was pregnant, I was eighteen, an art student at the Slade, divorced, recovering from rape and sodomy committed by my husband. That baby was my salvation, it helped me to recover the innocence that Tony had stolen. When Donald came into my life, I was seven months pregnant, and all he could say was how much he loved me and my child and if I didn't marry him he would die. Poor man, I couldn't bear it for him to hold my hand or even touch me. For the first few months after we married, every time he made love to me, I would shudder and scream inside. It took three years before I could look at him and know in my heart that I loved him." Her tears ran down her face. She made no move to wipe them away.

"I thought it was something like that. Tony seems to hate you on the one hand, and still love you deeply on the other." He reached across the coffee table and put his hand over hers.

"Don't ever say that. Loving someone has a different set of rules than the ones ordinary people play by. For Tony, love is owning someone, possessing someone, and when he's tired of her, he throws her away. He's a man without a soul, with a heart of evil."

"Juliet, he's going to die very quickly. His liver won't last another year, not with what he's done to it." Her answer was put aside, as she heard her son crossing the tiled floor.

"Mummy, Daddy said I was to come in here and let the doctor take my blood. Am I sick?"

"No, darling. But it's been a while since you had one, and Tony seems to have an infection of some sort, and Dr. Cohen wants to make sure that he didn't give it to you with the transplant."

"I don't feel sick or anything. Do I have to?"

"Yes, you do. It won't hurt much and we can do it right now." Her hand went out to stroke his hair, trembling with fear as she patted his cheek.

"You must be Carson. I'm Dr. Cohen. I don't know if you've ever seen these before, but these are called butterfly needles, because they're so tiny, just right for tiny veins, like yours. I have green, red or purple. Which color would you like?"

"Green, please. Are you Tony's doctor?"

Ben looked up and into Carson's eyes. Brown, with the soul of innocence shining through. His heart clenched as he thought of what was to come if this child was carrying HIV and syphilis. Another innocent, another victim of evil to rest on his conscience. He sighed and drove the needle home.

"Yes, I'm Tony's doctor." Ben looked up at Juliet, waiting for a signal. None came.

"Is he very sick?" Carson watched his blood running into the tube.

"Yes, I'm afraid so."

"Did he give it to me?" Ben thought his heart would shatter.

343

"I doubt it, but I just want to make sure. That's why I took three bottles of blood, so I can make a lot of tests. I have a Star Wars band aid, if you'd like one."

"Yes, thank you, I would." Carson smiled as Ben put it on.

"You're very brave, Carson, just like a Jedi knight."

The child grinned, an impish look crossing his face. He kissed his parents and ran from the room.

"When will you know?" Ben could hear the barely controlled fear in her voice.

"Not for a few days. If you give me a contact number, I can call you as soon as I get the results back." Slowly, he repacked his bag, waiting for the inevitable question.

"What if they come back positive?" Donald held his courage tightly, afraid that it would vanish.

"I don't know. It could be anything from IV antibiotics to protease inhibitors, or it could be worse."

"Worse?"

"Children don't always follow the pattern that you find in adults. But we're really jumping too far ahead. Why don't we wait until the results come back before we get depressed?" To himself, Ben recited a small prayer, in Hebrew, the one his father had taught him to protect the innocent.

"Thank you for coming all the way here, and then going all the way back to the hospital." Polite as ever, Donald controlled the urge to run screaming from the house.

"Actually, I'm having the tests done here, in Palm Beach. I don't want anyone to know that I'm doing this. With everything that's going on, I don't want Tony to know, not right away. We'll speak in a few days." Ben nodded and walked away as the door closed softly behind him.

*   *   *   *   *

Shutting the bedroom door, Donald held her in his arms, feeling her entire body trembling with fear and despair. He could feel the warm wetness of her tears as she wept without a sound, not daring to allow the depth of her fear to surface. Having no words of comfort to give her, he buried his face in her hair, seeking his own solace from its scented softness.

"I can't bear it, Donald. Everywhere I turn, I see Tony's evil, reaching out those fingers to trap and harm my child. I doubt that I will ever feel safe again."

"Of course you will, you'll see. We have to try and carry on as if nothing is wrong. Tomorrow we'll go to the beach and then maybe drive to Miami. And after that, we'll go back to London. And once the children are back in school, life will pick up its own rhythm and we will go along with it. There is a very good chance that Carson will not have any illness at all, and we have to focus on that. Promise me you will try."

She nodded, and burrowed herself into his body. Her head was down, the tears splashing across her hands. Consumed by fear himself, all that Donald could offer her in the way of comfort was to stroke her back, and make promises that could prove impossible to keep.

CHAPTER TWENTY

Tony lay in bed, staring at the ceiling. He was in a regulation private room, with a window looking out over the parking lot. The walls were painted in a soft blue, and there were two Monet prints on the wall opposite his bed. On the right side of the bed, the antibiotics fighting his syphilis hung from a hook, and on the left was the standard hospital issue nightstand. A stack of books shared the space with a pitcher of water and a glass, a box of tissues, and a bottle of hand lotion. Laurel and his parents had brought the books and a dozen magazines as well, but he didn't have the strength or the will to lift one off the table. It seemed like an eternity since he had been admitted to the hospital's AIDS unit, and he had noticed with alarm that he was beginning to feel his physical weakness increase with each day that passed. The final set of blood tests had come back positive for HIV, syphilis and liver disease. When he was told that it was very likely that his liver disease would kill him before the AIDS did, he had found the knowledge bitterly amusing.

Caught between fury and desperation, Laurel had said very little. She made the daily obligatory visits, and talked to him, trying to avoid any discussion of what kind of future he could expect. Today, she had told him that she had rented a small house nearby, so that when he was released to outpatient care, they would have somewhere to live that was convenient to the hospital. Deeply depressed, Tony could do little more than shrug his shoulders.

Jordan and Emily had been shattered by the news, she more so than he. She had wept openly after the doctors had told them that their son could be dead within a year. The doctors had promised to do everything to fight the syphilis with antibiotics, but had held out little hope for the future.

Jordan had taken the news grimly, saying little to his wife, other than the most superficial words of comfort and sorrow. There was a curious emptiness when he thought of his son. He dug as deep as he could, and came up with very little. Not only did he feel as if Tony was already dead, but almost as if all the years that his son had lived were slowly being erased. There was one emotion that did break through the emptiness, not anger, not rage, but fear, overpowering, paralyzing fear, not that his son might die, but rather that his grandson would. Night after night, he would lie awake, hating himself for putting Carson's life before that of Tony's, all the while hearing a small voice that repeated over and over that Tony was already doomed, but that the child, with any luck, might be saved. Emily's deep sleep, brought about by the medication prescribed by Ben Cohen, continued uninterrupted, oblivious to his tears and nightly agonies of conscience. Each day, he would go through the motions, calling the office, going to the hospital, playing with his granddaughters, trying to find something to hold on to as he watched the structure and familiarities of his life disintegrating a little more each day. Each evening, he would stare at the telephone, willing it to ring, to hear Carson's voice on the other end, the boy's sweetness like a gentle rain after a drought.

Any kind of meaningful conversation had become unbearable. Both Jordan and Emily were reminded of all the television shows they had watched, the couples portrayed in them barely able to carry on a dinner table dialogue. At bedtime, unable to offer him the comfort she herself longed for, she would hastily swallow her sleeping pill and wait for oblivion to help her pass the night away.

On the other side of town, near the hospital, Laurel would lie awake for hours, staring into the darkness. Feeling that her widowhood had already claimed her, she mourned for the life that although much desired, had always eluded her. Unable to stop, she relived her relationship with Tony, frame by frame, exposing it to a long delayed and now necessary pitiless reality. Night after night, she whittled away at any sentimentality that remained in her marriage, substituting instead the disillusionment and deep seated anger that she had repressed for years. Aware at last, she laughed at her stupidity, welcoming the bitterness that took the place of love.

By day, she followed the routines automatically, waking her daughters, feeding them, taking the twins to the new nursery school, waiting for the babysitter for Emily, driving to the hospital, buying ice cream as a treat to tempt Tony to eat, sitting in the room for hours, listening to the hatred and bitterness that was all her husband had left to offer, eating dinner with Jordan and Emily and the girls, and falling exhausted into bed, only to repeat the same things again the next day.

At the end of the third week, Tony was told that, as the syphilis was now under control, there was nothing else the doctors could do to help him. In two days time, he would be released to the outpatient program. The last item on the social worker's list was the name of the hospice whose workers would be coming to the house to help ease him into the reality of death. Strangled by fear and anger, he could barely nod in response to what the social worker was saying. For an instant, he weighed the prospect of escape in his mind. Escape from the hospital also meant escape from an inevitable and unpleasant future. Opening the closet, he gathered his clothes and headed into the bathroom to shave and get dressed. He shut the door and turned on the light. Turning around, he looked at himself in the mirror. Shocked, he stared at his reflection. A person he did not recognize was staring back at him. His face was yellow, as were the whites of his eyes. Amazed, he nodded at himself. He looked like a very sick person, someone else, not Tony Graniston, the man of steel, who could drink anyone under the table, and still perform in bed. Looking down at the pile of his clothes, he was suddenly so tired that he began to be afraid that he would not be able to make it back to bed. Gritting his teeth and sweating, he dragged himself across the room and collapsed onto the bed. Fifteen minutes later, he felt strong enough to pull the covers back over himself.

* * * * *

Juliet smiled as she watched her sleeping children. The departure of the Macallister company jet had come at exactly the right moment. The plane had just begun to taxi down the runway as all four had fallen asleep, having been sent to bed protesting every inch of the way. Only Isabel slept outside her crib, nestled in her father's arms, contented and smiling.

"Feeling better?" Donald bent and kissed the top of his daughter's head.

"Much. It was such a relief to hear Ben's voice telling us that there was no infection anywhere."

"For now."

"Right. For now. Only two more tests and then we don't have to worry again."

"Juliet, what are we going to do about Tony?" The baby stirred in her father's arms, bringing his gentle smile and a kiss to send her back to sleep.

"Nothing. He's finally getting what he deserves."

"That's not what I mean. The man is dying, quite quickly from what Ben told me. He's going to want to see Carson again."

"No. I allowed it twice, and look what happened."

"Tony will ask again, and I think, that with proper supervision, we should allow it. Carson will be fine, and I will make sure that he is never alone with him."

"Not good enough. He can go to the funeral."

"Compromise, let's wait and see what happens."

"Agreed."

"Change of subject. I thought that when they are back at school, we could fly down to Nice for a few days. I long to wake up and see you nursing Isabel in front of your window."

"Will you let me paint you holding her?"

"Perhaps. I'll think about it. She's stirring, so I know what that means. How about if Nanny changes her nappy, and then you can feed her in the bedroom."

"Donald, you have that look about you. You're in charge of locking the door after I feed her." She picked up the baby and disappeared into the back of the plane.

* * * * *

"I can't believe it, alone at last. Thank God my father volunteered to drive them all up to school. Tomorrow I must go to the office, and then it's off to Nice." Donald lay on the bed holding Isabel, fast asleep on his chest. He amused himself watching the baby move up and down as he breathed. In the background, he heard the telephone ring, and Juliet answer. She hung up the telephone, stricken with fear.

"That was Jordan. They're releasing Tony from the hospital at the end of next week. There's nothing more to be done. He sounded awful, Emily, too, like a sleepwalker."

"It can't be easy. Almost makes me feel guilty about pounding him the way I did." Suddenly alert, he watched her face carefully.

"He doesn't deserve your pity. He had it coming, and I'm sure that he has a few more surprises in store for me before it's over." She was shaking uncontrollably.

"Stop buying trouble. Darling, you have to stop imagining all these terrible things, most of which are never going to happen. Are you all packed? Plane leaves at five sharp tomorrow."

"All ready. All that remains is my paint case and the canvas. I can't wait to paint you holding our daughter."

*   *   *   *   *

The house that Laurel had rented was in a new development a quarter of a mile from the hospital. Tony's room faced a beautiful view of a man-made lake, complete with ducks swimming around the center of it, and the nurse had positioned his bed so that he could look out of the window whenever he wanted.

In the four weeks since he had been admitted to the hospital, he had lost twenty pounds, and had begun to show other symptoms of liver disease; sudden high fevers, nausea, and constant itching that drove him wild. His appetite had improved enough, however, to allow him to regain a little of the strength he had lost while in the hospital. As he grew stronger, he would sit in a chair by the window and watch his daughters playing in the yard. It was during these hours that he began to accept the inevitable and plan the end of his life.

*   *   *   *   *

Donald sighed, completely at peace with the world. It hardly seemed possible that after only three days away from London and the stresses and strains of his everyday life that he should be so relaxed. Fluffing up the pillow under his head, he watched his wife and daughter sitting next to the window, the same position Juliet and Carson had occupied nine years before. With the birth of his daughter, he could not help but feel that his life had been enriched beyond his imagination. Unlike the arrival of Miranda, when Delia had refused to nurse or care for the baby, and he had spent several frantic weeks until he had found a competent nanny, the arrival of Isabel had made his life come full circle.

"Donald, why don't you take her, she's fed and actually awake, ready to play. I want to make some sketches, so I can decide exactly how I'm going to paint you."

"I never said yes. Come here while I try and make up my mind."

"At this rate I'll never get any work done. I'm dying to do an Impressionist series of both of you, one now, one in a year and one in two years."

"We have all the time in the world today. Call the nanny to take her for a while, and come here so I can drive you to distraction. Besides, at this hour, there's not enough light to paint." Suddenly he could not wait another second. Getting out of bed, he firmly took the baby, and calling the nanny handed her through the door, and then closed and locked it.

"Donald, whatever will Francoise and Nanny think, at this hour of the morning?"

"What any normal person would think, that I am so much in love with my wife that if I can't get her into bed this minute, I will expire on the spot. I've never seen you so beautiful, right now, at this moment, in that robe standing against the window. Now if you don't come here, I'm going to have to come and get you."

Smiling, she teased him, leaning against the window.

"My God, you are so lovely, all I want is to make love to you over and over again."

"Donald, if you're not careful, I'll have two babies to feed in nine months." Giggling, she nuzzled his ear. For an instant, serious lovemaking had driven her worries from her mind.

"You can't be serious."

"No, but it brought back memories, that night in New York when we made Isabel." Smothering her laughter, she buried her face in the pillow.

"You shouldn't laugh like that, it's dangerous. Please, I want to make love to you and then I promise to feed you." Before she could answer, he had turned her over and was on top of her, drawing her into his passion. Her tears fell across his cheek as she surrendered her soul to his, crying his name, searching for more again and again.

*　　*　　*　　*　　*

Sighing as the gentle ticking of the grandfather clock broke the silence in his office, Jordan got up and walked to the window, looking down on the hurrying crowds on Madison Avenue. They had returned home two days ago, having had enough of the pain of watching Tony's life degenerating a little bit each day. He kept in touch with Laurel by telephone, assuaging his guilt by promising himself that he would return well before the end. Shaking his head, he watched the healthy as they hurried to their destinations, oblivious to anything but their own agendas.

His agony grew as he turned and looked around his office. He would be the last Graniston to occupy it. Whatever chances Tony might have had to redeem himself had become irrelevant. There was no more time to repair past mistakes, or to mend past behaviors. Jordan's face grew more haggard than it had been in the past weeks. A month ago it had been unthinkable that his son would die of AIDS and liver disease.

He had just had a lengthy conversation with Tony's doctors. Bitterly, he thought of his usual conference calls, closing deals for his clients, earning a fat fee in exchange for his services. Unhappy at having to bring bad news yet again, Ben Cohen had passed on the results of the latest blood work. His liver failing, Tony's immune system had shut down, and the rest of his healthy organs were being invaded and destroyed by the AIDS virus. That had been the last piece of devastating news that Ben had given him, Tony's HIV status had been upgraded to full-blown AIDS.

Now, Jordan had to prepare himself to make the unthinkable request, calling Juliet and begging her to let Tony see his son for the last time. A humanitarian request, designed to play on her generosity and sensitivity. He would make the promises he knew she expected to hear, that Carson would never be left alone with Tony, that the nurses and Laurel would make sure that the child was safe, all the while praying that she would say no. In spite of his conscious mind desperately wanting to believe that there was still something good left in his son, every nerve in his body, every instinct he had ever possessed screamed aloud that there was danger. His inner voice insisted that he should not make the call, that Tony hadn't earned the right to ask him to do it and that soon it wouldn't matter anyway, he would fall into a coma and mercifully, die. Hating himself, he knew he would ask, even beg if necessary, unable to resist the comparison with himself, knowing that if the situation were reversed, the possibility of redemption offered by the love of his child would be the only thing keeping him alive. Weeping, he pressed the intercom, and told Sheila to connect him to Donald Macallister, at Macallister Industries.

* * * * *

Licking his fingers, Donald polished off the last of the croissants that Francoise had brought on a tray, scolding him for keeping her waiting for so long. Her lunch, Madame's favorite, lobster salad, was now delayed, and it would not be her fault if it was not up to her usual standards. He had dutifully apologized, asking that she delay only an hour, serving at one instead of twelve. Humphing to herself, Francoise had departed, pausing to remark that lunch was to be served at twelve, not one, and therefore, they had delayed her dinner as well.

Consumed with laughter, Juliet had held her breath until Francoise had closed the door and gone back to the kitchen before she had exploded into throaty giggles. They had possessed her to the point where she had lain back on the pillows and laughed until she cried. Smiling at her amusement, Donald had served her coffee and croissants, finally scolding her as well for not eating the food while it was still warm.

"Isabel will go hungry if you don't eat. Here, there's jam and everything you like. Really, you're too wicked to make fun of her like that."

"I can't help it. She humphs so theatrically, she's too funny." She had taken a bite of croissant, scattering the rich, buttery crumbs onto her chest. The second bite stopped in midair, as she caught sight of his face.

"Stop looking at me like that. If you don't stop, I'll go in the other room and lock myself in while I eat."

"The crumbs, my darling, too delicious to pass up."

"Stop, you're not being fair."

"Juliet, that is what husbands are for, especially on vacation. Licking crumbs off the most delectable plate imaginable. Mmm, absolutely delicious."

"Stop, I hear the baby crying. Look at the time, she's way past her feed. Why don't you go and console her while I have a quick shower, and then afterwards, we can get our day started."

"What day? I think we should spend it right here, and after Francoise goes home, we'll lock Nanny in her nursery and go swimming, like we did last year."

"Scandalous, but enticing. Only if you promise me champagne with lunch, then I'll consider your offer." She had reached the bathroom door, and he could hear her laughter as she shut the door and turned on the shower. Sighing, he put on his robe and opened the bedroom door, getting the full benefit of his daughter's hungry screams.

*   *   *   *   *

Holding his daughter and rocking her to sleep after her meal, he watched the struggle between sleep and wakefulness. Her eyes would slowly close, only to open again, for fear of missing something. Overwhelmed by sleep at last, her eyes closed for the final time, and she sighed and snuggled into his chest. Completely relaxed, already far away from her father, she smiled in her sleep. Gently, he placed her in her crib, covering her up and kissing her fingers one last time.

The telephone was ringing as he walked back towards the bedroom. Thinking it was only for his wife, he ran the water in the sink, and lathered his face.

"No, Jordan, it's out of the question." Juliet's panic found its way into her voice. "I'm sorry for Tony, but I can't permit my son to go into a house with him. I don't care, you promised the last time that he would behave and look what happened. No, I won't change my mind and don't you dare go behind my back and ask Donald to make the decision instead. This is the last word on the subject, and please, don't call me again unless he's dead." Slamming down the receiver, she began to cry, silently, rocking back and forth.

"What's happened? Who was on the phone?"

"Jordan. According to him, the end is near, and Tony wants to see Carson one last time. I told him no, under no circumstances would I give my permission for him to go into a house to be alone in a room with Tony. I can't help it, I don't care how sick he is, or how convinced everyone else is that he's sick, I won't feel secure until he's dead." Her teeth chattering, she rubbed her arms, trying to warm away the cold dread taking over her heart.

"Juliet, he's dying. Carson is his child, no matter how much you might like to deny it. It's the human thing to do. If you refuse this, you're as bad as he is. Call Jordan back and tell him that we'll come, with Carson, at Easter, just before we go on the cruise.

Maybe by then, Tony will be in a coma and that will be that."

"You don't understand, that no matter how long it takes, his hate will keep him alive. He'll stay in bed, like a huge spider, waiting for Carson to come so that he can wreak some horrible revenge on him and on me. And don't tell me I'm exaggerating, because I'm not. If you insist on doing this, and something goes wrong, I will never forgive you."

*　*　*　*　*

"Donald Lord Macallister, Inspector Colin MacPherson of Scotland Yard. Have you a minute to talk to me about this dossier you submitted to us?"

"Yes, of course. Would you like me to come down to the Yard?"

"Would that be convenient, Your Grace? It would save a great deal of time for me."

"Within the hour?"

"Within the hour. My office is on the fifth floor."

*　*　*　*　*

"Lord Donald, I'm very grateful that you took the time to come all the way down to the Yard. I'm at the end of all the back and forth by the solicitors, and before I go and get this laddie, I wanted to explore a few details. Now, what if anything did your wife do in the period after the assault, say the first five hours."

"It's all in the dossier. She recovered consciousness and rang her father. He came with the ambulance and took her to hospital. Her father's solicitor, David Graham, came with a photographer, and took a statement from her, and of course, those ghastly pictures."

"She never called him on the telephone, or anything of that nature?"

"Graham wrote to him when Juliet discovered that she was pregnant with Carson, telling him he was going to be a father, and offering to share custody. His reply was a termination of rights, severing all his parental connections to the child. Considering what he did to her, it was not unexpected. Up until a year ago, she hadn't seen or heard from him in nine years." MacPherson watched Donald answer his questions. He wondered what kind of a man he was, what kind of woman his wife was. Whatever the answer was, he couldn't have done it, marrying a woman pregnant with another man's child.

"And the reason for this reunion?"

"At least you didn't say joyous, Inspector." Donald allowed himself a small smile. "Our son had leukemia. Juliet was not a match, so she went to New York to find Tony and ask him to be tested. He was our last hope. If he had refused, or not been a match, the boy would have died. Tony, needless to say, was overjoyed at the prospect of being a father to a son."

"And was he thrilled about being tested and giving his marrow?"

"No, he was not, by any means. I had to pay him three million dollars first." MacPherson winced.

"There must be more to it than just a test and a marrow donation, Lord Donald."

"There was. Apparently he never signed the divorce papers. Both of them had remarried in the interim, and were therefore bigamists. Signing them properly was part of the deal." The policeman leaned back in his chair and nodded.

"I gather that you and Countess Juliet have remarried?"

"As quickly as possible. We just had our first child together about four and a half months ago."

"Ah, congratulations. And tell me, do you know where this laddie can be found?"

"In Florida. At the moment, he is dying of liver disease and a host of other ailments, and is living in a rental home close to Northridge Hospital in Fort Lauderdale. You can get all the other information you need from Detective Paul Morales of the Fort Lauderdale Police Department. At this point, however, I can't see any good coming of going over there and arresting him. He'll be dead in a few months, anyway."

"A shame, Lord Donald. And here I was looking forward to him being at Her Majesty's pleasure for the next fifty or so years." MacPherson smiled, and leaned down towards the bottom drawer of the desk.

"A small toast, Lord Donald? To salute the intervention of the Almighty?" He filled two small glasses to the brim.

"To the Almighty, who protects the innocent and punishes the wicked." They raised their glasses, saluted each other and drained them all in one swallow. The two men shook hands.

"Inspector, could I prevail upon you to destroy that file? Utterly and totally destroy it."

"Lord Donald, it would be my pleasure to do it today, as soon as we're finished here. I wish both of you well."

"Thank you, Inspector. If you have any more questions, please do not hesitate to call me."

*   *   *   *   *

"Donald, I have something to say about this trip to Florida." Carson Macallister pulled out a chair in his son's office and sat down without being invited.

360

"Father, the discussion is over. We are going to Florida to pay Tony one last visit. He's dying, and Juliet must take this last chance, once and for all, to put her life with him behind her."

"And what does she say about it?"

"That she is convinced that he is planning some final act of revenge."

"I see. And you don't believe that for a minute."

"Why do I get the feeling that this is not going to be a simple conversation?"

"Because, son, this is not a simple situation. I thought that after nine years of marriage to her, that your understanding of her personality would have gotten beyond a ritual enforcing of your authority."

"She's behaving like a child. She refuses to talk to me, and she's moved into the guest room. The whole household is in an uproar, the baby screaming because she's hungry, Juliet crying all the time, it's an awful mess."

"Which, I might add, you and only you have created. Donald, your wife is unique among humans in that she has no repressive gene. What that means is that she has no need to control certain aspects of her personality, because frankly, they don't exist. She isn't deceitful, dishonest, thieving or anything like that. She has to work with what she has, an open, honest, almost otherworldly set of values, one which you will never be able to change. She has to live in a world where most people not only accept the existence of evil, but even learn to deal with it on a daily basis. Juliet is probably one of the few people in the world who understand evil, simply because they have no inbred defense against it. Once having had a brush with it, they recognize it and see it for what it really is. Her answer to evil is to avoid having to compromise herself to deal with it. Up until now, it worked well enough so that she was able to function. Forcing her to face Tony, which is how most people would handle this problem, will only succeed in one thing, son, and I don't think you want her to feel that you have abandoned her and Car III. Juliet sees Tony as the devil, waiting to snatch her child away from her. Donald, if anything should happen to the boy while he is on this visit, she may not forgive you."

"Why is it that everyone keeps telling me that she has no defense against evil? Frankly, I think that a big part of this is plain fear and cowardice."

"No, Donald, fear and loathing, perhaps, but never cowardice. Juliet is one of the bravest people I know. It's a shame that you don't appreciate her for what she really is. Do you remember the first time you brought her home to meet me? She was enormously pregnant, but so pure and unsullied, it took my breath away. Her innocence shone like a beacon, and I was content for you to marry her. After Delia, I felt that this one at least, would love you passionately to her last breath. And I was certain that you would protect that purity and innocence to your last breath as well. It seems that I was wrong. She hasn't changed, but you have. It's part of evil's insidious nature, Donald, it creeps inside your soul and changes you, a little bit at a time. Tony has some kind of power over you, I don't know what it is, but my greatest fear is that he will win in the end."

"Father, you're beginning to sound like Juliet."

"Son, I take that as the highest form of praise you can bestow." Carson left the office, closing the door quietly. Sick at heart, he put on his overcoat, unable to think or breathe.

* * * * *

The British Airways Concorde flight seemed to move more quickly than usual. Both mother and child watched the seconds ticking by, each one bringing them closer to Florida, closer to the meeting with Tony. Donald sat in his seat across from Juliet and worked out of his briefcase. Heavy hearted, he watched her face from behind one of his files. She looked exhausted, with huge circles under her eyes. Since he had forced the issue over Tony, she had eaten and slept very little. Isabel had spent two days and nights screaming with hunger, unable to nurse where there was no milk to give. Weeping, furious with recriminations, she had put the baby on bottled formula to quiet her screams.

In the past three weeks, his wife had not uttered more than two or three words to him at one time. Initially, he had made one attempt to talk to her and bring her out of her depression, a failure which had resulted in her moving into the guest room to sleep, locking the door each night. Unable to bring himself to let her have her way, he stood outside the locked door and listened to her sobs as she cried tears of pain and fury. Each day he went to work, and the door to the guest room was still locked. At night, when he returned, she was behind the locked door again. That morning, the three of them had made the trip to the airport, boarded the plane, and taken their seats, all without exchanging a single word. Trying to catch her eye, he had forced her to look at him, appalled by the empty look of desolation she had given in return. For the first time, he asked himself if trying to force her to come to terms with Tony had been the right decision.

Six hours later, they arrived at the house in Palm Beach, exhausted, silent and angry. Carson had wept when told he had to go to Florida, and had begged not to have to go. He had reminded Donald of his promise, that he would never have to see Tony again, and was told that at that time, no one had had any idea that he was dying, and besides, he was so sick that he couldn't do any harm anyway. Donald could have sworn that the look Carson gave him was one of pity, that for once, the child understood what was happening far better than his father.

CHAPTER TWENTY-ONE

Confined to bed for most of each day, Tony reviewed his plans over and over again. Each morning, when the nurse had finished bathing and dressing him, he would pretend to be tired so that he would be left alone for half an hour. As soon as the door closed behind him, he would reach into the nightstand, caressing the two shotguns, and the air rifle he had bought from a dealer he found in a gun magazine. Two hundred rounds of ammunition were more than he needed, but at the time he had not wanted to rouse any suspicions. He had given the gun dealer a story that his little boy was coming from England to stay with him, and after he recovered from his illness, he was going to teach him to shoot, first with the air rifle, and then with the shotgun.

Yesterday he had brightened considerably when his father had telephoned and told him that he had finally persuaded Donald and Juliet to bring Carson for one last visit. Laughing to himself at how gullible they all were, he rejoiced that the first part of his plan had gone off without a hitch. He even allowed the nurse to trim his hair, and shave him, a process that caused him hours of itching and the agony of not being able to stop it.

Jordan and Emily had boarded a plane for Florida, anxious to be present at the last meeting between Tony and Carson, each silently fearing the worst. He had tactfully avoided accepting Laurel's invitation to stay with them, pleading an important client in Hong Kong who would be telephoning at all hours of the night.

Living with Tony's deterioration first hand, Laurel watched as her husband seemed to lose more of his independence each day. Walking had become a problem for him, and he was now confined to a wheelchair, with a male nurse in attendance to help him in and out of the chair. Taking a great deal for granted, she completely misinterpreted the long hours he would spend staring out of the window as his final reconciliation with impending death. Lulled into a false sense of security, she was not at all suspicious when he would not allow her to send the children to her mother's house in Palm Beach for a few days, instead accepting his explanation, that they brightened up his otherwise miserable existence.

*   *   *   *   *

"Juliet, please, you must eat something. You haven't had a proper meal in three weeks."

"I'm not hungry. I want to go back to England. Carson wants to go back to England."

"No, that's not possible. Once and for all, both of you must understand that this is the humane thing to do. An hour in and out, and it will be all over."

"Why does this sound like a tooth extraction without an anesthetic? You're an even bigger fool that I realized, Donald. Excuse me, I'm going to bed." He heard the door to the guest room close and the lock snap shut even before he could answer. Turning to look at Carson, he saw that the boy's eyes were red from crying and that he hadn't eaten a bite. Hastily, the child excused himself and ran to his room, shutting and locking the door. Putting his head in his hands, all Donald could hear was the echo of his last conversation with his father.

*   *   *   *   *

366

Tony swallowed the last bite of cereal and shook his head. This morning, he had told Laurel that he was too weak to feed himself, and she had taken over, spooning the oatmeal to his mouth for him. Smiling, he looked over at her as she cleaned up the mess he had deliberately made, silently and without complaint. Half of each spoon had wound up all over the wheelchair and his pajamas, drooled out on purpose to add to her humiliation.

"You're a mess. I'll send Brian in to help you get dressed. They'll be here in an hour." Inwardly shuddering with disgust, her expression remained bland and noncommittal.

"Thanks, Laurel. I always knew you'd stick by me. Where are the kids?"

"I kept them home today, just as you asked. It's time they knew about him anyway."

"He has a name, it's Carson."

"She has a name, too. It's Juliet, and that's what all this is about, isn't it?"

"I'm married to you, aren't I?" He watched as tears of frustration slid down her cheeks. "Don't cry. She's not worth it." Turning his head away, he was able to hide a smile of triumph from her.

*   *   *   *   *

"We'll meet you at Tony's at eleven. I'll be waiting on the front porch to take the boy inside."

"No, Jordan, I'm bringing him in myself. I'll wait for him outside the room. The door will be left open, so that I can hear and see everything."

"Donald, that's not what Tony wants. He wants to see the boy alone. You can't blame him for that. In a few months, he'll be dead. It's not too much to ask."

"Yes, it is. You don't understand what's going on over here. My wife and son won't talk to me, neither of them has eaten in days, and I'm afraid that she's going to leave me. After three weeks of sleeping alone, and not having her talk to me, I've started asking myself if agreeing to Tony's dying wish is worth it."

"I'm sorry, I had no idea she was so upset over all of this. I think it's much ado about nothing. Tony's in a wheelchair now, has to be carried around, and from what Laurel tells me, he can't feed himself anymore either."

"All of this had better be true, or I'm dragging my son out of there and all bets are off. We'll be there on time." Turning around, he saw her standing by the door. A haunted look passed over her face, and he noticed that her clothes seemed to be too big for her.

"How long have you been standing there?"

"Long enough. You're quite right about one thing, Donald. And that is that after this is all over, Carson and I will be returning to England, alone."

"I see."

"Do you? I'll be collecting Isabel and moving out, as quickly as possible. You should be proud of yourself. Patronizing me, telling me I had to face up to Tony, when the last thing in the world any sane person should want is to be anywhere near him. Bad enough to do it to me, but to force Carson to do this, and after you promised him he would never have to see Tony again, I won't ever forgive you. Tony is probably laughing himself sick. You know why, don't you, Donald? You're turning out just like him." The last words hit him like a hard slap across the face. Before he could answer, she was gone.

The car ride to Ft. Lauderdale was torture. Val Lenox, brought over as extra security drove the rented limousine. Inside, all three were silent, each living in his own dread of what was to come.

"Donald, it's not too late. You can still call and say you've changed your mind. Please, for all our sakes, especially Carson's, do it." Tears flowed down her face, unchecked.

"No, I can't and I won't. Blackmail doesn't work with me, Juliet, you should have learned that by now. Wait, Val, why are we stopping?"

"Picking up another passenger, Lord Donald." He got out and opened the door.

"Grandpa, what are you doing here?" Donald saw his son's face brighten, thinking bitterly that this was what life had been like, only three short weeks ago.

"Donald, Juliet, thought I'd come along for the ride. I brought your American mobile phone, you left it at the office. Take it, you might need it."

"Thank you, Father." Donald looked out of the window, signaling that the conversation was over.

Juliet looked down and saw her father-in-law's hand over hers. He patted it, and winked. She smiled and suddenly felt less abandoned and alone. Carson sat back in his seat, his arm around his grandson, patting his shoulder. Silently, they sat, waiting for the worst, as the car turned into the driveway. Jordan, as promised, was waiting on the front steps, with Laurel at his side. Tony was nowhere to be seen.

"Let's get this over with. Val, why don't you park across the street? If you hear anything you don't like, use the car telephone to call the police. Ask for Detective Paul Morales." Donald took Carson's hand and turned to his wife.

"Are you coming in?" Nodding, she strode ahead, shunning any physical contact with him.

"Thank you for coming. I know what it must have cost you, after everything that's happened. Come in and sit down, I believe that Tony is ready for you." Laurel turned on her heel and walked into the house. Inside his room, Tony had finished loading the two shotguns. He set the safeties, and replaced them in the bottom of the nightstand. They had arrived right on schedule. All that was now required was for the other players to follow the script he had created.

"Tony, they're here. Why don't you come out and say hello?" He could hear his mother's voice through the locked door.

"Sure, I'm ready. Ask them to bring the boy in here." Emily's footsteps faded away towards the living room. His wristwatch read five after eleven, a good enough time as any. Pushing himself up, he got out of the wheelchair and stretched. Listening for the sound of footsteps, he hoisted the two shotguns out of the nightstand, flipped off the safeties and hid them under the sheets.

"Tony, unlock the door. Carson is here." Laurel stood in front of the door.

"Tony, answer me. We're waiting." Beginning to be exasperated, she tried the handle, and turned it, swinging open the door. Carson, as instructed, walked into the room. In the shadows, Donald waited, his palms sweaty, his heart racing.

They were all unprepared for what followed. A single shotgun blast killed Laurel instantly, its force flinging her body out into the hallway. The door slammed shut an instant later, leaving the boy, now screaming hysterically, alone with the murderer.

"Macallister, you out there? Listen carefully, I want you and my parents out of the house or I kill the boy right now. And no police, or he dies, in front of his mother. Juliet and the boy and my daughters stay here. Now, go get her and bring her here."

"How do I know you won't hurt her or Carson?"

"You don't. You'll have to trust me, it should be a new experience for you. Now do it, I'm getting tired of talking to you." Donald heard a scuffling sound, followed by his son's voice.

"Daddy, please, he's got me by the throat, and he has a gun pointed at my head."

"All right. Mummy will be right back." Dragging his feet, Donald tried to plan what to say to his wife. She had been right all along, everything his father had said had been right and true. He had been blind sided by his own arrogance, his over-confidence that he was a better judge of Tony's character than his wife and father. And now, the nightmare was beginning. Evil lived in that room, its claws stretching out to destroy his family. It was all happening exactly as she had predicted.

The living room was empty, except for Juliet. She was standing near the window, her head down, weeping openly.

"Where is everyone?"

"They went outside to show Tony's daughters the ducks. How is it going?"

"You didn't hear anything?"

"No, I was outside as well. I was restless, so I came inside. Donald, don't look at me like that. What's happened?"

"Everything you promised me. Laurel is dead, he killed her with a shotgun."

"And Carson?"

"Locked in the room with that monster, with a gun at his head."

"Donald, you're not making any sense."

"He means to kill you and Carson, and his children. And then, I imagine, himself, going out in a blaze of glory."

"That doesn't sound like Tony at all. He'd never put himself in a situation where he would be discovered, or thought of as a murderer."

"Juliet, he's dying. That changes things."

"So what does he want?" Her voice seemed to grow further and further away.

"All of us to leave, except you, Carson and the girls. I'm going to send Jordan and Emily away, but I'll stay, hiding if I have to. I won't leave you alone now, not after I betrayed you. I'm sorry, I've been a bloody fool." He looked steadily at his wife, not knowing what her reaction would be.

"I wish that you had realized this before, but I won't hold it against you. Come here so I can forgive you properly." Softly, she brushed his lips.

"I may never forgive myself." He held her tightly.

"Darling, it doesn't matter any more. We have more important things to worry about. Right now we need to make a plan to save our child."

"He said no police, or he would kill Carson."

"That sounds like a bad movie. Donald, he wants an audience, he always loved that. Swaggering and bragging, I remember that, when we were first married, he loved to show me off. Pride of ownership, I think it's called."

"So what shall we do?"

"You still have that phone on you? Call Paul Morales and have him bring someone who can pose as a reporter. Let Tony think that the press is going to print his sordid little story. And now, I'm going to try to rescue my child. Donald, I love you, always remember that I loved you to my last breath, and if something happens, tell Isabel about me, don't let her forget me. And Donald, please, take Laurel away somewhere she can get the respect he never gave her." She was gone, quietly walking away, without looking back.

372

＊　　＊　　＊　　＊　　＊

"Stop sniveling, you little brat! God, your mother's ruined you, turned you into a baby." Tony dragged Carson away from the window.

"Now just behave and in a minute, I'm sure that your mother will come running to save you." Tony began to smile. His plan was working perfectly, just as he had mapped it out.

"Tony, it's Juliet. Open the door." Holding her breath, not daring to look at the floor where Laurel's body lay, she tensed, waiting for the door to open.

"Are you alone?"

"Yes, the others have all gone. They were outside anyway, and Donald told them to leave."

"All right, you get one look at our son, the last one you'll ever have, and then I want you to leave, too. My daughters come inside and you leave."

"Tony, this is madness. What are you planning to do?"

"Make sure that I have company when I go to wherever it is that I'm headed. Now, you get to see the change in our boy. He's even calling me Daddy now, just like he's always lived here with me. Carson, come here and say goodbye to Mommy. She's going out for a while." Shuffling, the child walked towards her, his head down. Her hand went out, under his chin, bringing his face up to hers. Clamping down on her feelings, she forced herself to ignore the bloody lip and the eye almost swollen shut. She held him close, feeling his arms around her.

"Do whatever Daddy tells you, darling. Nothing will happen to you if you do."

"Promise?"

"Yes, darling. Now kiss me, and I'm off. I love you, Carson. Remember that, Daddy and I love you always."

"That's enough. My son and I have some things to do."

As the door began to swing shut, she reached out and grabbed the child by the arm. Twisting her body, she moved backwards into the shadows, keeping him behind her. Bracing herself, she waited for the shotgun blast. Don't be fooled if it takes longer, she kept repeating to herself, over and over. As she waited in the shadows, Tony slipped into the bathroom adjoining his bedroom, his hand on the doorknob, waiting for the moment of surprise.

The house was almost silent. Nothing moved or made a sound, no dripping faucet, no ringing telephone, no radio, only the blare of the television. Moving carefully, she walked backwards against the wall, always pushing Carson behind her. She passed the entrance to the living room, seeing the three little girls in front of the television set. Suddenly, she could feel that someone else was in the room. A heightened awareness told her that evil was standing behind her. She began to scream.

"Run, Carson, run away from here as fast as you can." In the next instant, she heard soft laughter. A moment after that, she felt herself separated from her child, her body flying across the room. Horrible screams told her that Carson was again a prisoner of that evil, and before she could move back across the room, she heard the slamming of a door in the back of the house. Taking a deep breath, she crept closer and put her ear to the door, biting her hand to keep from screaming as she listened to the abuse raining down on her son. She would be killed if she insisted that Tony open the door again, it would be a useless sacrifice. As she moved towards the front door, she went through the downstairs, opened the windows and took off all the screens.

She passed the kitchen on her way to the front door. Almost as an afterthought, she stayed long enough to make some sandwiches for the children. It felt surreal, she didn't even know if anyone in the house would still be alive when it came time to eat them.

*   *   *   *   *

Outside, across the street, the others waited. At last, they saw the front door open and Juliet come out of the house.

"Oh, God, she's safe. Donald, look, he let her go. Don't go. Let her walk by herself. He may be watching." Carson grasped his son's arm and pulled him back to safety.

Slowly, Juliet crossed the street, willing herself not to run. Courage was what she needed to show now, strength for her husband and child.

"Did you see Carson?" Bewildered, she looked into their faces, for a moment not recognizing any one.

"Darling, wake up. Did you see Carson?" Donald shook her slightly.

"He's alive. Tony beat him, he has a bloody lip and a swollen eye. He's cooperating, calling him Daddy. I got him out of the room, and I was almost at the door when he took him again. The girls are in the living room, watching television. I opened all the windows downstairs and took off all the window screens. Perhaps the police can go in and bring them out later on. Tony has to go to sleep sometime." Her voice was a monotone, a sing song narrative given by someone who has retreated from the ugliness of the real world.

"Pray that doesn't happen soon. He may just kill the kids before he passes out." Paul Morales trained his binoculars on the windows of the house. "Right now, I don't think he'll do anything, he's enjoying his power over the boy too much. But it won't last forever." Donald held her close, feeling the trembling lessen.

"No, Paul, we know it won't. It can't."

*   *   *   *   *

"Carson, go in the kitchen and get Daddy a beer. Go on, the door is unlocked, it's in the refrigerator." The boy walked unsteadily towards the door.

"And don't take forever. You know what happens to boys who disobey." His hand came up and he smacked the child across the face.

"Just so you remember. Now go, I'm thirsty."

Bewildered and in shock, Carson walked slowly through the house, looking for a way out. It would be dark soon, a perfect time for an escape, before something worse happened. He saw his sisters, all three of them, sitting on the floor, with sandwiches in front of them, watching television, as if nothing had happened.

"Carson, your mother made these. You want some?" Amanda offered him a half-eaten sandwich. Shaking his head, he turned and noticed that all the windows were open, and the screens were off. Encouraged, he went to get Tony's bottle of beer out of the refrigerator. Abigail followed him in to the kitchen.

"Is anyone else here besides us and my Dad?"

"No, it's just us in here. Look, I have an idea, how I can get all of you out of the house safely, away from him."

"What about you?"

"I'm the one he wants. The boy, you can see how much he wants me." Wide-eyed, Abigail looked at the bruises and cuts on his face and nodded.

"Can I count on you and your sisters to move when I tell you?"

"I think so, but Emily's only a baby. She has to be carried." He picked up the beer and made his way out of the kitchen.

"It took you long enough. What were you doing?"

"Giving my sisters a glass of water, and changing Emily's diaper."

"Aren't you the good brother?" Tony's hand came up and slapped him hard across the back of the head.

"Liar, you don't think I believe you, do you? You were trying to escape."

"I don't care if you believe me, Daddy, it's the truth." Carson faced him steadily, bracing for the next slap, which came across his face.

"You'd better not be lying, or you'll be sorry." Tony drank the beer greedily, spilling some of it on his shirt, licking up the excess foam that had run down the side of the can after it was opened. For the next two hours, he sat in the wheelchair and said nothing. Carson sat in the corner, watching and waiting for his chance.

*　*　*　*　*

"What do we do now?" Donald sat on the curb, next to his wife, who was explaining the layout of the house to the police.

"Mr. Macallister, we're going to call the house when it gets dark, get him talking, wear him down a bit, let him tell us his side of the story. As long as he's talking, he can't be killing the kids at the same time."

"And when he's finished talking?" Asking the question required an immense effort of will. Thinking about the answer was something she wished she didn't have to do.

"I just don't know, Mrs. Macallister, I just don't know."

* * * * *

"Carson, get me another beer and some food. And make it snappy, no diaper changing this time."

"Sure, Daddy. I'll be right back." Carson held his breath as he opened the door.

"I don't like the way you said that. Too eager, what are you going to do out there? That's not being a good boy, Carson. I've a good mind to give you a beating you won't forget, at least until tomorrow. What a good idea. Take off your pants, now." Carson shook his head. Tony leaned over and yanked down his shorts and underpants.

"Bend over. You deserve to get a good beating." Shaking and sobbing, Carson bent over, praying that it would end. Over and over again, Tony smacked his son with his belt, changing hands when one got tired. Carson bit back his screams, willing himself not to make a sound. Soon the welts turned to blood as Tony, in a frenzy of hate and frustration, continued beating him. After half an hour, Carson fainted, collapsing in a pool of his own blood. Tony continued to beat him, screaming at him to wake up and stop being a weakling.

"God, you are so useless. Maybe I should just shoot you now, but that would deprive your mother of the joy of watching me kill you, right in front of her."

"Please, Daddy, don't hurt me any more. I'm sorry."

"What a worthless piece of shit you are, you're a poor excuse for my son. Get dressed and go and get me that beer and a sandwich." Silent and aching, Carson pulled up his shorts and shuffled out of the room. His agony was complete. He had been beaten, abused and humiliated by someone who wanted to be called Daddy. Now, all Carson could think of was to escape, back to the loving arms of his mother.

"Are you all right? You look awful." Abigail sat in the kitchen, waiting for something to happen.

Carson opened the refrigerator to get the beer and a sandwich. As he straightened up, the phone rang once. The light was on, Tony must have picked up the extension in his bedroom.

"Look, get Amanda and Emily in here and wait for me to come back. And don't move or make any noise." He looked out of the window as he walked by. It was dark outside, the only light provided by the single bulb on the porch, and some bright lights across the street. If they could manage it and get out of a window, all they had to do was get across the street, where he knew his parents were waiting.

"Took you long enough." Tony grabbed the beer and the sandwich.

"You know who's on the phone, waiting to talk to me? The New York Times, that's who. That reporter actually wants me to tell my story for tomorrow's paper. I may even let you live long enough so that you can read all the wonderful things I'm going to say about your mother. Now get out and leave the door open. And stay away from the front door, I'll know if you open it." He turned back to the telephone, talking rapidly and laughing.

Cautiously, Carson backed away from the door and edged along the corridor. At each light switch, he turned off the power, putting another section into darkness. In the living room, he turned off the switches and unplugged the lamps. The only thing he left on was the television, hoping that the noise would convince Tony that they were all obediently sitting in the living room and waiting. The three little girls were sitting in the kitchen, huddled together, their eyes focused on his face, relying on him for guidance.

"Right. We're all going out of a window on the other side of the house. My mother took off all the screens and left the windows open, so if you're very quiet, we might get away."

"I'm scared." Amanda sucked her thumb.

"It's all right. I'm scared, too. Can the two of you each take Emily's hand? When we get to the window, I'll boost one of you out first. After you get outside, run to the house next door, and don't make a sound. With all the windows open, Tony will hear you. Just be quiet, wait, and then run across the street to where my mother is waiting."

"What about Emily?"

"She's too little to run. I'll have to carry her, and one of you will have to stay under the window long enough to grab her so I can climb out. Any questions?" They shook their heads, too terrified to talk.

He turned around to make sure the telephone light was still on. Holding out his hand, he led his sisters through the darkened house, into the dining room. Motioning to Abigail, he boosted her up on the window sill, and held her hands as he lowered her down to the grass. She stood up and nodded. Her twin came next. Amanda slithered to the ground and began to run to the house next door. Abigail stayed under the window, lifting her arms up for her baby sister. Quietly, Carson kissed her and lowered her out of the window. Without a sound, he climbed out after her, took her in his arms, and motioned Abigail to run for safety. Ducking down low, he placed his hand over the baby's mouth and began to run across the grass, headed for the sanctuary of the house next door.

"Carson, you little sneak, where are you?" Tony walked through the darkened house, flicking the lights on. He carried a shotgun over each shoulder, his finger on the trigger, just in case there was trouble around the corner. The house was silent, except for the noise he made walking through the rooms, and the hollow laughter of the television set.

"Amanda, Abigail, you get out here this minute." When the little girls did not answer, he walked into the kitchen. It was deserted, quiet, still tidy after Laurel had cleaned up the breakfast dishes. Turning around, he headed towards the dining room. As his eyes adjusted to the darkness, he noticed the open window and the screen leaning against the wall next to it. Cursing, he peered outside, seeing nothing at first, and then noticing Carson as he ran across the grass. Laughing aloud, he aimed the shotgun and fired. The first round went wild, as Carson picked up speed and sprinted up the porch steps. The second did not miss, but found its mark, hitting the boy in the back and flinging him across the porch. To his credit, he held on to his sister, saving her life.

Tony lingered near the window, listening to Juliet's screams as she called Carson's name. Smiling to himself, he walked back through the house, pausing only long enough to fire two rounds from the other gun through the living room window. He could hear the sound of breaking glass, and swearing, as the onlookers ran for cover.

"How do you like that, you bitch. He's mine now, in every way. Tony Graniston, Jr. and I made sure that he will never be a Macallister again." Leaning out of the window, Tony laughed and fired off a few more rounds, hoping to hit something.

Even as he knew his revenge was almost over, he felt a moment of regret that he had freed Juliet too early. He should have stretched it out, enjoying all the begging and pleading she would have done in exchange for their son's life. They could have made very convenient hostages, their lives in exchange for anything Tony could have desired. And Juliet, at last she wouldn't have been able to avoid him. He could have made her love him, as many times as he wanted, before he killed her.

Heading to the kitchen, he opened the refrigerator and took out the last three beers. Placing them carefully on the bedside table, he sat back on the bed, thinking about what he had done.

"It was all Juliet's fault. She should have never married someone else, she should have told me I had a son." A solitary tear of self-pity edged its way down his face. Angrily, he brushed it away and popped the first can of beer. One after the other, he drank them all, enjoying the sensations of being drunk, something he had missed since he had been ill.

He looked around the room that had been his prison for the past month. In it were all the reminders of his mortal weakness, the hated trappings of a fatal disease. At last, he could admit the truth that he had been hiding from for the past ten years. The minute he had thrown her away there had been nothing left to live for. For a second he debated not going through with the last part of his plan, but then he remembered that at the end of it all was escape from the misery of his life. He put the shotgun against the inside of his mouth and pulled the trigger. As the sound of the gunshot rushed out of the open window, the noise was deafening to the ears of those waiting across the street.

CHAPTER TWENTY-TWO

Shaking as the final shotgun blast echoed down the street, Juliet waited for a few seconds, and then sprinted across the street. She no longer cared about her own life, her child was all that mattered. Faintly, she could hear a baby crying and she followed the sound up onto the porch. The dimness of the porch light showed her Emily's face, blood streaked and wet with tears. As she went closer, she whispered her son's name, over and over, without an answer.

Concentrating on the baby's cries, she tripped over something lying on the floor of the porch. As she looked down, she saw her son's leg, covered with blood. Crying and bending over, she lifted up the baby and called to Carson to open his eyes, that Mummy was here and that nothing could ever hurt him again.

Carson was still alive, almost unconscious, but he could hear his mother calling him. With a supreme effort of will, he dragged open his eyes, trying to focus on her face.

"Mummy, I'm sorry. I tried to do what you wanted, I'm so sorry."

"Darling, Daddy and I are to blame that all this happened. We should never have allowed you to go into that house."

"He would have killed my sisters, then. They're safe now. Mummy it hurts, where he shot me. And it's dark and I'm cold."

"Carson, keep talking. The doctor is on his way, and he's going to make you better. You'll see, and then we'll take the cruise next week, and maybe fly to New York for next half term, and stay in a wonderful hotel, just like last time."

She could hear Donald's step on the stair. He knelt down and took off his jacket.

"Carson, here, this will keep you warm. I'll hold you so you won't be scared. Talk to me, I love you so much."

"I want to go to sleep. Daddy, hold me while I sleep, I'll be safe then."

"No, Carson, not yet. Wait for Dr. Cohen. He's coming and wants to see you before you go to sleep."

Carson's eyes closed, and his body went limp. Weeping, Donald felt for a pulse, it was faint, but steady.

"He's still alive, there's a pulse. Where is that ambulance?" A siren howled faintly in the distance. Donald kept his hand on Carson's pulse, rejoicing every time he felt its beat. He talked to his son, urging him to stay alive, to fight for every second. Agonized, he accused himself of the most terrible things he could think of, all the while begging the child not to die.

"Donald, let me take care of things now. There's nothing else you can do." Ben Cohen stood on the porch, his heart breaking in two at what he saw. The anguished parents, the wounded child, the all too familiar scenario he had dreaded since the moment Tony had told him that the boy was coming for a visit. The paramedics worked on Carson, trying to stop the bleeding, hooking him up to oxygen and an IV, and finally putting him, with infinite care, on a gurney, to be taken away to the hospital. The parents, clinging to each other and to Emily as they stumbled, followed their son down the stairs.

At the foot of the stairs, Jordan and Carson waited, each anxious for their grandson. Meeting Donald's eyes, Carson shook his head, and followed his son across the lawn. At the edge of the curb, Emily stepped up and took the baby out of Juliet's arms.

.

Numbed, Donald and Juliet followed his father into the ambulance, taking their places beside their son.

"Jordan, what have we done?" Emily held on to the baby, while her eyes followed the lights of the ambulance, until they were out of sight.

"We've killed him, that loving little boy, as surely as if we had taken that shotgun and pulled the trigger ourselves. He gave his life to save his sisters. He never even got to know them, he just knew that they had to be saved. Oh, God, my life is over, in an instant, it just ended." Weeping, he sat down on the curb, his head in his hands.

*   *   *   *   *

Donald and Juliet sat in the emergency room, holding each other's hands, each praying silently for the life of their child.

"Donald, do you think that someone will come and talk to us soon?" Carson's voice trembled as Donald shook his head.

"Then I'll go and get you some tea and some food. It will be a long night. And I'll send for some fresh clothes so you can get cleaned up." Dazed, Juliet nodded and looked up at her father-in-law.

"What will I do if he dies, my precious darling child? He's my life, my reason, my art, everything. His innocence was his strength, my strength, too. He could see it, the evil in Tony, he knew it was dangerous, but he went because his love was stronger than his fear."

"Juliet, don't. Please, try and hang on." Helpless, Carson looked to his son for support. Donald was in another world, a broken man.

"Father, you were right all along, about everything. I was going to teach Tony by example, show him what being a wonderful father means. What a lot of garbage. I should have killed him myself."

It seemed as if the waiting would be forever. Carson brought them tea and some soup and sandwiches. Val Lenox appeared with changes of clothes. The staff gave them a room with a bathroom, so that they could wash their child's blood away. Weeping, their sobs echoing around the tiled walls, they washed each other, previously always an act of sheer physical delight, now a grisly task they would just as soon never wished to have done. With trembling hands, they put on fresh clothing, and groping for sanity, they crept back to their chairs to begin the wait again, each dreading the unthinkable.

In another part of the emergency room, Jordan Graniston also waited for news of his grandson. Shamed and full of self-hatred, he waited for word of Carson's condition. One question kept running through his brain. Why had he trusted Tony? What character flaw had prevented him from seeing the horror before it happened?

Paul Morales pulled up in front of the hospital emergency room and parked in the space reserved for the police. Deeply depressed, he went inside, hoping against hope that the news would be good.

"Donald, any news?"

"No, nothing."

"Try to hang on. If it were bad, you would have heard by now. Would you like me to stay and drive you home?"

"No, thank you. We'll be staying." Juliet gave a small smile, her good manners automatic.

"I have to go back to the station, I'm still on duty, but I'll find you in the morning." He patted Donald's shoulder and turned away. In his heart, he felt only sorrow for Donald and Juliet. All of his policeman's instincts told him that the child would not live. It was beyond imagination to think of what would come afterwards.

"Mr. Macallister, I'm Deborah Cohen. Ben called me from the ambulance. I'm so sorry about your son. I came right away, because I can get upstairs and find out what's going on. Just let me change into scrubs and I'll come back as soon as I know anything." She was gone before Donald could answer.

*   *   *   *   *

The operating room was running at frantic speed. The shotgun blast had hit several blood vessels, and although the spine had been spared, there were wounds to the spleen and the small intestine, blood loss had been significant, and Carson's heart had already failed once.

Ben Cohen looked up and saw his wife standing in the observation tower. He signaled her, shrugging his shoulders, then pointing to the paddles used to shock the heart. Deborah gasped and watched as the team struggled to save the boy's life. With a will of their own, her eyes gravitated to the monitor keeping track of his heartbeat. For now, the rhythm of the boy's heart appeared normal.

Minutes later, out of the corner of her eye, she watched the monitor go to flat line and the movements of the team change. The paddles were placed against Carson's chest, shocking him, but there was no change to the monitor. Again and again, Ben worked to get Carson's heart beating, until at last the head surgeon grasped his wrist, signaling that it was over. Weeping, she covered her mouth with her hand, controlling an overpowering urge to vomit. Standing up, she rapped on the glass to signal her husband, making a cutting motion, and curling her fingers to simulate a massage.

Galvanized, Ben grabbed a scalpel and opened the chest cavity up further, reaching inside to massage Carson's heart. His hand came away dripping with blood. She could see from the motion of his head that he was swearing and shouting for help. Deborah watched as her husband reached into the chest cavity, trying to clamp the aorta. Carson's heart had not beaten for two minutes. The head nurse irrigated the chest with saline solution, clearing the way for him to repair the damage. As the seconds ticked away to minutes, she could see them working feverishly over the child. The clock registered five minutes when the signal was given to try and start the heart again.

She could hardly bear to watch as again and again an electric current was applied to Carson's heart. After nine minutes, Ben took off his gloves and signaled the resident to close the openings. Frustrated, he kicked the surgical tray across the room and turned off the heart monitor as he staggered out of the operating room. She was waiting in the hall when the door opened.

"That poor little boy. I don't envy his parents." She buried her head in his shoulder.

"Such a waste. He was really a terrific kid. What were they thinking to let him go into that house and be alone with that monster?" She winced as his grip tightened.

"Ben, sometimes people don't recognize evil when they see it. Only the truly good and innocent can, and then no one else believes them until it's too late."

"His mother, she's like that. I saw it when I went to draw his blood. She reminded me of what my father once said, about the pure of heart, how they can see sin and evil as clearly as their own image in a mirror."

"We have to go and tell them. They should hear it from us."

"I can't. It will be like killing him all over again. I'll be killing them, too. For the rest of their lives, they won't be able to remember him without remembering that I couldn't save him, that I sentenced them to death at the very moment that he died." He held her tight, his tears falling warm and wet onto her shoulder.

"Ben, you can't show them how you really feel. We have to do these things every day, and try our best not to let personal feelings get involved with our professional ones. That is the way of our world. All we can hope for is that they'll eventually learn to forgive you and themselves." She stood on tiptoe and kissed his cheek. "Let's get it over with." Holding hands, they walked slowly towards the elevator.

They sat in a corner of the emergency room, red-eyed and numbed. Juliet looked up as Deborah approached and began to cry when she looked at her face. Ben looked into her eyes, knowing that if he lived to be a hundred, he would never forget what it meant to see innocence at the point of death.

"Juliet, I'm so sorry. His heart stopped, there was a hole in the aorta. We just couldn't fix it in time."

"He's gone? My baby's gone?" The keening wail came from her heart, as it too lay dying, spreading a chill over the emergency room. Juliet rocked back and forth, weeping. Donald sat as if turned to stone, barely breathing, alone in his grief. Feeling the crushing weight of his responsibility, Carson Macallister took charge again, as he had so many years before, after the avalanche that had killed his wife.

"When will he be ready to come home with us?" His voice shaking, a single tear found its way past his iron control. Automatically, his hand came up to brush it away. Later, when he was alone, he could cry and mourn for as long as he wanted, but now he had to be strong, unable to bear shaming his grandson's memory.

"He's in a viewing room now, if you'd like to see him. Afterwards, your funeral home can make the arrangements with the morgue to transport him back to England."

"Scotland, that's where the Macallisters come from. That's where he will go, to sleep and rest with his family."

"I'm so sorry that I couldn't save him. He was really a wonderful child." Carson looked over at Ben Cohen, feeling his guilt and sorrow.

"You did everything you could. We all loved him, he was just that kind of person. Everyone who came close to him loved him, and he loved them back, with such innocence and purity. Only Tony, he was the devil, and the boy feared him as he feared nothing else in his life." Unable to listen any longer, Ben turned away.

"Juliet, listen to me carefully. I put Carson in a room so that you can see him and say good-bye. Why don't you and Donald go with his father and see him one last time?" She heard Ben's voice, calm and gentle, through the fog of her pain. Bowing her head, she nodded and turned to her husband. He had not moved at all, still sitting upright in the chair, his tears flowing unchecked, soaking the front of his shirt.

"Donald, darling, he's waiting. We have to say farewell and Godspeed now, and send our darling off to be with your mother and my grandmother. He's going to people who love him, who will care for him." She touched his cheek with her hand, and leaned her head on his shoulder. He stirred and reached his hand up to stroke her hair.

They had become elderly in an instant, getting out of the chairs slowly, and with infinite care, fearful that they would shatter, the fragments of their lives then beyond repair. They moved like sleepwalkers, their arms supporting each other as they followed the doctor down to the morgue. Behind them, his back straight and his eye clear, his heart and soul screaming for all to hear, Carson Macallister followed his son and daughter-in-law on the longest journey they would ever take.

In later years, none of the three would remember anything about the farewells other than a memory of each individual experience. One would remember the sound made by the door as it closed behind them, another the coldness of his little hands, and the last, a kiss of ice, as her lips brushed his cheek, whispering her love and advice for his long journey.

*   *   *   *   *

"HOSTAGE DRAMA ENDS IN TRAGEDY, THREE DIE IN VENGEANCE KILLINGS"

The headline that screamed across the front page of the Miami Herald put the agony of three families into a single sentence. Jordan tossed the newspaper aside and walked to the window with a sigh. Now he understood what people meant when they described horror and tragedy as unreal, a nightmare from which they were sure they would awaken, if only someone would come and wake them up. It didn't matter that both he and Emily had taken the sleeping pills offered by Ben Cohen. Sleep would never again seem the safe haven it had always been, not when waking up to what had been normal life was now impossible.

After the arrangements had been made, they had all gone back to Palm Beach, Jordan and Emily, Carson, Donald and Juliet, and the three little girls. The mundane tasks of finding rooms for everyone, and putting food for a meal on the table had served as a temporary reprieve.

Abigail and Amanda had wept and clung to Juliet as if they were drowning. Jordan had thought of them as limpets, magnetizing themselves to a receptive host. He knew he was being unfair to think of his granddaughters in such impersonal terms, but he had never warmed to their whining and combative natures and could not find the sympathy he knew they were entitled to, no matter how often or deeply he searched his heart.

The telephone call Juliet had had to make to her parents had been a scene he wished he had never had to witness. Juliet had dialed the number, and when Bertram had answered, had said only, "Daddy," and then had burst into tears. Further words were unnecessary. Rose and Bertram, the others who had had to tolerate Tony as a son-in-law at the beginning of this long odyssey, were grief stricken at the loss of their grandson, but would be waiting at the airport when they arrived, the day after tomorrow.

*   *   *   *   *

She could hear the ringing sound. It couldn't be the telephone, it was a Saturday and she was still sleeping. Everyone in New York was still sleeping. The answering machine finally picked up. Probably another telemarketer from AT&T trying to sell her long distance again. She rolled over and tried to think about sleep, just at the moment that the prerecorded message ended.

"Vivian, wake up. This is important. Oh, for pity's sake, get up and answer the phone. It's me, Jane, your secretary, and you have to answer this call. Vivian, please don't make me come to the city all the way from Queens to make you talk to me." Moaning, Vivian reached across the nightstand and picked up the telephone.

"Tell me, Jane, have we been invaded by hordes of fat Martians in paper dresses?" She looked at the clock. It was 7:15 in the morning. Of course, she had forgotten about Jane's daily two mile run, which began around 6 A.M. and always put her at home, with all the papers at seven.

"The most terrible thing has happened. It's all over the papers, even the Times. Oh, that poor woman and that little boy." Suddenly awake and alert, Vivian sat up and calmly tried to get her secretary to make some sense.

"Now look, Jane. I want details, the same way you do it in the office. What woman and what little boy?" I wish she would stop sniffling into the phone.

"Your friend, Juliet Macallister. Her son is dead, killed by his father, what's his name, the scumbag you keep mumbling about?" Vivian felt as if she had been transported to another universe.

"Let me organize this. Tony Graniston has killed Carson Macallister, Juliet's son?" Vivian ran the water in the sink so that she could make coffee. It was going to be a very long day.

"Right. Anyway, I called the office. They're sending over all the dailies, and the Miami papers as well. I'll be there in about an hour and a half. Leave a message if you need something extra."

"Plane tickets. Two to Palm Beach, first class. One for me and one for a Mr. Paul Townsend. Get us on the first available flight after one this afternoon. Then make the return open, from London to New York. As soon as you have them, bring them over here, no later than noon. Thanks, Jane, I don't know what I would do without you."

Get a grip, Vivian, and don't start leaping all over the place. Get organized, then you can leap around all you want. She poured her first cup of coffee and picked up the telephone. It was 7:30.

"C'mon Paul, answer the phone already. Why aren't you in bed sleeping like other normal citizens of New York?" At least there was one small mercy in all of this, Paul didn't believe in answering machines, so the phone could ring off the hook. It would, until he felt good and ready to answer it. Answering machines, he had told her loftily the last time she had complained about trying to reach him, don't match my image. After all, how can I justify the way I am if I run out and buy every modern convenience that comes on the market?

Vivian hung up and redialed, putting the call on the speaker as she rummaged in the closet to get out a suitcase. She stopped listening after the tenth ring, concentrating on finding enough warm and cold weather clothes to wear for the next week. It had rung thirty times before she disconnected and redialed. He picked it up on the fifth ring.

"Darling, whoever you are, don't you know what time it is? Can't a man bathe without being interrupted?" Vivian could hear the amused whine behind his complaint.

"It's me, Paul, Vivian. Let me guess, you were fixing the glue on that hairdo of yours. And don't get all offended. I have a good reason for calling at this hour of the morning. I'm usually asleep at this time." She could sense his polite attention through the telephone.

"I'm waiting, Vivian. My soft boiled egg is getting a chill."

"Paul, I'm afraid it's about to catch pneumonia. Have you seen today's papers?"

"No, not yet. I was just about to open the door and bring them in. Why do you ask?" Control, girl, complete control. You can cry and scream later.

"There's been a horrible tragedy. My secretary called and woke me up. I'm packing right now, and you should, too."

"Vivian, you haven't told me anything. Are you going on a trip somewhere? Is that why you called me?" His impatience was breaking through.

"Paul, that's not why I called you. I'm having a hard time because I don't know how to tell you that Tony has gone and killed Carson." She was gulping for air, struggling for control.

"That's not possible. I talked to Juliet the day before yesterday. They were in Palm Beach, visiting that scum. He's in a coma, or something like that." The horror began to creep in, silently, slowly, blanketing everything with its dark numbness.

"No, Paul. He did it, he killed that wonderful little boy. And now we have to be there for them. Pack your bags and be ready to go by noon. I'll swing by and get you at about twenty after. And please, bring something for Florida, so you don't look so uncomfortable in tweeds." She could feel the tears beginning to slide down her face.

"My poor girl. How could it happen? What were they thinking, letting Carson go into a room with that devil? I have to hang up now. I'll be ready in two hours. Can you get us on an earlier flight?"

"I doubt it. Anyway, I'm going to need a few hours to make all the other arrangements. Bring a dark suit for the funeral. Oh, Paul, I'm going crazy here. I don't think I can stand it." He could hear the sound of noisy crying.

"Darling, you have to stand it. Both of us have to. Juliet needs us now, more than ever." She could hear the gentle disconnect. Wiping her eyes, she reached for her telephone book. She had one more call to make.

*   *   *   *   *

"Emily, the coroner just called. He wants to know who is going to pick up Tony's body." Jordan sat down next to his wife and held her hand.

"It all sounds so easy. Just tell someone to come and get him, and then put him in a place where we never have to look at him, or think about him, ever again. How does it happen? Tony was our son, we loved him and raised him, and tried to teach him the lessons that all parents teach their children. How did it go so wrong? Who would have thought that such a sweet little boy could wind up as a murderer?" She covered her face with her hands, trying without success to hide from the truth.

"I'd love to be able to say it wasn't anyone's fault, except Tony's, but I would be wrong. Somewhere along the line, we missed the signs that he was evil, a monster dressed in a skin that looked like mine. And that is a fact that we both have to learn to live with. If we're lucky, Juliet and Donald won't blame us too much." He hugged her close.

"They won't. They'll eat themselves up with guilt, and blame themselves. They'll be sure that believing us about Tony's condition was their fault. And they will never be quite able to forgive themselves for being human and caring, even about a monster like our son." Emily dabbed at her eyes.

"And we do deserve it, me more than you. If only I hadn't wanted to believe that there was some good left in him, Carson would be alive right now, and we would still be able to..." He swallowed, trying to get past the lump in his throat.

"Save your strength. We're going to need it over the next week. We still have to talk to Laurel's parents about the girls, and then there are the funerals. I wish it was over, right now."

"I know just what you mean. I was thinking about cremation for Tony, and then putting him somewhere very isolated. A place where we can put him and never have to go back again."

*   *   *   *   *

The funeral home had been accommodating. Not overly anxious, but very businesslike and matter of fact. Michael Sims, the director, had been tempted to charge more for the cremation, and for Laurel's casket, but one look at Jordan's face had convinced him that doing so would be the same thing as killing someone who didn't know he was already dead.

Jennifer Markham stood together with her husband, Herb, and their two daughters, just behind her parents. Somehow the mausoleum didn't quite match its location, in the outskirts of Fort Lauderdale. It was dark and dank, and smelled of death and grief. She fidgeted, waiting for it to be over quickly.

Jordan and Emily willed the pastor to read the service faster. It had been a mistake, asking the minister who had come to call on all of them to read the service. It seemed to them as if he was deliberately taking his time, drawing out the agony for as long as possible. At last, he closed his prayer book, and the director picked up the urn with Tony's ashes. He walked away without looking back, knowing they would be unable to resist the unspoken command to follow.

It was over. Jordan nodded with a small smile. Tony had been interred exactly as he had requested. Alone, in the darkest part of the building, with the assurances of the director that since he had purchased every single spot on the wall, his wish that no other person ever be interred near Tony would be fulfilled.

Laurel's body had been shipped north, to Connecticut, where her grieving parents would put her to rest. Bob and Lucy Davenport had refused to discuss the funeral arrangements, icily telling Jordan that his and Emily's presence there would be undesirable. In the next breath, they had disowned their granddaughters, saying that the sooner they could forget everything that concerned their connection to the Granistons, the better off they would be.

* * * * *

The little group of mourners stood huddled together against the late March chilly dampness. Inside the Macallister family crypt, the pallbearers laid Carson Macallister III to rest. His beloved brother and sister, his grandfathers and his uncles, Paul and Herb, had all helped to see him on his way. The parting words had been spoken by his grandmothers Rose and Emily, their voices breaking as they bid their grandson a safe journey.

His eyes rimmed with red, Donald Macallister had not uttered a word during the service, his agony plain for all the world to see, any words he might have said superfluous. Enveloped in a fog, Juliet had not needed a doctor to sedate her. Since that awful day, she had clung to her other three children, and to Vivian and Paul, as if they were life preservers God had thrown to a drowning woman. She continued to live, to breathe and to exist, but her heart had been battered into unconsciousness, her innocence hovering at the edge of death. The last sound, of the door of his place in the family crypt slamming shut, would be the one she would remember until the day she died.

The Macallister jet taxied down the runway and took off for London, bearing its cargo of pain and grief. Stunned and heartbroken, the passengers sat with their thoughts, each unwilling to break the heavy silence.

*　*　*　*　*

For Miranda and Dylan, this was their first experience with death, loss and grief. They had both been at school when their brother had been murdered, and were unable to comfort their parents and each other until a few days after the initial shock. For the first time since their babyhood, both children had insisted on sleeping in their parents' bedroom, afraid to leave their mother and father alone with their guilt.

Both of them had always accepted that their mother was unusual in her innocence. As children, they too had believed in the goodness that they could see shining in her eyes, but once they had gone off to the local comprehensive, and then to board away from home, they had quickly realized that the world was a place in which the innocence of their mother was considered a unique psychological aberration, something that others neither understood nor appreciated.

Bertram, Rose and Carson were united in their fear that Donald and Juliet might never recover from the loss of their son. Only too aware of the unique connections that had tied mother and child together, they watched her agony, trying but unable to offer her any real comfort. Vivian and Paul, distraught and suffering as well, had stayed close at hand for as long as they dared, but ten days after the funeral, they had said their sad goodbyes and returned to New York.

Donald retreated inside his grief, carrying on, well-behaved and amenable as always, but politely telling everyone else to leave him alone and mind their own business. Each day he would follow his routine, getting up, going to the office, conducting his business as if nothing had happened, returning home for dinner, playing with Isabel and going to bed, only to repeat the same sequence the next day, holding ironly to every minute, as if any divergence would shatter his life completely.

At night, he would lie awake, unable to sleep, concentrating on every noise that he could hear. His wife, numbed and exhausted, slept without dreams, deeply and completely. Jealous of her unconsciousness, he had tried taking the sleeping pills that Ben Cohen had prescribed, but had stopped them after the third day. Sleep was a constant replay of blood and death, guilt and self abomination. Better to stay awake than to have to relive the death of his child in dreams night after night. Three weeks after the funeral, ashen faced and with dark bruises under his eyes, he had collapsed during a board meeting. Carson had woken him up, loaded him into a limousine and taken him home.

"Donald, I have watched you now for three weeks, watched you slowly killing yourself with guilt. I won't allow you to do this. I miss him as much as you do, but life must continue. If you don't go on, you will be shaming his memory. You have three other children to

400

take care of, and a wife who is losing touch with reality. Do you know what she does when you leave the house? Now that Miranda and Dylan are back at school, she doesn't get dressed at all. She sits in his room, and rocks in that chair, for hours, and doesn't shed a tear. Dylan told me she has padlocked the studio. She told him that she will never paint again. And yesterday his box arrived from Templeton. Those bloody fools, I told them to burn everything. Your housekeeper called to tell me to come. When I got to your house, she had taken everything out of the trunk and she was lying on the pile, weeping and keening. Apparently, she had been doing that for hours."

"It's all my fault. He'd still be alive if I hadn't been such a bloody arrogant fool. She warned me, she begged me, she even threatened to leave me, just to keep Carson away from him. And I forced her to go there, and I forced him to go there, too. She locked herself into the guest room every night and cried herself to sleep for the three weeks before we went to Florida. And even then, all I could think of was that I knew better and she was wrong. And now, I have nothing left, no love, no happiness, no hope. It's all over, and night after night, I can't sleep, because I see him in my dreams, calling me, crying, 'why didn't you save me, Daddy?'"

"Have the two of you been out of the house at all?"

"No, I'm afraid to ask her, afraid that she'll tell me she never wants to be with me again."

"Donald, her heart is broken, and that takes some time to heal. She needs you to love her, to tell her that nothing has changed, that she is still the same person you have always loved, and that love is the only thing that will save both of you."

"Is that what you did, when Miranda died?"

"I tried, with your mother. I never blamed her, it was an accident. She took all the responsibility on herself. It was impossible for her to forgive herself. It poisoned everything, like a sickness. You saved us, all of ten years old, and you became my hero, because you helped us learn to love each other again. Now, I want to help you to do the same thing for yourself and for Juliet. Go home, pack her up and go to Nice for a week. No Isabel, no problems, just the two of you. You have to try, Donald, or you'll lose her forever." Carson resisted the urge to shake his son and wake him up.

"I'm so tired, I don't think I can. All I want is to sleep without dreaming. Right now, nothing else matters." He could feel his eyes closing, even as he spoke.

"Then go to France with her, and sleep, for days if you have to. You'll see, it will be different." Carson looked into his son's face and sighed.

Two days later, fearing the worst, Carson packed up Donald and Juliet and forcibly put them on the plane for Nice. They had complied, protesting, exhausted, not daring to look each other in the eye. His predictions were correct. Once in the house in Nice, they had slept for an entire day, without dreams or guilt. After sharing the dinner tray that Francoise had prepared, they had begun to talk to each other, Donald to ease the torture of his guilt, Juliet to finally be able to come to terms with the death of her child.

She wept for hours, mourning Carson's loss. He held her, unable to promise her that life would ever return to the way it had been. That night, he made love to her for the first time in weeks, tentatively, afraid of her reaction, touching her the same way that he had the first time they had made love. Gratefully, she responded, his tenderness the first step on the long road back.

By the end of the week, they had drawn closer again. The dreams that had invaded his sleep began to disappear, the weight of his guilt to lighten. He even began to remember feeling joyful, when on the last morning, Juliet confirmed that she was pregnant.

"Tell me, Donald, are you happy?"

"More than you can imagine. In fact, I'm so happy about it that I'm going to send for Isabel so that we can stay here for another week, and I promise that this time I will sit if you still want to paint me." She had smiled through her tears and kissed him.

*　　*　　*　　*　　*

Donald and Juliet Macallister sipped champagne and waited for the ribbon cutting ceremony. Their recovery had been slow, filled with guilt and remorse. After the initial hesitant steps back into the world, their pain had been eased when, eight months after Carson's death, Juliet had given birth to another son. Michael Macallister's arrival had put his parents firmly on the long road back. Dark haired, with his father's eyes, he was a child of boundless affection, the redeemer of his grieving parents. Miranda and Dylan and even Isabel, now three and with a personality to match the color of her hair, adored their younger brother.

"Almost time. You'll be all right up there, speaking?" Donald checked his watch.

"Of course I will. I have you and the others to make me strong. And I know that he's watching us, making sure we don't miss him too much." She touched the braided bun at the back of her head, and then readjusted her pale peach hat. Her hand strayed to her pearl necklace, the one Donald had given her when Isabel was born, and then to the edge of her suit jacket, pulling it into place.

"Mummy, up!" Michael, dressed for the occasion in an Eton suit, gazed at her with pleading eyes.

"Michael, darling, let Daddy give you up today. My hat will fall off, and I have to draw the curtain over the paintings." Solemn and wide-eyed, chewing his fist, he nodded and raised his arms to his father.

"Juliet, he's so adorable. Too soon he'll be off to school. Look at Isabel, three and already a heartbreaker." Donald kissed Michael's cheek and blew on his neck, bringing delighted giggles from his son.

"No matter, darling. Just think, by the time he's three, who knows what the stork will bring." Smiling wickedly, she kissed him on the cheek.

"You can't be serious, can you?"

"It's all your fault, that week-end in Nice last month. All that celebrating, I did warn you that it was dangerous."

"I thought you were a bit, you know, but I convinced myself that it was just wishful thinking."

"We'll have to move, for sure this time. We are out of bedrooms, and it would be nice to have a larger place, perhaps with space for a large party. You do realize that Miranda is going to be presented next year, and you know what that means. Ah, there's the signal. We need to pay attention now. There's your father, and mine, and Jordan."

The three men stood quietly on the stage, ill at ease for a moment until the chatter of the crowd ceased. By agreement, only Carson Macallister would speak on behalf of all three grandfathers.

"Ladies and gentlemen, allow me to introduce myself and my two companions. I am Carson Lord Macallister, Earl of Dunodeen, and with me are

Bertram Sadler and Jordan Graniston. All three of us have one thing in common. We shared the joy of being grandfathers to a marvelous, loving human being, our grandson, Carson Lord Macallister, the third of his name.

"I won't bore you with the distressing details of his passing, but I will tell you how much love he not only inspired, but gave in return. He was an innocent, a boy who loved everything that life had to offer. It is a great tragedy that his life was cut short. And that brings us to the ceremony taking place today. All three of us wanted to do something concrete to commemorate his life, something of which he would have approved, something that will continue to mean something to his family long after today's ceremony. We decided among ourselves that we would donate all the money to create something that would have meant a great deal to Carson if he were alive today." He nodded slightly, and Bertram and Jordan walked towards an easel which stood in the middle of the stage.

They raised their right hands and together they unveiled the architect's drawing of their project.

"Ladies and Gentlemen, I present to you the drawing of our project. I will, however, leave it to the next speaker to explain the details behind the drawing." Slowly, Juliet got out of her seat and walked up to the podium, standing to the side of a large mass covered by a tarpaulin.

"Ladies and gentlemen, I present to you Countess Juliet Macallister." The three men applauded, and then took their seats. Juliet took a deep breath before she spoke.

"Ladies and gentlemen, three years ago, my beloved son, Carson was killed. After the shooting, two of Northridge's doctors tried valiantly to save his life. Their care and love and efforts made his loss a bit less painful.

"Today is the culmination of all the planning and effort that his grandfathers put into this project. Therefore, I would like to welcome all of you to the ground breaking of the Carson Macallister III pediatric wing at Northridge Hospital." The murmurs of the audience rushed towards her. Breathless herself, she waited until the audience had fallen silent.

"This wing will have one hundred and fifty beds for critically ill children of all countries and of all nationalities. These children will be treated here with the finest medicines and by the finest doctors money can buy. For those unable to pay the full cost, and for those without insurance, the family of Carson Macallister will make up the difference. In addition, next year, a home for the parents of these children will be built right next to the wing, so that when a child is critically ill, he does not have to be alone, and so that the parents do not have to worry about anything except the health of their child." The applause was deafening. Juliet stood calmly, a tear running down her cheek, but still in control.

"The grandfathers made the wing and the parents' home a complete project, but I wanted to give something of my own, something my son would have been proud of, something that would have meaning for the future health and happiness of all children. My donation to the Carson Macallister III pediatric wing is the funding of the Deborah and Benjamin Cohen Research Laboratory at Northridge Hospital. With gratitude for their loving and sensitive treatment of my son, I present the Doctors Cohen and Northridge Hospital with 'Carson's Tree.' The paintings will be sold at auction and the proceeds used to help build the finest research laboratory in the world." Looking out over the audience, she saw Deborah and Ben hugging each other and motioned to them to come forward. With a radiant smile, she waited for them to join her.

Motioning to them, she waited while they drew aside the sheeting. The three glowing paintings, all renditions of the tree outside his hospital room so long ago, drew gasps from her audience and tears from the artist. Deborah and Ben hugged her and shook her hand before leaving the stage.

Catching her husband's eye, she motioned to him to join her on the stage. Carrying Michael and followed by Miranda and Dylan, they surrounded Juliet, hugging and kissing her. Not to be ignored, Isabel broke away from her grandmother and ran to the podium to be with her mother. Eluding Rose's frantic efforts to stop her, she planted herself in front of the paintings and stamped her foot, saying over and over, "Me, too, Mummy. Me, too."

Smiling through her tears, Juliet scooped up her wayward daughter and kissed her cheek. The uncanny resemblance between mother and child brought smiles to the faces of the audience, and a sigh of appreciation from Donald. Both he and Juliet had traveled a great distance in the two years since their son had been murdered. Their progress on that journey had been, for the most part, agonizingly slow. At each turn, painful memories had stopped their progress, forcing them to regroup and begin again.

Nothing in their relationship had remained the same after Carson's death. Juliet had lost some of the security that her innocence had given her, Donald had been forced to reevaluate his understanding of his wife's uniqueness and admit that she was far better at identifying evil than he could ever be. Gone was his naivete, the belief in his immunity to the blandishments of evil. Gone as well was the Juliet who had existed before Carson's death. In her place had grown a wiser woman, one who had learned her lessons the hard way. Both had learned the terrible truth, that evil respects no boundaries or temperaments.

For a moment, Donald felt a rush of gratitude, knowing how close he had come to losing everything that was important in his life, and in the end both he and Juliet had survived and flourished. Unconsciously, he tightened his grip on Michael, making the child squirm.

"Daddy, stop." Smiling, Donald relaxed his grip and held his present close.

ABOUT THE AUTHOR

Monica Ruthizer has spent her professional life teaching history and expository writing. *Carson's Tree* is her first work of fiction. She lives in Northern Westchester, in New York State, with her family. She is currently at work on a novel set during World War II.

SM Tried to sound British
why?
how?
Did you write this with a TV movie
in mind?

You use dialog to
describe a feeling or
a predicament — but
its not a natural way
to talk. p.73

— Who feels sexy + beautiful while
your son is dying?

Do you have any familiarity
with leukemia?

Printed in the United States
6861

9 781403 311511